D0957261

IRENE HANNON

It Had to Be You

&

All Our Tomorrows

HARLEQUIN LOVE INSPIRED CLASSICS

Recycling programs for this product may not exist in your area.

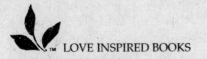

LOVE INSPIRED BOOKS

ISBN-13: 978-0-373-65167-2

IT HAD TO BE YOU AND ALL OUR TOMORROWS
Copyright © 2014 by Harlequin Books S.A.

The publisher acknowledges the copyright holder of the individual works as follows:

IT HAD TO BE YOU
Copyright © 1999 by Irene Hannon

ALL OUR TOMORROWS
Copyright © 2006 by Irene Hannon

www.Harlequin.com

Printed in U.S.A.

CONTENTS

Books by Irene Hannon

Love Inspired

*Home for the Holidays
*A Groom of Her Own
*A Family to Call Her Own
It Had to Be You
One Special Christmas
The Way Home
Never Say Goodbye
Crossroads
†The Best Gift
†Gift from the Heart
†The Unexpected Gift
All Our Tomorrows
The Family Man
Rainbow's End
**From This Day Forward
**A Dream to Share

**Where Love Abides
Apprentice Father
††Tides of Hope
††The Hero Next Door
††The Doctor's Perfect Match
††A Father for Zach
Child of Grace
§Seaside Reunion
§Finding Home
§Seaside Blessings

*Vows
†Sisters & Brides
**Heartland Homecoming
††Lighthouse Lane
§Starfish Bay

IRENE HANNON,

who writes both romance and romantic suspense, is the author of more than forty novels, including the bestselling Heroes of Quantico and Guardians of Justice series. Her books have been honored with two coveted RITA® Awards (the "Oscar" of romantic fiction), a National Readers' Choice Award, a Carol Award, a HOLT Medallion, a Retailers Choice Award, a Daphne du Maurier Award and two Reviewers' Choice Awards from *RT Book Reviews* magazine. *Booklist* also named one of her novels a "Top 10 Inspirational Fiction" title for 2011. A former corporate communications executive with a Fortune 500 company, Irene now writes full-time from her home in Missouri. For more information, visit www.irenehannon.com.

IT HAD TO BE YOU

Remember not the events of the past,
the things of long ago consider not.
—*Isaiah* 43:18

With deepest gratitude to the One
who makes all things possible.

Prologue

"I'm sorry, Maggie, but…I just can't go through with it."

Maggie Fitzgerald stared in shock at the man standing across from her, his words echoing hollowly in her ears. He looked like Jake West, the man she'd loved since she was sixteen years old. But he didn't sound like that Jake. Not even close.

Maggie felt a cold chill crawl up her spine despite the Midwest heat and humidity, and she wrapped her arms around her body for warmth. He was only an arm's length away, close enough to touch, and yet she suddenly felt more alone than ever before in her life. Because always, through all the losses in her life— her mother, her father, and just three weeks before, the tragic deaths of her sister and brother-in-law in a small-plane crash—she'd still had Jake. He'd been her friend for as long as she could remember, and though their relationship had transitioned—quite unexpectedly— to romance, their friendship remained strong and sure.

But now he was leaving—less than five weeks before

she was scheduled to walk down the aisle as his bride. It was inconceivable. Incomprehensible. But true. The stoic expression on his face told her so more eloquently than his words.

The knot in Maggie's stomach tightened as she sank down onto the couch, her legs suddenly too shaky to support her willowy five-foot-six, hundred-and-ten-pound frame. Nothing in her twenty-four years had prepared her for this...this *betrayal*. Maybe that was a harsh term. But what else could you call it when the man you loved bailed out just because things got a little rough?

Even in her dazed state, however, Maggie had to admit that "a little rough" wasn't exactly an accurate description of the situation. The sudden responsibility of raising six-year-old twins—one of whom needed ongoing medical care—wasn't a minor complication. Not when they'd planned to spend the first ten years of their marriage child-free, exploring some exotic new corner of the world each year on vacation, living the adventures they'd always dreamed of. It was a situation that demanded huge compromises, and Maggie knew it marked the death of a dream for both of them. But she had wanted to believe that Jake would realize there simply was no other option. As their only living relative, Maggie *had* to take her sister's girls. But clearly Jake hadn't been able to accept it. And where did that leave her?

Apparently alone.

As Jake sat beside her and reached for her hand, she glanced at him with dazed eyes, blind to the anguish in his. The strongly molded planes of his dear, familiar face were only a misty blur. When he spoke, the appealing, husky cadence of his voice—edged with that smoky quality that was distinctly his—sounded suddenly foreign to her ears, and his words seemed to come from a great distance.

"Maggie, I'm sorry," he whispered, knowing the words were inadequate, his gut twisting painfully at the wretched, abandoned look in her eyes.

So was she. Ever since her sixteenth birthday, when their relationship changed forever—from childhood friends to sweethearts—she'd never even looked at another man. She'd built her whole future around Jake. A future that was now crumbling around her.

"This…situation…doesn't change how I feel about you," he continued when she didn't respond. "But… well, I guess I never expected a ready-made family. It would be bad—" He cut himself off and deliberately changed the term. "Hard…enough if they were normal kids. But they've just lost both parents, and Abby has years of medical treatment ahead of her. And what about our plans for seeing the world? For not being tied down by responsibilities, at least in the beginning? And I'm not ready to take on the responsibilities of parenthood. I just feel so…trapped," he finished helplessly. With a sigh, he reached for her cold hands, his gaze locked on hers. "Do you understand at all?"

Slowly Maggie shook her head, trying desperately to restrain her tears. "No," she replied brokenly. "No, Jake, I don't. I thought…well, I know we haven't actually said the vows yet, but I thought, in our hearts, we'd already made a commitment. For life. For better or for worse. What if this had happened six weeks *after* the wedding instead of six weeks before? Would you have walked out then, too?"

Jake cringed, and he felt his neck grow hot. He deserved that. It was more or less the same question his father had coldly asked. Though his mother had been less vocal in her disapproval, he had seen the look of disappointment in her eyes, as well. But if the vows had actually been spoken, he would have stuck it out.

"You know better, Maggie."

She looked at him, suddenly skeptical. "Do I? I'm not so sure anymore, Jake." She shook her head and gave a short, mirthless laugh. "But I guess it was a lucky thing for you it happened now. You won't be put to that test. You're free to walk away."

God forgive him, but he'd thought that very thing. That he *was* lucky this had happened *before* the wedding. He felt like a heel for even thinking it, but he couldn't deny that he'd been relieved.

Maggie watched his face, realized that though her words had been spoken harshly, they did, in fact, mirror his thoughts. Her stomach clenched even tighter. Until this very minute she'd half expected him to rethink his decision and do what she considered the honorable thing. But as her gaze searched his eyes, she knew he wasn't going to bend, and a powerful wave of fear suddenly crashed over her.

When she spoke again, her voice was tinged with desperation. "Jake, I—I don't want to lose you. I don't know why the Lord gave us this burden, why He's testing our commitment like this. I wish I did. I wish there was an easy answer to this problem. But I can't see any other option. Can you?"

He stared at her helplessly. There was only one other option as far as he could see: put the two bereft six-year-olds into the hands of a foster family. But leaving them in the care of strangers would be wrong, and he knew it. That was why he hadn't asked her to choose between that or him. After much soul-searching he had decided that the best solution was for him to break the engagement. He didn't feel particularly noble about it, and his father's few choice words about duty and honor were still ringing in his ears, but in the end he had to make his own decision. And as much as he loved Maggie, he feared that if he went into this marriage feeling trapped, it would lead to resentment and, ultimately, heartbreak.

But now, sitting here with her ice-cold hands in his, her vulnerable eyes pleading with him to reconsider, he wondered if this was any better.

"Maggie, are you sure Charles didn't have any relatives who might take the girls?" he asked, already knowing the answer. They'd been over this before.

She shook her head. "He was an only child, born late in life. His parents died years ago. There isn't anyone else, Jake."

With a sigh of frustration, Jake rose and strode restlessly across the room, stopping at the window to stare unseeingly into the night.

Maggie watched him, frantically searching for words that might change his mind. She couldn't lose Jake! Since her sixteenth birthday, all she'd wanted out of life was to be Mrs. Jake West. Maybe modern women were supposed to want a career and independence. But those things paled in comparison to being Jake's wife. What better "career" could she find than spending her life loving Jake, first traveling with him all over the world and then creating a home for him and their children? Her throat tightened painfully, and she choked back a sob.

"Jake…maybe we should just postpone things. Maybe if we give it a little time…"

Her voice trailed off as he turned to face her. There was a tightness to his jaw, a sudden resolve in his face, that made her realize there was something he hadn't told her yet, something that she knew intuitively was going to seal their fates.

"That's not really an option, Maggie. I…" He paused, and she could see the struggle on his face as he searched for the words to tell her the thing that was going to make her world fall completely apart.

"Jake." The panic in her voice was obvious, even to her own ears. She didn't want to hear what he was going to say. "Please, can't we think about this a little more?"

She heard him sigh, saw the sudden sag in his shoulders, watched with trepidation as he walked slowly back to the couch and sat beside her again. More than anything in the world she wanted him to pull her into his arms and tell her that everything was going to be all right, as he had on so many other occasions through the years. But she could see that wasn't his intent. He kept himself purposely at a distance and made no attempt to touch her.

Jake lifted a hand and wearily rubbed his forehead, then drew in a deep, unsteady breath. When he spoke, his voice was gentle but firm. "Maggie, I joined the navy. I leave in five days."

Maggie stared at him blankly, her eyes suddenly confused. "Leave?" she parroted. "You're leaving? You joined the navy?"

"Yes. I signed all the papers this morning. I've known for a week I was going to do it, but I just couldn't seem to find the words to tell you."

"But…but why?"

"It's my chance to see the world, Maggie. It won't be the same as if we were going together, I know, but with my advanced degree I should get plum assignments. That's what they told me at the recruiting office, anyway. I go directly to officer training school. It's a great opportunity."

"But…but you have a job already."

"I know. But it's just a job, Maggie. In two years the most exciting thing I've done with my engineering skills is design hydraulic systems for elevators. I don't want to do that the rest of my life."

"But…but why the navy?" she asked, still trying to make sense of this unexpected twist.

Because I knew if I didn't do something irrevocable like that, I wouldn't be able to go through with the breakup, not when you look at me like this, he thought in silent anguish. But he couldn't say that.

He studied her now, this woman he loved, as he debated how to answer. From the first time he kissed her, Maggie had been the only woman he ever wanted. They'd played together as toddlers, hung around as teenagers and fallen in love that one magical day on Maggie's sixteenth birthday when he'd suddenly begun to realize that she was growing up. For the first time, he had really looked at her—the way a man looks at a woman who attracts him. Maggie wasn't exactly a great beauty, with her wavy, flyaway red hair and turned up nose. But those attributes were more than offset by her gorgeous, deep green eyes and porcelain complexion. Suddenly she wasn't just a "pal" anymore, but a woman who brought out unexpected feelings and responses in him.

And as time went by, he'd begun to notice other things, too. Like how close to the surface her feelings lay, how transparent they were, clearly reflected in her expressive eyes. And he'd noticed something else in her eyes, too—a maturing passion, flashes of desire, that set his blood racing. But she had a discipline he could only admire. For, in an era of questionable morals, she made no apology for her traditional Christian values, believing that the ultimate intimacy should be reserved for marriage, expressed only in the context of a lifetime commitment. He'd always respected her for that.

Yet despite Maggie's strong faith, she had a certain air of fragility, an aura of helplessness, that always brought out his protective instinct. And it was this latter quality that he knew would do him in tonight unless he had an airtight out, an ironclad escape—like joining the navy.

And *escape* was an accurate word, he admitted. He was running away because he was running scared. It was as simple as that. But he couldn't very well tell her all that.

"The navy seemed to offer some great career and travel opportunities," he replied, the reason sounding lame—and incomplete—even to his own ears.

Maggie stared at him, wide-eyed and silent. She'd hoped he'd at least help her get settled with the twins. She'd even begun to think that maybe he would change his mind if he saw that caring for them wasn't so bad after all. But he wasn't going to give himself that chance. He was bailing out.

An aching sadness overwhelmed her as she recalled all the tender words they'd said to one another, all the plans they'd made with such eager anticipation. She thought of the hours they'd spent poring over maps, dreaming of places that would take them far from their Midwest roots, planning their future travels around the world—beginning with their honeymoon in Paris. A honeymoon now destined never to take place, she realized. Cold fingers clutched at her heart and tightened mercilessly, squeezing out the last breath of hope. He'd made his decision. It was done. There was nothing more to say.

She gazed at Jake, and suddenly she felt as if she was looking at a stranger, as if the man she'd fallen in love with had somehow ceased to exist. That man had been caring and kind, someone who could be relied upon to stand beside her, no matter the circumstances. The stranger sitting beside her seemed to possess none of those qualities. He'd said he loved her. And maybe he thought he did. But his actions didn't even come close to fitting her definition of love.

Maggie took a deep breath, struggling to make sense of everything that was happening. Her life had changed so dramatically in the last three weeks that there was an air of unreality about it. She'd lost her only sister. She'd been given responsibility for two young, newly orphaned children, one of whom needed ongoing medical care. And now the final blow. She was losing the man she loved. Only her faith kept total despair at bay. But even *with* her faith, she was finding it hard not to give in to self-pity. Why was the Lord testing her this way? she cried silently. She just couldn't see any purpose to it.

Unless…unless it was the Lord's way of letting Jake show his true character now, before they formalized their commitment, she thought, searching desperately for an explanation that made *some* sense. She supposed it was better to find out now how he reacted in adversity. But frankly, at this moment, it didn't give her much consolation.

"Maggie?"

Jake's concerned voice drew her back to the present. The familiar warmth and tenderness were back in his eyes, and for just a moment she was tempted to tell him she'd do whatever he wanted, just so long as they could be together.

But with sudden resolve, she straightened her shoulders and lifted her chin. She'd already practically begged him to rethink his decision, and he'd rejected her plea. Well, she had *some* pride. If Jake didn't love her enough to stick by her through this, then she didn't want him, either. She could survive on her own. Okay, so maybe she'd relied too much on Jake to take care of things, make all the decisions. That didn't mean she couldn't learn to do those things herself. Especially since it was clear she *had* to. She needed to take her life in her own hands. Beginning right now.

Abruptly Maggie rose, and Jake stared up at her, startled by her sudden movement.

She took a deep breath, willing herself to get through the next few minutes without breaking down. Her heart might be tattered, but there would be time for tears later, when she was alone. Plenty of time, in fact. Like the rest of her life.

"Jake, I don't see any reason to prolong this, do you? You've said what you came to say. It's obvious you've set a new course for your life. I have to accept that. And I wish you well."

Jake rose more slowly, his face troubled. There was

a quality in Maggie's voice he'd never heard before—a quiet dignity, tinged with resignation. This wasn't at all the reaction he'd anticipated. He'd expected tears and pleading right up to the final goodbye.

"Look, Maggie, I don't want to just walk out and leave you to totally fend for yourself. I'd like to at least help you out financially, make sure you're settled."

As far as Maggie was concerned, offering money was the worst thing Jake could have done. Maybe it would appease his conscience, but she wanted nothing from this man who, until half an hour ago, had been the center of her world, whose love she had mistakenly believed to be unshakable and true.

"I don't want your money, Jake. I have a job. A good job. Graphic design is a growing field. I might even branch out into illustration. And Becky and Charles had insurance, so the girls will be well provided for. We'll be fine."

Jake looked at Maggie, noting the uncharacteristic tilt of her chin. She'd always been so compliant, so accepting of his help, that he was a bit taken aback by her refusal. And he was even more surprised when she removed her engagement ring and held it out to him.

"I think this is yours."

"Keep the ring, Maggie," he protested, surprised at the unevenness of his own voice.

"Why? It's a symbol of something that no longer exists. I'd rather you take it back." She reached over and dropped it into his hand. Then she walked to the door, opened it and turned to face him. "I don't think we have anything else to say to each other, do we?"

Jake looked at Maggie. Her beautiful eyes were steady, and for once he couldn't read her feelings in

their depths. But he knew she was hurting. Knew that
she must feel exactly as he felt—devastated and bereft. But she was hiding it well. Slowly he followed her
to the door.

"I'll take care of canceling all the…arrangements."
He could at least spare her that.

"Thank you," she said stiffly.

"I'm sorry, Maggie." He knew words were inadequate. But they were all he could offer.

"So am I." Her voice caught on the last word, and
for a moment he thought she was going to lose it. He
almost wished she would. He didn't know how to deal
with this aloof, controlled Maggie. He wanted to take
her in his arms one last time, wanted to cry with her at
the unfairness of life, wanted to mourn the passing of
their relationship. It was clear, however, that she had a
different sort of parting in mind.

"Well…I guess there's nothing left to say."

"No."

"Maggie, I hope…" His voice trailed off. What did
he hope? That someday she would find it in her heart
to forgive him? Unlikely. That she would eventually
be able to remember with pleasure their good times?
Again, unlikely. That a man worthy of her love would
one day claim her heart?

That thought jolted him. No, that wasn't at all what
he wanted. His Maggie in the arms of another man? The
idea repelled him. And yet, how could he wish her less?
She deserved to find happiness with a man who would
love her enough to stand by her through the tough times
as well as the happy ones. Someone who would do a
much better job at that than he had.

"What do you hope?" she asked curiously, a wistful note creeping into her voice.

He considered his answer, and settled for one that didn't even come close to expressing the myriad of conflicting emotions in his heart. "I wish you happiness, Maggie."

The smile she gave him was touched with bitterness, telling him more eloquently than words that she considered that a vain hope. "Thanks, Jake. Goodbye."

And then she very gently, very deliberately, shut the door behind him.

Maggie walked numbly back to the couch and sat down. She felt chilled to the bone and suddenly she began to tremble. For the first time in her life she was truly alone. She'd told Jake that she would be all right. But those words had been spoken with more bravado and pride than confidence. She didn't have a clue how she was going to cope. Not without Jake.

Jake, with his gentle touch and laughing eyes, his confidence and optimism, his sense of adventure. He had filled her world with joy and brightness. The events that had transpired in this room during the last hour couldn't erase the memory of all they'd shared, of the love she had felt for him. Without Jake, the future stretched ahead like a dark, aching void, filled with overwhelming responsibilities, yet empty of the warmth and companionship and love that made all trials bearable. How could she go on alone?

And then she thought of the twins. They needed her. Desperately. They, too, had been deprived of the people they loved most. She had to be strong for them, if not for herself. Together they would move forward. For the three of them, love had died—for the twins, physically; for her, emotionally. But the death was equally final in both cases.

Which meant that, for the first time her life, her future lay solely in her own hands. She had no one to consult, no one to make decisions for her, no one to reassure her that she could handle the task before her. It was up to her alone.

Well, maybe not quite alone, she reminded herself suddenly. There *was* Someone she could rely on, Someone who would stand by her through whatever lay ahead. And so she took a moment, before the demands of her new life came crashing down on her, to close her eyes and ask for His guidance.

Please, Lord, show me what to do. Help me be strong. Help me to know that I'm never truly alone. That You're always with me. And help me to accept, even without understanding, the hardships You've given me, and to believe in my heart that You would never give me a cross too heavy to bear.

The short prayer brought Maggie a momentary sense of peace and renewed confidence. She could almost feel the Lord's loving presence beside her. And for that she was immensely grateful. For she knew, beyond the shadow of a doubt, that she would need Him desperately in the months and years to come.

Chapter One

Twelve Years Later

Give it up.

The word's echoed in Jake's mind as the swirling Maine mist wrapped itself around his small rental car, effectively obscuring everything beyond a thirty-foot radius. He frowned and eased his foot off the accelerator. Should he continue the short distance to Castine or play it safe and pull in somewhere for the night?

A sign appeared to his right, and he squinted, trying to make out the words. Blue Hill. He glanced at the map on the seat beside him. Castine was less than twenty miles away, he calculated. But he suspected that these narrow, winding—and unfamiliar—roads weren't too forgiving, and dusk was descending rapidly. Not a good combination, he decided. Besides, he was tired. He'd driven up from Boston, then spent what remained of the day exploring the back roads and small towns of the Blue Hill peninsula. If he wanted to feel rested and fresh for his interview at the Maine Maritime Academy tomorrow, it was time to call it a day.

As if to validate his decision, a sign bearing the words Whispering Sails B&B providentially loomed out of the mist. Talk about perfect timing! he mused. He pulled into the gravel driveway and carefully followed the gradual incline until he reached a tiny parking area, where one empty space remained. Hopefully, the space was a good sign.

Jake eased his six-foot frame out of the compact car and reached into the back seat for his suit bag, slinging it effortlessly over his shoulder. As he made his way up the stone path, he peered at the house, barely discernible through the heavy mist. The large Queen Anne-style structure of weathered gray clapboard was somewhat intimidating in size, its dull color offset by the welcome, golden light spilling from the windows and the overflowing flower boxes hugging the porch rail. Definitely a haven for a weary traveler, he decided.

Jake climbed the porch steps, read the welcome sign on the door and entered, as it instructed. A bell jangled somewhere in the back of the house, and he paused in the foyer, glancing around as he waited for someone to appear. The house was tastefully decorated, he noted appreciatively, with none of the "fussiness" often associated with this style of architecture. In fact, the clean, contemporary lines of the furnishings set off the ornate woodwork beautifully, and he found the subtle blending of old and new eminently pleasing. A soft, warm color palette gave the house a homey feel—no small accomplishment for high-ceilinged rooms of such grand proportion. Clearly the house had been decorated by someone with an eye for design and color.

His gaze lingered on the ample fireplace topped by a marble mantel, which took up much of one wall, and he was sorry the month was July instead of January. He wouldn't mind settling into the large overstuffed chair beside it with a good book on a cold night. There was something…restful…about the room that strongly appealed to him.

As Jake completed his survey, a door swung open at the back of the foyer and a young woman who looked to be about twenty hurried through.

"I thought I heard the bell," she greeted him breathlessly, her smile apologetic. "I was on the back porch changing a light bulb. Sorry to keep you waiting."

He returned the smile. "Not at all. I was hoping you might have a room for the night. I was trying to make it to Castine, but the weather isn't cooperating."

She made a wry face and nodded. "Not exactly Maine at its best," she concurred sympathetically as she slipped behind a wooden counter that was half-hidden by the curving stairway. "You're in luck for a room, though. We're always booked solid in the summer, but we just received a cancellation." The young woman smiled and handed him a pen. "If you'll just fill out this card, I'll help you with your bags."

"No need. I just have a suit bag. But thanks."

He provided the requested information quickly, then waited while the young woman selected a key and joined him on the other side of the desk.

"I'll show you to your room. It has a private bath and a great view of the bay-well, it's a great view on a clear day," she amended with a rueful grin over her shoulder as she led the way up the steps. "Maybe by tomorrow morning it will be clear," she added hopefully. "Anyway, breakfast is between eight and nine in the dining room, which is next to the drawing room. Checkout is eleven. My name's Allison, and I'll be on duty till ten if you need anything. Just ring the bell on the desk." She paused before a second-floor door at the front of the house and inserted the key, then pushed the door open and stepped aside to let him enter.

Jake strolled past her and gave the room a quick but thorough scrutiny. It seemed that the hand of a skilled decorator had been at work here, as well. The room was done in restful shades of blue. A large bay window at the front of the house would afford a panoramic view of the sea in clear weather, he suspected, and a cushioned window seat beckoned invitingly. A four-poster bed, antique writing desk, intricately carved wardrobe and comfortable-looking easy chair with ottoman completed the furnishing. His gaze paused on the fireplace, noting the candle sconces on the mantel, and again he wished it was cool enough for a fire.

"I hope this is all right," Allison said anxiously.

He turned to her with a smile. "Perfect. The room is very inviting."

Allison grinned. "My aunt has a way with color and such. Everybody says so. And she makes all the guests feel real welcome. That's why we have so many regulars. You know, you're really lucky to get this room. It's the most requested one. Especially with honeymooners."

Jake grinned. "I can see why. It's quite…romantic."

Allison blushed and fumbled with the doorknob. "Well, if you need anything, just let me know. Have a pleasant evening, Mr. West."

As the door clicked shut, Jake drew a deep breath and stretched tiredly, flexing the tight muscles in his neck. He'd been on the road since early morning, but the time had been well spent. Before he decided to make this area his permanent home, he intended to check it out thoroughly.

He strolled over to the window and stared out thoughtfully into the gray mist. Home, he repeated silently. Surprisingly enough, the word had a nice sound. After twelve years of roaming the globe, his worldly possessions following him around in a few small boxes, the thought of having a home, a place to call his own, had a sudden, unexpected appeal. But he shouldn't be too surprised, he supposed. For the last couple of years he'd been plagued with a vague feeling of restlessness, of emptiness, a sense of "Is this all there is?" Even before his brother's phone call, the notion of "settling down" had crept into his thoughts, though he'd pushed it firmly aside. It wasn't something he'd seriously considered—or even *wanted* to consider—for a very long time. In fact, not since he was engaged to Maggie.

Jake frowned. Funny. He hadn't really thought much about Maggie these last few years. Purposely. During the early years after their breakup, she'd haunted his thoughts day and night, the guilt growing inside him with each passing month. It was only in the last three or four years that he had met with some success in his attempts to keep thoughts of her at bay. So why was he thinking of her now? he wondered, his frown deepening.

His gaze strayed to the chocolate-chip cookies, wrapped in clear paper and tied with a ribbon, resting between the pillows on the bed. He'd noticed them earlier, had been impressed by the thoughtful touch. Maybe they had triggered thoughts of the woman he'd once loved, he reflected. She used to bake him chocolate-chip cookies—his favorite—he recalled with a bittersweet smile.

But Maggie was only a memory now, he reminded himself with a sigh. He had no idea what had become of her. She'd moved less than a year after their parting, breaking all ties with the town which held such unhappy memories for her. Even his parents, to whom she had always been close, had no idea where she went. It was better that way, she'd told them. They understood. And he did, too. But though he'd initiated the breakup, he had nevertheless been filled with an odd sense of desolation to realize he no longer knew Maggie's whereabouts. He didn't understand why he felt that way. Didn't even try to. What good would it do? All he could do was hope she was happy.

Jake walked over to the bed and picked up the cookies, weighing them absently in his hand. Here he was, in the honeymoon suite, with only memories of a woman he'd once loved to warm his heart. For a moment, self-pity hovered threateningly. Which was ridiculous, he rebuked himself impatiently. His solitary state was purely his own doing. He'd known his share of women through the years, even met a few who made him fleetingly entertain the idea of marriage. But that's as far as it ever went. Because, bottom line, he'd never met anyone who touched his heart the way Maggie had.

He sat down in the chair and wearily let his head fall against the cushioned back. He'd never really admitted that before. But it was true. Maybe that was the legacy of a first love, he mused, that no one else ever measured up. Most people got over that, of course, moved on to meet someone new and fall in love again. He hadn't. As a result, he'd never regretted his decision to remain unmarried. Until now. Suddenly, as he contemplated a future that consisted of a more "normal" land-bound existence instead of the nomadic life he'd been living, the thought of a wife and family was appealing. For the first time in years, he felt ready to seriously consider marriage—and fatherhood.

Of course, there was one little problem, he thought with a humorless smile. He hadn't met the right woman.

Then again, maybe he had, he acknowledged with a sudden, bittersweet pang of regret, his smile fading. But it was too late for regrets. To be specific, twelve years too late.

"I mean, this guy is gorgeous!"

Abby looked at her sister and grinned as she scrambled some eggs. "Are you sure you're not exaggerating?" she asked skeptically.

"Absolutely not." Allison peeked into the oven to check the blueberry muffins, then turned back to her twin. "Tall, handsome, dark hair, deep brown eyes. And you know what? I think he's single."

"Yeah?" Abby paused, her tone interested. "How old is he?"

Allison shrugged. "Old. Thirty-something, probably. But for an older guy, he's awesome."

"Let me serve him, okay?" Abby cajoled.

"Hey, I saw him first!" Allison protested.

"Yes, but you had your chance to talk to him last night. It's my turn. That's only fair, isn't it, Aunt Maggie?"

Maggie smiled and shook her head. "You two are getting awfully worked up about someone who will be checking out in an hour or two."

Allison sighed dramatically. "True. But we can dream, can't we? Maybe he's a rich tycoon. Or maybe he's lost his beloved wife and is retracing the route they traveled on their honeymoon. Or maybe he's a Hollywood producer scouting the area for a new movie. Or..."

"Or maybe you better watch those muffins before they get too brown," Maggie reminded her with a nod toward the oven.

Allison sighed. "Oh, Aunt Maggie, you have no imagination when it comes to men."

"I have plenty of imagination. Fortunately, I also have a good dose of common sense."

"But common sense is so...so boring," Allison complained.

"He just came in," Abby reported breathlessly, peering through a crack in the kitchen door. She grabbed the pot of coffee before Allison could get to it, and with a triumphant "My turn," sailed through the door.

Maggie smiled and shook her head. One thing for sure. There was never a dull moment with the twins. At eighteen, the world for them was just one big adventure waiting to happen. And she encouraged their "seize the moment" philosophy—within reason, of course. Because she knew that life would impose its own limitations soon enough.

When Abby reentered the kitchen a few minutes later, she shut the door and leaned against it, her face flushed.

"Well?" Allison prompted.

"Wow!"

"See? Didn't I tell you? What's he wearing?" Allison asked eagerly.

"A dark gray suit with a white shirt and a maroon paisley tie."

"A suit? Nobody ever wears a suit here. He must be a business tycoon or something."

"Sorry to interrupt with such a mundane question, but what does he want for breakfast?" Maggie inquired wryly.

"Scrambled eggs, wheat toast and orange juice," Abby recited dreamily.

Maggie was beginning to regret that she'd missed this mysterious stranger's arrival. But the church council meeting had run late, and their unexpected guest had apparently retired for the night by the time she arrived home. It *was* unusual for a younger, apparently single, man to stay with them. Most of their guests were couples. Maybe she ought to check this guy out herself, she thought, as she placed two of the freshly baked blueberry muffins in a basket. Just for grins, of course. It would be interesting to see how she rated this "older guy" the twins were raving about.

Maggie picked up the basket of muffins and a glass of orange juice and headed for the door. "Okay, you two, now the mature woman of the world will give you her expert opinion."

The twins giggled.

"Oh, Aunt Maggie. You've never been anywhere but Missouri, Boston and Maine," Abby reminded her.

Maggie felt a sudden, unexpected pang, but she kept her smile firmly in place. "True. But that doesn't mean I haven't had my romantic adventures."

"When?" Allison demanded pertly.

When, indeed? There'd only been one romantic adventure in her life. And that had ended badly. But she'd never told the girls much about it. Only when they reached the age when boys suddenly became fascinating and they'd begun plying her with questions about her own romantic past had she even mentioned it. And then only in the vaguest terms. Yes, it had been serious, she'd told them. In fact, they'd been engaged. But it just hadn't worked out. And that was all they ever got out of her, despite their persistent questions. She never wanted them to know that it was because of their arrival in her life that her one romance had failed. They'd had a hard enough time adjusting to the loss of their parents; she never wanted to lay the guilt of her shattered romance on them, as well. And she wasn't about to start now. "I think I'll remain a woman of mystery," she declared over her shoulder as she pushed through the door to the sound of their giggles.

Maggie paused on the other side, taking a moment to compose herself. For some reason their innocent teasing had touched a nerve. She'd always claimed she had no time for romance, that she was perfectly happy living her life solo. She'd pretty much convinced them of her sincerity through the years. She'd almost convinced herself, as well. In many ways, her life *was* easier this way. Only occasionally did she yearn for the life that might have been. But she'd learned not to waste time on impractical "what-iffing." Her life was the way it was, and for the most part she was happy and content and fulfilled. The Lord had blessed her in many ways, and she was grateful for those blessings. In fact, she had more in the "blessings" department than most people.

Her spirits renewed, she glanced around the small dining room. All the tables were filled, but it was easy to spot their "mystery" guest. He sat alone, angled away from her, his face almost completely obscured by the daily paper he was reading. Yet she could tell that for once her assessment matched that of the girls'. They'd been right on target in their description of his physical attributes. He was impeccably dressed, his dark hair neatly trimmed above the collar of his crisp white shirt. His long legs stretched out beneath the table, and his hands seemed strong and capable.

As Maggie started across the room, the man lowered the paper and reached for his coffee, giving her a good view of his strong, distinguished—and very familiar—profile.

It was *Jake!*

Even as her mind struggled to reconcile his presence with the astronomical odds of him appearing in her dining room, her heart accepted it. She knew that profile—the firm chin, the classic nose, the well-shaped lips. It was him.

Maggie felt suddenly as if someone had delivered a well-placed blow to her chest, knocking every bit of wind out of her lungs. Her step faltered and the color drained from her face. She had to escape, had to get back to the kitchen and regain some control, before he spotted her.

But it was too late. As he lifted the coffee cup to his lips he glanced toward her, and their gazes connected— Maggie's wide with shock, Jake's changing in rapid succession from mild interest to curious to stunned.

Jake stared at the red-haired woman standing less than ten feet away from him and his hand froze, the coffee cup halfway to his lips. His heart stopped, then raced on. *Maggie!*

Maggie didn't even realize her hands were shaking

until the basket of muffins suddenly slipped out of her grasp. She tore her gaze from his and bent down, just as he rose to join her. Some of the juice sloshed out of the glass, leaving a sticky residue on her fingers as it formed a puddle on the floor. She looked at it helplessly, but a moment later Jake was beside her, wiping it up even as he retrieved a wayward muffin. Then he reached over and took her hand.

Her startled gaze collided with his, their eyes only inches apart.

"Let me," he said softly, the husky cadence in his voice exactly the same as she remembered it. With difficulty she swallowed past the sudden lump in her throat as he carefully wiped the sticky juice off her fingers with the clean side of the napkin. She stared down numbly, watching his strong, bronzed hand gently hold hers. She used to love the way he touched her, she recalled, her breath lodging in her throat. His hands—possessive, sure, tender—could work magic. A sudden, unexpected spark shot through her, and in confusion she jerked free of his grasp and rose unsteadily to her feet.

He stood up, as well, and then gazed down at her, his eyes warm, a shadow of incredulity lingering in their depths.

"Maggie." The way he said her name, gently and with wonder, made her heart lurch into triple time. "It's been a long time."

"Yes. It has." A tremor ran through her voice, but she didn't care. She was just grateful she could speak at all.

"Is this your place?"

"Yes. Listen, I'm sorry about the muffins and juice. I'll go get you some more. Excuse me." And then she turned and fled.

Jake watched her go, aware for the first time that the two of them were drawing curious looks from the other guests. With one last glance toward the kitchen, he slowly turned and walked back to his table. His first inclination had been to follow Maggie, but he understood that she needed some time to adjust to this strange turn of events. He knew he did.

Jake reached for his coffee, noting that his hand was trembling. He wasn't surprised. A bizarre coincidence like this was more than a little unsettling. Only yesterday he'd been thinking of Maggie, and his dreams last night had been filled with her. Then he'd awakened to a reality that didn't include her, reminding himself that she was part of his past. Until now.

For twelve years, Jake had felt as if the two of them had unfinished business. Now, after all these years, it seemed he was being given a second chance to make amends. And he intended to take it. He didn't expect her to welcome him back with open arms. But he hoped they could at least find some sense of resolution and inner peace.

Peace wasn't exactly the word Maggie was thinking as she burst through the kitchen door, breathless and pale. Her emotions were anything *but* peaceful. Her heart was banging against the wall of her chest as furiously as if she'd just finished a hundred-yard dash. She felt strangely light-headed. And more than a little annoyed. What was wrong with her? Why should a man whom she hadn't seen in twelve years, who had walked out when she'd needed him most, still have such a powerful effect on her? It didn't make any sense. And Maggie didn't like things that didn't make sense.

"Aunt Maggie?" Allison's concerned voice penetrated her thoughts, and she glanced up.

"What's wrong?" Abby asked, her face alarmed at her aunt's pallor.

Maggie forced herself to take a deep breath. "I'm fine. I just…well…that man you two have been talking about, I—I used to know him."

"You *know* him?" Allison repeated incredulously. "How? When?"

"A long time ago. I haven't seen him in years. It was just a…shock, that's all. I'll be okay in a minute."

Abby sent Allison a worried frown. Maggie never got rattled. "So who is he?" Abby persisted.

Maggie walked over to the center island and put two new muffins in the basket, then filled a glass with orange juice, aware that her hand was shaking. She knew the twins would notice. She also knew they weren't going to let her get away without explaining this uncharacteristic behavior. With a sigh, she turned to find them staring at her, their expressions intent—and concerned.

"He's a man I used to date…a long time ago."

Suddenly the light dawned on Allison's face. Though Maggie teased them about her past beaux, as far as they knew she'd only been really serious about one man in her entire life. Certainly none since they could remember. And it would take someone who had once been important to her to make their aunt…well, come unglued.

"Aunt Maggie, this is *him,* isn't it?" Allison's voice was slightly awed.

"Him who?" Abby demanded.

Allison turned to her twin, suddenly excited. "*Him.* You know, the guy Aunt Maggie was engaged to once."

Now it was Abby's turn to look incredulous. "Aunt Maggie, is that true?"

Maggie had always been glad that the twins had grown into insightful, perceptive young women. Until now. She might as well admit the truth, she thought with a sigh. They'd get it out of her sooner or later.

"Yes, it is."

"Wow!" Allison breathed.

"Yeah, wow!" Abby echoed. "It's so romantic!"

Maggie could think of other words to describe it. *Disruptive,* for one. *Upsetting,* for another. *Scary,* for a third, although why that word popped into her mind she had no idea. She turned to the twins and gave them a stern look.

"Now look, you two, the man is leaving shortly. It's just sheer coincidence that he turned up on our doorstep last night. I'll admit I was surprised. Shocked, even. But don't make a big deal out of this."

"But Aunt Maggie, don't you think it's…well, like a movie or something, that he appeared out of the mist at your B&B after all these years? You know, where long-lost lovers are reunited and rekindle an old romance?" Abby asked dreamily.

"First of all, we are *not* long-lost lovers. We didn't get lost. We broke up. On purpose. And second, neither one of us has any interest in rekindling an old romance. I'm perfectly content with my life just as it is. And even though he's not wearing a ring, Jake could very well have a wife and five kids somewhere."

"I'll bet he doesn't," Allison predicted smugly.

"Now why on earth would you say that?" Maggie demanded impatiently, turning to find the other twin peeking through the crack in the door.

"Because he keeps looking this way, like he's waiting for you."

"He probably just wants his orange juice," Maggie pointed out, trying desperately to keep her voice from reflecting the turbulence of her emotions.

As she picked up the glass and added it to the tray with the basket of muffins she could feel the twins' gazes on her back, knew they were silently communicating with each other about this exciting development in their aunt's lackluster love life. But in truth, she didn't want to go back out there. Talking to Jake would only stir up old, painful memories best left at rest. Yet, refusing to see him would be childish. Their relationship was history, after all. Whatever they once felt for each other had long since evaporated. They would simply carry on a calm, mature conversation, and then she'd bid him farewell. She could handle that, she thought as she lifted the tray and walked toward the door.

Couldn't she?

Chapter Two

Jake was on his feet the moment Maggie stepped through the door, but when she was detained by guests at another table, he slowly sat back down. In a way he was grateful for their intervention, because as they engaged her with questions about local sights, he had a chance to look at her unobserved.

She'd changed, he reflected, as his discerning gaze swept over her. She was still slender, her trim figure shown to good advantage in a pair of well-fitting khaki slacks and a green, long-sleeved cotton blouse that was neatly tucked in and secured with a hemp belt. But the girlish figure he remembered had changed subtly—and attractively—as she'd matured.

His appreciative eyes moved to her hair. The vibrant red color had mellowed slightly, but was no less striking, he noted with pleasure. He'd always been partial to red hair, and Maggie's was especially beautiful, shot through with gold highlights. Apparently she'd never quite tamed its waves. Despite her efforts to pull it sedately back, loose tendrils had escaped around her face, giving the no-nonsense style a winsome, feminine appeal. She still had her freckles, too, he observed with a smile, but they appeared to have faded slightly. He assumed she was grateful for *that* change, recalling how she'd always complained about them.

But there was something else...different...about her, he realized. The Maggie he remembered had been dependent, always waiting for him to take the initiative. The woman he now observed seemed anything *but* dependent. She was gracious, poised and self-confident. A woman who not only took charge of *things* but was quite capable of taking care of *herself.* It was a surprising—but intriguing—transformation.

There was one thing, though, that hadn't changed at all, he discovered a moment later when their gazes connected and his pulse flew into overdrive. He found her every bit as attractive as he had twelve years before. His spirits took a swift and surprisingly strong upswing— only to nosedive a moment later. Just because *he* felt the old chemistry didn't mean *she* did. And even *if* she did, he doubted that she'd want to renew their friendship, let alone anything more. Why should she, after what he'd done to her twelve years ago? Yet, he couldn't quite stifle the hope that suddenly surged through him.

Maggie moved toward him then, and he stood as she joined him, noting the slight flush on her cheeks. One more thing that hadn't changed, he tallied with pleasure. She still blushed. It was a quality he'd always found endearing.

"I wasn't sure you'd come back out," he confessed quietly.

She served the juice and muffins, avoiding his gaze. "Why wouldn't I?"

There was a moment of silence before he responded. "I wouldn't have blamed you if you hadn't," he told her, instead of replying to the question.

She risked a glance at him then, praying that her fragile composure would hold. "That was a long time ago, Jake." Much to her surprise—and relief—her voice was steady, and she congratulated herself for sounding so calm and controlled when her insides were churning.

Jake eyed her speculatively, debating whether to pursue the subject. "Maybe so," he responded carefully. "But some things are hard to forget."

A shadow crossed her eyes, come and gone so quickly he almost missed it. Anyone else would have. But once he had been keenly attuned to the nuances of her emotions. Apparently he still was. No matter what she said next, he knew that the hurt was still there, possibly buried so deeply in her heart even *she* didn't realize it still existed. But it clearly did, and his gut twisted painfully as he came face-to-face with the lingering effects of his actions twelve years before.

Instead of responding directly to his comment, she shrugged, and when she spoke, her tone was straightforward. "Life goes on, though. We all learn to cope."

He wanted to ask if life had been good to her, if she'd found the happiness she deserved, if she'd had much trouble raising the twins…if her heart belonged to another man. She wore no ring. He'd noticed that right away. But you didn't ask someone personal questions after twelve years. Not when you'd long ago forfeited the right. He had to settle for a less probing query. "So you've managed all right, then, Maggie?"

Maggie looked into his eyes—warm and compelling and intense—and remembered with a bittersweet pang how easily she used to get lost in his dark gaze. How, with a simple look, he could make her heart soar. His eyes were still expressive, still powerful, she realized. But she wasn't susceptible to their magnetism anymore, she told herself resolutely. A lot of things had changed. She'd changed. And this man, once the center of her world, was really nothing more than a stranger to her now.

She tucked the tray under her arm and forced herself to smile. "Well, as you can see, I have a business. The girls are well. We've done fine. I hope your career has been as satisfying as mine."

"The navy has given me a good life," he acknowledged. "I have no regrets about that choice, anyway."

But he had regrets about other choices? Better not to ask, though, she decided quickly.

"Well, I have things to attend to, Jake," she said brightly. "I hope your stay with us has been pleasant—"

The words died in her throat as he reached out and touched her arm.

"I know this situation is somewhat…awkward…but I can't help thinking our paths crossed again for some reason." He paused, searching for a convincing way to phrase his request. Finally he drew a deep breath, his eyes reflecting the intensity of his feelings. "I don't want to walk away without at least talking to you," he told her honestly, his gaze steady and direct. "Will you give me half an hour or so? For old times' sake, if nothing else?"

Maggie tried to ignore the entreaty in his eyes as she considered his request. But it was hard to think rationally when the warmth of his hand was seeping through the sleeve of her blouse. She really didn't want to talk to him. What good would it possibly accomplish after all these years? It seemed far…safer…to leave the past where it belonged—in the past.

But she had to admit that, like him, she was thrown by the odd coincidence that had brought them together. A coincidence so odd that it seemed somehow more than coincidence. She recalled how she'd prayed for just such a "coincidence" more often than she cared to admit in the early years, when she was struggling to earn a living and cope with the challenges of single parenthood. There were so many times when a simple touch, a warm, caring hand holding hers, would have lightened her burden immeasurably. But the Lord hadn't answered those prayers. Not in the way she'd hoped for, at least. Instead, He had helped her find hidden reserves of strength, spirit and determination that had seen her through the rough times. In the end, she'd made it on her own, and in so doing, discovered that she was a capable and competent woman who didn't need to rely on a man to survive. The experience had bolstered her self-esteem, and she had learned to make choices and plans decisively and with confidence.

So why had the Lord sent Jake now, long after she'd stopped asking? Why disrupt her world now, when she had not only resigned herself to a solitary life, but made her peace with it? Maggie didn't have a clue. But there must be a reason for this unexpected meeting, and maybe she should at least try to find out what it was.

"Please, Maggie," Jake persisted. "It would mean a lot to me."

She drew a deep breath and nodded. "All right, Jake. The girls can finish up the breakfast."

His answering smile was warm and grateful—and

relieved. "Thank you." He glanced at his watch. "I need to make a quick call. Then we can talk."

"There's a phone in the drawing room. Next to the fireplace."

He nodded. "I'll be right back."

Maggie watched him leave, then sank down into the closest chair. Her seat afforded her a discreet view of the drawing room. He was turned slightly away from her as he used the phone, and she took advantage of the opportunity to observe him.

He'd changed, she noted thoughtfully. He'd filled out, the lanky frame she remembered maturing into a trim, well-toned body. The style of his dark brown hair was familiar, though shorter than it used to be. And a faint brush of silver at both temples gave him a distinguished air. The few lines on his face, which hadn't been there when they parted, spoke more of character than of age. Maggie had to admit that he was even more handsome now than he had been twelve years before.

But there was something else different about him, something beyond the physical that she couldn't quite put her finger on, she realized with a frown. He radiated a quiet confidence, a decisiveness, a sense of determination and purpose. It was reflected in his body language, in the very way he moved, she thought, as he hung up the phone and made a few quick notes on the pad beside it. The Jake she had known was eager, restless and searching. This Jake was polished, self-assured and at peace with his place in the world.

And yet…there was a certain indefinable sadness in his eyes, a world-weariness, that tugged at her heart. It was almost as if he'd searched the world for something but had come up empty, and ultimately had resigned himself to that fact.

Maggie had no idea where that insight came from, or even if it was accurate. Nor did she have a clue what it meant. Still, she knew instinctively there was a void of some sort in Jake's life that troubled his soul.

But the state of Jake's soul was *not* her concern, she reminded herself sternly as he walked toward her. Her energies would be better focused on conducting a civil, rational conversation.

Jake smiled as he sat down across from her. "Well, that buys me an hour."

"You have an appointment?"

"Mmm-hmm. But I wish I didn't."

His comment, as well as the familiar tone in his voice, startled Maggie. She didn't know how to respond, so she remained silent, uncomfortably aware that he was studying her.

"The years have been good to you, Maggie," he said finally. "You look great."

This wasn't at all the polite, impersonal conversation she'd expected, and the warm, husky note in his voice rattled her. "Th-thanks. So do you," she replied, berating herself for letting him fluster her.

"So tell me about this place." He made an all-encompassing gesture. "Have you been doing this long?"

That was more like it, she thought with relief. Questions like that she could handle. "Eight years. I moved to Boston about a year after…" She started to say, "after you left," but changed her mind. The less she talked about *them*, the better. "…after I got the twins," she continued. "I worked in a graphic design firm there for three years. By then Abby was finished with all her operations and therapy, so there was less need to stay in a big city. And I thought it would be better for the girls to grow up in a small town. We'd visited Maine on vacation once and loved it, so we came up and looked around one summer. This place happened to be on the market at a good price. It had been vacant for a while, and even though it was structurally sound, it needed lots of cosmetic help and some updating. Before I knew it, I was the proud owner of a B&B. I did freelance design work for a while to tide us over until we established a clientele, and I still sell some of my watercolors to a greeting card company."

She paused and took a deep breath. "The early years here were a little rough, and it took a lot more hard work than I expected to get established, but I've never regretted the move," she finished.

Jake eyed her speculatively, making no attempt to conceal his admiration. "I'm impressed, Maggie. It took a lot of courage to make such a radical life-style change. Not many people would have risked it."

She shrugged dismissively, but was oddly pleased by the compliment. "I did a lot of research before I made the move. This is a popular area, and the B&Bs do well. I drew up a pretty solid business plan, so it wasn't too difficult to get a loan for the necessary improvements. And I found ways to keep the capital expenditures reasonably low."

Jake stared at the woman across from him, struggling to reconcile the Maggie he knew with this savvy businesswoman. His Maggie would not have had a clue about business plans or capital expenditures. Apparently she'd changed even more than he suspected. But it wasn't an unpleasant change, he realized, a faint smile touching his lips.

Maggie noted the smile and eyed him cautiously. "What's wrong?"

"Nothing. It's just that the Maggie I remember had very little interest in business. I'm surprised, that's all."

"The Maggie you knew didn't *need* to be interested in business, Jake. This one does."

There was no hint of recrimination in her matter-of-fact tone, but the old, familiar guilt tugged at Jake's conscience. If he'd honored his commitment to her, Maggie wouldn't have had to struggle alone to build a life for herself and the twins. It couldn't have been easy, though she'd downplayed the difficulty. Which only made him admire her more.

"You seem to have done a good job," he said quietly. "This place is obviously a success. And the twins seem like fine young women. Abby looks as if she's recovered fully from the accident."

Maggie nodded. "She has. She needed two more operations after…after I took them in, and therapy after that for three years. But she's fine now." She glanced toward the kitchen, her eyes softening. "They've been a tremendous help to me through the years. I couldn't have made this place a success without them. And they've brought a great deal of joy to my life."

Now was the perfect opening to ask the question that was most on his mind. He reached for his coffee and took a sip, trying to phrase it the right way. "Has it just been the three of you all these years, then?"

Maggie turned and looked at him directly. "If you're asking me whether I'm married, or have ever been married, the answer is no."

"Why not?" The indiscreet question came out before he could stop it, and he felt hot color steal up the back of his neck. He shook his head and held up his hands. "Listen, forget I asked that, okay? It was way out of line."

She toyed with the edge of a napkin, then gave a little shrug. "It's all right. The simple fact is, you weren't the only one who didn't want to take on a ready-made family, Jake. Especially one with medical problems."

He flinched. She'd scored a direct hit with that comment, whether she intended to or not. "I guess I deserved that," he admitted.

She frowned. "I didn't mean it that way. It's just that I eventually realized my situation was an awful lot for anyone to take on, especially in the early years. And as time went by, I simply lost interest in romance. I have a nice life. Why should I change it? But tell me about you," she urged, adroitly shifting the focus before he could pursue the subject. "What are you doing here?"

He took her lead readily, grateful she hadn't taken offense at his rash question. "Actually, I'm interviewing this afternoon at the Maine Maritime Academy."

Her eyes widened in surprise. "For a job?"

"Yes. To make a long story short, I'm leaving the navy and Dad is coming to live with me."

"What about your mom?"

"She died five years ago, Maggie."

"Oh." Her face looked suddenly stricken, and he reached across and laid his hand over hers. Maggie had always gotten along famously with his parents. They'd held a special place in her heart, especially after her own parents died.

"It was a shock to all of us," Jake continued gently. "She had a stroke about five years ago. She lived for about six months after that, and Dad took care of her at home. That's where she wanted to be. Mom was a great believer in families taking care of their own. In fact, before she died, she made Rob and me promise that if Dad ever got to the point where he couldn't live alone, one of us would take him in rather than relegate him to a retirement or nursing home."

"And he isn't able to live alone now?"

Jake shook his head regretfully. "No. He had a heart attack about eight months ago and went down to stay with Rob and his family in Atlanta while he recovered. Except that he never did recover very well. He's gotten pretty frail and a little forgetful, and Rob and I finally realized that he couldn't ever go home. Rob was perfectly happy to have Dad live with them—the kids love having their grandpa around—but three weeks ago he lost his job in a corporate downsizing, and Jenny— Rob's wife—had to go back to work. What with three kids and lots of uncertainties, life has been pretty stressful for them. And they really can't give Dad the attention he needs. So the younger son—namely me—was called in to pinch-hit. That's why I'm here."

"You mean you're giving up your navy career to take care of your dad?"

Jake dismissed the implied sacrifice with a shrug. "I never intended to spend my life in the service. And even though it was a good life in many ways, I have to admit that I'm getting a little tired of being a nomad. The idea of settling down in one place is beginning to appeal to me. Rob may be having some career problems at the moment, but I'm starting to envy his life—the wife, the kids, the picket fence."

"So you've been…alone all these years?" she said tentatively.

"I never married, either, Maggie," he told her quietly.

A strange feeling of lightness swept over her, but she ignored it and focused on a less volatile topic. "So how does your dad feel about this move?"

Jake's face grew troubled. "Not happy, I'm afraid. You know how independent Dad always was. He hasn't taken kindly to having to rely on his kids to take care of him. Rob says it wasn't too bad at first, when Dad thought he'd eventually be able to go home. But since we decided that's not an option, he's been pretty despondent. He knows we're right, but that hasn't made it any easier for him to accept. And it's even worse now that he realizes he'll be stuck with me instead of Rob, at least for a while."

Maggie eyed Jake assessingly. His last comment had been made lightly, but she suspected his tone masked deeper feelings. She knew his parents hadn't been happy when he'd walked out on her. They'd apologized on his behalf more times than she could count. But surely, after all these years, his father didn't still hold a grudge against his son on her behalf. There had to be more to their troubled relationship than that.

"I take it you and your dad don't get along that well," she probed carefully.

Jake gave a short, mirthless laugh. "You might say that. As I'm sure you know, Dad was very disappointed in me after I…after we broke up. And he didn't hold back his feelings on the subject, either. So I made fewer trips home, which only seemed to fuel the fire. I did go home more often after Mom's stroke, but not enough to suit Dad. He figured I'd abandoned them, too, I guess."

Maggie looked at him in surprise. Abandoned them, too? That was an incriminating word choice. Did it mean that he regretted his decision twelve years ago to break up with her? Had guilt followed him all these years as he roamed around the world? She'd never really considered that. She figured once he'd made his decision he's simply gone on with his life, that eventually memories of her and their time together had faded. But his words implied otherwise.

"Anyway, like it or not, we're stuck with each other," Jake continued. "And I'm determined to make the best of it. In fact, to be perfectly honest, I hope we can mend the rift between us. Dad and I used to be close, and… well, I've missed that all these years."

Once again, Maggie was taken aback by Jake's admission. He'd never been the kind of man who talked much about feelings. Maybe the willingness to do so had come with maturity, she speculated. Once you felt comfortable with your life and had proven your abilities, it was easier to admit other limitations without feeling threatened. Jake struck her as being a very secure man in most aspects of his life. Confident and in control. Yet he'd been unable to reestablish a good relationship with his father. And he wasn't too proud to admit it.

"Well, the opportunity will certainly be there now," Maggie pointed out encouragingly. "I'm sure your dad will come around."

Jake shook his head skeptically. "I'm not so sure. But I have to try at least. Rob has his hands full, and we can't go back on our promise to Mom. Besides, Rob's done more than his share with Dad since Mom died. It's only right I take my turn."

Maggie stared at Jake. The man was full of surprises.

Through the years she'd gradually convinced herself that he was a self-centered, spoiled, irresponsible man who had probably grown even more so with age. But the decisions he'd made regarding his father, his acceptance of his duty, his willingness to honor the promise to his mother at the expense of his career, weren't the actions of a selfish man. They spoke of integrity and principal and dependability. Maggie had to admit that his behavior was admirable. But it was a grudging admission, and certainly not one she cared to verbalize.

"Excuse me, but there's a call for you, Mr. West," Abby interrupted, pausing beside the table, her gaze blatantly curious as it moved from Jake to Maggie. "A man named Dennis Richards."

Jake frowned. "He must not have been able to switch the time for the first interview after all. Will you wait, Maggie? I'll be right back."

"Yes."

"You can take the call on the phone in the foyer, at the desk," Abby told him.

She watched Jake leave, then turned to Maggie, her eyes shining. "Were you really engaged to him once?" she asked incredulously.

Maggie briefly glanced in the direction Jake had disappeared and nodded. "It's a long story, honey. And it happened a long time ago."

"But he's back now," Abby pointed out eagerly. "Who knows? Maybe—"

"Maybe we should try not to let our imaginations run away with us," Maggie advised, cutting off her niece's fanciful speculations.

"But what's he doing here?" Abby persisted.

"He's on his way to Castine. He's considering a job at the Maritime Academy."

"You mean he might be living less than twenty miles away?" Abby was clearly elated.

"Maybe," Maggie admitted reluctantly.

"Wow!" Abby repeated. "Wait till I tell Allison!"

Before Maggie could respond, Abby turned on her heel and disappeared into the kitchen. Maggie shook her head helplessly, then propped her chin on her hand, a pensive frown on her face as she considered the situation.

Jake had reappeared in her life after twelve years. "Shock" was hardly adequate to describe her reaction. But somehow she'd made it through the last half hour or so. Perhaps the Lord had taken pity on her and sent an extra dose of courage her way. Still, it had taken every ounce of her willpower and fortitude to act as if Jake's presence hadn't been a jolting experience that left her reeling emotionally.

She had succeeded, though, and congratulated herself for that. But a thirty-minute encounter was one thing. How on earth would she cope if the man lived just down the road? If she knew every time she went out that she might run into him—at the grocery store, on the street, in the park? The thought unnerved her completely.

What unnerved her even more was the realization that the man still had the *power* to unnerve her. She resented that. After all, he was nothing to her anymore. Her life was full and rich as it was. She had two loving "daughters," an artistic talent that gave her great joy, a satisfying career and a solid faith that continued to sustain her. What more could she ask for?

But Maggie knew the answer to that question, she admitted with a sigh. Though she'd long ago reconciled herself to the fact that the single life seemed to be God's plan for her, deep in her heart she still yearned for someone to share it with. Having once loved deeply, she knew what joy love could bring. She didn't think about it often, though. Idle wishing was fruitless. But seeing Jake again had reawakened those yearnings, made her recall the heady feeling of being in love.

Her lips curved up into a wistful smile as she thought back. It had been a wonderful time, those days of awakening emotions and eager plans for a future together, when the world stretched before them, infinite in its possibilities. How differently her life would have turned out if those plans had come to fruition. But the Lord had had a different future in store for her. And she shouldn't complain. Her life had been blessed in many ways.

"It looks like I'll have to leave sooner than I wanted to." Jake's regretful voice interrupted her reverie.

"I understand."

"Listen, Maggie, I'd like to continue our conversation. We barely got started. Can I call you tomorrow?"

She frowned and slowly shook her head. "I'm not sure that's a good idea."

"I guess you've been kinder to me already than I have any right to expect," he acknowledged soberly. "You probably still hate me, and I can't say I blame you."

"I never hated you, Jake. I was just…hurt. But I got over that a long time ago."

He looked at her, wanting to believe that was true, but finding it difficult to accept. In her place, he doubted he'd be that forgiving. "Really?"

She nodded. "Really."

"Then why won't you talk to me?"

Because I'm scared, she cried silently. *I feel like a tightrope walker who's about to lose her balance. And I don't want to fall, Jake. Not again. Not ever again.*

But of course she couldn't say that. "It's awfully busy this time of year. I just don't have the time to socialize."

"How about a phone call, then? Surely you can spare a few minutes for that."

They both knew she could. And Maggie didn't want to give Jake the impression that she still held a grudge. That would make her seem small and unforgiving. Not to mention un-Christian. With a sigh, she capitulated.

"All right, Jake. Give me a call when you have a few minutes."

She was rewarded with a smile so warm it seemed like sunshine on a lazy summer day. "Thank you, Maggie. I appreciate it. I've already taken care of my bill and loaded my car, so I'll say goodbye for now." He stood up and held out his hand. She had no choice but to take it, trying to still the rapid beating of her heart as her fingers were engulfed in his firm, warm grip.

"I know this encounter has upset you, Maggie," he murmured, the familiar husky timbre of his voice playing havoc with her metabolism as his discerning gaze locked on hers. "And I'm sorry for that. I never want to upset you again. But I'm not sorry our paths crossed. I think it happened for a reason."

Maggie didn't respond. She couldn't.

Jake held her gaze a moment longer, then released it—as well as her hand. "I'll call you soon," he promised. With that he turned and strode away.

Maggie sank back into her chair, his words echoing in her mind. He'd said he thought their paths had crossed for a reason. She couldn't dispute that. It was too odd a coincidence to accept at face value. He'd also said he was glad it had happened. On that point she disagreed. Maggie wasn't glad at all. Because now that Jake had walked back into her life, she somehow knew it would never be the same again.

Chapter Three

"Earth to Maggie, earth to Maggie. Are you with me over there?"

Maggie abruptly returned to reality, blushing as she sent Philip, her lunch partner, an apologetic look. "Sorry about that," she said sheepishly.

"No problem. So what if you don't find my company fascinating? Why should I be insulted?"

Maggie grinned at his good-natured teasing. "You're a good sport, you know that?"

"So I've been told. So what gives?"

She shifted uncomfortably. "What do you mean?"

"Maggie, I've known you for what…seven, eight years? In all that time I've never once seen you distracted. So I figure something's happened—something pretty dramatic. Therefore, I repeat…what gives?"

Maggie looked down and played with her fork. She should have known she couldn't hide her inner turmoil from Philip. He was way too perceptive. And maybe it wasn't such a bad idea to tell him about Jake. Philip had been a trusted friend and firm supporter for years.

Without his encouragement, she might never have taken up serious painting again. Even now he had several of her pieces displayed in his gallery. He'd been a good sounding board through the years, too. A widower with two grown daughters, he'd offered her valuable advice about the girls on numerous occasions. Maybe it wouldn't hurt to run this situation by him, get his take on it.

"Okay, you win," she capitulated. "Something pretty...dramatic...did happen today."

He tilted his head and eyed her quizzically. "Well, I can't say you look unhappy exactly. It must not be anything too terrible."

"I'm not so sure about that," she murmured, shaking her head. She stirred her ice tea and took a deep breath. "You remember I mentioned once that years ago I was engaged?"

"Mmm-hmm."

"Well...Jake—that was his name—he...he stayed at the inn last night."

Philip frowned. "You mean he came to see you?"

"No, nothing like that," she said quickly. "He got caught in the fog and just happened to stop at our place. Allison checked him in. I didn't even know he was there until this morning at breakfast, when the girls kept talking about this...this nice-looking man who'd checked in. It turned out to be Jake."

Philip stared at her. "That must have been a terrible shock."

Maggie gave a short, mirthless laugh. "That's putting it mildly. I've been off balance ever since it happened. Which is odd, since my relationship with him was over long ago. I can't figure out why his reappearance has disturbed me so much."

Philip studied her for a moment. "It does seem strange," he concurred. "After all, whatever you two shared is obviously history."

"Right."

"And it isn't as if he even means anything to you anymore."

"Right." This time there was a hint of uncertainty in her voice.

"What was he doing here, anyway?"

"He's interviewing for a job at the Maritime Academy."

"You mean he might actually move up here?"

"Yes. And that makes me even more nervous. Which is ridiculous, because we're really no more than strangers to each other now."

"It's probably just the shock of seeing him," Philip reassured her. "Where has he lived all these years?"

"All over, I guess. He's been in the navy. I think he still would be if it wasn't for his father." Maggie briefly explained the situation to Philip.

"Hmm" was his only cryptic comment when she finished.

Maggie tilted her head and looked at him quizzically. "What's that supposed to mean?"

He shrugged. "I guess I'm a little surprised. And impressed. Not many people would give up their career, start over, change their whole life to keep a promise basically made under duress. He sounds like a very honorable man."

Maggie frowned. "Yes, he does," she admitted. "And

it's so at odds with the image I've had of him all these years."

"Well, people do change."

"I suppose so," she admitted reluctantly. "I just wish I didn't feel so off balance."

"Things will work out, Maggie," he told her encouragingly. "They always do. You've successfully weathered a lot of storms though the years, and you'll ride this one out, too. I know. And I'm always here if you need a sympathetic ear. Don't forget that." He touched her hand lightly and smiled, then switched gears. "In the meantime…when do I get a preview of the new painting?"

"Will next week be okay?"

"Perfect. I'll reserve a spot right near the front for it. You know, you have a large enough body of work now to consider your own show."

Maggie grimaced. "I just don't feel…well…good enough…to have an official show."

"Why don't you let me be the judge of that? Besides, you'll never know till you try. It's not like you to back off from a challenge."

"I know. But my painting is so…personal. If I got bad reviews it would be devastating. I'm not sure I'm ready to face that."

"First of all, they wouldn't be bad. And second of all, you can face anything, Maggie Fitzgerald. Because you are one of the strongest women I know."

Maggie wanted to believe him. As recently as yesterday she might have. But a lot had happened since then. And at this particular moment, she didn't feel very strong at all—thanks to one very unforgettable man named Jake West.

* * *

"Jake called twice. Will call again tomorrow."

Maggie's heart leapt to her throat as she read the note on the kitchen counter. She should have figured he'd call while she was out. She hoped the girls had explained where she was. She didn't want him to think she was trying to avoid him. It was just that she led a very busy life. Her days—and evenings—were filled. Like tonight. The zoning board meeting had run far later then she expected, because of some heated discussion. And she still had a few breakfast preparations to make, even if it was—she glanced at her watch and groaned—ten-thirty. There always seemed to be too much to do and not enough time.

As Maggie methodically set about assembling the egg and cheese casseroles that were tomorrow's breakfast entrée, she reflected on the hectic pace of her life. For most people, simply running an inn and raising twins would be a full-time job. But she had made other commitments, as well. Like serving on the church council. And on the zoning board. Not to mention the watercolors she did for the greeting card company and, in recent years, pursuit of more serious art in her limited "spare" time. Why did she take so much on? she wondered with a frown. Could it be that she wanted to keep herself so busy that she had little time to dwell on the one thing that was lacking in her life?

With an impatient shake of her head, Maggie beat the eggs even harder. She didn't usually waste time trying to analyze her life choices. If some of them were coping mechanisms, so be it. They worked, and that was all that mattered. Or they'd worked up until today, she amended. Jake's reappearance had changed everything and, much to her surprise, rattled her badly.

But what surprised her even more was the fact that when she looked at him, it wasn't the hurt she remembered, but the intense, heady joy of being in love. In some ways, it would almost be easier to remember the pain. Because that had no appeal. But love—that was a different story. That had a whole lot of appeal. It was just that the opportunity had never come along again. And it wasn't here *now,* she reminded herself brusquely as she slid the casseroles into the refrigerator. Jake had had his chance. She wasn't about to give him another.

Abby looked up from her seat in a wicker chair on the porch and grinned as she saw Jake stride up the path.

"Did you come to see Aunt Maggie?" she asked eagerly, laying her book aside.

"Please don't tell me I missed her again?" He'd been trying unsuccessfully for the past two days to reach her, and the frustration was evident in his voice. If every minute of his stay in Castine hadn't been packed, he would have simply driven over and planted himself in her drawing room until she had time to talk to him. But he knew one thing for sure. He wasn't leaving Blue Hill until he saw her again, even if that meant tracking her down wherever she might be now.

"Don't worry, you didn't. She's in the studio, Mr. West."

He felt the tension in his shoulders ease, and he smiled. "Call me Jake. And where's the studio?"

"It's the little room off the kitchen."

"Would it be all right if I go back?"

"Sure. Aunt Maggie won't mind," Abby said breezily,

ignoring the worried look that Allison sent her way as she stepped outside. "It's just down the hall and through the door at the end."

"Thanks." Jake turned to find Allison in the doorway.

"Hello, Mr. West," Allison greeted him.

Jake grinned at her. "No one's called me 'Mr.' in years. Just Lieutenant. And both of those sound too formal now. So how about we just make it Jake?"

Allison smiled. "Okay."

"Good. I'll see you ladies later."

Allison watched him disappear, then turned to her sister with a worried frown. "Why did you send him back there?" she demanded urgently. "You know Aunt Maggie said never interrupt her when she's painting, unless it's an emergency."

Abby gave her sister a condescending look. "Allison, Aunt Maggie's love life *is* an emergency."

Allison clamped her lips shut. How could she argue with Abby—especially when her sister was right?

Maggie tilted her head and frowned. She wanted the seascape to convey restlessness, inner turbulence, the sense of impending fury. But she wasn't quite there yet. Considering her firsthand knowledge of the ocean, and given that her own emotional state paralleled the scene she was trying to paint today, it ought to be easy to transfer those feelings to canvas. But the mood was eluding her, and that was frustrating.

A firm tap sounded on the door, and Maggie glanced toward it in annoyance. Why were the twins bothering her? They were old enough now to handle most of the so-called crises that occurred at the inn. But maybe there truly was an emergency of some kind, she thought. In sudden alarm she reached for a rag to wipe her brush, psyching herself up to deal with whatever crisis awaited her. "Come in."

The "crisis" that appeared when the door swung open was *not* one she was prepared for, however. What on earth was Jake doing here, in her private retreat? She stared at him in surprise as her heart kicked into double-time. Try as she might, she couldn't control the faint flush that crept onto her cheeks, or stop the sudden tremble that rippled over her hands.

Jake smiled engagingly. "Abby said I could come back. I hope you don't mind. But I'm on my way back to Boston, and this was my last chance to see you before I left. We didn't seem to have much success connecting by phone."

"Y-yes, I know." Why did her voice sound so shaky? "Sorry about that. I was at a zoning board meeting the first night you called, and running errands the other times." That was better. Steadier and more in control.

"So the girls told me." He propped one shoulder against the door frame and folded his arms across his chest. "You continue to amaze me, Maggie. I don't remember that you ever had any interest in politics or government, local or otherwise, and now you're on the zoning board?"

She carefully set the brush down and reached for a different rag to wipe her hands on, using that as an excuse to escape his warm, disquieting gaze. "Well, I'm part of the business community of this town. It's my home. I feel a certain sense of responsibility to do my part to make sure Blue Hill retains the qualities that attracted me in the first place."

"Once again, I'm impressed."

"Don't be. A lot of people do a whole lot more than me."

He didn't agree, but rather than debate the point, he strolled into the studio, his gaze assessing. It was a small room, illuminated by the light from a large picture window on one side. Unlike his image of the stereotypical messy artist's studio, however, this one was neat and orderly. A couple of canvases in various stages of completion stood on easels, and several other finished works were stacked against one wall.

But what captured his attention most were the posters. Vienna. Florence. Rome. Paris. London. Athens. As his gaze moved from one to another, he realized that these were the places he and Maggie had planned to visit together. And he realized something else, as well. He'd seen most of them, while Maggie had been confined to rural Maine, coping with responsibilities that even now her slender shoulders seemed too fragile to bear. His dream of travel had become reality; hers had remained a dream.

He looked down at her slim form silhouetted against the window, the sun forming a halo around her hair, and his throat tightened. He wished with all his heart that he could take her to all the exotic places pictured on her walls. She would love them, he knew, would be as awed as he had been on his first visit. But maybe…maybe she'd managed to see one or two, he thought hopefully.

He nodded toward the walls. "Nice posters," he remarked casually. "Are any of them souvenirs?"

She gave him a wry smile and shook her head, dashing his hopes. "Hardly. B&B owners may cater to travelers, but they do very little traveling themselves.

Especially with two girls to raise. I've stayed pretty close to home all these years. I expect you've made it to some, or all, of these spots, though."

He nodded, trying to stem the surge of guilt that swept over him. "Yes."

"Are they as wonderful as we…as people say?" she asked, the slightly wistful note in her voice producing an almost physical ache in his heart.

"Mmm-hmm." He cleared his throat, but still the huskiness in his voice remained. "I'm sorry you never got to see them, Maggie."

"Oh, but I will," she said brightly, suddenly aware that he felt sorry for her. She didn't want his sympathy. "I'm going to Europe right after Christmas. Actually, the trip's been in the works for years. I decided what with the twins going away to college this fall, it was time I started a new phase of my life, as well. I'm going to close the B&B for four months and visit all the museums and take some art classes and just soak up the ambiance. It should be wonderful!"

The sudden spark of enthusiasm in her eyes lit up her face, giving it a glow that warmed his heart. "That sounds great. I know you'll enjoy it, especially with your art background." He nodded toward the canvases stacked around the room. "I guess I never realized just how talented you are. I remember you sketching and doing some watercolors, but not painting. I don't know that much about art, but these look very impressive to me."

Despite herself, Maggie was pleased by his compliment. "Thanks. I'm not that good, though. I really don't have any formal training. But Philip—he owns a local gallery—has encouraged me. He even displays some of my work. And he's been trying for the last year to convince me to have a show at a gallery in Bangor that's owned by a friend of his. But I'm just not sure I'm ready for that."

"You look ready to me," Jake told her sincerely. There was a quality to her work, an emotion, a power, that radiated compellingly from the canvases. Even with his untrained eye he could sense it.

"Philip says so, too. But I haven't committed to it yet."

"Is this Philip someone whose judgment you trust?"

She nodded confidently. "Absolutely. About everything except my painting, that is. We've been friends for a long time, and I'm afraid he may not be completely impartial."

An alarm bell rang in Jake's mind. Maggie had used the term *friend,* but when she spoke of this Philip, the warmth and familiarity in her voice implied something more. And that possibility disturbed him. Which was wrong. He certainly had no claim on her heart. He should be glad that she'd found a male companion. Considering all the love she had to offer, Maggie wasn't the kind of woman who should spend her life alone. But even as he acknowledged that his reaction was selfish and wrong, he couldn't change the way he felt. The thought of Maggie in love with another man bothered him. It always had.

"Well, I think he's right," Jake said, biting back the question that he longed to ask her about Philip.

"We'll see," Maggie replied noncommittally. "So... you're heading back to Boston. How did the interview go?"

"I'll tell you all about it in exchange for a cup of coffee," he bartered with a smile.

"Oh! Sure. I thought maybe you only had a few minutes."

"I've got an early flight out of Boston tomorrow morning, so I'd like to get back at a reasonable hour. But I can stay for a little while," he told her as he followed her into the large, airy kitchen.

"Flight?" she asked over her shoulder as she filled two cups.

"Rob and I are meeting at the old house. Before we put it on the market we have to sort through everything and decide what we want to keep. The rest will be sold at an estate sale."

Maggie turned to him with a troubled frown. "This must be awfully hard on your dad."

"I'm sure it is," he agreed with a frown. "He's accepted the necessity of it, though, and other than a few specific items he's asked us to save, he's pretty much left the disposition of everything in Rob's and my hands."

"That won't be an easy job, Jake," Maggie empathized.

Jake hadn't really thought that far ahead. But he'd been gone from his childhood home for a long time. The emotional ties had loosened long ago. He expected he'd cope just fine. He couldn't very well say that, though. It would sound too coldhearted somehow.

"Well, Rob and I will be doing it together. That should help," he replied.

She placed his coffee on the table and sat down, motioning for him to join her. "So how did the interview go?"

"I guess it went well. They offered me the job."

Her breath caught in her throat as her heart stopped, then lurched on. "So you'll be moving to Castine?" she said carefully.

He nodded. "In about three weeks."

Three weeks! That hardly even gave her time to adjust to the idea! "That fast?"

"Well, Rob's in a bind. The sooner I take Dad off his hands, the better. And I think I'll like the job a lot. I've been an instructor for a few classes in the navy, and I enjoy teaching. And this job will let me stay close to the sea, which is a real plus."

His voice had grown thoughtful, and Maggie looked at him curiously while he took a sip of coffee, again struck by the sense of maturity and quiet confidence that he radiated. The high energy she remembered—exhilarating but sometimes undirected—seemed to have been tamed and channeled toward specific goals.

"So, since I had a lot of leave accumulated, I'm taking a month off while they process my discharge— to get things squared away for my new life. I found a nice two-bedroom cottage that's available right now and signed the papers yesterday," he finished.

"It seems like you have everything pretty much under control."

"Logistically, yes. Dealing with my father...that's another story."

"Well, he's had an awful lot to adjust to, Jake. Maybe he just needs some time."

"Time I can give him. I'm just not sure that's all it will take." He glanced at his watch regretfully and drained his cup. "I've got to go. It's a long drive back to Boston. But I'll be back, Maggie. And I was hoping...

well, I thought maybe we could have dinner then to finish catching up and celebrate my new job."

She looked into warm brown eyes that, with a single glance, had once been able to fill her heart with light and hope and promise. But that was then. This was now. And she wasn't the starry-eyed bride-to-be that she'd been twelve years ago.

And yet…sitting here with him now, she felt an awfully lot like the young girl she used to be. Which was not a good sign at all. Her best plan would be to avoid him until she straightened out the emotional tangle she'd felt ever since his reappearance.

"So what about it, Maggie? How does a dinner celebration sound?"

She looked down and ran a finger carefully around the rim of her cup. "I'm not sure that's a good idea, Jake."

He didn't respond immediately, and she refused to meet his gaze, afraid that if she did, her resolve would waver. Finally she heard him sigh, and only when he made a move to stand up did she look at him.

"Would you think about it at least?" he asked quietly. "Don't give me an answer now. I'll call you when I get back. And I'm sorry about interrupting your work. I'll let myself out."

Maggie didn't protest. And as she watched him disappear through the door, she took a sip of her cold coffee. She had no intention of changing her mind. For one very simple reason. She wasn't at all sure there was anything to celebrate.

Chapter Four

With a weary sigh, Jake flexed the muscles in his shoulders, then reached for yet another dusty box. Thank heavens Rob hadn't been called back to Atlanta for that job interview until all of the big items at the house had been dealt with. Only a couple of closets remained for Jake to clean out alone. But it was slower—and more difficult—going than he'd expected.

It seemed that Maggie had been right. Even though he'd cut most of his ties with this small house and the town where he grew up, for some reason he found it surprisingly difficult to be in his childhood home for the last time. He'd come to realize that though his ties to this place were few, they were stronger than he'd suspected. The process of cutting his roots with such finality was unexpectedly unsettling.

As he and Rob pored over the old scrapbooks, sometimes laughing, sometimes lapsing into quiet, melancholy remembrance, the good days came back to Jake with an intensity that startled him. The days when they'd all lived here together under this roof, happy and content. The days when he and his dad were not only father and son, but friends.

He'd lingered longest over the faded photos. The photos of himself, flanked by his parents at high school graduation, their eyes shining with pride. Photos older still, of his dad teaching him to ride a bike and to pitch a baseball. For years, Jake hadn't allowed himself to remember those happier times. The memories only made him sad. Though he'd denied it to himself for more than a decade, the truth was he'd always cared what his father thought about him. But he'd failed him twelve years ago, and many times since in the intervening years.

Jake sighed. He almost wished he didn't care. It would make things easier. But he did. He still loved his father, despite the older man's opinionated views and stubborn disposition. Not that he'd done much to demonstrate that in the last decade, he admitted. After his father's sound rejection of his initial overtures, he hadn't wasted time or energy on further attempts.

His mother was a different story. She had been disappointed in his choices, as well, but she'd never let that interfere with her love for him. The rift between her youngest son and husband had always caused her distress, and in her quiet way she'd tried—unsuccessfully—to bring them together on several occasions. One of her greatest disappointments was that she hadn't lived to see a reconciliation.

Maybe his father would have softened over time if Jake had admitted he'd made a mistake. And maybe Jake would have admitted his mistake if his father's attitude had softened a little. But instead it became a standoff. It was a shame, really, Jake thought with a pang of regret. Because as he'd grown older he'd come to realize the enormity of his betrayal in walking out on the woman he had professed to love.

Jake had considered admitting that to his father a few times through the years, but the older man had never offered him an opening. And Jake didn't want it thrown back in his face.

Sometimes he wondered if his father harbored regrets, too. If he did, he'd never let on. Jake suspected that pride was at the root of their problem. But knowing the source didn't necessarily suggest a solution. And dwelling on the past wasn't helping him finish today's job, he reminded himself.

Jake glanced at the box he had just withdrawn from the closet and was surprised to find his name written on it in his mother's neat, careful hand. As he sifted through the contents, he realized that she had saved every letter he'd written, as well as every clipping he'd sent. He blinked rapidly to clear the sudden film of moisture from his eyes. His mother's death had been hard on him. He missed her deeply, as well as the direct link she had provided to home. Although he'd continued to write, his father never responded. It was only through Rob that Jake kept tabs on him. He wasn't sure if his father even opened his letters.

Suddenly Jake's gaze fell on the clipping announcing his promotion to lieutenant two years before. His mother couldn't have put that in the box. Nor the article about the special commendation he'd received last year, he realized, shuffling through the papers. Which only left one possibility. His father had not only *opened* his letters, but *saved* them. Which must mean he still cared.

With a suddenly lighter heart, Jake worked his way steadily through the remaining boxes, eating a hastily assembled sandwich as he made one more circuit of the house to ensure that none of the furnishings had gone untagged. Most items were to be sold. A few were to be shipped to his cottage in Maine. Everything seemed to be in order, he thought with satisfaction, as he stepped into the garage and glanced around. There really wasn't much of value out here, certainly nothing he planned to take to Maine. Unless...

His gaze lingered on the boxes containing his father's woodworking tools. He knew from Rob that they had lain unused since his mother's death. But why not hang on to them, just in case? Without stopping to reconsider, Jake quickly changed the instructions on the boxes, then headed back inside.

By the end of the emotionally draining day, Jake had reached the last "box"—a small fireproof safe stored in the far corner of the closet in his parents' bedroom, under the eaves. He read the label, written in his mother's hand, with a puzzled frown. "Important Documents." As far as he knew, he and Rob had already located and dealt with all the "important documents."

But the mystery was cleared up a moment later when he opened the lid. He should have guessed the kinds of things this box would contain, knowing his mother's definition of "important," he thought with a tender smile. Carefully, one at time, he withdrew the items. Her own mother's handwritten recipe for apple pie. A poem she'd clipped from the newspaper about taking time to enjoy a quiet summer night. Jake's kindergarten "diploma." An embossed copy of the Twenty-third psalm, given to her on her wedding day by her father. These sentimental items were his mother's real treasures, Jake knew. These "important documents"—not expensive rings or necklaces—had been her jewels.

Every item touched his heart—but none more so than the last one. As he withdrew the single sheet of slightly yellowed paper, memories came flooding back of a hot summer day more than a quarter of a century before. The document contained few words, but as his eyes scanned the sheet he remembered with bittersweet intensity the strong emotions and deep sincerity that had produced them.

It had been a long time since that document had seen the light of day. But as he carefully replaced the paper and gently closed the lid, he hoped that its time would come again soon.

"Is Maggie here?"

The unfamiliar woman behind the desk at Whispering Sails shook her head. "No, I'm sorry. Is there something I can help you with?"

Jake sighed wearily. It had been a hectic and emotionally taxing three weeks since he'd left Maine, and he'd had a very long drive up from Boston. He should have just gone directly to his cottage in Castine and contacted Maggie tomorrow. This was obviously a wasted detour.

"No. I was just hoping to see her for a minute. I should have called first."

The woman looked at him uncertainly. "Are you a friend of hers?"

"Yes." Jake wasn't sure Maggie would agree, but from his perspective the statement was true.

"Well…then I guess it's okay to tell you what happened. Allison was in a car accident, and Maggie's at the hospital."

Jake's face blanched. "How badly is she hurt?"

"I don't know. Maggie got the call about two hours ago, and I haven't heard from her yet."

"Where's the hospital?"

The woman gave him directions, and with a clipped "Thank you," he strode out the door and to his car. Less than a minute later he pulled out of the driveway in a spray of gravel, his foot heavy on the gas pedal, oblivious to the speed signs posted along the route.

By the time he reached the hospital, his body was rigid with tension. He scanned the emergency room quickly, but there was no sign of Maggie.

"Sir...may I help you?"

He glanced at the woman behind the desk. "I'm looking for Maggie Fitzgerald. Her niece, Allison Foster, was brought in some time ago. A car accident."

"Oh, yes. Ms. Fitzgerald is just around the corner." She inclined her head to the right.

"How is Allison?"

"The doctor is still with her, sir. We'll let you know as soon as we have any word."

He acknowledged her reply with a curt nod, then covered the length of the hall in several long strides, pausing when he reached the door to the cold, sterile waiting room. It was empty except for the lone figure huddled in one corner.

Jake's gut clenched as he looked at Maggie's slim form, every muscle in her body tense, her face devoid of color. He tried to swallow, but it was difficult to get past the sudden lump in his throat. How many of these kinds of crises had she endured alone, without even the reassuring clasp of a warm hand for comfort?

Jake had never thought of Maggie as a particularly strong woman. But his assessment of her had changed radically in the last few weeks. She was clearly capable of handling emergencies alone. If she wasn't, she couldn't have survived the last twelve years. But that didn't mean she had to, not anymore. Not if he had anything to say about it, he decided, jamming his hands into his pockets, fists clenched, as a fierce surge of protectiveness swept over him.

The sudden movement caught Maggie's eye and she jerked convulsively, half rising to her feet as she turned to him. The frantic look in her eyes changed to confusion as his identity registered. Was that Jake? she asked herself uncomprehendingly. And if so, why was he here? She hadn't prayed for him to miraculously appear to comfort her, to hold her, to help her survive, as she had so many times in the past during times of trauma. And yet…here he was. Or was it just a dream? she wondered, closing her eyes as she wearily sank back into her chair and reached up to rub her forehead.

The warm hand that clasped her icy one a moment later wasn't a dream, though, and her eyelids flew open.

"Jake?" Her voice was uncertain, questioning, as if she couldn't believe he was really there.

"Yeah, it's me," he confirmed softly as he reached over and pried a paper cup of cold coffee out of her other hand, then took that hand in his warming clasp, as well.

"But…what are you doing here?"

"I stopped by Whispering Sails, and the woman on duty told me you were here. What happened, Maggie?"

She drew a deep, shuddering breath and spoke in

short, choppy sentences. "Some guy ran a stop sign. Rammed Allison's car on the passenger side. He walked away. But her…her head hit the window. It knocked her out. She was still unconscious when they brought her in. They haven't told me anything yet. But I'm afraid…. She's so young, and… Oh, Jake!" A sob rose in her throat and she bowed her head as a wave of nausea swept over her. *Dear God, please let Allison be all right,* she prayed fiercely. *Please! She has her whole life still to live!*

Jake watched helplessly as Maggie's slender shoulders bowed under the burden of desperate worry. Without even considering what her reaction might be, he put his arm around her and pulled her close.

For a moment, Maggie was sorely tempted to accept the comfort of his arms. A part of her longed to simply let go, to burrow into the haven he offered, to let his solid strength add stability to a world that at the moment seemed terribly shaky. Part of her wanted that badly.

But another part sounded a warning. *Don't get used to this, Maggie. Don't even think about leaning on this man. You did that once, remember, and where did it leave you? Alone, to pick up the pieces. You've handled crises before. You don't need him to make it any easier. Because even if he helps you through this one, he won't be there the next time. And it will be that much harder to face if you accept his support even one time.*

Jake felt her go absolutely still, and he waited, holding his breath. He hoped she would simply let him hold her, that she would accept his actions at face value—as the compassion of a friend. But when her body grew rigid and she pulled away, he knew he'd lost this round. Reluctantly he let her go.

"Ms. Fitzgerald?"

Maggie's head shot up and she was on her feet instantly. "Yes."

The white-coated figure walked into the room and held out his hand. "I'm Dr. Jackson." He turned to Jake quizzically as he took Maggie's hand.

"Th-this is Jake West," Maggie told him. "He's a…a friend of the family."

The two men shook hands, and then the doctor turned his attention back to Maggie. "Let's sit down for a minute, okay?"

Jake watched her carefully. He could tell from the rapid rise and fall of her chest that she was scared to death, and despite her rejection moments before, he decided to risk taking her hand. Maybe she'd allow that minimal intimacy. He wanted—needed—her to feel a connection between them, a tactile reassurance that she was not alone. And this time she didn't protest his touch, he noted with relief. In fact, she almost seemed unaware of it, though she gripped his hand fiercely.

"Your niece has a slight concussion, Ms. Fitzgerald, and a bruised shoulder. Nothing more, it appears. She was very lucky that the other driver hit the passenger side of the car. We'd like to keep her overnight for observation, but she should be fine."

Jake could sense Maggie's relief as her body went limp. "Thank God," she whispered fervently.

"You can see her now if you'd like."

"Yes." She nodded and rose quickly. "If you'll just show me the way, Doctor…"

"Of course."

"I'll wait here for you," Jake told her.

She stopped and turned back to him with a frown. "You don't have to."

"I want to."

Maggie was too exhausted to argue. Besides, she had a strong suspicion it wouldn't do any good anyway. "I'm not sure how long I'll be."

"I'm in no hurry." Before she could argue further, Jake settled into one of the chairs and picked up a magazine.

Short of telling him to get lost, Maggie was left with no choice but to follow the doctor.

She reappeared in thirty minutes, and Jake looked at her in surprise, rising quickly when she entered. "Is everything all right?" he asked.

"Yes. Allison's all settled now. She wanted me to go home and get some rest." She didn't tell him that when Allison found out Jake was there, she'd just about pushed her aunt out the door.

"I think she's right. You look done in, Maggie."

"Yeah, well, it's been a long day." She brushed a hand wearily across her eyes, and Jake noted that her fingers were still trembling. She was clearly in no condition to drive, he realized.

"Listen, Maggie, why don't you let me take you home?"

Her startled gaze flew to his. "But…my car is here."

"Do you need it for anything else today?"

"No."

"Then leave it here. I'll bring you back tomorrow to pick up Allison."

"That's too much trouble, Jake. I couldn't let you do that."

Couldn't or wouldn't? he wondered, deciding to try a

different tact. "Come on, Maggie," he cajoled. "I know you're a strong woman and very capable of running your own life, but it's okay sometimes to let other people help. Besides, my mother always taught me to do at least one good deed a day. If you cooperate, I can count this for today."

Maggie was torn. In all honesty, she felt too shaky to drive. And she *was* exhausted. But she definitely did *not* want to feel indebted to Jake, didn't want to owe him *anything*.

"Look, Maggie, this is an offer with no strings, okay?" he assured her, as if reading her mind. He'd been pretty good at that once, she recalled. It was rather disconcerting to think he still was. "And if you feel that you have to do something to repay me, here's a suggestion. You can go with me to pick up Dad at the airport next week. A familiar face might help smooth over what's sure to be a rocky beginning."

Maggie considered his request. It seemed like a reasonable trade.

"Okay," she agreed. "That seems fair."

A relieved smile chased the tension from his face. "Great. Let's head home."

When he took her arm and guided her toward the door, she didn't pull away as she had earlier. His protective touch felt comforting. Not that she'd let it happen again, of course. Tomorrow, after a good night's sleep, she'd feel stronger. And then she'd keep her distance.

"Well, this is it."

Maggie turned to look up at Jake as they waited near the exit ramp of the plane, noting his tense expression. She wanted to reassure him that everything would be all right, but she wasn't sure that was true. From what Jake had told her, he and his father wouldn't have an easy time of it. Still, she wished there was some way to ease his mind, offer him some hope. With sudden inspiration she reached up and touched his arm.

"Jake, do you remember the verse from Proverbs? 'Entrust your works to the Lord, and your plans will succeed.' It's been a great comfort to me through the years. I know you face an uphill battle with your dad, and I'm not sure anyone can make it any easier for you. But there is a greater power you can turn to, you know. Prayer might help."

Jake glanced down at her with a wry smile and covered her hand with his. "Well, it sure couldn't hurt."

Just then the passengers began to emerge, and Maggie felt Jake stiffen, almost as if he was bracing for a blow.

A few moments later Howard West appeared. At least she thought it was Jake's father. But the frail figure trudging wearily toward the waiting area bore little resemblance to the robust man Maggie remembered. There was nothing in his dejected posture or delicate appearance to suggest the man she had once known. Maggie's grip on Jake's arm tightened, and she felt a lump rise to her throat.

Jake looked down at her. He should have prepared Maggie for his father's deteriorated appearance, he realized.

"He's changed a lot since Mom died," Jake murmured gently. "And even more since the heart attack."

She nodded silently and he saw the glint of unshed tears in her eyes. "I guess I should have expected something like this," she admitted, a catch in her voice. "But somehow I never thought that…well, I don't know, he just seems so…so lost…"

Jake glanced back toward his father and nodded. When he spoke, his own voice was slightly uneven. "I know. He should have made a better recovery. But after Mom died, he lost interest in a lot of things, and once he had the heart attack he just sort of gave up on life. He keeps getting more frail. It's hard to accept sometimes. He was always so strong."

Howard looked up then. His gaze fell first on Jake, and his eyes were so cool, Maggie could almost feel the chill. His mouth tightened into a stubborn line and he lifted his chin slightly, defiantly as the two men looked at each other across a distance that was more than physical. They remained like that for several seconds, until finally, sensing a need to break the tension, Maggie took a step forward and smiled.

Howard transferred his gaze to her, and the transformation in his face was astonishing. The glacial stare melted and the line of his lips softened as a genuine smile of pleasure brightened his face.

"Hi, Pop," she greeted him, using her pet term of endearment for him.

"Maggie." He held out his arms. "Nobody's called me that in years. Aren't you going to give this old man a hug?"

She stepped into his embrace, and his thin, bony arms closed around her. There was almost nothing to him, she realized in alarm as she affectionately returned the hug. When they finally drew apart there was a telltale sheen to his eyes.

"Maggie girl," he repeated, still holding her hands. "You look wonderful. A sight for sore eyes, I can tell you. I heard you were here, but I didn't expect you to come and meet me. I'm glad you did, though. It does a body good to see such a friendly face in a strange place."

Maggie knew Jake was right behind her, knew he'd heard his father's comment. She was sure it had cut deeply. And she was equally sure that was Howard's intent. Clearly the gulf between the two of them had widened dramatically through the years, she thought in dismay.

"Hello, Dad."

Howard reluctantly transferred his gaze from Maggie to Jake. "Hello," he said flatly.

"Did you have a good trip?"

"It was bumpy. And long."

"Then let's get your luggage and head home so you can rest."

"I don't need to rest."

Before Jake could respond, Maggie tucked her arm in Howard's and began walking toward the luggage carousels. "You're a better traveler than me, then," she declared with a smile. "I'm always tired after a long plane trip. And Atlanta to Maine certainly qualifies."

"Well, I might be a little tired," he admitted.

"Maybe a short nap would be nice when you get home."

"Maybe it would."

Although Howard conversed readily enough with Maggie, and his eyes even took on their old sparkle a couple of times, she quickly became aware that he was doing his best to ignore his son. Several times she tried to draw Jake into the conversation, but Howard would have none of it. Finally she gave up.

When Jake pulled into the parking lot of Whispering Sails, Howard leaned forward interestedly. "Is this your place, Maggie?"

"Yes. And the bank's," she teased.

"Well, it's mighty pretty. And a nice view, too."

"Thanks, Pop. It's been our home for a long time now. We love it here."

"I can see why. What's that over there?" He pointed to a small structure of weathered clapboard about a hundred yards from the house.

"That's our cottage. It's a little roomier and more private than the house. Some of our guests come back and stay there every year. I'll give you a tour soon, if you'd like."

He nodded eagerly. "That would be great."

She reached back then, and clasped his hand warmly. "You take care now, okay, Pop?"

He held on to her hand as if it was a lifeline, the strength of his grip surprising her. "Is that tour a promise, Maggie?"

The plea in his eyes made her throat tighten, and her heart was filled with compassion and affection for this man she'd once loved like a father. Cutting her ties with Jake's parents had been very painful, but at the time it had seemed the best way to preserve her sanity and start a new life. She'd never stopped missing them, though. And she was more than willing to do what she could to ease the difficult transition for this man who had lost not only his wife, but his health, his home and now his independence.

"Of course. Give me a call once you're settled and we'll have lunch."

"I'd like that." When he at last reluctantly released her hand, she reached for the door handle.

"I'll walk Maggie to the door, Dad."

"That's not necessary, Jake," she said quickly.

"I insist."

"At least some of your good manners stuck with you," Howard muttered.

A muscle in Jake's jaw clenched, but he didn't respond. Maggie quickly stepped out of the car and met him at the path to the house, deciding not to protest when he took her arm. She wasn't going to give him the cold shoulder, too.

"It's pretty bad, isn't it?" she conceded quietly.

"And not apt to get much better any time soon, I'm afraid."

He paused when they reached the porch and raked his fingers wearily through his hair. "Thanks for going today, Maggie. I think it was good for Dad to see a friendly face, as he so bluntly put it."

There was a touch of bitterness—and despair—in Jake's voice, and though Maggie had her own unresolved issues with this man, she couldn't help but feel compassion for his plight. Impulsively she reached over and laid a hand on his arm. "I'll keep you both in my prayers, Jake," she promised with quiet sincerity.

"Thanks. We could use them. Goodbye, Maggie."

As he walked back to rejoin his father, Jake thought about Maggie's last comment. He wasn't much of a praying man, not anymore. In fact, it had been so long since he'd talked to the Lord that he doubted if his voice would even be recognized. But maybe the Lord would listen to Maggie.

Jake hoped so. On his own, he wasn't sure he could

ever make peace with the stony-faced man waiting in his car. It would take the intervention of a greater power to bring about such a reconciliation. In fact, it would take a miracle. And unfortunately, Jake thought with a sigh, he hadn't witnessed many of those.

Chapter Five

Jake slowly opened his eyes, glanced at the bedside clock with a groan, then pulled the sheet back over his shoulder and turned on his side. Even after all his years in the navy, living by rigid timetables that often included unmercifully early reveille, he'd never adjusted to getting up at the crack of dawn. Okay, so maybe eight o'clock didn't exactly qualify as the crack of dawn. But it was still too early to get up on a Sunday morning.

He had just drifted back to sleep when an ominous clatter in the kitchen rudely awakened him. Obviously his father was up, he thought wryly. As he'd discovered in the last couple of days, Howard was an early riser. But he usually tried to go about his business quietly until Jake appeared. Clearly, however, his father was in no mood to humor him this morning.

With a resigned sigh Jake swung his feet to the floor. He supposed he should look on the bright side. At least they hadn't come to blows yet. On the other hand they'd barely spoken since Howard's arrival. Jake had tried to engage his father in conversation, but the older man's responses were typically monosyllables or grunts.

Jake frowned as Howard noisily dropped something onto the counter. For whatever reason, his father appeared to be in a worse mood than usual today.

Jake pulled on his jeans and combed his fingers through his hair. Might as well find out what was in the old man's craw. Whatever it was, Jake had a sinking feeling that it had something to do with him.

He padded barefoot toward the kitchen, pausing on the threshold to survey the scene. Howard had apparently already eaten breakfast, judging by the toast crumbs on the table and the almost-empty cup on the counter. A crusty oatmeal pot added to the unappetizing mess. Jake jammed his hands into his pockets and took a deep breath.

"I would have made breakfast for you, Dad."

"I might starve waiting for you to get up," the older man replied brusquely.

Jake felt a muscle tighten in his jaw, but he tried to maintain a pleasant, civil tone. "I spent a lot of years in the navy getting up early, Dad. I like to sleep in when I can. I'll be on my new job in less than a month, back to a regular schedule. I'm enjoying this while I can."

"At the expense of God, I see."

Jake frowned. "What's that supposed to mean?"

Howard spared him a disparaging glance, disapproval evident in his eyes. "It doesn't look to me like you plan on going to church today. I guess you've turned your back on God, too."

So that explained why his father was wearing a tie, Jake thought distractedly as he considered Howard's caustic remark. The fact was, the older man was right—

and Jake felt guilty about it. Since he'd left home, he'd slowly drifted away from his faith. Oh, he still believed all the basics. He just hadn't seen much reason to demonstrate those beliefs by going to church. And gradually, as time went by, his faith had become less and less a part of his life. But clearly it was still very much a part of his father's.

"Give me a few minutes to get dressed," he said shortly, turning on his heel and retreating to his bedroom.

"What time are the services?" his father called.

Jake ignored the question—because he didn't have a clue. But Maggie would. He knew beyond the shadow of a doubt that her faith still played a pivotal role in her life. There was probably a church somewhere near Castine, but if he had to go, he figured he might as well use it as an excuse to see her. He reached for the phone, praying she hadn't left yet.

By the time Jake reappeared in the kitchen fifteen minutes later, in a navy blue blazer and striped tie over khaki slacks, his father had cleaned up the kitchen and was sitting at the table reading the paper. He looked up and adjusted his glasses when Jake stepped into the room, and for the briefest second Jake could have sworn he saw a flash of approval. But it was gone so fast, he couldn't be sure.

"So what time are services?"

"Ten o'clock."

"When do you want to leave?"

"Nine-thirty should be fine. I'm going to grab some breakfast first."

His father silently perused the paper as Jake toasted a bagel and poured some coffee. Except for the rustle of paper as he turned the pages, the house was quiet. Jake didn't even try to converse with him this morning. The last few days had been draining, and he was tired. The tension in the air between them was so thick, he could cut it with the proverbial knife. Jake found himself on edge all the time, constantly bracing for his father's next dig.

The drive to the church also passed in strained silence. But the sight of Maggie waiting outside for them, just as she'd promised, brought a wave of relief. Funny. As far as he was concerned, Maggie had more reason than his father did to treat him badly. Yet despite her wariness and her obvious attempts to keep him at arm's length emotionally, she was at least civil. That was more than he could say for his father.

"Hello, Pop. Hi, Jake."

Jake smiled at Maggie as they approached. She looked especially lovely today, in a teal green silk dress that clung to her lithe curves, her hair sending out sparks in the sun when she moved. In the soft morning light, she hardly looked older than she had twelve years before.

"Hi." He smiled at her, and their gazes connected for a brief, electric moment before hers skittered away.

"Maggie, you're a sight for sore eyes." Howard's tone was warm, and for the first time since the day they'd picked him up at the airport, the older man smiled. It was amazing how that simple expression transformed his face, Jake reflected. Gone was the cold, prickly, judgmental man who shared his house. In his place was a congenial stranger, easygoing and good-natured. He seemed like the kind of person who could get along with anybody. Anybody but his youngest son, that is, Jake thought grimly.

"How have you been, Pop?"

He shrugged. "Kind of hard to adjust to a new place. I'm looking forward to that lunch and tour you promised me, though."

"How about tomorrow?"

"That would be great!" His eyes were actually shining and eager, Jake noted.

"Jake, would you like to come, too?" Maggie asked politely, turning to him.

The idea of spending time with Maggie under any circumstances was appealing to Jake. But he knew his presence would ruin the treat for the older man. Slowly he shook his head. "I'm afraid I can't. I need to go over to school and get some things squared away." Without even looking, he could sense his father's relief.

"Another time, then," Maggie replied.

Did she mean it? he wondered. She'd done little to encourage his attention since that first morning at the B&B when he'd reappeared in her life. She was polite, pleasant, completely civil. But he sensed very clearly that she'd also posted a No Trespassing sign on her heart. She would be nice to him because she was a lady and because she'd been brought up in a faith that taught forgiveness. But he suspected that she had set clear limits on their relationship.

Maggie took Howard's arm and led him into the church, leaving Jake to follow in their wake. In Maggie's presence Howard stood up straighter, walked more purposefully, Jake realized. It was obvious that Maggie was good for his father. And maybe…maybe that was why their paths had crossed, he speculated. Not because the two of them were destined to renew a failed romance, but because Maggie would be able to help Howard.

It was a sobering thought, and not one Jake especially liked. It wasn't that he begrudged his father the joy Maggie seemed to give him. But somehow he'd hoped that…well, he didn't know exactly what he'd hoped would come out of their chance meeting. He only knew it had something to do with him and Maggie—*not* Maggie and Howard.

As Jake took a seat beside Maggie, he tried to recall the last time he'd been to a Sunday service. Eight or ten years ago, maybe? Probably during one of his few visits home on leave. It felt strange to be back. Strange, and yet… He couldn't quite put his finger on it. It was just that here, in this peaceful place, with the familiar words of Scripture ringing in his ears and Maggie and his father beside him, he felt oddly as if he'd come home. Which made no sense, given that his father hated him, Maggie—though polite—was distant, and he hadn't darkened a church door in years. The Lord probably didn't even recognize him. Nevertheless, he couldn't shake the sense of homecoming. For whatever reason, being in this place with these people felt good. And right.

When the service ended, Maggie accompanied them outside, then turned to say goodbye. But Jake didn't want her to leave, not yet. She was the only bright spot in his day, and he was in no hurry to return to the silent, tension-filled house with his father.

"Where are the girls today?" he asked, trying to buy himself a few more minutes in her presence.

"Minding the store. We take turns going to services

on Sunday. What time would you like me to pick you up tomorrow, Pop? We don't take guests on Sunday night, so my Monday mornings are free."

"I'll drop Dad off, Maggie. It will save you a trip," Jake said.

She considered his offer for a moment, then gave a shrug of concession. "All right. How about ten o'clock, Pop?"

"The sooner the better as far as I'm concerned."

"I'll see you tomorrow, then." She reached over impulsively and gave Howard a hug, and for a moment Jake actually envied the older man. Though she was only a whisper away from him, she was as distant as some exotic locale where he'd been stationed. The breeze sent a whiff of her perfume his way, and he inhaled the subtle, floral scent. Nothing dramatic or sophisticated, just refreshing and filled with the promise of spring. It seemed somehow to capture her essence.

"Goodbye, Jake," she said pleasantly as she stepped out of his father's embrace. The sizzling connection was there again as their gazes met, sending a surge of electricity up his spine. His eyes darkened, and her own dilated ever so slightly under the intensity of his gaze, her lips parting almost imperceptibly. How was it possible that she could move him so after all these years with no more than a look?

"See you tomorrow, Maggie," Howard said brightly.

With a nod, she turned and walked rapidly away. Too rapidly, Jake thought. It was as if she was running away from him. He knew she didn't want to feel anything for him. He understood that. He also understood that she had no choice. *They* had no choice. The emotional ties that had once bound them might be tattered. But the chemistry was most definitely still there.

"She always was a real special girl," Howard declared warmly as he watched her disappear around the corner. "It sure is nice to see that some things never change."

Jake glanced at his father, prepared to take offense. But for once the older man's potentially barbed remark didn't seem to be directed at Jake. His eyes were thoughtful, sad even, as he stared after Maggie. Maybe his father was thinking of all the things that had changed in his life these last few years, Jake mused. Death, illness, loss of independence—they'd all taken their toll.

Both his father and Maggie had clearly changed through the years. And so had he. For the better, he thought. The challenge was to convince these two very special people of that.

"This sure is a wonderful place, Maggie," Howard complimented her as they finished their tour of Whispering Sails. "And you did all this yourself?"

"All the decorating. And a lot of the minor renovations. It's amazing what you can learn from a library book. Plumbing, wallpapering, electrical repairs, carpentry—it's all there."

Howard shook his head. "I would never have believed it. I don't recall you ever showing an interest in that kind of thing in the old days."

"Well, what's that old saying—'Necessity is the mother of invention'? You can learn an awful lot when you have to. And it's a whole lot more economical than paying someone to do it. So how about a quick look around town before we have lunch?"

By the time Maggie pulled up in front of Jake's cottage to drop Howard off, it was nearly three o'clock. She could tell that the lonely older man was reluctant to see their outing come to an end, and her throat tightened in empathy. If only he and Jake could reach some understanding. This rift had to be hard on both of them.

"Maggie, would you come in and have a cup of coffee?" Howard asked, the plea in his eyes tugging at her heart. "Jake's not back yet. His car's still gone."

Maggie hesitated, but only for a moment. As long as she didn't have to worry about running into Jake, she could spare a little more time for Howard. And maybe she could find some words that would help these two strong-willed men breach the gap between them. "All right. For a few minutes," she agreed.

Half an hour later, sitting at the kitchen table with Howard, Maggie carefully broached the subject. "So how have you and Jake been getting along?"

Howard's response was a wry face and a shrug. Which pretty much confirmed her suspicion. She took a sip of her coffee, then wrapped her hands around the mug, choosing her words carefully. "You know, Pop, it would be easier if you and he could find a way to make some sort of peace."

He glanced down at his coffee. "Not likely."

"I feel guilty about the two of you, you know. Like the rift between you is my fault."

"That's not true, Maggie. At least not now. Jake's decision to walk out on you did *start* everything. What kind of man would do a thing like that? I thought I raised him better." He shook his head sadly and sighed.

"But things just went downhill from there. I guess I made my feelings pretty clear—I never have been one to mince words—and he just quit coming around. Oh, once in a while on leave he'd show up for a few days. More for his mother than anything else. He did love her, I'll give him that. But he should have come around more often. She was always sad he didn't. It was almost like he cut us off because we reminded him of something he was ashamed of. Even when Clara was sick, we didn't see much of him. Not till the end. Barely made it home before she died, in fact. That wasn't right."

"Where was he at the time, Pop?" Maggie asked gently.

"Japan."

"That's pretty far away," she reflected. "I don't suppose the navy would have looked kindly on too many trips home."

Howard studied her curiously. "Seems strange, you defending him, Maggie. After what he did to you."

She shrugged and took a sip of her coffee. "It was a long time ago, Pop. We were different people then. I was devastated for a long time. But in the end I put it in the hands of the Lord, asked for His help. And eventually I was able to leave the past behind and move on. I won't lie to you, Pop. The scars are still there. It was a very tough road alone. But the girls, and my faith, helped a lot."

"I can see you've made a nice life for yourself, Maggie. But...well, I hope you won't think I'm being too nosy...I just wondered how you feel about living this close to Jake again after all these years."

Maggie took a moment to consider that question as she poured herself another cup of coffee. It was the same question she'd been asking herself for weeks. And it was a question that became even harder to answer after Sunday services, when one sizzling look from Jake had not only sent her blood pressure skyrocketing, but made her feel as shaky as a newborn colt.

So far she hadn't come up with an adequate answer. Her feelings were all jumbled together...shock, anger, trepidation. She was nervous and jumpy and confused. Mostly confused. Because she'd long ago relegated her relationship with Jake to history. She'd even gotten to the point where weeks went by when she didn't think of him. She had finally convinced herself that he no longer meant anything to her. So she had been stunned and unsettled to discover that the powerful attraction between them hadn't died after all. It had simply lain dormant—and undiminished. She felt it spark to life every time he was near her. She sensed that he did, too. And she didn't like it. Not in the least. But she didn't know what to do about it.

Maggie glanced up and realized that Howard was still waiting for an answer. "I really don't know, Pop," she replied honestly as she stood and gathered up their cups. "I'm still trying to sort it out." She deposited the cups in the sink and turned on the faucet. "I suppose I'm still in..." She paused and peered down. "Say, Pop, did you know your sink isn't draining too well?"

He rose and joined her. "Yeah. We called the owner but he hasn't done anything about it yet."

"This could back up anytime. Let me take a quick look in the garage. There might be a few tools."

Howard showed her the way, but after poking around between the boxes Jake had shipped from his father's house, she gave up. "I don't see anything. But I have some in the... Pop, what's this?" she asked curiously, leaning close to examine a label on a box. "Do you still do woodworking?"

Howard peered at the box. "Haven't in years. Not since Clara died. Hmmph. Can't imagine why Jake brought all that stuff. Guess I ought to look around and see what else he dragged up here." He glanced at the small accumulation of boxes, and his shoulders sagged dejectedly. "Not much to show for a lifetime, is it? A couple dozen boxes of junk."

Maggie reached over and gently touched his arm. "Pop, you know the important things aren't in boxes. They're here." She laid her hand on her heart.

He nodded. "You're right about that. But I haven't done too well on that score, either, I guess."

"It's never too late."

He considered that in silence for a moment, then turned to her and planted his hands on his hips. "But first things first. What about my clogged-up sink?"

She smiled. "I have some tools in the car. Let me run out and get them."

A few minutes later Maggie was wedged under the sink, Howard standing over her. "Can you hand me the wrench?" she asked, her voice muffled.

He rummaged around in her toolbox and passed it to her. "Maggie, are you sure you know how to do this?"

She grinned. "Trust me. Now, do you think you could round up some rags or old towels? There's probably water in here that will run out when I loosen the pipes."

"I'm pretty sure there are some rags out in the garage. I'll check."

Maggie shifted into a more comfortable position as she waited. It was too dark under the sink to get a clear view of the pipes. When Howard returned she'd ask him to hold the flashlight while she worked. In the meantime, she might as well see how tight the corroded connections were, she decided, reaching up to clamp the wrench onto the pipe.

When Jake pulled up in front of the cottage, he was pleasantly surprised to discover Maggie's car still parked in front. He had expected her to be long gone by the time he returned. He had no idea how his father had convinced her to come inside, but he owed the older man one for that coup. Just seeing her would brighten up his otherwise mundane day.

Jake strolled into the house, pausing in the living room to listen for voices. But the house was totally silent. Maybe they were sitting out back.

Jake strode quickly through the living room, heading toward the back door. But he came to an abrupt halt when he reached the kitchen doorway and his gaze fell on a pair of long, clearly feminine legs, in nicely fitting tan slacks, extending out from under his sink. Maggie, of course. But what in heaven's name was...

"Pop? Listen, could you hold the flashlight for me? It's pretty dark under here. And hand me the rags. I think the wrench did the trick. It's starting to give."

Silently Jake walked over to the sink, sorted through the items in the unfamiliar toolbox on the floor and withdrew a flashlight. He clicked it on, then squatted beside the prone figure, impressed by her deft handling of the wrench. She was full of surprises, that was for sure. As he recalled, she didn't know pliers from a screwdriver in the old days. With a smile he pointed the light toward the tumbled mass of red hair. "Sorry. I don't have any rags," he said in an amused tone.

Maggie's startled gaze flew to his, and she tried to sit up, whacking her forehead on the pipe in the process. "Ouch!" She clapped her hand to her head and let the wrench drop to the floor.

Jake was instantly contrite. "Maggie, are you all right?" Without waiting for a reply, his hands circled her slender waist and he gently tugged her into the open until she sat on the floor beside him, her head bowed.

"I can't believe I did that," she muttered, rubbing her forehead. "After all the sinks I've been under, to pull a stupid stunt like that..."

"I shouldn't have startled you. Let me check the damage." He pried her hand off her forehead and frowned at the rapidly rising lump. "This needs ice right away." He rose and reached for her hand, drawing her swiftly to her feet in one smooth motion, then guided her to a chair. "Sit tight. What were you doing under there, anyway?" he asked over his shoulder as he headed toward the freezer.

"Pop said it was clogged. I figured I could probably fix it. I was checking it out when you walked in."

"I found some rags, Maggie. They were right where..." Howard stopped abruptly at the garage door. "What happened?" he asked in alarm.

"I hit my head," Maggie explained quickly. "Jake is fixing me an ice pack."

"I knew I shouldn't let you tackle that plumbing. That's not woman's work," Howard fretted.

"Oh, Pop, don't be silly. I do this all the time at home. Women are liberated these days, you know." Jake handed her the homemade ice pack—ice cubes in a plastic bag wrapped in a dish towel——and she clamped it against her head, wincing as the cold made contact with her tender skin. "Thanks. I think."

Howard snorted in disgust. "Liberated! You mean free to do all the dirty work? Doesn't sound very liberating to me."

Maggie chuckled. "I've never heard it put quite that way, but you have a point," she conceded.

"We seem to be in short supply when it comes to tools around here, Maggie, but if you'll let me borrow a couple of these, I'll fix the drain," Jake said.

"Are you sure? I really am pretty good at this. I don't mind finishing up."

"Let Jake do it," Howard told her. "He should have done it in the first place anyway."

Maggie looked at Jake, saw his lips compress into a thin line at the criticism, and decided that this was a good time to make her exit. "Well, in that case, I'll head home. We have a full house tonight, and I need to be on hand to greet the guests."

"I'll bring the tools back in a day or so," Jake promised as he walked her to the door.

"No hurry. Hopefully I won't need them before then anyway." She turned and smiled at Howard, who had followed them. "Goodbye, Howard."

"Goodbye, Maggie. Thank you for the tour. And lunch. It was real nice."

"You're very welcome. I enjoyed it a lot."

Maggie turned to go, only to find Jake's hand at her elbow. She looked up at him questioningly.

"I'll see you to your car."

Maggie shrugged. "Suit yourself."

They walked in silence, and even though Maggie's

head was starting to throb, she was acutely conscious of
Jake's nearness, of the warmth of his hand on her bare
skin and the faint, woodsy scent, uniquely his and ach-
ingly familiar. She had all but forgotten that scent. But
standing so close to him now, she was reminded with
startling intensity of all the times this man had held her
in his arms, had caressed her face, had claimed her lips.
But how could she still find him attractive after what
he'd done to her? She'd been burned once. Shouldn't
she be immune to his appeal?

Jake glanced down at Maggie's bowed head as they
approached the car. She seemed lost in thought. *Where
are you, Maggie?* he asked silently. *Are you remember-
ing, as I am?* Gently, as unobtrusively as possible, he
rubbed his thumb over the soft skin on her arm, recalling a time when she'd welcomed his touch. His happi-
est memories, his times of greatest contentment, were
linked with this woman, he realized.

His gaze lingered on her glorious hair, as beautiful as ever. It was the kind of hair a man could get lost
in—full and thick and inviting his hands in to play. But
those old, sweet days were gone, he reminded himself.
And yet…he felt the same as he had twelve years before.
The astounding attraction—physical, emotional and intellectual—was still there. Did she feel it as intensely
as he did? he wondered. And was it real? Or was it just
fed by memories of what had once been, reawakened
temporarily by the strange coincidence of their reunion?

"I'll hang on to the ice bag, if that's all right," Maggie interrupted his thoughts when they reached the car,
trying with limited success to keep her voice steady.

With an effort he forced his lips up into a grin as he

opened her door. "Such as it is. And thanks for taking time for Dad today. I know he appreciated it."

"It was no effort. He's a good man, Jake. He's just dealing with an awful lot right now."

"I know it's tough for him. I wish I could make it easier. But I can't reach him, Maggie. He shuts me out." He sighed and raked the fingers of one hand through his hair as he glanced back toward the cottage. "I had hoped that if we actually lived under the same roof he might come around. But I'm beginning to lose hope."

"Give it some time," she urged, impulsively laying her hand on his arm. "You and he have been apart for so long that you need to get to know each other again before you can feel comfortable together."

Jake smiled gently as he glanced down at her hand resting on his arm, then covered it with his. "You know, when I talk to you, I don't feel quite so hopeless. Why is that, Maggie?"

Her gaze locked with his, and for just a moment, the tender look in his eyes, the warmth of his voice, made her feel sixteen again. Made her want to *be* sixteen again. Which was bad. What was past could never return. She needed to remember that. She was not going to get caught up in the romantic fantasies that Abby and Allison were weaving. They were eighteen. She was almost thirty-seven—far to old to believe in fairy tales and happy endings.

With an abruptness that momentarily startled Jake, Maggie removed her hand and stepped away.

"I don't know. But maybe I should bottle it," she said with forced brightness as she slid into the car. "Call it Dr. Maggie's elixir. See you later, Jake." She started the engine, put the car in gear and drove away without a backward look.

Jake watched her go, a troubled look on his face, then slowly walked back to the house. His father met him at the door.

"She going to be all right? That was a nasty bump."

"She'll be fine, Dad." Physically, at least. Emotionally, he wasn't so sure. About either of them.

Chapter Six

Great. Just great.

Maggie stared down in disgust at the decidedly flat tire. Naturally this couldn't have happened in town. That would be too easy. It had to happen in the middle of nowhere—namely, an isolated spot on the remote Cape Rosier loop.

A drop of water splashed onto her cheek, and she closed her eyes with a sigh of resignation. Now it was raining. That figured. And it only made sense that the air would take a turn toward the chilly side. Where was the warm sun and lovely light she'd had earlier while she was painting?

Gone, obviously, she thought with a disgusted glance at the rapidly darkening sky. As were her hopes of anyone appearing along this stretch of deserted road, she concluded. Other than walking two or three miles to a house, her only option was to change the tire herself. Suddenly she sneezed, groping in her pocket for a tissue as she sniffled. On top of everything else, she seemed to be coming down with a bug of some kind. So what else could go wrong today? she wondered in dismay.

Maggie climbed back into the car, allowing herself a moment to regroup before tackling the job ahead of her. She put her forearms on the wheel and wearily rested her cheek against them, angling her head away from the bruised spot on her temple that was a souvenir of her plumbing adventure the week before. She hadn't seen Jake since then, although Howard had called once in the middle of the week. He said he was just checking to see how she was, but she suspected that he was simply lonely. It was so sad, the two of them sharing a house yet both so alone. Jake was trying—she knew that. But his attempts at reconciliation were rebuffed at every turn. In a way she felt sorry for him.

It was odd, this feeling of sympathy she had for Jake. And it was certainly a surprising—and ironic—twist, considering their history. But what surprised her even more was the spark between them. How could her response to him suddenly reactivate after lying in disuse for so long? One smoky look from those deep brown eyes was all it had taken to make her feel sixteen again. It has been so long since she'd felt the tremulous, breathless sensation of physical attraction that she'd even forgotten how to handle it. And she didn't want to relearn that lesson. What she *wanted* to do was turn those feelings off. That, however, didn't seem to be an option, she admitted with a sigh. But she *could* choose not to act on them. And she so chose.

For the moment, though, she would do better to focus her attention on a more pressing problem. The flat tire wasn't going to fix itself, after all. So, with a resigned sigh, she got out of the car and opened the trunk.

Maggie eyed the spare tire and jack uncertainly. She'd changed a tire before, of course. Once. A long time ago. In a basic car-maintenance class she'd taken. Under the watchful eye of the instructor. The procedure was a bit hazy after all this time. But it would come back to her, she told herself encouragingly.

Maggie removed the spare tire without too much difficulty, then got down on her hands and knees to look under the car, trying to figure out where to put the jack. She was so intent on her task that she didn't even realize a car had stopped until she heard a door shut. Before she could fully extricate herself from under the car to check out the new arrival, an amused voice spoke beside her.

"How is it that I always seem to find you repairing things?"

Maggie scooted back and turned to stare up at Jake.

"What are you doing here?" she asked in surprise.

"I think the more important question is, what are *you* doing here?"

"At the moment, changing a tire," she replied dryly.

"I can see that. What I meant was, what are you doing on this road? It's pretty isolated."

She shrugged. "I come here to paint. There are some lovely coves out this way." Suddenly she sneezed again, then reached into the pocket of her jeans for another tissue.

Jake frowned. He'd noticed right off that her voice was a bit husky, and a closer look revealed that her eyes were red. "Are you sick, Maggie?"

She wiped her nose and shook her head. "Of course not. I never get sick."

He reached for her hand then, and before she could protest he drew her to her feet and placed a cool palm against her forehead. It was warm—too warm—and his frown deepened.

"You have a temperature."

"No, I don't. I'm fine." She pulled away, disconcerted by his touch. If her face hadn't been flushed before, it was now. She walked around him toward the trunk and started to reach for the jack, but his hand firmly restrained her.

"Yes, you do. And standing out here in the drizzle isn't going to help matters. Go wait in my car while I change your tire."

"You don't have to do that," she protested.

He sighed in frustration. "Maggie, just accept the help, okay? I would have stopped no matter who it was."

In all honesty, she really wasn't feeling that great. In fact, she was fading fast. With a sigh, she capitulated. "All right. Thank you."

Maggie couldn't believe that she actually dozed in Jake's car while he changed her tire, but he had to nudge her shoulder gently to wake her up when he finished. Her eyelids felt extraordinarily heavy as they flickered open.

"All done," he declared as he slid in beside her.

The drizzle had escalated into a steady rain during her brief nap, producing a soft, rhythmic cadence on the roof. Her gaze flickered to Jake's blue shirt, which had darkened in color with moisture and now clung damply to his broad chest, and stuck there as her pulse accelerated.

"How are you feeling?" he asked solicitously.

"Your shirt's wet," she murmured inanely, her gaze still on his chest.

He shrugged her concern aside. "It'll dry. I'm more worried about you. Are you okay to drive?"

With a supreme effort, she transferred her gaze to his face. "Sure. I—I guess I picked up a bug or something. I felt fine this morning. This just came over me in the last hour or two. I'll be okay by tomorrow."

"I don't know," he replied doubtfully. "You look pretty under the weather."

"As opposed to under the sink? Or under the car?" she teased.

That drew a brief smile in response, but then he grew more serious. "You don't have to put on an act in front of me, you know. I can tell you're feeling rotten. You always got a certain look when you were sick. Something in your eyes…" His gaze locked on hers, and for a moment her heart actually stopped beating. Here, in this cocoon of warmth, sheltered from the rain, she felt as if they were alone in the world. He was only a few inches away, close enough to touch, to lean on, to kiss…

Her breath caught in her throat as the impulse to do just that intensified. This was all wrong. She didn't want to feel this way, not about Jake. How could she even consider letting herself get involved with him again? Yes, he seemed different. More responsible, more mature. But it was too soon to know. Far too soon. But even though her mind accepted that logic, her heart stubbornly refused to listen.

Jake watched Maggie's face, his perceptive gaze missing nothing. She had always been easy to read. She wanted him to kiss her just as badly as he *wanted* to kiss her. But it was too soon. One of the things he'd learned in the navy was to control his impulses, think things through. An impulsive move in battle could cost you your life. And an impulsive move right now could cost him Maggie. Intuitively he knew that, and it wasn't a risk he was willing to take.

Reluctantly he released her gaze and turned to look at the road, which was now partially obscured by fog. He took a deep breath, willing his pulse to slow down, struggling to control his erratic respiration. He didn't want to scare Maggie away by revealing the depth of his attraction.

"I think we'd better head back or we might be marooned here," he said conversationally, striving for a light tone. "Not that I'd mind, you understand, but I think you need to change into some dry clothes and get some rest."

Maggie drew a shaky breath and reached for the door handle.

"You're right." She started to push the door open, then turned back to him with a frown. "By the way, you never did tell me how you happened to be out here today. It's not exactly a well-traveled route."

He sighed and wearily shook his head. "Dad and I had an argument. Again. I decided to go for a drive until I cooled down, and this road caught my eye. Lucky for you, I guess."

"I take it things haven't improved much in the last week between you two?"

"I think that would be a fair assumption."

"I'm sorry, Jake. I wish there was something I could do."

He shrugged. "We'll just have to work it out between the two of us. But I appreciate your concern."

"Well, tell Pop I said hi. And…thanks, Jake."

"You're welcome. Now go home and get some rest."

"I'll try, although I do have a business to run, Jake. But Eileen—you met her the night Allison was in the hospital, remember?—she comes by to fill in when we need someone, and she helps with the cleaning every day for a couple of hours. So I don't have to do much when I get home. Since I don't take guests on Sunday night, I'll actually be a lady of leisure until tomorrow afternoon."

"Good. Take advantage of it. The best way to fight a virus is to rest."

"Yes, Doctor," she teased.

"Hey, I learned a lot in the navy. One of my best buddies was a medic." He reached across to push her door open, and as his arm brushed against hers her heart lurched.

"I'll follow you until we get to the main road." Did his voice sound huskier than usual, or was it only her imagination? she wondered. "And Maggie...don't worry about my problems. I'll deal with the situation. I'm sure you have enough problems of your own to handle."

He was right, of course, she thought, as she dashed through the rain to her own car. She did have her own problems. And a glance into the rearview mirror revealed her biggest one.

With a sinking feeling, Maggie played back the answering machine again. As she listened a second time, her spirits nose-dived. Eileen had the flu, too, and wasn't going to be able to come over in the morning to help with the cleaning.

Maggie hit the erase button and wearily pushed her hair back from her face. This had most definitely *not* been a good day, she decided. A flat tire, a flu bug and four guest rooms plus the cottage to clean before two o'clock tomorrow. If the twins were here it would be manageable. But they had signed up months ago to volunteer for a week at a camp for disadvantaged children, and they wouldn't be home until tomorrow afternoon. Which meant the housecleaning chores fell squarely on her shoulders.

She trudged into the kitchen to make herself a cup of tea, detouring for two aspirin on the way. She was generally able to overlook minor aches and pains and work right through normal fatigue, but this was different. She honestly felt that if she didn't lay down, she might fall down. Maybe Jake was right. A little rest might help. Perhaps if she gave herself an hour or so she'd feel good enough to tackle a couple of the rooms tonight. Then she could finish up in the morning.

Maggie dragged her protesting body up to the third floor, which had been divided into two dormer bedrooms—one for her, one for the girls. She sank down onto her bed, too tired even to remove her shoes as she stretched out. The twins would give her a hard time about that, she thought with the ghost of a smile as her eyelids drifted closed. She'd always been such a stickler about keeping shoes off beds and furniture. But the thought didn't linger long. In less than fifteen seconds she drifted into oblivion.

As consciousness slowly returned, Maggie lifted her heavy eyelids and stared at the ceiling feeling disoriented. Then she turned her head to look at the clock on her bedside table. When it finally came into focus, she frowned. Eight o'clock? She'd slept for two hours? But no, the light wasn't right, she thought in confusion, glancing toward the dormer window. It was at the wrong angle.

With a sudden jolt, the truth hit home. It was *morning!* Propelled by panic, she quickly sat up and swung her legs to the floor. The room tilted crazily, and she dropped her head into her hands as she waited for everything to stop spinning.

The sudden ringing of the phone on her nightstand made her jump, and she groped for the receiver with one hand.

"Hel..." Her voice came out in a croak and she tried again. "Hello?"

"Maggie? Is that you?"

"Yes," she replied groggily. "Hi, Jake."

She could hear the frown in his voice. "You sound awful."

"Thanks a lot."

"How are you feeling? Or does your voice tell the story?"

Yes, she thought to herself, it does. The numbing lethargy still had a grip on her body, and her aches hadn't dissipated much, if at all. "I'll live," she assured him, striving for a flippant tone. "It's just a flu bug or something. And in this business there are no sick days. The guests just keep coming." She reached for a tissue and tried to discreetly blow her nose.

Jake realized that he'd never really thought about that. The few times he'd been under the weather in the navy he'd simply gone on sick call. But Maggie didn't have that luxury. In fact, as far as he could see, she didn't have many luxuries, period. And that bothered him. "I guess you're right," he admitted. "But the girls can help, too, can't they?"

There was no way to avoid such a direct question. "They could if they were here. But they've been gone all week and won't be back until late this afternoon. So I'm the official greeter today."

"But your cleaning woman is coming today, isn't she?"

"Monday is one of her regular days to come," Maggie hedged.

"Well, try to take it easy, okay?" he replied.

"I'll try," she said, knowing that she could try all she wanted to—the house still had to be cleaned. It was a daunting task when she was well; "impossible" was a more appropriate descriptor today, considering how she felt. But she'd manage somehow. She always did.

"I'll check back with you later, Maggie."

"Okay. Thanks for calling, Jake."

Slowly she replaced the receiver. Then, summoning all her reserves of energy, she forced herself to stand up. At least she was already dressed, she thought wryly as she made her way unsteadily down the stairs to the utility closet. *You can do it,* she encouraged herself. *The girls will be back to help later today. Just make it through the next few hours, take it one room at a time, and you'll be fine.*

And with that she reached for the mop.

By the time Maggie started on the third room, however, she was on autopilot. She went through the motions mindlessly, every movement more of an effort than the last. In fact, she was so out of it that it took several rings before she realized someone was at her front door. Her gaze flew to the steps in panic. *Please, Lord, not a guest,* she prayed as she made her way stiffly down the stairs. *Not yet. Not this early.*

This time her prayers were answered. When she swung the door open, she found Jake, not a guest.

In one swift, assessing glance he came to the obvious conclusion. She was sick as a dog and, judging by the faint scent of disinfectant cleaner drifting his way and the mop in her hand, she was *not* resting. Without a word he took her arm and ushered her inside, forcing her to sit in the closest chair before he knelt beside her. He put his hand on her forehead, and this time it was not only hot but clammy. A muscle in his jaw clenched and he frowned.

"What are you doing with that mop?" he demanded.

"Cleaning."

"What happened to Eileen?"

"She has the bug, too."

"Why didn't you tell me that earlier?"

"What good would that have done?"

He ignored that comment for the moment. "Have you called the doctor?"

"It's just a bug, Jake. Something's been going around. I was just lucky till now. I guess it was my turn."

He didn't look convinced, but he didn't argue the point. Instead, he stood up and held out his hand. "Come on. You're going back to bed."

She shook her head. "Jake, you don't understand. I have ten guests arriving this afternoon beginning at two o'clock. I've only cleaned two of the four rooms and I still have the cottage to do. I'll barely make it as it is. I can't lay down now."

"Maggie, you're sick. You should never have gotten up today in the first place."

She sighed, blinking away the tears of weariness that sprang to her eyes. "Jake, try to understand. Eileen and the girls are my only backup. There isn't anyone else I can call."

"Yes, there is."

She gave him a puzzled look. "Who?"

"Me. I learned to wield a pretty mean mop in the navy. They don't tolerate slobs, you know," he said, flashing her a brief grin.

She stared at him. Jake West cleaning a house? It was incomprehensible. As she recalled, he had always put housekeeping duties on a par with going to the dentist.

"Don't look so shocked," he admonished her gently, with that disconcerting habit he had of reading her mind. "Times change. People change. You can trust me to do a good job. I promise your guests won't complain."

"It's not that…" She was still having a hard time comprehending his generous offer. And even if he was sincere, it was too much to ask. "Jake, I can't let you do my work. It's not right. And don't give me that good deed business. This goes way above and beyond that."

He crouched down beside her once again, his warm, brown eyes level with hers, and took her cold hand in his. "Maggie, I *want* to do this, okay? You're sick. You'll only get sicker if you push yourself." He paused a moment, then took a deep breath. "Look, I know that you're still trying to grapple with this whole situation between us. To be honest, so am I. But fate, or whatever you care to call it, brought us back together. I don't know why. But at the bare minimum I'd like to be your friend—whatever that takes, and despite the fact that I don't deserve it. And friends take care of each other. Let me take care of you today, Maggie. As a friend."

She listened to Jake's heartfelt speech in silence, unable to doubt the sincerity in his eyes—or ignore the tenderness. He cared for her, that was clear. And, God help her, she was beginning to care for him again. She didn't want to. She told herself it was unwise. That it was risky, that she could get hurt again. But she couldn't help it. Because the Jake that had walked back into her life not only had all the good qualities she remembered, he had become even better. Under other circumstances, he was the kind of man she could easily fall in love with. There was nothing in his present behavior to make her cautious.

It was his past behavior that worried her. His track record wasn't good. And that made her *very* cautious. Her wariness wasn't something that could be overcome in a week, or a month, or maybe even a year. She'd been burned once before by this man and left with scars—plus a very real fear of fire.

Jake scrutinized her face, but for once he couldn't read her thoughts. He didn't want to push himself on her, but he'd already decided he wasn't going to walk away and let her face the housecleaning task alone. If necessary, he would insist—and deal with the consequences later. But he hoped she would just accept her limitations and be sensible.

"Maggie?" he prodded gently, exerting slight pressure on her hand when she didn't respond.

Jake's voice brought her back to the present. She was deeply touched by his offer, whatever his motivation. And like it or not, she needed help today. The Lord had obviously seen that need and provided for it. Maybe the help wasn't in the form she would have chosen, but who was she to question His motives?

"All right, Jake. Thank you. To be honest, I—I'm not sure I could have made it anyway."

Considering how she prided herself on her self-reliance, Jake knew she must be a whole lot sicker than she was letting on, to admit that she wasn't able to handle the task in front of her. Once more he stood and gently reached for her hands, drawing her to her feet. He put his arm around her shoulders, and as they walked slowly up the stairs she leaned on him heavily—another indication of her weakened physical state. No way would she lean on him—literally or figuratively—unless she was in bad shape.

He paused at the landing, giving her a chance to catch her breath.

"Where's your room?"

She nodded toward the back stairway at the end of the hall. "Third floor."

By the time they made it up the much narrower stairway to her bedroom, he could feel her quivering. They passed an open door that revealed a spacious, gaily decorated dormer room with two twin beds. Obviously the twins' domain, he thought with a smile, noting the posters of the girls' latest movie heartthrobs.

Maggie's room was much smaller, squeezed under the eaves near the front of the house. It was very simply furnished and decorated, as if she'd poured all of her attention into the rest of the house and simply not bothered with her own little piece of it. As he gently eased her down onto the narrow twin bed, his throat contracted with tenderness and admiration for this woman who had struggled against all odds to overcome traumas and challenges that would have overwhelmed most people. Jake didn't know where she had found the strength to face each day, especially in those early years. But as he knelt to remove her shoes, his eyes fell on the Bible

on her nightstand, and he suspected that was probably
its source. She'd always had a strong faith, and it clearly
had sustained her spiritually through the difficult years.

But how had she managed emotionally? he wondered. Maggie had so much love to give. Had it all been
directed to the girls? He suspected so. As he tucked
the covers around her shoulders, he felt that the single bed in the small attic room spoke more eloquently
than words of her solitary state. He started to speak,
then realized that she had already fallen asleep. Gently
he reached down to brush a wisp of hair off her forehead, his fingers dropping to linger on her cheek. As
he gazed at her pale face, a fierce surge of protectiveness washed over him.

Ever since their paths had crossed, Jake had felt in-
creasingly drawn to the woman who had once, long
ago, claimed his heart. At first he'd looked upon their
reunion as a chance to at last find a way to ease the
guilt that had plagued him for so long. Only a few minutes ago, he'd told Maggie that he hoped they could be
friends. But now, as he stood beside her, he knew that
his interest wasn't motivated by guilt, and that his feelings went far beyond friendship.

He loved her. It was as simple—and as complicated—as that.

As he gazed tenderly down at her, he thought of
the Maggie he'd once loved. All the essential qualities
he'd cherished were still there. But she'd changed, too.
And he found that he loved the new Maggie, with her
self-reliance and confidence and decisive manner, even
more than he had loved the dependent young woman
who had once deferred to his every decision. He liked

her grit and her spunk and her strength—and her soft heart, which hadn't changed one iota.

Jake walked slowly to the door, pausing at the threshold to glance back once more at Maggie's sleeping form. She was quite a woman, he thought. She deserved to find a man who would love her and stand by her no matter what, who believed in honoring commitments and wasn't afraid of responsibility, who could be counted on to stand with her through good times *and* bad.

Jake had failed her once on that score, but he vowed silently that he never would again. The question was, how could he convince her of that?

Jake didn't have the answer. But he knew one thing with absolute certainty. He would find a way. Because suddenly a future without Maggie was not something he was willing to consider.

Chapter Seven

"See, Allison, I told you it was him!"

Abby's triumphant voice heralded the arrival of the twins at the kitchen door, and Jake glanced up from the pot he was stirring. "Hello, ladies," he greeted them with an engaging grin.

They simultaneously dumped their knapsacks on the floor and joined him.

"What are you doing here?" Abby asked curiously. "And where's Aunt Maggie?"

"She's in bed with the flu. I'm making her some soup."

"You're cooking?" Allison was clearly impressed.

Jake grinned. "I don't think heating up a can of soup exactly qualifies as cooking."

"How sick is she?" Abby asked with a frown of concern.

"Pretty sick."

"Where's Eileen?"

"She's got the same bug."

"But...but what about the cleaning?" Allison asked

in alarm. "What will we tell the guests when they arrive?"

"The guests have already arrived and they're all settled in," Jake informed them calmly as he transferred the soup to a bowl and put it on a tray. "Your aunt started the cleaning, and I finished up."

"You mean...you mean *you* helped clean the rooms?" Abby asked incredulously.

Jake gave them a look of mock indignation. "Don't you think I'm capable of wielding a mop and broom?"

"It's not that," Allison said quickly. "It's just that... well, guys don't usually offer to pitch in on stuff like that."

"Well, let me tell you ladies a little secret," Jake said conspiratorially. "Men know how to clean. They just pretend they don't. So keep that in mind whenever you meet Mr. Right."

"I bet you had trouble convincing Aunt Maggie to let you help," Allison speculated.

"A little," he admitted with a grin.

Suddenly Abby frowned. "Gosh, she must be really sick if she gave in and went to bed."

"It's just the flu," Jake assured them as he added a cup of tea and some crackers to the tray. "But she's probably not going to have a whole lot of energy for a few days. Do you think you two can pick up the slack?"

"Sure. No problem. This is our summer job, anyway. We'll just put in a little overtime. Aunt Maggie's done it often enough for us."

They really were good kids, Jake reflected. Maggie had raised them well. "Great. Now, if you two can get the breakfast preparations under way, I'll take this up to your aunt."

The twins watched him disappear through the door, then Allison sank down on a convenient chair and sighed. "Wow! Talk about Sir Galahad!"

Abby joined her on an adjacent chair and propped her chin dreamily in her hand. "Yeah."

There was silence for a moment while they both mulled over this latest turn of events, and then Allison turned to her sister. "Do you think maybe something might come of this after all? I mean, I know Aunt Maggie keeps saying that their relationship is in the past and all that, but how many guys would clean toilets for a woman they don't care about?"

"I think it has very interesting possibilities," Abby replied with a thoughtful nod. "I think Aunt Maggie still cares, too. She just won't admit it—to us or herself. But maybe we can find a way to give her a nudge."

"And how do you propose we do that?"

Abby smiled smugly. "Well, as a matter of fact…I have a plan."

Jake eased Maggie's door open with one shoulder and cast a worried glance toward the bed. He'd checked on her a couple of times during the afternoon, and she'd been sleeping soundly. Now, however, she was sitting up, bent over, struggling to tie her shoes.

He pushed the door all the way open and strode inside. "What are you doing?" he demanded with a frown. He deposited the tray on the dresser and turned to face her, clamping his hands on his hips.

She looked up, startled. "Jake, it's after five! I'm surprised none of the guests have arrived yet," she said, her voice edged with panic.

"They have arrived. All of them."

Her eyes widened in alarm. "Oh, no! What did you tell them?"

"I told them hello. Then I welcomed them to Whispering Sails and asked if I could help with their luggage. I think that's the spiel, isn't it?"

Her frantic hands stilled on the laces and she stared him. "You mean...you checked everyone in?"

"Mmm-hmm. I looked them all up in the guest book on the desk in the foyer. It was a piece of cake." He picked up the tray and came to sit beside her. "Dinner," he explained, placing it on her lap.

She stared down at the soup, then back at him. "Jake, I..." Her voice choked, and she looked down in embarrassment. She was usually able to keep her emotions under control, but she couldn't stop the tears that sprang to her eyes. It had been a long time since anyone had stepped in as he had to ease her burden. The twins were great, of course. And they certainly would have helped if they'd been here. But they were family. Family members did those kinds of things for each other. But Jake wasn't family. He was... Well, she wasn't sure exactly what he was. He said he wanted to be her friend. But a moment later, when he took her chin in gentle fingers and turned her head toward his, the look in his eyes said a whole lot more than friendship.

"Did I pick the wrong kind of soup?" he asked with a tender smile.

She shook her head. "No. Th-this is fine."

"Then, what's wrong?"

She swallowed with difficulty. "It's just that I—I appreciate all you did today, Jake. It was too much to ask."

"You didn't ask."

"No, but…well, I feel like you were sort of forced into this."

"I wasn't forced into anything," he assured her firmly. "I wanted to help."

"I guess I owe you now," she replied with a sigh. "Big-time."

Jake cupped her flushed face with both hands, and his gaze locked on hers. It was difficult to concentrate on his words when his thumbs began to stroke her cheeks. But she tried.

"Maggie, you don't owe me a thing. If I spent the rest of my life trying to ease your burdens, I could still never make up for what I did to you."

Maggie's spirits took a sudden, unaccountable nosedive. Was that the only motivation for Jake's good deed—to make amends? Was that the reason he'd offered her his friendship?

Jake saw the sudden dark cloud pass over her eyes and frowned. "What's wrong now?"

She shrugged and transferred her gaze to her soup, playing with the spoon. "Nothing. Just tired, I guess."

Jake studied her a moment, then nodded toward the tray. "Well, eat your soup and get back in bed. Everything's under control downstairs. The girls will take care of breakfast."

"I feel better since I slept, Jake. I can—"

"Maggie." He cut her off, his voice gentle but firm. "I want you to promise me you'll take it easy until at least tomorrow afternoon. You need the rest." When she didn't reply, he sighed. "Look, if you won't do it for yourself, do it for me, okay? Otherwise I'll be awake all night worrying about you."

She looked at him curiously, started to ask, "Why?"

but stopped herself in time. She could deal with those kinds of questions later, when she'd regained her strength. In the meantime, after all he'd done for her today she could at least give him some peace of mind in return.

"All right, Jake," she agreed.

"Good." He glanced at his watch, then grinned ruefully. "Well, I better get home and put together some dinner for Dad and me. Or maybe I can convince him to go out. He hasn't been in the mood yet, but it's worth a try tonight," he mused. "Now eat your soup."

She gave a mock salute. "Aye, aye, sir."

He grinned sheepishly. "Sorry. I got used to giving orders in the navy. It's a hard habit to break. How about, please eat your soup?"

"That's better," she conceded.

He sat there for another moment, his eyes soft on her face, and Maggie felt her breath catch in her throat. She knew that look. It was the look he used to get at his most tender moments, right before he kissed her, and her pulse went into overdrive.

Jake's gaze dropped to her full lips and a surge of longing swept over him. With a supreme effort he forced his gaze back to hers.

His eyes had deepened in color, Maggie noted, and she stared back into their unfathomable depths as he reached over to stroke her cheek with a featherlike touch. A pulse began to beat in the hollow of her throat as he slowly, very slowly, leaned toward her.

Maggie knew she should resist while she still could. But instead of listening to logic, her eyelids fluttered closed and she leaned ever so slightly toward him, inviting his kiss. She felt powerless to stop herself.

And then his lips, warm and tender, gently—and briefly—brushed her forehead. That was it. The kiss was over in an instant, so quickly that Maggie, who had expected so much more, was momentarily left off balance. Her eyelids flew open and she stared at him as he abruptly stood up.

"Good night, Maggie. I'll call you tomorrow."

And then he was gone.

She stared after him, still trying to figure out what had just happened. She thought he was going to kiss her. Really kiss her. And she'd offered no resistance. But instead of the passionate kiss she'd expected, he'd given her a brotherly peck on the forehead.

Why? Was it because he really did care about her only as a friend? Or was he just being noble, refusing to take advantage of her weakened physical condition?

Maggie didn't have a clue. But she knew one thing very clearly. Jake's brotherly kiss on her forehead just hadn't cut it. For better or worse, she wanted more.

Jake pulled up in front of his cottage and turned off the engine. It had taken the entire drive from Maggie's place to his for him to regain some semblance of control over his emotions. And he was still shaken by how close he had come just now to blowing it with her. Thank God he had found the discipline to back off, to stop at that brotherly kiss on the forehead, when what he really wanted to do was claim her tender lips with a kiss that expressed all the passion and love that was in his heart.

As each day passed, he knew with greater certainty that his feelings for this special woman had never died. During all the years of separation they had simply been stored in a quiet corner of his heart, growing in intensity as they waited for the opportunity to be given full expression. Now that the opportunity was at hand, they were clamoring for release.

But he had to be cautious. He felt sure that Maggie wasn't yet ready to accept such an admission on his part, that she was still very confused about her own feelings, grappling with questions and doubts, just as he had been initially. She needed time. He needed patience.

Jake drew a slow, deep breath. Only now was his pulse returning to normal, his respiration slowing. He'd known any number of women through the years who attracted him, but he'd never come this close to losing control. The only woman who had ever been able to do that to him was Maggie, beginning that summer when he was seventeen. She obviously hadn't lost her power over him.

Jake stepped out of the car and walked toward the house, trying to psyche himself up for the long evening ahead with his father. He didn't feel up to that ordeal— or to cooking. Wearily, he pushed the door open, took one step inside, then stopped in surprise. Appetizing aromas were wafting his way, and he frowned in puzzlement. Warily he made his way to the kitchen door, where a quick survey revealed the table neatly set for two and his father at the stove.

"Dad?"

Howard turned in surprise. "Oh. Didn't hear you come in. Dinner will be ready in fifteen minutes. You have time for a shower if you want one."

His father turned back to the stove and Jake stared at him, speechless. "Dad...are you making dinner?"

"Looks that way, doesn't it?" he replied gruffly.

"But...why?"

The older man shrugged. "You worked all day over at Maggie's. That was a nice thing to do, with her sick and all. Figured you'd probably be hungry when you got home. I didn't have anything else to do anyway."

Jake struggled to grasp this unexpected turn of events. His father actually sounded...well, if not friendly, cordial at least.

"Dad...I bought some sparkling cider when you first arrived," he said on impulse. "I thought we could have it with our first dinner here in the cottage. But...well, things didn't quite work out. If you'd like to have it tonight, it's in the cabinet next to the dishwasher."

His father's only response was a grunt, which Jake couldn't interpret. But when he reappeared ten minutes later after a quick shower, dinner was on the table. And so was the cider.

"Maggie, my dear. How are you feeling today?"

Maggie glanced toward the familiar voice of Millicent Trent and smiled at the older woman seated in a wicker settee on the front porch.

"Hello, Millicent! Welcome back to Whispering Sails. I'm much better today, thank you. And I'm sorry I wasn't on hand to greet you when you arrived."

"Don't give it a thought. The young man who showed me to my room last night was very nice. And he seemed quite concerned about you."

Maggie flushed. "It was just a flu bug, I think."

"Well, I must say you still look a bit peaked," Millicent observed, peering over her glasses.

"I'm a little tired, but I feel fine," Maggie assured the older woman. "I'm sure I'll be completely back to normal by tomorrow. The girls won't let me lift a finger today, so I'm getting lots of rest."

"Well, then, can you spare a few minutes to visit with an old lady?"

Maggie smiled. "I don't know about an old lady, but I certainly have time to visit with you."

Millicent chuckled. "You do have a way with words, my dear. Oh, Allison, would you mind bringing your aunt and me some tea?" she called when the younger girl stepped outside.

"Not at all, Ms. Trent. I'll be back in a jiffy."

"Now then, we can have a nice visit. Let's start with that young man. Who is he, my dear? I've never seen him around here before, and you know I've been a regular since the first year you opened."

Maggie took a moment to settle into an adjacent wicker chair, trying to decide how to answer the older woman's question. Millicent had become almost part of the family through the years, her annual two-week visits as predictable as the tides. She'd retired ten years before, apparently from a very prestigious position in publishing, and she had no family to speak of, as far as Maggie knew. But although she and Millicent had shared many a cup of tea and discussed everything from philosophy to the latest books and plays, they never talked about more personal matters. But for some reason, Maggie felt comfortable confiding in her about Jake.

"Jake is…an old friend," Maggie replied carefully. "He's recently moved to this area, and our paths just happened to cross."

Millicent eyed her shrewdly. "A friend, eh? His interest seemed somehow more than friendly to me."

Maggie blushed. Millicent might be old in body, but

her mind was still as sharp and perceptive as someone half her age.

"To be honest, Millicent, I'm not sure what his interest is," Maggie admitted. "The fact is, we were...well, we were engaged once, many years ago."

"My dear, I had no idea!" Millicent exclaimed, laying her hand on the younger woman's arm. "I always suspected there was an unhappy romance in your past, but I never wanted to pry."

"It wasn't an unhappy romance," Maggie corrected her. She leaned back against the cushions and gazed thoughtfully into the distance as Allison deposited their tea, her lips curving into a sweet smile as she retreated to memory, oblivious to the view of the bay spread out before her. "It was a wonderful romance. Jake was my first love. In fact, he was my only love. But a few weeks before we were to be married, he... Something happened, and we... The wedding was called off. Jake joined the navy and I left the Midwest and moved to Boston, then eventually here. I hadn't seen him in twelve years when he literally appeared out of the fog at the inn a few weeks ago."

"My!" Millicent breathed softly, clearly mesmerized by the story. "What an odd coincidence."

Maggie nodded. "I still have a hard time believing it myself."

"And he lives here now?"

"Yes. In Castine. He'll be teaching at the Maritime Academy in the fall." Maggie briefly explained the events that had precipitated his move.

"My!" Millicent repeated. "That's quite a story, my dear. I take it your Jake has never married?"

"No."

"Hmm. And what do you intend to do about the situation?"

"Do?" Maggie repeated with a frown.

"Yes. Do. I would say the man is quite taken with you still, my dear. I can see it in his eyes when he talks about you."

Maggie flushed. "You sound like the twins," she declared.

"Well, the young and the old often have a clearer vision of life than you people caught in the middle," Millicent observed. "But I suppose the most important thing is how you feel about this young man."

Maggie sighed. "I really don't know, Millicent. I loved him once. With all my heart. But...well, I got hurt. He...he wasn't there when I needed him the most. I'm afraid to...well, take that risk again."

Millicent nodded sagely. "I can understand that, my dear. Perhaps the best thing to do is give yourself some time to become acquainted again. People can change, you know. And twenty years from now you don't want to look back with regrets."

Maggie studied her curiously. The bittersweet quality in the older woman's voice tugged at Maggie's heart. "Millicent...I don't want to pry, either, but...well, it sounds like maybe you had a similar experience."

The older woman took a sip of tea and nodded slowly. "Yes, Maggie, I did. Many years ago. Long before you were born, in fact. It's one of the reasons I come back here each year, in fact. You see, this is where I fell in love."

"You lived in this area?"

The older woman smiled. "Actually...I lived in this house."

Maggie stared at her. "Here?" At the woman's nod of confirmation, Maggie frowned. "But…but I researched the history, and I never saw the name Trent."

"That's because I took my mother's name when I moved to New York. I thought it had more of a literary ring to it."

"You mean you actually lived at Whispering Sails?" Maggie repeated incredulously.

"Yes. It wasn't Whispering Sails then, of course. It was just home. My father owned a very successful shipping company, and Robert—that was my beau's name—was a merchant seaman who sometimes worked on my father's ships."

She paused, a smile of sweet remembrance lifted the corners of her mouth.

"We met the summer I was twenty-two. He was a handsome man, with sun-streaked brown hair, tall and strong, with the bluest eyes you could ever imagine. Bluer than the sea on a cloudless day. We fell in love, madly, passionately, with the intensity reserved for the very young. But my father would have none of it. His daughter deserved better than a seaman, he informed me. And what of the career I'd planned? He'd sent me to college, much against his better judgment, and now that I had the degree I'd so desperately wanted, he expected me to do something with it.

"Robert and I had a wonderful summer together, and when it was drawing to a close he asked me to marry him. I thought about it a long time, Maggie. I loved him as I had loved no one before or anyone since. But he was poor, and content with his lot, and I was wealthy and ambitious. I wanted to make something of my life outside of Blue Hill, and I had just been offered a prestigious position with a publishing company in New York. Plus, much as I hate to admit it, my father had finally convinced me that I was too good for a mere seaman. So in the end, I turned him down."

She gazed out over the water, and her voice grew quiet. "I regretted my decision within a year. New York wasn't nearly as glamorous as I'd expected, and living among so many different kinds of people made me realize how arrogant my attitude had been. I wasn't any better than anyone else. Not as good as most, in fact. And I missed Robert desperately. To love with such intensity…what a gift that is. And what a sin to waste it."

Her voice faded, and Maggie leaned toward her. "But why didn't you tell him you'd changed your mind?" she pressed.

Millicent turned to her with a smile of regret. "At first I was too ashamed—and too proud, I suppose—to admit my mistake. But eventually, after two years, I realized what a fool I'd been. And so I wrote to him, and asked him to meet me on his next trip to New York. I didn't tell him why, because I wanted to apologize in person, to beg him to give me one more chance."

"And did he come?"

She shook her head. "No. You see, by then he was engaged to another woman. He was an honorable man, my Robert, and I knew he wouldn't break his engagement. Nor would I ask him to. So I simply wished him well."

"And you never saw him again?"

"No," she replied sadly. "But we corresponded after that, each Christmas, until he died five years ago."

"So you…you never married, Millicent?"

She shook her head. "No. Not that I didn't consider it.

But no one ever again touched my heart the way Robert did. And I wasn't willing to settle for less."

Maggie knew exactly what she meant. It was the same legacy Jake had left with her.

"I'm so sorry, Millicent," she murmured, deeply touched by the sad story.

The older woman nodded. "So am I. Especially after I received this." She withdrew a slender chain from beneath her blouse and fingered two jagged pieces of silver which, when fitted together, formed one heart. "Robert gave me half of this in the middle of our special summer," she related softly. "He said that part of his heart now belonged to me and asked me to keep this always, and that he would do the same with his. I've worn my half faithfully, all my life."

She paused and gently fingered the two pieces of silver. "When he died I received a package with the other half from his daughter, along with a letter saying that her father had always carried it in his wallet and had left instructions for it to be sent to me when he died."

Maggie's eyes filled with tears as Millicent brought her story to a close. Her heart ached for the older woman and the sailor named Robert, whose abiding love had never been fulfilled.

Millicent leaned toward her then, her gaze earnest and intent. "My dear, love is a precious and beautiful gift, but it's easily lost. Pride, ambition, fear—so many things can get in the way. I don't know what made you and Jake break up years ago. I don't know how deeply he hurt you. But a lot can happen in twelve years. People change. Circumstances change. But true love endures. And if that's what you have, don't let it slip away. Because not very many people get a second chance at love."

Chapter Eight

A second chance at love.

Those words had been playing over and over in Maggie's mind ever since Millicent Trent planted the thought. And especially so today. Birthdays always made her wonder what the next twelve months would hold. But even in her wildest imagination she'd never considered on her last birthday that before the next one Jake would be back in her life.

Maggie took a quick glance in the rearview mirror and shook her head. She didn't feel thirty-seven. Not physically, anyway. Emotionally...well, that was a different story. She'd lived through a lot, especially in the last dozen years. But she honestly didn't think she looked her age.

Obviously, though, the twins did, she mused with a rueful smile. Why else would they have given her a day of "rejuvenation" at the new one-day spa that had opened in Bangor? Frankly, she'd been taken aback by the gift—not to mention appalled at the cost. Maggie wasn't accustomed to such self-indulgence, had opened her mouth to point out that the money could have been better spent on more practical items for the upcoming school year. But the girls had been so excited about their gift, had received so much pleasure from the giving, that she couldn't dampen their spirits. So she'd bitten her tongue and accepted it with a smile.

Then they'd topped off the first indulgence with a second—they were going to cook her a special birthday dinner tonight. Since neither of the girls was particularly interested in cooking, the chore usually fell to Maggie. And she was pretty good at it, if she did say so herself. Jake had always liked her cooking, she recalled with a smile.

Jake. He'd been more and more in her thoughts these last few days. Did he remember that today was her birthday? she wondered wistfully. Probably not. In general, men weren't very good about those kinds of things. But he'd changed a lot in the last dozen years. She thought of Millicent's words. Was Maggie being offered a second chance at love? And if so, was it a chance she was willing to take?

She didn't have the answer to those questions. And she didn't even want to think about them for the next few hours. The twins had told her to relax and enjoy the spa experience, and she couldn't very well do that if she thought about Jake. So with a discipline that surprised her, she forced all disruptive thoughts from her mind and focused on the moment. She wanted to get her money's worth—make that the twins' money, she corrected herself—out of this extravagant gift.

And as it turned out, she did. She was coddled and massaged and manicured, then treated to a facial, makeup session and haircut and style. It was pure indulgence, pampering like she had never before experienced, but much to her surprise she enjoyed it. Thoroughly. She emerged feeling invigorated, renewed, pretty and—strangely enough—younger than when she went in. It was wonderful!

By the time she climbed into her car for the drive back to the inn, Maggie was completely relaxed and looking forward to the special dinner the twins were preparing. She loved them dearly for the effort, no matter the result.

They were obviously watching for her, because when she stepped inside they were waiting, their faces shining, eyes expectant.

"Wow!" they breathed in unison, their voices reflecting their awe at the glamorous transformation in their aunt.

Maggie grinned. "Not bad for a thirty-seven-year-old innkeeper, huh?" she teased.

"Aunt Maggie, you look great!" Abby enthused. "That makeup really brings out your coloring. And I love your hair!"

"Yeah," Alison agreed. "It's a great cut. It looks really...sophisticated."

Maggie smiled. The haircut *was* good, she had to admit as she glanced at her reflection in the oven door. Nothing dramatically different than before, but expertly shaped and tamed to bring out her gentle, natural waves. She rarely left it down around the inn, but now, as it softly brushed her shoulders and flatteringly framed her face, she had to admit that wearing it loose and full made her feel younger. And very chic.

"Thanks. And thank you both for today. I hate to

admit this, since it was such a wild extravagance, but I loved every minute of it!"

The girls beamed.

"We hoped you would. Now go up and dress for dinner. We laid out your clothes. And take your time," Abby instructed. "We aren't going to eat for an hour."

"Well, I won't argue," Maggie replied, trying to ignore the chaotic mess. "I may not be going to a ball, but I must admit I feel a little like Cinderella at the moment. So I'll enjoy it while it lasts."

As Maggie closed the kitchen door she heard the girls begin to whisper, and she smiled indulgently. They were terrific young women, she thought, allowing herself a moment of pride. Despite her novice-level child-rearing skills, despite her many mistakes, despite the absence of a father figure in their home, the girls had turned out just fine. It hadn't been easy to raise them alone, she reflected, but she'd done okay.

Then again, she'd never been totally alone, she reminded herself, as she stepped into her room and her gaze fell on the Bible beside her bed. She'd turned to the Lord many times through the years, asking for His guidance and support. And He'd always answered her. Not necessarily in the way she expected, but always with a wisdom that it sometimes took her years to appreciate.

She picked up the volume and opened it to the well-worn pages in Matthew that had given her comfort and calmed her troubled soul on so many occasions. "Ask, and it shall be given you; seek, and you shall find; knock, and it shall be opened to you. For everyone who asks, receives; and he who seeks, finds; and to him who knocks, it shall be opened." She flipped forward a few pages. "Come to me, all you who labor and are burdened, and I will give you rest. Take my yoke upon you, and learn from me, for I am meek and humble of heart, and you will find rest for your souls. For my yoke is easy, and my burden light."

Maggie couldn't remember the number of times through the years when she had read those pages before going to bed, asking the Lord to help her make the right decisions, to ease her burden. And always she had felt His loving presence beside her. She paused now to thank Him in the silence of her heart for His steadfast presence throughout her life, but especially during these last twelve, often tumultuous years.

When Maggie gently closed the book, she felt even more renewed. She replaced it on the nightstand, then turned her attention to the clothes the girls had laid out. Her eyebrows rose in surprise when she realized that they had chosen her fanciest dress—a black chiffon, with rhinestone-studded spaghetti straps and a straight-cut bodice softened with a cowl-like draping of fabric. The full skirt swirled softly beneath a wide belt that was also studded with rhinestones. It was a lovely outfit—but good heavens, what were the girls thinking? she wondered in amusement. This was a cocktail dress, better suited to an elegant black-tie affair than an at-home dinner, no matter how "fancy" they were trying to make it. In fact, she'd only worn the dress once before, to an opening at an art gallery Philip had invited her to a couple of years before. She smiled and shook her head. Obviously the girls were trying to make this as nice an evening as possible. She couldn't find it in her heart to disappoint them.

She reached for the dress, and discovered a small, gift-wrapped package from the girls. It was a bottle of her favorite perfume, one she rarely bought because of the high cost. The twins had really outdone themselves this year, she thought with a soft smile.

When she was dressed, Maggie paused to glance in the mirror behind her door. She felt a little silly, all dressed up and nowhere to go. But she had to admit that her rejuvenating day at the spa, her new makeup and expertly styled hair—along with the dress, which emphasized her trim figure—made her feel terrific.

Suddenly she wondered what Jake would think if he saw her now. Would he be awed by her "glamour"? Would that flame of desire she so clearly remembered from years ago spark to life in his eyes? Would he be tempted to pull her into his arms and kiss her fiercely, with the simmering, barely restrained passion she recalled so well?

Although Maggie impatiently dismissed those questions, the answers were nevertheless waiting for her a few moments later when she walked into the dining room and came face-to-face with the man himself. They were obvious from the look in his eyes—yes, yes and highly likely.

Jake rose slowly from the table set for two in the center of the dining room, his gaze smoldering, hers confused. What on earth…?

A movement to her left caught her eye, and she turned to find the twins watching the proceedings with undisguised glee.

"Surprise!" they chorused.

I'm going to ground them until they're thirty, Maggie thought fiercely, hot color suffusing her face as she realized what they'd done. Now everything made sense. The spa. The clothes. The perfume. The two conspirators had decided to fill their aunt's social vacuum by planning a romantic evening for her—down to the fresh flowers and candles on the table and the bottle of sparkling cider chilling in the silver cooler, she noted with a dismayed glance. What must Jake think? she wondered, her mortified gaze meeting his. But he didn't look upset. Not in the least. In fact, he seemed amused. He was wearing that lopsided smile he used to give her when they were sharing a private joke. Thank goodness he was being a good sport about the whole thing! she thought gratefully. But she was so embarrassed, she wished the floor would just open up and swallow her.

"There's cheese and crackers on the table to start," Abby announced. "Take your time. We'll bring in the salad in a little while."

And then the twins disappeared.

Maggie stared helplessly at the tall, distinguished man in the dark gray suit who stood across from her.

"Jake…I'm so sorry," she choked out apologetically, her blush deepening. "I had no idea…. This isn't at all what…" Her voice trailed off and she shook her head. "Wait till I get my hands on them," she added vehemently.

He chuckled, a deep, pleasing rumble that somehow helped soothe her tattered nerves. "Oh, don't be too hard on them. Their hearts were in the right place."

"Maybe. But I've explained to them over and over that we're…well, that our relationship was in the past… they knew better than to pull a stunt like…I just can't believe they did this," she finished in exasperation, realizing how inarticulate her disjointed jumble of words sounded. But she was so upset, she couldn't think straight, let alone form a coherent sentence.

Jake, on the other hand, seemed the epitome of calm as he strolled toward her. But his casual stance was at odds with the flames flickering around the edges of his eyes, and her breath caught in her throat. "Let's humor them," he said quietly. "They've gone to a lot of trouble, Maggie. And it is your birthday. What will one dinner together hurt?"

Maggie was afraid it might hurt a great deal. But she couldn't very well say that. And Jake was right. The girls meant well, even if their intentions were misguided.

"I suppose you're right," she capitulated with a sigh.

He smiled, then tucked one of her hands through his arm as they strolled back to the table. He pulled out her chair with a flourish and wink before sitting down next to her. The girls had set the two places at right angles instead of across from each other, Maggie noted. Another transparent attempt to make this an intimate dinner.

Jake poured their drinks, then raised his glass in a toast. "To Maggie—the most beautiful thirty-seven-year-old I've ever known—and the most memorable woman I've ever met," he murmured huskily.

Maggie watched as he took a sip, his gaze never leaving hers, and suddenly she found it difficult to breathe.

"You really are beautiful, you know," he said softly. "Especially tonight. I like your hair down, Maggie. It's too lovely to pull back all the time."

She swallowed with difficulty. "Th-thanks." Despite her best efforts, she couldn't stop her voice from betraying her turbulent emotions. She glanced down and played with the edge of her fork. It had been a long time since anyone had treated her as a desirable woman. It had been an even longer time since she *felt* like one.

But with Jake...it was different. He made her feel special...and alluring...and not at all like Maggie the aunt, or Maggie the innkeeper. With him she felt like Maggie the woman.

Suddenly his hand covered hers, stilling her restless fingers.

"Maggie?"

She took a deep breath and looked up.

"Do I make you nervous?"

Of course he made her nervous. But she couldn't say that without saying *why,* so she forced herself to smile. "I'm just embarrassed by this whole thing, Jake. It's very...awkward. You must feel very uncomfortable."

"Frankly I don't."

She looked at him in sudden suspicion. "Did you know about this?"

"No. The girls just invited me to a birthday dinner. I had no idea it was only going to be the two of us. But to be honest, I'm not sorry. I've been wanting to..."

Suddenly soft music began to play, and Jake paused as Maggie uttered a soft groan. "Oh, no! Now we have music, too."

He listened for a moment, then another chuckle rumbled out of his chest. "Mmm-hmm. Can you place this singer?"

Maggie focused on the music, and then she, too, had to smile. The vocalist was one who had been popular in her parents' courting days.

"Just how old do they think we are?" Jake asked in a low tone, his eyes glinting with mirth.

"Ancient," she replied dryly, struggling to contain her own smile.

"Oh, well." He stood up and held out his hand. "I

have a feeling the twins conveniently cleared the floor so we could…do the minuet maybe? That's a little beyond my capabilities, but I have mastered a pretty mean fox-trot. So…may I have this dance?"

"Jake, you'll only add fuel to the fire," she admonished him. "The girls' imaginations are active enough without any encouragement."

"Oh, come on, Maggie. One dance. It's a nice song— even if it *is* old."

When he had the beguiling look in his eyes, she found him difficult to refuse. And he *was* being a good sport about the whole thing. After being brought here under false pretenses, he had a right to be angry. Instead, he was playing along, taking the whole thing in stride. In fact, he seemed to be enjoying it. She supposed she might as well try to, as well. It was her birthday, after all. But dancing with Jake, being held in his arms—the mere thought of it made her feel shaky inside.

"One dance, Maggie?"

Face it, Maggie, she told herself as she stared up into his warm, brown eyes. *You want to dance with the man. Don't fight everything so much. Remember Millicent's advice. Give it a chance.*

With a sigh of defeat, she rose silently, and Jake gave her a smile of encouragement as he led her to the center of the floor. Then he took her into his arms, and for just a moment, Maggie thought every bone in her body was going to dissolve simultaneously.

She closed her eyes to better savor the sensations washing over her. His hand was firm but gentle in the small of her back, feeling familiar to her yet new. He entwined the fingers of his other hand with hers and pressed her trembling hand against his solid, muscled chest. The scent of him—masculine, unique, utterly appealing—surrounded her and set a swarm of butterflies loose in her stomach. She could easily stay like this forever, she decided, as a wave of pure contentment washed over her. With a small, almost inaudible sigh, she let her cheek rest against his shoulder and slowly relaxed in his arms, putting aside for just a moment all of the doubts and questions that plagued her about this man. For once, for the space of this brief dance, she would simply enjoy being held in his sure, strong arms.

Jake felt the stiffness in her body ease as she nestled against his shoulder. He dropped his chin and brushed his cheek against her hair, inhaling the subtle, sweet fragrance that clung to it. She felt so good in his arms. She always had. Soft and appealing and somehow fragile, in a way that brought out his protective instinct and made him want to keep her safe and sheltered. In fact, he would like nothing better than to spend the rest of his life doing exactly that.

For the first time all evening, he relaxed, too. Until this very moment he'd been afraid that she would bolt. It was obvious that she was uncomfortable with the contrived situation. And he was sure the twins would hear about it later. But personally, he had no complaints. In fact, he'd been trying for weeks to figure out a way to get Maggie alone so that he could try to begin rebuilding a relationship with her. So far he'd failed miserably.

He couldn't fault her caution. And at least she was pleasant to him, which was more than he would probably be in her place, he admitted. It was a start. But only a start. Before he could hope to make any progress, he had to find a way to break through the barrier she'd erected between them so that he could begin to rebuild her trust level, make her realize that he was a different man than the one who had walked out on her twelve years ago. And tonight was a good time to start, thanks to the twins.

When the music ended they drew apart reluctantly, and Jake smiled tenderly down into her dreamy eyes.

"See? That wasn't so bad, was it?" His tone was teasing, but unmistakably husky.

She shook her head, not trusting her own voice.

The twins appeared with their salads then, and slowly, as they worked their way through the meal that had been prepared with love, if not finesse, Maggie began to truly relax. Jake told her amusing stories about his travels, and she found herself admiring his wit and self-deprecating humor. He also gave her an update on his relationship with his father—still strained, though improving—and the progress he was making on his lesson plans for the coming school year.

But he also drew her out, skillfully and with sincere interest. Maggie didn't know if it was the romantic atmosphere that loosened her tongue, or just Jake's adept probing, but she opened up more than she expected. She even admitted her secret aspiration to give serious art a try, now that the girls were grown and ready to leave for college.

"I think you should, Maggie. I've seen some of your work, and I'm very impressed. I'm no expert, but didn't you say that your friend—the gallery owner—had encouraged you, too?"

She nodded. "But Philip and I...well, we go back a long way. He has a wonderful eye for art, but I'm afraid he may not be that impartial when it comes to my work."

This was the opening Jake had been waiting for ever since the day in her studio when she'd made a similar remark, and he wasn't about to let it pass. Even though he wasn't sure he wanted to hear the answer, he had to know. "You've mentioned him before," he remarked with studied casualness. "I suppose you might have a point about the impartiality issue if you and he are... well, close."

Maggie tipped her head and studied him.

"If you want to know whether Philip and I are romantically involved, why don't you just ask, Jake?" she said bluntly.

He felt his neck grow red. "I guess I didn't want you to think I was prying, and take offense."

She shrugged. "Actually, we explored a romantic relationship once. Shortly after I moved here. But there just wasn't any...*passion* might be the best word, I suppose. Philip's wife died ten years ago, and even though he's lonely, no one ever came along who compared to her, I guess. As for me, well, it was kind of the same story. Plus, I had a ready-made family in tow." Before he could ask a follow-up question about her "same story" comment, she quickly asked one of her own. "And what about you, Jake? Why didn't you ever marry?"

He looked at her steadily. "For the same reason you didn't, I suspect."

They gazed at each other for a moment in silence, and then she glanced down, suddenly uncertain. Did he mean what she thought he meant? Had he cared about her all these years, as she had cared about him, held back unconsciously by a love that had never died?

He reached for her hand then, and she was forced to meet his gaze. "However, lately I've been thinking more and more about settling down, getting married, raising a family—the whole nine yards."

His implication was clear. But even clearer was his comment about wanting a family, Maggie thought with a frown, that single reference suddenly casting a pall over her evening. She vaguely recalled that he'd mentioned a family once before, but it hadn't really registered at the time. Now it hit home.

He saw the sudden furrow on her brow, and a mirror image appeared on his own. Had he revealed too much too soon? "Maggie? Is something wrong?"

She forced herself to smile. "No. It's probably a good time for you to…to get married and start a family, if that's what you want. Raising kids is an experience everyone should have."

One time. She hadn't said that, but the implication was clear, Jake realized. She was telling him that she'd done the family scene, that if a family was in his future, it wouldn't be a future that was linked with hers. He could understand how she felt. Raising twins, especially when one had had a medical problem, would have been difficult enough for two people, let alone one. But it was different when the responsibility was shared.

Before he could suggest that, however, the twins appeared at the door carrying a birthday cake topped with glowing candles. As they launched into a spirited rendition of "Happy Birthday," Jake gave her a look that said, "We'll continue this later" before joining in the refrain.

The twins set the cake before Maggie with a triumphant flourish.

"Make a wish, Aunt Maggie," Allison instructed.

"But don't tell," Abby added. "Or it won't come true."

It was the same instruction she'd always given them, and she smiled. Her gaze met Jake's over the golden light of the candles, but she couldn't read the enigmatic expression in his eyes. Was he wondering whether her wish would have anything to do with him? she reflected. But that would remain her secret.

She took a deep breath and blew out the candles on the first try, to the applause of her small audience. Then Jake reached down next to the table and retrieved two small packages, which he held out to her.

"Happy birthday, Maggie."

"Oh, Jake, you didn't have to do this!" she protested.

"Of course I did. What's a birthday party without presents? Actually, the small one is from me and the larger one is from Dad, who sends his best wishes."

Maggie took them as the girls quickly and efficiently cut and served the cake. Then, despite her entreaties to stay and join the celebration, they whisked the cake away and returned to the kitchen to enjoy their dessert, leaving the guest of honor once more alone with her dinner companion. Maggie shook her head resignedly.

"Their single-minded determination is amazing. Especially when I think about all the years I struggled to get them to concentrate on their homework," Maggie noted wryly.

Jake chuckled. "I have to admit, I'm impressed by their thoroughness." He took a sip of coffee and nodded toward the packages on the table. "Aren't you going to open your presents?"

She chose Howard's first, exclaiming over the intricate pair of wooden candlesticks that were nestled in tissue. "Oh, Jake, these are lovely! Did Pop make them? I thought he didn't do woodworking anymore?"

"He doesn't. He's had these for years. He made them right before Mom died."

Maggie's face grew thoughtful. "I saw all his wood-working equipment in the garage the day I tried to fix your plumbing," she reflected. "You know, it would probably be really good for him to get back into this. It's not too taxing physically, and it would give him something productive to do."

"I agree. But he hasn't show any interest in picking it up again."

"There's a fair coming up at church," Maggie mused aloud. "We have it every fall. A lot of area crafters exhibit and sell their work. And the church sponsors a booth where we sell donated items. Maybe Pop would make a few things for us, since it's for charity. It might be a way to get him back into it."

"It's certainly worth a try," Jake concurred. "But I doubt he'll be receptive to the idea if it comes from me."

"Then I'll talk to him tomorrow," Maggie decided, carefully laying aside the candlesticks as she turned her attention to Jake's present. When she tore the wrapping off she was delighted to discover a leather-bound travel diary, with a note scrawled on the first page.

To Maggie,
May all your travels be exciting—and may they
all lead you home.
Jake.

She looked over at him, touched by the thoughtful gift—and the thought-provoking inscription. "Thank you, Jake."

"You're welcome. I hope your upcoming trip is the first of many."

They focused on the cake, then, and just as they finished the twins made another appearance.

"Why don't you two go sit on the porch while we clean up," Abby suggested.

Jake grinned. "Sounds good to me." He stood up and reached for Maggie's hand. She glanced over at the twins who were, as she expected, positively beaming. She intended to have a long talk with those young women later, but for the moment she'd let them hold on to their misguided romantic fantasy. So, with a "Why fight it?" look, she placed her hand in Jake's and stood up, strolling with him in silence to the front door.

Once outside, she carefully withdrew her hand from his. The evening was drawing to a close, and though she'd enjoyed spending the time with Jake, she didn't want to get used to it.

"Those two," she declared in exasperation, stepping away from him to stand at the porch railing and look out over the moon-silvered bay. "What would they have done if my birthday hadn't been on a Sunday? Any other day the inn would have been full of guests."

Jake noted the physical separation she'd established. And he knew why. Her defenses had started to crumble just a bit tonight, and she was scared. But he wasn't about to let that wall come back up, not yet, anyway. He moved behind her and brought one hand up to rest lightly on her shoulder.

"Somehow I think they would have found a way."

Maggie heard the amusement in his voice, felt his breath close to her ear. So much for her plan to put some space between them. He was so close that she was afraid he would be able to tell that she was trembling. "You're probably right," she admitted, grateful that at least her voice wasn't shaking.

"Well, shall we sit? Or would you rather walk a little?"

Maggie glanced at the wicker porch swing, a perfect invitation to romance—obviously what the twins had in mind—and quickly made her choice. "Let's walk."

"I think the girls will be disappointed," Jake countered with a grin.

"Too bad. They've had their way all evening."

Maggie moved purposefully toward the porch steps, certain that walking was a far safer alternative than sitting next to Jake on the porch swing. But when he reached for her hand, laced his fingers through hers and led her into the moonlit night, she suddenly wasn't so sure.

Chapter Nine

"Are you chilly?"

Maggie glanced up at Jake. Obviously he'd felt her shiver, but she could hardly tell him it was caused more by the warm, tingly feeling his presence evoked than by the cool night air. She swallowed and shook her head.

"No. I'm fine."

Which wasn't true, either. Not when he was stroking her clasped hand with his thumb and smiling at her with that tender look in his brown eyes.

"Well, you're welcome to my jacket if you need it."

That was the *last* thing she needed at the moment, Maggie decided. Having him place his jacket around her shoulders would not do a thing to calm her rapidly accelerating pulse rate.

"Thanks."

Jake seemed content to stroll in silence after that, and Maggie gladly followed his lead. She didn't trust her voice anyway.

After a few minutes, Jake paused and nodded toward the water. "Looks like a good spot for a view of the bay. Can your shoes handle the path?"

Maggie glanced down at her slender-heeled pumps, then at the gravel path he'd indicated. Her shoes would handle the detour with no problem, she decided. But she wasn't so sure about herself. The path led to a small dock that jutted out into the silver-flecked water—the perfect spot for a romantic tryst. Is that what Jake had in mind? she wondered nervously. Better to play this safe and take the out he'd offered her, she concluded. But when she opened her mouth to decline, different words emerged instead.

"They should be okay."

He smiled then, a smile so warm and tender, it made her toes tingle and her stomach flutter—and convinced her that she'd just made a big mistake.

But he didn't give her time for second thoughts. He took her arm and silently guided her down the narrow path to the water's edge, then onto the rough wooden planks of the dock. They walked to the railing, and as she gazed over the moonlit sea, she realized that the gentle cadence of the waves lapping against the shore was much steadier than her pulse. That was even *more* true when Jake draped an arm casually around her shoulders, making her heart jump to her throat. What had she gotten herself into? she thought in sudden panic. She was attracted to Jake, yes. But she wasn't ready for this. Not yet. And maybe never. She still had too many tangled issues and emotions to work through.

Jake felt Maggie trembling, knew she was scared, knew she was still grappling with her feelings for him and fighting their mutual attraction every step of the way. He couldn't blame her. She was afraid of being hurt again, afraid to let herself believe that maybe this time things would be different. But they had to get past that eventually if anything was ever to develop between them. Which was exactly what he had in mind.

Once upon a time, he had never even considered a future without Maggie. He felt the same way now. The challenge was to convince her of that.

A drop of water flicked against his cheek, and he glanced up at the sky with a frown, surprised to discover that a dark cloud had crept up behind them. But he wasn't ready to go back to the inn. He nodded toward the small, abandoned shed they'd passed at the end of the dock and took Maggie's arm.

"Come on. I'd hate to see that spectacular dress ruined."

She followed his lead unprotestingly, pausing only when he stopped to push open the rickety door of the structure. The hinges objected with a loud squeak, but the door reluctantly gave way, and he ushered her inside.

Maggie took a quick inventory of the shed as she stepped over the threshold. When the girls were younger she'd brought them to this dock a few times to fish, not wanting to deprive them of any of the experiences they might have had with a father. She'd peeked into the old fishing shack, but never ventured inside. It looked more dilapidated than ever, she assessed, noting that the spaces between the weathered gray clapboards had widened considerably through the years. The floorboards had long since rotted away, leaving hard-packed dirt and rock in their place. But at least it was relatively even, she thought, as she walked over to a framed opening in the wall that had once been a window. Amazingly enough, the roof still seemed reasonably watertight. It would do as a shelter from the storm, she decided.

But what about the storm inside of her? she wondered, as memories of another rainy day suddenly came flooding back with an intensity that took her breath away. In a shed much like this one, her life had changed forever, she recalled. It was her sixteenth birthday—twenty-one years ago—but right now it seemed like yesterday.

Maggie glanced up at the sky and wrinkled her nose as the first raindrops splattered again the asphalt, leaving dark splotches in their wake.

"Oh, great! Now it's going to rain on my birthday!" she complained as they pedaled side by side down the country lane.

Jake laughed. "Sorry about that, squirt. But I have no control over the weather."

She made a face at him. "Very funny. And will you please stop calling me that?"

He grinned. "Why?"

"Because I'm not. At least, not anymore."

"My, my. Aren't we getting uppity now that we're sixteen," he teased.

Maggie made another face, then pointed to a small, seemingly abandoned shed off to the side of the road. "Let's go in there till the rain stops." Without waiting for him to reply, she rode off the pavement and onto the bumpy ground.

Jake followed her lead, and as they reached the ramshackle structure the rain suddenly turned into a downpour. They dropped their bikes and dashed for cover.

"Wow! Where did *that* come from?" Maggie said breathlessly. When they'd loaded their bikes into the rack on Howard West's car earlier in the day, there hadn't been a cloud in the sky. Nor had there been any when they'd started their ride an hour ago.

"I guess the clouds crept up behind us while we were riding," Jake replied easily. He glanced up at the sky. "I think it will pass quickly. Might as well make ourselves comfortable in the meantime."

Maggie glanced around skeptically. The rain beat a noisy refrain on the rusted tin roof, but at least the floor was dry, she noted, as she started to sit down.

"Watch that mouse!" Jake exclaimed, then laughed when Maggie jumped. "Just kidding."

She glared at him. "Very funny."

He looked around. "Actually, I think we're alone here. But I promise to defend you if any cheese eaters show up." He lowered his tall frame to the floor and leaned back against the wall, drawing his knees up and clasping his hands around his legs.

Maggie looked around doubtfully, then sat down gingerly in the middle of the floor where she could keep a three-hundred-and-sixty-degree lookout for small, unwanted visitors. She dusted her hands on her khaki shorts and crossed her legs, then glanced at Jake. Her eyes widened in alarm and she gasped, pointing behind him.

"Is that a poisonous spider?"

Jake jerked away from the wall and turned to look. Maggie's sudden eruption of giggles told him he'd been had.

"Gotcha!" she declared gleefully.

Jake's eyes narrowed and he gave her a disgruntled look. "How old are you again? Sixteen—or six?"

"You did it to me," she pointed out.

"Once is okay. Getting back isn't," he declared with a tone of superiority.

Maggie gazed at him speculatively. In a way she was glad it had rained, glad they'd found this isolated shelter. Because she had something she wanted to ask him. After all, Jake was more than a year older than she was. He was popular with the girls, dated a lot. In another week he'd be going off to college. Today would be her best chance to pose the question that had been burning in her mind for weeks. But she just wasn't quite sure how to go about it.

"Jake?" Her voice was suddenly tentative, uncertain. "Can I ask you something?"

"Sure." His eyes were closed now, his head dropped back against the rough planks of the wall. He looked very comfortable, and Maggie hated to bother him with this, but he was her only hope.

"Um…well, I've been wondering…I mean, I know this is kind of a weird question, but…well…how do people learn how to kiss?"

That got his attention. His eyelids flew open and he stared at her, startled.

"What?"

Her face grew pink and she dropped her gaze. "I need to find out how people learn to kiss," she repeated, acutely embarrassed.

He grinned. "Ah, the squirt must be growing up."

She blushed furiously and scooted back against the far wall, suddenly wishing some poisonous creature *would* bite her and put her quickly—and mercifully—out of her misery. "Just forget I asked, okay?" she muttered, her shoulders hunched miserably.

Jake looked over at her bowed head, instantly contrite. He and Maggie had been friends since his parents moved onto her block when he was six, and he'd enjoyed their easy give-and-take ever since. She was a good sport and lots of fun to be with. More fun than anyone he'd ever met, in fact. But she was also easily hurt. Obviously she'd had to muster all of her courage to ask him about such a personal subject, and instead of realizing how embarrassed she was, he'd given her a hard time. Jake scooted over and sat in front of her, reaching out to touch her stiff shoulder.

"Maggie, I'm sorry." His voice was gentle, all traces of teasing gone.

She refused to look at him. "It was a dumb question anyway."

Her voice was muffled, and she seemed on the verge of tears. Which only made him feel worse.

"It's not a dumb question."

"Yes, it is."

"No, it's not. And I'm sorry I made a joke of it. I guess I just never thought about you growing up and thinking about those kinds of things."

She sniffed and risked a glance at him, her eyes frustrated. "Well, I am, Jake. And I do. Most of my friends date now. They talk about…stuff…and I feel so ignorant. I don't even know how to kiss, and they…they're way past that stage. I even turned down a date with Joe Carroll last week because I'm afraid he'll think I'm… well, that I don't know what I'm doing. And I don't!" she wailed.

Jake frowned darkly. "Joe Carroll asked you out?"

She nodded. "Why are you so surprised? Don't you think I'm the kind of girl guys would want to ask out?"

Actually, he'd never thought about it one way or the

other. But the idea of Maggie going out with Joe Carroll, who acted like he was the next Casanova, made his blood run cold. Maggie was too sweet and innocent to go out with a guy like that.

"I'm not pretty enough. Is that what you think?" Maggie's miserable voice interrupted his thoughts when he didn't respond.

Jake stared at her. He'd never thought about that, either, to be honest. Maggie was…well, Maggie. She was cute. She had pretty hair. He liked her turned-up nose. He'd just never thought about her in those kinds of terms. But clearly she needed some reassurance, and the least he could do was build up her confidence—and give her some warnings.

"Of course you're pretty," he declared gallantly. "Too pretty, maybe. You need to be careful around guys like Joe. He expects a whole lot more out of a date than a kiss, from what I hear."

"Really?" She stared at him wide-eyed.

"Uh-huh."

She sighed. "Oh, well, it doesn't matter anyway. I don't even know how to do *that,* let alone anything else."

"You just need to practice," Jake told her. "That's how I learned."

"Yeah?"

"Mmm-hmm."

"But…who would I practice with?"

He looked at her for a moment as an idea suddenly took shape in his mind. "Well, I suppose you could practice with me," he offered slowly. "*I* could teach you."

She stared at him again. "You?"

"Yeah. What's wrong with me?" he asked, offended.

"Well…I don't know. It just seems kind of…weird,

you know? I mean, it's not exactly…romantic…or any-thing."

"So? That's probably good. This way there's no pres-sure."

She considered the idea for a moment, her head tipped to one side. "Yeah, you're right," she conceded. In fact, the idea made a lot of sense, the more she thought about it. She scooted closer and looked up at him expectantly. "Okay. What do I do?"

Jake shifted uncomfortably. He was in this too far now to back out, but it *was* weird, as she said. Besides, *she* might think he was an expert at this. But at the moment his limited experience seemed hardly adequate to qualify him as an instructor. However, his seventeen-year-old ego wasn't about to let him admit that. He'd just have to try and pull this off.

"You don't really have to *do* anything. The guy usually takes the lead." Like Joe Carroll, Jake thought grimly. He took more than the lead if he had half a chance, to hear him boast. Maggie needed to be pre-pared for guys like that, had to learn not to be swept away by their nice words and what, to her, would be sophisticated technique. The more she knew before she got into a situation like that, the better.

"So when he *does* take the lead, is that when the kissing starts?"

"Yeah. Usually."

"Okay." She looked up at him, but when he remained unmoving she frowned. "So…are you going to show me?"

Jake took a deep breath. Maggie now seemed at ease. He was the one who suddenly felt uncomfortable. He *had* made a promise, though. "Yeah, I am." He took a deep breath and leaned forward, and she followed his lead. But instead of their lips connecting, their noses collided. Maggie threw back her head and erupted into a fit of giggles.

"This isn't how it happens in the movies," she declared, her shoulders shaking with laughter.

Jake gave her a stern look. "This isn't going to work if you keep giggling," he admonished her.

Maggie stifled the giggles—with difficulty. "Sorry. Can we try that again?"

This time their lips briefly connected, but when Jake backed off and checked out her reaction, *disappointed* was the only word that came to mind. He frowned at her in irritation.

"Now what's wrong?"

"Is that it?" she asked, crestfallen.

Jake's seventeen-year-old pride took a nosedive. This lesson was getting a lot more complicated than he'd anticipated.

"Maggie, are you really sure you want me to teach you all this?"

Her face fell. "I don't have anyone else to ask, Jake," she replied quietly. Then she dropped her gaze and played with the edge of her shorts. "But if you don't want to, that's okay. I understand."

The plaintive note in her voice tugged at his heart, and he reached down and tilted her chin up with a gentle finger. "I said I'd teach you, and I will," he told her softly. Then, calling on every bit of his limited experience, he set out to do just that.

He reached over and touched her hair, surprised at its softness as it drifted through his fingers. Then he cupped her face with this hands and combed back through her flame-colored tresses, loosening her barrettes in the process until her hair tumbled freely around her shoulders. He stroked her face, the skin soft and silky beneath his fingers. But she was too far away, he decided. He reached down to her waist and pulled her toward him, until her knees touched his as they sat cross-legged facing each other, their faces only inches apart.

At this range, Jake noticed the flecks of gold in her deep green eyes. Funny, he'd never even paid any attention to their color before. But they were beautiful eyes, he realized, expressive and—at the moment—a bit dazed. So maybe his technique wasn't so bad after all, he thought, pleased. His confidence bolstered, he reached over and traced the outline of her lips with his fingertip, a whisper-soft touch that made her gasp. Her lips parted ever so slightly—and oh-so-invitingly. She'd be putty in Joe Carroll's hands, he thought, suddenly glad they'd pursued this today. At least now she'd have some idea what to expect, be a little more prepared if some guy tried to take advantage of her innocence and inexperience.

Jake let his hands drop to her shoulders, then framed her face with his hands, marvelling at the incredible softness of her skin. As she gazed up at him, so trustingly, his heart suddenly did something very strange. It stopped, just for a second, then raced on.

Jake didn't pause to analyze his reaction. Instead, he leaned forward to claim her lips, softly tasting them, before he captured her mouth in a kiss that was perhaps a bit short on technique but very long on passion.

Maggie had no idea what was happening to her. This had all started out so innocently, two old friends out for a bike ride. Her request of Jake had seemed simple enough: Tell me how people learn to kiss. But the results were far from simple. From the moment he'd begun running his fingers through her hair, her heartbeat had gone haywire. Her stomach felt funny, and she couldn't seem to breathe right. And now…now, as his lips possessed hers, she thought she was going to drown in the flood of sensations washing over her.

How could he never have noticed before that she had grown up? Jake wondered in amazement. It was obvious in her delicate curves, in her softness, in the small sounds she made as he continued to kiss her. He'd always thought of Maggie as a kid, a pal, someone to ride bikes and shoot baskets with. But he didn't think of her as a kid right now. The frantic beat of the rain on the tin roof couldn't compete with the beating of their hearts as their embrace escalated.

It was Jake who finally realized that things were moving too fast and he broke away abruptly. Somewhere along the way this "lesson" had gotten out of hand, their roles changing from instructor and student to man and woman. And as Jake gazed down into Maggie's dazed eyes, he realized something else had changed, as well. Namely his life. Somehow he knew it would never be the same again.

Maggie stared up at him, then reached out to wonderingly trace the contours of his face. She heard his sharply indrawn breath, then he captured her hand in his, stilling its sensual movement. She could see the tension in his face, feel the thudding of his heart and realized with awe that she had drawn this passionate response from him. But she felt no less moved. She drew a deep, shaky breath, and when she spoke her voice was unsteady.

"Wow!" she breathed.

He tried to smile but couldn't quite pull it off. "Yeah. Wow!"

"Jake, I...I never expected to feel like...well, anything like this. I feel so...I don't know...fluttery inside. And shaky. And scared. But good, too. All at once. Is it...is it because I've never done this before?"

Slowly he shook his head. "I don't think so, Maggie. I feel the same way, and I've kissed a fair number of girls."

She struggled to sit up, and he saw with a frown that her hands were shaking badly. He should have been gentler, moved more slowly, he chided himself. She'd never even been kissed before. Of course, better him than Joe Carroll, he consoled himself. At least he'd had the decency to back off. He doubted Joe would have been as noble.

Jake put his arm around Maggie and pulled her against him until her head rested on his shoulder, smiling as he rubbed his cheek against her hair.

"You know, I never thought of you—of us—romantically before," she said in a small, uncertain voice.

"Me, neither. But I do now." He stroked her arm. "And you know what? I like it."

"So do I," she replied softly.

"You know something else? I have a feeling this may be the start of something pretty wonderful."

She snuggled closer. "I have the same feeling."

He backed off just far enough to look down into her emerald eyes, and the warmth of his smile filled her with joy. "Happy birthday, Maggie." And then he leaned down and claimed her lips in a tender kiss filled with sweet promise.

* * *

Maggie drew a deep, shaky breath as she stared at the silvered bay through the rough opening in the wall. She wrapped her arms around her body, holding the memories close for just a moment longer, memories of the day their friendship had ripened into romance. The images had seemed too vivid, so real—so lovely. She hated to let them go.

Had taking shelter in the old fishing shack prompted similar memories in Jake? she suddenly wondered, turning toward him. He was gazing at her silently.

"Seems like old times, doesn't it, squirt?" he said quietly, and she had her answer.

Maggie swallowed with difficulty, and turned back to the window. "Yes," she whispered.

She felt him move behind her, and her breath caught in her throat as he placed his hands on her shoulders and stroked them lightly.

"It's still there, isn't it, Maggie?" he murmured, his voice rough with emotion.

"What?" she choked out, knowing only too well what he meant.

With firm but gentle hands he turned her to face him so that she had to look directly into his eyes.

"This," he replied, and slowly reached over to trace the soft curve of her mouth with a whisper touch.

She closed her eyes and shuddered, willing herself to walk away, knowing she couldn't.

"Jake, I...things have changed. We're not the same people anymore."

"Not everything has changed."

She swallowed, and a pulse began to beat erratically in the delicate hollow of her throat. His gaze dropped to it for a moment, swept over the expanse of skin that had turned to alabaster in the moonlight, then came back to her eyes.

"We should go back," she suggested, a touch of desperation in her voice.

"I wish we could," he replied, and she knew he wasn't talking about the inn. "But the best we can do is start over. Tonight. Right now."

And then slowly, very slowly, he leaned toward her until his lips, familiar and warm and tender, closed over hers.

With a soft sigh, Maggie gave up the fight and melted into his arms. She'd intuitively known this moment would come since the day she stepped into the dining room seven weeks ago and found him there. It had been a losing struggle from the beginning, she acknowledged. Right or wrong, she wanted this moment in the arms of the man she'd always loved.

She was aware that the muscular contours of his chest were more developed, harder, than she remembered. And his arms were stronger, more sure, than she recalled, holding her with a practiced skill that had been absent twelve years ago. His mouth moved over hers with a new adeptness. The passion, though—that was the same. Just more intense.

Mostly she simply gave herself up to the moment, reveling in the exquisite joy of Jake's embrace. She returned his kiss tentatively at first, but his lips coaxed hers into a fuller response. She sighed softly as he cradled her head in one palm, his fingers tangled in her hair. Jake deepened the kiss, and she could feel the hard, uneven thudding of his heart as he pressed her closer. She offered no resistance. Couldn't have even if she'd wanted to.

Jake wasn't usually a man who lost control. He'd learned a great deal about discipline over the last dozen years, but it was a virtue that deserted him at the moment. Even as he told himself not to push, it was almost as if he was trying to make up for twelve long, parched years in one kiss. He had been so afraid she would reject his overture, that her fear would make her back off. But the fact that she had allowed him to claim her lips gave him hope for the future.

With a shuddering sigh, Jake at last raised his head and pressed hers close against his chest, holding her tightly. He had to stop now, before this got out of hand. He wasn't seventeen anymore, even if he felt like he was.

For several minutes neither spoke. Jake could feel Maggie trembling in his arms, and he didn't feel any too steady himself. Not only had their attraction endured through the years, it had intensified, he realized. The question now was, what were they going to do about it?

When her quivering finally eased, and when he finally felt able to carry on a coherent conversation, he gently pulled away from her, though he kept his arms looped around her waist. Their gazes met—his smoldering, hers dazed. With great effort, Jake summoned up the semblance of a smile.

"Wow."

"I…I think that's my line," she replied in a choked voice.

"I'm stealing it."

"Jake, I—I don't know if this is wise. I don't think I'm ready to…to…"

"Trust me again?" he finished softly, when her voice trailed off.

She stared at him, and warm color suffused her face at his blunt—and accurate—assessment of her feelings.

"It's okay, Maggie," he assured her softly. "I'm not asking you to—not yet, not after all these years. We need to give this some time. But the magic is still there. We both know that. I'd like to see where it leads."

Maggie swallowed. He was being direct about his intentions, and she respected that. She owed him no less. "Jake, I have a good life now. I've been…content. I thought that love had…that it wasn't the Lord's will for me. But I think I could…that we might…" She paused and turned away in frustration, reaching up to swipe at an errant tear. "See what you do to me? I'm a wreck. And it will be worse if I let myself…if I let myself care and then…" She paused, and Jake stepped in to finish the sentence again, much as he hated to.

"And then I disappear."

She turned to look at him and nodded slowly.

"I'm not going to leave again, Maggie," he promised her, his intense gaze locked on hers. "I'm here to stay this time."

She searched his eyes, wanting desperately to believe him. But he'd turned her world upside down once, and she had vowed never to let anyone do that again. How could she be sure this time?

Jake read the uncertainty in her eyes. "Just give me a chance, Maggie. That's all I ask. Spend some time with me. Just the two of us."

Maggie sighed. After tonight, there was no way she could refuse. She might be foolishly walking headfirst into danger, but Millicent Trent was right. Not very many people got a second chance at love. She'd be a fool to let it slip by without even considering it.

"All right, Jake. But right now we really do need to get back. The twins will be wondering what happened to us."

He grinned. "I think their imaginations will fill in the blanks. They're probably celebrating the success of their strategy right now."

Maggie took the hand he extended, and as he laced his fingers with hers, she suspected he was right. She knew that the notion of a rekindled romance between their aunt and Jake made the twins feel hopeful and excited. She ought to chastise them for their unrealistic expectations. But how could she, when her heart suddenly felt the same way?

Chapter Ten

Jake tossed his jacket onto the couch, set his briefcase on the floor and reached up to massage his neck. It had been a day full of meetings as the faculty prepared for the new school year, and he was tired. Classes started in a week and Jake was inundated with lesson plans and paperwork. The latter was no problem, of course. His years in the navy had prepared him for that, he mused, his mouth quirking up into a wry smile.

The lesson plans were another story. Teaching a course here and there during his career in the service was one thing. Planning a full load of classes for an entire semester was another. But not much could dampen his spirits after yesterday's dinner with Maggie. His heart felt lighter than it had in years.

A sudden thud from the direction of the garage drew his attention. What in the world was his father up to? he wondered, heading out to investigate.

When Jake reached the door to the garage, he paused only long enough to note that Howard was struggling to lift one of the boxes containing his woodworking tools.

Then he strode rapidly across the floor and reached for it before the older man could protest.

"This is too heavy for you, Dad."

"I could have managed it," Howard declared stubbornly.

Jake didn't argue the point. They both knew he wasn't supposed to do heavy lifting or strenuous work of any kind. Making an issue out of it would only lead to an argument or cause his father to retreat into miffed silence. So instead, Jake nodded toward the once neatly stacked boxes, which were now in disarray. "What are you doing anyway?"

Howard stuck his hands in his pockets. "Maggie called. They need some craft items for a booth at the church fair, and she asked me if I'd make a few things. I couldn't say no, not after she's been so nice and all since I got here. But I need to set up my equipment."

Jake deposited the box on the floor and surveyed the garage. There was a workbench in one corner, and he nodded toward it. "Will that spot work?"

"That'll do. I just need to set up the saw and lathe."

"I'll take care of it for you after dinner."

"I can do it myself."

Jake planted his hands on his hips and turned to face his father. They were going to have to address the issue anyway, it seemed. "Dad, this equipment is too heavy for you to lift," he said evenly. "You know that. Why didn't you just wait until I got home?"

Howard shrugged. "Didn't want to be a bother."

Jake's tone—and stance—softened at the unexpected response, and he reached over and laid a hand on his father's stiff shoulder. "You're not a bother, Dad."

The older man glanced down, his shoulders hunched.

"I just feel in the way these days. Maybe I can at least do something productive for the church."

Jake frowned. Did his father really feel that useless? Maggie had intimated as much, but Jake had been so busy getting ready for school—and worrying about his relationship with her—that he hadn't really thought much about how his father was feeling. Maybe he needed to.

"Well, we'll set it up tonight. Tomorrow we can run into Bangor and buy whatever wood and supplies you need. And a couple of space heaters, so you can work out here when the weather gets cooler."

Howard looked at him warily. "I don't want to put you out."

Jake's gaze was steady and direct. "I'm glad to do it, Dad," he said firmly.

As Jake prepared for bed later that night, he thought about his conversation with his father and how they'd worked side by side earlier in the evening to set up the workshop, Jake doing the physical work, Howard providing the direction. It reminded him of younger, happier times with his father. Maybe, just maybe, they were finally taking the first tentative steps toward a true reconciliation, he thought hopefully.

He recalled Maggie's promise to pray for them, and his own conclusion that it would take a miracle to put things right between him and his father. Jake had always been skeptical of miracles. But perhaps he was about to see one come to pass after all.

"Please, Aunt Maggie?"

Maggie stared at the twins. They'd ganged up on her again, and she couldn't seem to come up with a reason to say no. Ever since her birthday the week before, they'd been grinning like the proverbial Cheshire cat, dropping hints about her and Jake, urging her to call him, to accept his invitations for dinner, to sit on the porch with him when he dropped by unexpectedly in the evening. But she needed some space to mentally re-group after their last tumultuous encounter. Those few minutes in the fishing shed had caused her too many sleepless nights.

"Won't you do it for *us,* Aunt Maggie?" Allison ca-joled.

Maggie sighed, realizing she'd lost this battle. If the twins wanted her to invite Jake to accompany them to the airport in Bangor when they departed for college in two days, how could she disappoint them?

"All right. You guys win. I'll ask. But remember, he's getting ready for school, too," she warned. "So don't be surprised if he can't make it."

"He'll make it," Abby predicted with a knowing smile.

And she was right. In fact, he not only agreed to go, he offered to drive.

When the big day arrived, Jake showed up right on time, dressed in a pair of khaki slacks and a cotton fish-erman's sweater that emphasized the broadness of his chest and enhanced his rugged good looks. His smile of welcome for her was warm and lingering, and the smoky look in his eyes wasn't missed by the percep-tive twins. She saw them exchange a secret smile and shook her head. Hopeless romantics, the two of them.

The twins chattered excitedly all the way to Bangor, plying Jake with questions about his overseas travels, and Maggie was content to just sit back and listen to the lively banter. Between her sleepless nights and the rush to take care of all the last-minute details that going off to college entailed—not to mention running the inn—she was exhausted. Up till now the girls' enthusiasm had been contagious and had kept her adrenaline flowing. It was a happy, exciting time for them—the start of a new life—and she was pleased that their excellent academic performance had earned them both scholarships to the universities of their choice. Those scholarships, combined with their parents' insurance money—most of which had been put into a trust fund—would offer them security for many years to come. Their futures looked bright, and they had much to be happy and thankful for.

But late at night these last couple of weeks, when all the tumult ceased and she lay alone in bed, Maggie was overcome with a vague sense of melancholy. For the twins, college was a beginning. For her, it was an ending. Their departure marked the end of the life she had known for most of her adult years. Their laughter and teasing had filled her days, and the girls had provided her with an outlet for the bountiful love that filled her heart. Now they would build their own lives, apart from her, and eventually, special men would come along to claim their hearts. That was what she hoped for them anyway. She wanted their lives to be full and rich, filled with love and a satisfying career and children. It was just that she would miss them terribly. They had been her purpose, her anchor, and she felt suddenly adrift and strangely empty.

It wasn't until Abby was getting ready to board the plane that the girls themselves got teary-eyed. They'd never been apart for any great length of time, and now they were heading in two different directions, away from each other and the only home they could remember. Abby clung first to Allison, then to Maggie, as Jake stepped discreetly into the background.

"I'll miss you both so much!" she said, her voice suddenly shaky and uncertain.

"Call me every day, okay?" Allison implored.

"I promise."

"Goodbye, Aunt Maggie. And thank you…for everything."

Maggie's own eyes grew misty, but she struggled to maintain her composure as she hugged Abby again. She wanted this to be a happy moment for them, not a sad one. "Believe it or not, I loved every minute of it. Even the old days, when you and Allison used to delight in confusing me about who was who."

"I guess we were pretty bad about that," Abby admitted with a sheepish grin.

"Well, I survived. I even managed to guide two girls through adolescence at once without losing my sanity. Don't I get a medal or something?"

"Would a kiss and a hug do instead?" Abby asked with a laugh.

Maggie smiled. "I think that would be an even better reward."

Abby embraced her, and Maggie blinked back her tears.

"Now get on that plane before it leaves without you. I can't run after the plane like I used to run after the school bus!"

Abby grinned. "Yeah, I remember. Alli, you'll call, right?" Her voice was anxious as she hugged her twin.

"Count on it."

"You, too, Aunt Maggie?"

"Absolutely. Now scoot. The bus is leaving," Maggie teased, trying valiantly to keep her smile in place.

"Okay." She hefted her knapsack and headed down the ramp.

Maggie and Allison waved until she was out of sight, and then, half an hour later, it was Allison's turn.

As Jake watched in the background, giving the two a moment alone, he wondered what was going through Maggie's mind. She seemed upbeat, happy. But he'd caught the glimmer of tears in her eyes more than once today. And as Allison disappeared from view, the sudden slump in Maggie's shoulders confirmed his suspicion that saying goodbye to the twins was one of the more difficult moments in her life. She suddenly looked lost—and very alone. He tossed his empty disposable coffee cup into a nearby receptacle and quickly strode toward her.

Maggie felt Jake lace his fingers through hers, and she blinked rapidly before looking up at him, struggling to smile. The understanding look in his eyes made it even more difficult to keep her tears at bay.

"You did a good job with them, you know," he said quietly, brushing his thumb reassuringly over the back of her hand. "They're lovely, intelligent, confident young women with their heads on straight and hearts that reflect an upbringing filled with kindness and love."

How was it that he'd known exactly the right thing to say? she wondered incredulously, trying to swallow past the lump in her throat. In the moments before he'd walked over, she'd been asking herself those very kinds of questions. Had she done everything she could to prepare them for what was ahead? Would the values she'd instilled in them survive their college years? Had their single-parent upbringing provided enough love and support and stability? Had she given them an adequate sense of self-worth, a solid enough grounding in their faith, to sustain them through whatever lay ahead? Jake seemed to think so. She didn't know if he was right. But hearing him say it made her feel better, and for that she was grateful.

"Thank you. I tried my best. I suppose that's all any of us can do. And I hope you're right. I hope it was good enough."

He draped his arm around her shoulders. "I don't think you have to worry about those two, Maggie. You raised them to be survivors. But then, they had a good example to follow."

Suddenly she was immensely grateful that the girls had insisted Jake come along today. His presence somehow helped ease the loneliness of their departure.

"Thank you for coming today, Jake. It was a lot tougher than I expected, saying goodbye. I—I'm going to miss those two! It will be so strange to be alone after all these years."

Jake turned to face her, letting one hand rest lightly at her waist as he tenderly stroked her cheek. "You're not alone, Maggie."

She searched his eyes, discerning nothing but honesty in their depths. His intense gaze seemed to touch her very soul, willing her to believe the sincerity of his words. And she wanted to. Dear Lord, she wanted to, with every fiber of her being! But she had to be cautious. She had to be sure. She still had too many doubts, too many questions. She would move forward, yes. But

slowly. Because only time would provide the answers—
and the assurance—she needed.

"By the way, the date's set."

"What date?" Maggie asked distractedly as she
snagged another forkful of chicken salad. The mid-
September weather was absolutely balmy, and when
Philip had called and asked her to meet him for lunch
at the outdoor café overlooking the bay, she couldn't
refuse. Even now, her attention was focused more on
enjoying the warmth of the sun seeping into her skin
than on their conversation.

"The date for your show."

She stared at him. "What show?"

"The show we've been talking about for a year—
remember?"

"You mean the show I never agreed to?"

"That's the one," he verified cheerily, reaching for
his iced tea.

Maggie set her fork down with a clatter. "Philip, you
didn't! You know I'm not ready!"

"You're ready, Maggie. You have been for a couple
of years."

"But...but I never agreed to a show!"

"True. And why is that?"

Maggie bit her lip. "This is too close to my heart,
Philip. You know that. I just can't take the chance. What
if...what if I fail?"

Philip leaned forward and took her hand. "Maggie,
there's no growth without risk. You've lived a very predictable, quiet life here for as long as I've known you.
You think things through and try as hard as you can to
make everything perfect. And that's worked well for

you with the inn. You have a successful business and a comfortable life. But some things can't be worked out on a spreadsheet. Sometimes you have to just trust your heart. I know it's risky. I know how much your art means to you. It comes right from your heart, exposes your soul. That's why it's so good—and also why rejection is so scary. But I'm telling you, as your friend and a professional art dealer, that the risk of a show is minimal. I've shown some of your work to my friend in Bangor, and he agrees with my assessment. It will be a great opportunity for you to launch a more serious career. I'll cancel the show if you really want me to, but I think it would be a big mistake."

She frowned. "When is this show supposed to be?"

"The opening is scheduled for the first Friday in December. It will run for a month."

Maggie took a deep breath. It was a scary commitment, but Philip was right. If she ever wanted to pursue serious art, she had to make her work available for critique and review. She needed to take this opportunity.

"All right, Philip. I'll do it," she told him with sudden decision. "I guess it's time to test the waters, take a chance."

He smiled. "You won't be sorry, you know."

"I hope you're right."

"And what about the other…risky…situation in your life at the moment?" he asked, purposefully keeping his tone casual.

"What situation?"

"Jake."

Maggie glanced down and played with her chicken salad. "I'm not so sure about that one. It's even scarier."

"Well, it would be a shame to walk away from something good just because you're afraid. And that's true for everything—from a show to a relationship. Now, suppose I get off my soapbox and change the subject to something less heavy. Tell me about the girls. How are they adjusting?"

The rest of the lunch passed in companionable conversation. But Philip's words kept replaying in her mind. Was her fear protecting her—or keeping her from something good, as he had suggested? Maggie didn't know. But as she left Philip in front of the restaurant and returned to her car, she turned to the source of guidance she always relied on in times of uncertainty.

Lord, I'm confused, she confessed in the silence of her heart. *I'm starting to fall in love with Jake again, but I don't know if that's wise. He hurt me badly once, and I don't ever want to go through that pain again. But I feel You sent him here for a reason. If it's Your will that I give our love a second chance, please help me to find the courage to trust again. Because otherwise I'm afraid I'll let it slip through my fingers. And I don't want to live the rest of my life with regrets, the way Millicent has. Please—please—show me the way!*

"Pop! Over here!"

Jake turned at the sound of the familiar voice and smiled at Maggie.

"She's over there, Dad." He laid one hand on Howard's shoulder and gestured toward the church booth with the other.

"Well, let's go say hello."

Jake was more than happy to comply. He hadn't seen enough of Maggie these last two weeks, not since the girls left. September was a popular month at the inn, and she was busier than ever, without the girls to help. But no more busy than him. He had been a bit overwhelmed by the workload at school and had been left with virtually no free time. It was not a situation he was pleased about, but until he adjusted to school and her business slowed down for the winter, there didn't seem to be much he could do about it. He had to take whatever limited time he could get with her. And accompanying his father to the church fair—especially knowing Maggie was working at the booth—was as good an excuse as any to take a break from correcting papers.

He gave her a lazy smile as they approached. "Hi, Maggie."

The smoky, intimate tone in his voice brought a flush to her cheeks. "Hello, Jake." With an effort she dragged her gaze from his and turned her attention to Howard. "Hi, Pop."

"Hi, Maggie. How's business?"

"That's what I wanted to tell you. All of the things you made sold already!"

"Really?" he asked, clearly pleased.

"Yes. And not only that, Andrew Phillips—he owns the local craft alliance—wants to talk to you. They'd like to take some of your things on consignment, and he was even interested in having you teach a class."

Howard's eyes lit up. "He liked my work that much?"

Maggie nodded emphatically. "Absolutely. He said… wait, there he is over there. Andrew!" She waved at a tall, spare young man with longish hair and gestured for him to join them. He strolled over, and she made the introductions.

"I told Howard you were interested in talking with him," Maggie explained.

"Yes, I am. Could you spare me a few minutes now? Maybe have a cup of coffee or something?"

Howard was actually beaming. "Sure, sure. That is, if my son doesn't mind waiting." He glanced at Jake, suddenly uncertain.

Jake propped his shoulder against the corner of Maggie's booth and folded his arms across his chest. "Not at all. Take your time, Dad."

He watched the two men wander off toward the refreshment area, then turned to Maggie with a smile and shook his head. "Now that, Ms. Fitzgerald, is a miracle. Did you see the way my dad's face lit up?"

She smiled. "Yes. It makes all the difference in the world when a person believes they have something to contribute. Pop just needs to feel like he can still do something worthwhile."

"Thanks to you, he does."

Maggie blushed again and shook her head. "No. You were the one who thought to bring the woodworking tools."

"But you were the one who convinced him to use them."

She shrugged. "Well, it doesn't really make any difference where the credit belongs. The important thing is that Pop seems interested in something again. And he's looking better, too, Jake. Are…are things improving at all between you two?"

"They're better. But even though we're more comfortable with each other, there's still a…a distance, I guess is the best way to describe it. I don't feel like we ever really connect at a deeper level. And frankly, I'm not sure what else I can do. School is pretty demanding right now, and I just don't have the time to focus on Dad the way I'd like to. I'm not used to dealing with boys that age, and it's a real challenge. In fact, to be perfectly honest, I sometimes feel like I'm in over my head."

"Your father raised two boys," Maggie said thoughtfully. "Maybe he could offer you a few tips. Have you talked to him about your job, or any of the kids?"

Jake frowned and shook his head. "I don't think he's interested. He's never asked about my work."

"Maybe he's afraid that you don't want his advice."

Jake considered that. She might have a point. During the last twelve years he hadn't exactly shared a lot of his life with his father. Why should the older man expect him to start now?

"I guess it couldn't hurt to try," Jake conceded.

"Well, most people are flattered when asked for advice. And your father really does have a lot of experience with boys. You might actually…"

"Next Wednesday, then?"

Andrew's voice interrupted their conversation, and they turned as the two men approached.

"Let me check with my son." Howard looked at Jake. "Andrew would like me to come by the shop next Wednesday and look things over, maybe work out a schedule for a class. Would it put you out to run me over after school?"

"I'd be happy to, Dad."

Howard turned back to Andrew and stuck out his hand. "It's nice to meet you, young man."

"My pleasure. I'll see you Wednesday."

"Sounds like things went well," Maggie observed with a smile.

Howard nodded, looking pleased. "Yes, they did.

Nice young fellow. He's a potter. It's good to talk to people who appreciate handcrafted work."

"Could be a whole new career for you, Pop," Maggie pointed out.

"Could be, at that." He turned back to Jake. "I appreciate the ride Wednesday," he said stiffly.

"No problem, Dad."

"Well, if I'm going to be making things for the shop, I need to take inventory. You ready to go?"

"Sure." Jake turned to Maggie, the warmth of his smile mirrored in his eyes. "Thanks."

Before she realized his intent, he reached over and touched her cheek, then let his hand travel to her nape. He exerted gentle pressure and drew her close for a tender kiss. When he backed off she was clearly flustered, and Jake wondered if he'd been too impulsive. But it had been three long weeks since her birthday, three weeks with nothing but the memory of their embrace in the fishing shack to sustain him. He needed to reassure himself that she hadn't had second thoughts about pursuing their relationship.

He searched her eyes, and when their gazes locked for a mesmerizing moment, he had all the reassurance he needed. "I'll be by later this week, Maggie," he said in a voice only she could hear. "We need to talk."

She nodded, unwilling to trust her voice.

He smiled, then glanced at his father. "Ready, Dad?"

The older man nodded. "Whenever you are." Howard looked at Maggie quizzically, then turned and walked away.

"I'm surprised she let you do that," he muttered as Jake fell into step beside him.

"I think she's beginning to realize that I've changed, Dad," Jake replied quietly. "At least, I hope she is."

The older man paused and regarded his son silently for a moment. Jake tensed, waiting for a derogatory comment, but instead Howard simply turned and continued toward the car. "Let's go home," he said gruffly, over his shoulder. "I've got some projects to start."

Jake followed, trying to absorb the significance of what had just occurred. Not only had his father refrained from making a disparaging remark, but even more important, he had used the word *home* for the first time. It was a small thing, Jake knew. But it was a start.

Chapter Eleven

Jake dropped his briefcase on the couch and sniffed appreciatively. Since the beginning of the school year, his father had taken over the chore of cooking dinner. The meal was never fancy, given Howard's limited culinary skills, but the gesture was greatly appreciated by Jake. He was usually tired when he got home, and definitely not in the mood to cook. His father's willingness to step in and handle KP was a godsend. Especially tonight.

As Jake strolled toward the kitchen, he mulled over the encounter he'd had with one of the freshmen this afternoon. Actually, *confrontation* might be a better description, he thought grimly. The last thing he needed in this "learning-the-ropes" phase of his new career was a smart-aleck kid mouthing off at him. He supposed he could—and perhaps should—report the insubordination to the dean. But that could be the death knell for a budding maritime career, and he was reluctant to take such a drastic measure so early in the semester. Besides, there was something about the boy that troubled him. A look in his eyes of…bleakness; that was the word that came to mind. And desperation. They were barely discernible under his veneer of insolence, but they were there, Jake was certain. He just didn't know what to do about it.

"Hi, Dad." He paused in the doorway. "What's for dinner?"

His father shrugged. "Just meat loaf. I used to make it for myself at home sometimes, after your mother died. She made it better than I do, though."

"Well, it sure smells good."

Howard turned to set the table, pausing for a moment to study Jake. "You look tired."

Jake sighed and reached around to rub the stiff muscles in his neck. "It was a long day."

"Well, I imagine teaching is quite a change from the navy. Takes a while to get used to, I expect." Howard placed the cutlery beside the plates. "Go ahead and change if you want. Dinner'll be ready in fifteen minutes."

When Jake reappeared a few minutes later wearing worn jeans and a sweatshirt, his father nodded to the table. "Have a seat. It's almost ready."

"Can I help with anything?"

"Two cooks in the kitchen is one too many. That's what your mother always used to say, and she was right."

Jake eased his long frame into the chair, watching as Howard bustled about. His father was moving with much more purpose and energy these last few days, he realized. Thanks to Maggie. Getting his father back into woodworking had been a terrific idea, and she had known just how to go about it. Considering the success of that strategy, he decided to talk to his father about school, ask his advice. Maggie had been batting a thousand so far, after all. And he *was* at a loss about how to deal with his problem student. Perhaps his father could offer a few insights. It couldn't hurt to ask anyway.

Halfway through the meal, his father gave him the perfect opening.

"I saw some of the students from the academy walking down the road today. They look like fine young men," he observed.

Jake nodded. "They are. Most of them. But I've got one freshman—I just can't figure out what's going on in his head."

Howard looked over at Jake quizzically. "What's his problem?"

Jake sighed. "I wish I knew. I checked his transcripts, and he's obviously bright. But he's only doing the bare minimum to survive in my class—and apparently in his other classes, as well. He's sullen and withdrawn and just itching for a fight. We had a confrontation after class today, as a matter of fact. I told him I expected more, and essentially he said that as long as he turned in the assignments it wasn't any of my business how well he did. That I should just grade his papers and buzz off."

"Sounds like somebody needs to give that boy a good talking to."

Jake nodded. "You're right. But he doesn't let anybody get close enough. Whenever I see him he's alone."

"Well, I'm not surprised, with that kind of attitude."

"The thing is, Dad, he has a sort of…hopeless…look in his eyes," Jake said pensively, his brow furrowed. "Like he's worried and scared and…I don't know. I just sense there's something wrong. I'd like to reach out to him, try to help, but I don't know how," he admitted with a frustrated sigh.

Howard stopped eating and peered across the table at Jake, obviously surprised by his son's admission. There was a moment of silence, and when he spoke, his voice was cautious.

"Sounds like something's on his mind, all right. Probably could use a sympathetic ear. But you're a stranger, Jake. It's pretty hard to trust a stranger, especially one who's an authority figure."

"Yeah. I suppose so."

"You know, going away to school can be a pretty scary thing. That could be part of it. But it sounds to me like maybe something's going on at home, too. Something that's tearing him up inside. Lots of times people get belligerent when they're faced with a situation that scares them, especially if it's something they can't control."

Jake wondered if his father realized that insight might apply in his own case, but as the older man thoughtfully buttered a piece of bread, his focus was clearly in the past.

"I remember one time when Rob was in sixth grade, the teacher called us up and said he was picking fights," he recalled. "Well, you know that wasn't like Rob at all. So I took him out to the woods the next weekend to help me chop some logs. Just the two of us. Your mother packed a nice lunch, hot chocolate and sandwiches, and while we were eating I started to ask about school, casual-like, and how things were going. Just kind of opened the lines of communication, I think they call it these days. Anyway, 'fore we left, I found out Rob was scared to death your mother was sick. Overheard us talking about the Nelsons, but misunderstood and thought it was your mom who had to have surgery. Amazing how things improved once he got that worry off his mind."

Jake stared at his father. "I never knew anything about that."

Howard shrugged. "No reason for you to. Anyhow, might not be a bad idea, if you really want to find out what's going on with this boy, to take him out for a cup of coffee or something. Let him know you're willing to listen, away from the classroom. More as a friend than a teacher—you know what I mean? Sounds like he could use a friend."

Jake looked at his father speculatively. Maggie was right, it seemed. Not only did the older man have some good insights, but he'd been more than willing to share them.

"That sounds like good advice, Dad," he said with quiet sincerity. "Thanks. I'll give it a try."

The older man gave what appeared to be an indifferent shrug, but Jake knew his father was flattered.

"Might not work. But it couldn't hurt to try," Howard replied. Then he rose and began clearing the table. "How about some apple pie? Can't say I baked it myself, but you'll probably be just as happy I didn't."

Jake sent his father an astonished look. This was the first time in years he had shown Jake any humor. Could a gesture as simple as a mere request for advice make such a difference? Jake marveled. Apparently it could. Because as Howard deposited the dishes in the sink and prepared to cut the pie, something else astonishing happened. For the first time in years, Jake heard his father whistle.

* * *

Maggie glanced at her watch for the tenth time in fewer minutes and told herself to calm down. Just because Jake was coming over was no reason for her nerves to go haywire. Unfortunately, her nerves weren't listening to reason, she thought wryly, as another swarm of butterflies fluttered through her stomach.

She sat down in the porch swing, hoping its gentle, rhythmic motion would calm her jitters. She was certain that Jake wanted to pick up where they'd left off the night of her birthday, and she was afraid. Afraid that by allowing their relationship to progress, she was exposing her heart to danger. But she still cared for him. To deny it was useless. She still found him attractive, still responded to his touch. But more than that, she still felt as she had so many years ago—that God had meant Jake and no one else to be her husband. In fact, she felt it even more strongly now than before. Which seemed odd, after all they'd been through.

The crunch of tires on gravel interrupted her thoughts, and her heartbeat quickened as her gaze flew to the small parking lot. She recognized the small, sensible car Jake had purchased—a far cry from the impractical sporty number he used to crave—and watched as he unfolded his long frame and stood gazing out to sea, his strong profile thrown into sharp relief by the setting sun. He stayed there, motionless, for a long moment, seeming to savor the scene. It was a lovely view, and Maggie herself had often paused to admire it. But it was not something Jake would have appreciated—or even noticed—a dozen years ago, she reflected. It was just one of the many things about him that had changed.

And yet, at least one thing had stayed the same. He

was every bit as handsome as he'd always been—tall, confident in bearing, with an easy, heart-melting smile that could still turn her legs to rubber. He was the kind of man who would stand out in any gathering—and who could have had his pick of women through the years.

And yet...he'd never married. Had even implied that she was the reason for his single status. Maggie wanted to believe that was true, wanted to think that the love he'd once felt for her had endured—just as hers had for him.

At the same time, she wasn't a starry-eyed sixteen-year-old anymore. She was an adult who knew better than to let her emotions rule her life. She was determined to approach the situation as logically and as objectively as she could. It was true that everything she'd seen since he'd returned indicated that Jake had matured, that he was now a man who understood the concept of honor and responsibility, who could be counted on in good times *and* bad. And Maggie *wanted* to believe the evidence that was rapidly accumulating in his favor. But only time would tell if the changes were real—and lasting.

He didn't notice her in the shadows, so as he reached to press the bell she spoke softly.

"Hello, Jake."

He turned in surprise, and a slow, lazy smile played across his lips. She looked so good! he thought. Her shapely legs, covered in khaki slacks, were tucked under her, and she'd thrown a green sweater carelessly over her shoulders to ward off the evening chill. In the fading light, her flame-colored hair took on a life of its own. She wore it down tonight, as he preferred, and it softly and flatteringly framed her porcelain complexion. Right now, at this moment, she looked no older than she had that summer twenty-one years before, on the day of their eventful bike ride. And she made him feel exactly as he had on that same memorable, long-ago day—breathless, eager and deeply stirred. But he wasn't a seventeen-year-old bundle of hormones anymore, he reminded himself. Even if he did *feel* like one. *Control* was the operative word here.

"Hi." The deep, husky timbre of his voice was something he *couldn't* control, however. And it wasn't lost on Maggie, he realized, noting the soft blush that crept up her cheeks.

"Would you like some coffee?"

He shook his head. "No, thanks. Why don't we just sit out here for a while?"

"Okay." She lowered her feet to the floor and scooted over to make room for him. The swing creaked in protest as he sat down, and he turned to her with a grin.

"Are you sure this is safe?"

No, she thought in silent panic as he casually draped an arm across the back of the swing and gently brushed his fingers over her shoulder. *It isn't safe at all. Not for me!*

"Perfectly safe," she replied, struggling to keep her voice even. "We check it every season."

He smiled at her then, that tender smile she knew so well. "I've missed you," he told her softly.

"You just saw me at the fair."

"That was four days ago. And besides, there were too many people around."

The corners of her mouth tipped up. "That didn't stop you from…"

When her blush deepened and her voice trailed off,

he grinned. "Kissing you? No, as a matter of fact it didn't. It could easily become a habit," he warned, reaching out to seductively trace the contours of her lips with a gentle finger.

Maggie's breath caught in her throat at the intimate gesture, and her heart began to bang painfully against her rib cage.

"But I have to admit I prefer more privacy. Take this spot, for instance. I think the twins had the right idea on your birthday. It's very romantic here." He cupped her chin in his hand and let his gaze lovingly, lingeringly caress her face. The conflict in her eyes, the war between desire and prudence, was apparent. But equally apparent was the longing in their depths—and the invitation.

Jake tried to resist. Valiantly. He told himself that she wasn't even aware of her silent plea. That he needed to move slowly. That he needed to reach deep into his reserves of discipline and simply back off. But he was only human, after all. And desire suppressed for twelve long years was a difficult thing to control, especially when the object of that desire sat only inches away, looking so appealing and ready to be kissed.

With a sigh of capitulation to forces stronger than he seemed able to resist, Jake gave up the fight and leaned down to tenderly claim the sweet lips of the woman he loved. His intention was to keep the kiss simple and swift. Make it long enough to let her know he cared and had missed her, but short enough not to make her nervous, he cautioned himself. But somehow it didn't turn out that way.

Because from the moment their lips met, Jake was overwhelmed by a sense of urgency that took his breath away. Maggie felt so good in his arms, so right, as if she belonged there always. He framed her delicate face with his strong hands, his lips eager and hungry as he kissed her with an abandon that surprised them both. The initially gentle, tentative touching of lips escalated rapidly to an embrace that spoke eloquently of love and longing, reflecting twelve long years of parched emotions.

What surprised Jake more than his unexpected loss of control was Maggie's acquiescence. He had felt her tense initially, as if taken aback by the intensity of his embrace, but within seconds she was returning his kiss with a passion that equaled his own. Without breaking contact with her lips, he shifted their positions so that she was cradled in his arms. She sighed softly, and he continued to kiss her, with a hunger that only Maggie's sweet lips could satisfy.

Maggie was only vaguely aware of their change in position. All she knew was that she wanted to stay in Jake's embrace forever, feeling cherished and loved and desired. With a sigh, she put her arms around his neck and strained to draw him even closer, letting her fingers explore the soft hair at the base of his neck. Jake reciprocated by combing his fingers through her thick tresses, and she felt her heartbeat quicken at his touch.

Jake was thrown by the feelings of tenderness and desire that nearly overwhelmed him. How had he lived without her sweet love to sustain him all these years? he asked himself wonderingly. Now that he'd found her again, he couldn't imagine a future without her.

When at last Jake reluctantly released her lips, she lay passively in his arms, staring up at him with a slightly dazed expression that he suspected mirrored his own. He hadn't intended their evening to begin this way. But once in her presence, all his good intentions had evaporated, he acknowledged, as he gently brushed a few errant tendrils of hair back from her face. She tentatively reached up, as if to touch his cheek, then dropped her hand.

"Why did you stop?" He took her hand and laced his fingers through hers, then pressed it against his cheek.

She colored and removed her hand from his, then eased herself to the other side of the swing. She wasn't sure what had come over her just now, but if taking things slowly was her plan, this was not exactly the way to start. Distractedly she ran her fingers through the tangled waves of her hair, trying futilely to restore it to order.

"Jake…I think that…well, I think it's obvious that we're still…attracted to each other on the…on the physical level," she stammered. "But there are other levels that are equally important—if not more important. I—I need to focus on those, but I can't even think straight when you…when I'm…when we're close," she said haltingly, obviously flustered. "And there are issues we need to deal with—*I* need to deal with— things I still need to work through. I don't want to lose sight of those."

That wasn't exactly what Jake wanted to hear, but he saw her point. All of the other realities of his life—and their relationship—got pretty fuzzy for him, too, when her soft, pliant body melted against him and her lips were warm and willing beneath his. He drew a deep, slightly unsteady breath.

"So…no more kissing—is that what you're saying?" He tried for a teasing tone but didn't quite pull it off.

"No, of course not. It's just that…well, I think we need to keep it in perspective, that's all."

He wondered if she had any idea just what she was asking. Maintaining his perspective—let alone his equilibrium—around Maggie was almost impossible. But if that's what she wanted, he'd give it his best shot, he resolved. With a crooked grin, he draped his arm casually around her shoulders, though he felt anything but casual. His body was clamoring with unfulfilled needs—which weren't going to be fulfilled anytime soon, it appeared. So he'd better just get used to it.

"How about the old arm around the shoulder? Is that out of bounds, too?"

"No." She snuggled close and pulled her legs up beside her as Jake set the swing gently rocking.

It was sweet agony to have her soft curves cuddled so close, but he'd get through this, he resolved, gritting his teeth. He had to. *Change the subject,* he told himself desperately. *Focus on something else.* He struggled to find a topic, and was immensely grateful when Maggie took the initiative.

"Your dad seemed pleased about the fair Sunday."

"He was. He spent the rest of the afternoon making a list of supplies. I drove him over to Bangor to pick up everything yesterday. He's happy as a clam—or should I say lobster, here in Maine?—now that he's got a project. I have to practically force him to stop every night. You were right about him needing to have something to do that would make him feel worthwhile. And you were right about something else, too."

She turned to look up at him. "What?"

"Your idea to talk to dad about school. I tried it Monday night. I think he was a little shocked, but he did open up. And offered some pretty good advice along the way, I might add. Thanks to him, I think I'm finally starting to connect with one of my problem students."

"Really?" Her eyes were bright, her smile warm and genuine. "I'm so glad, Jake! What did he suggest?" She listened interestedly as he recapped his father's suggestion. "And it's working?"

"So far. I invited Paul—that's the student's name—to meet me in the canteen for coffee yesterday. I wasn't sure he'd come, but he did. He hasn't said much yet, but I picked up enough to suspect that there was a major trauma of some sort in his life shortly before he left for school. Something to do with his parents, I think. I invited him to meet me again tomorrow between classes, and I'm hoping he'll come. I'd like to help him through this, whatever it is, if I can."

"Did you tell your father?"

He chuckled. "You've heard the phrase, 'Pleased as Punch'?"

Maggie smiled and settled back against Jake. "That's good. I'm glad you two are getting along better."

"We still have a long way to go, Maggie."

"But at least you're moving in the right direction."

They swung quietly for a few minutes, her head nestled contentedly on his shoulder, the muffled night sounds peaceful and soothing. When Jake finally broke the silence, his husky voice was close to her ear.

"It's good to have you in my arms again, Maggie."

She swallowed past the lump in her throat. "I was just thinking the same thing," she confessed softly.

"I know you need some time. And I'm not trying to rush you. But I think you know where I hope this is heading."

She'd have to be a fool not to. But there was so much still to be dealt with. So much that she wasn't yet *ready* to deal with. And she hadn't expected him to be quite so up-front about his intentions—not yet, anyway. "There are…issues… Jake."

"You mean beyond the obvious?" They both knew he was referring to her struggle to overcome lingering doubts about his reliability and honor.

She nodded. Maggie hadn't really planned to get into a heavy discussion tonight. But there was one issue in particular that had to be discussed sooner or later, and sooner was probably better from a self-preservation standpoint. Jake wasn't going to like what she had to say. In fact, he might dislike it enough to reconsider his feelings. But it would be better to know that now, before she got any more involved, she told herself resolutely as she drew a deep breath.

"You mentioned once that you wanted a family." Her voice was quiet, subdued. "But I've already had a family, Jake. I don't regret a minute of it, but it's a demanding job, and I've spent the last twelve years doing it. So much of my adult life has been spent doing what I *had* to do. Now…now I want to focus on the things I *want* to do for a while. Like go to Europe, pursue my art." She paused and stared down unseeingly, absently running her finger over the crease in her slacks. "I guess that sounds selfish, doesn't it?" she finished in a small voice.

Jake frowned and stroked her arm comfortingly. "No. *Selfish* is hardly a word I would use to describe you, Maggie."

She leaned away and looked up at him in the dim light, trying to read his eyes. "Do you understand how I feel, Jake?" she asked anxiously.

"Well, it's not exactly what I wanted to hear," he admitted, "but I do understand." He stroked her cheek and gave her a rueful smile that was touched with melancholy. "Our timing always seems to be off, doesn't it? First you were saddled with responsibilities that tied you down. Now you're free, and I'm saddled with responsibilities that tie me down. And as for a family—it would be different this time, you know. Two people sharing the responsibility for one child is a whole lot easier than one person trying to raise two children."

"I accept that in theory, Jake," she conceded. "But life has a way of tearing theories to shreds. And plans can fall apart in the blink of an eye."

He couldn't argue with that. Their own broken engagement was a perfect example of plans gone awry. And his presence here in Maine was another. Three years ago, if someone had told him he'd end up being a land-bound teacher, sharing a cottage with his father in rural Maine, he'd have laughed in their face.

Maggie frowned as the silence between them lengthened. She'd known since the day he talked about a family that her feelings on the subject could be a major hurdle to their relationship, had dreaded having to deal with the issue. They were at two ends of the spectrum. Jake wanted a family. She didn't—at least, not in the near future. And with her biological clock beginning to tick rather loudly, it might come down to the near future—or not at all.

Maggie felt a wave of despair sweep over her. Why did the Lord always make the choices so difficult? she wondered helplessly. Twelve years ago, her choice had been a family or Jake. Now it seemed that it might come down to Jake and a family—or no Jake. That thought chilled her, but she saw no way around it. Not unless she gave up her own dreams. And she'd done that once. She couldn't do it again—not even for Jake.

"I'm sorry, Jake," she said quietly at last. "I do understand your desire for a family. It's a beautiful thing, raising children, watching them develop and grow and become caring, responsible adults. But I—I can't make any promises. Maybe in a year or two I'll feel differently, but right now I'm just not ready to even consider it."

Jake absently brushed his fingers up and down her arm, his frown deepening. He'd been so caught up in his rediscovery of Maggie that he really hadn't thought much about the family issue, though she had alluded to her feelings on the subject a few weeks before, he admitted. It just hadn't been something he wanted to deal with at that moment. Or at all, if he was honest. There had been enough barriers already between himself and the woman he loved. Why did life often seem to consist entirely of hurdles and detours? he railed silently.

Jake sighed. The evening had taken an unexpectedly heavy turn. He still hoped that when her trust level grew, the notion of a family based on shared responsibilities would become more palatable. In the meantime, she needed the space, the freedom, that the twins' departure had given her. He didn't begrudge her that. She'd earned it. He wanted her to make that trip to Europe, to see all the places she'd always dreamed of. He only wished he could go with her.

"I'm not sure what the answer is, Maggie," he admitted, gently stroking her arm. "But maybe it's one of those things we should just place in the hands of the Lord. I can't help but believe He brought us together for some reason. Maybe, if we give this some time, He'll eventually let us in on His plans and show us the way."

She turned and looked up at him, tipping her head. "That's funny, Jake. I can't ever remember you talking about faith or trust in the Lord before."

He chuckled softly. "Well, Dad's been dragging me to church every Sunday. Some of it must be rubbing off." Then his voice grew more serious. "Besides, the older I get, the more I realize how much help I need finding my way through this maze of a world. Going back to church, thinking about my faith again—well, it's been a great help. It seems to give me more of a sense of direction. I'm beginning to realize what I've been missing all these years by not turning to the Lord when I needed help."

Yet another new dimension to Jake, Maggie thought wonderingly. And he was right about trusting in the Lord. He would reveal His plan for them in His own time—which, as she'd learned through the years, wasn't always *her* time. She just needed to be patient.

"All right, Jake. Let's just give it some time."

"How about starting Sunday? We could go hiking over on Isle au Haut. I hear it's spectacular."

She nodded. "It is. The twins and I have spent some lovely days over there. It's wild and rugged and isolated—a wonderful spot to get away from it all."

They swung in silence for a few moments, and when he spoke, his voice was thoughtful. "Maggie?"

"Mmm-hmm?"

"You know that comment you made earlier? About keeping kissing in perspective?"

"Mmm-hmm."

"It's not going to be easy, you know. Not when it's

the first thing I think of every time I'm near you—and most of the time when I'm not."

She blushed at his frankness. "It's—it's a problem for me, too," she admitted.

She heard a chuckle rumble deep in his chest and was relieved that at least he seemed to be taking her ground rules in good humor. "Well, as long as I don't have to suffer alone, maybe it won't be so bad."

"Besides, I didn't rule out kissing entirely, you know," she reminded him. She doubted whether she could even if she wanted to.

"Are good-night kisses acceptable, then?" he inquired hopefully, a smile tugging at the corners of his mouth.

"Absolutely."

"Well, in that case..." He glanced at his watch and feigned a yawn. "I think it's time to say good-night. Don't you?"

She chuckled and shook her head. "You're incorrigible, you know."

"Guilty," he admitted promptly. And then his eyes grew serious. "At least when it comes to you." He reached over and drew a finger gently down the line of her cheek. "Good night, Maggie," he murmured softly, and then his lips closed over hers.

This time the kiss was gentle, a thing to be slowly savored as they absorbed each exquisite nuance of sensation. Now that they had agreed to let time be their friend, the earlier urgency of their embrace was replaced by a tender exploration and leisurely rediscovery that spoke of understanding and promise and hope.

Maggie had no idea what the future held for them. But for the first time since Jake had come back into her life, she felt a sense of peace and calm. For now that she had stopped struggling so hard to resolve their issues on her own and had put her trust in the Lord, her soul felt refreshed. She didn't know the destination of their relationship, but her heart felt sure that He would guide them in right paths.

Chapter Twelve

As the blaze of fall colors began to burn brightly on the coastal landscape, so, too, did the blaze of love burn with ever-growing fervor in Maggie's heart. Sundays became "their" day, and after early-morning services together she and Jake explored the back roads and quaint byways of their adopted state. Sometimes Howard went with them, but usually he declined their invitation, insisting that three was a crowd.

And so, from popular Acadia National Park to remote Schoodic Point, their love blossomed once again on the splendor of the Maine coast. The twins regularly demanded progress reports, and though Maggie tried to play it low-key, even *she* could hear the joyful lilt in her voice every time she mentioned Jake. The girls, of course, were delighted—but no less so than Maggie. She'd been so afraid that her fragile bubble of happiness would burst, that one day she'd wake up to find herself once more alone. Yet her fears seemed groundless. Each moment she spent with Jake was more perfect than the last.

In fact, everything seemed almost *too* perfect. And life was far from perfect, as she well knew. Yet her hours with Jake disputed that reality. Each time he protectively enfolded her fingers in his strong, bronzed hand; each time his warm, brown eyes smiled down into hers; each time he held her in his arms and tenderly claimed her lips, Maggie felt a renewal, a rebirth, a reawakening. Joy and hope filled her heart as the love she'd kept locked away for so long gradually began to find release. For Maggie, who had long ago ruthlessly stifled romantic fantasies and the notion of happy endings, it was a dream come true.

That "dream-come-true" quality was brought home to her most clearly on Thanksgiving Day when she glanced around the table, her heart overflowing with love. The twins looked radiant and vivacious, chattering about college life and clearly thriving in the challenging academic environment. Howard had filled out and looked well on the road to recovery. And Jake… Maggie's eyes softened as they met his warm, intimate gaze across the table. Jake made her understand the real meaning of Thanksgiving. Loving him, and being loved in return, filled her with gratitude—and hope. For Maggie sensed they were close to a resolution of their issues.

In fact, she had a feeling this Christmas might bring a very special present her way, one she'd thought never to receive again. She glanced down at her bare left hand as she reached for the basket of rolls. Maybe…maybe in a month it wouldn't look so bare, she thought, as a delicious tingle of excitement and anticipation raced along her spine. And wouldn't the girls love a spring wedding?

* * *

Jake turned the corner and drove slowly through the pelting, icy rain, a troubled frown on his face. Though Paul had eventually opened up and taken Jake into his confidence, in the end it hadn't made much difference. He was withdrawing at the end of the semester.

Jake let out a long, frustrated sigh. The boy had been dealing with a lot, no question about it. First, a few weeks before leaving for school, his parents had announced their intention to divorce. That was hard enough to accept. But the reason had made it even worse. His father, whom Paul had always looked up to and admired, had admitted to an affair and made it clear that he wanted to marry the other woman. Paul had not only felt betrayed and abandoned himself, but as the only child he'd been left to comfort his devastated mother. It was a difficult position to be in at any age, but especially for a seventeen-year-old still in the process of growing up himself.

Jake believed that his talks with Paul had helped a great deal, that the sympathetic ear he'd offered had provided a much-needed outlet and sounding board for the angry, hurt young man. Slowly, over the last few weeks, he had begun to calm down, settle in. His work improved and he began to socialize more.

And then he'd been hit with the news that his mother had cancer, so far advanced that there was nothing the doctors could do. She'd been given four to six months, at best. And because she had no one else to love and support her through the ordeal to come, he had decided to go home, to be with her during the difficult days ahead. Jake knew Paul had struggled with the decision, knew he didn't want to withdraw from school. In the end he'd made a courageous choice, and Jake admired him for it. But it was just so unfair, he thought in frustration, his fingers tightening on the wheel as he pulled to a stop in front of the cottage.

Jake forced himself to take a long, steadying breath before he slowly climbed out of the car and turned up his collar against the biting wind and cold rain. He slammed the door and strode up the walk, stopping abruptly when he realized that there was a ladder directly in his path. He frowned and glanced up—to find his father perched precariously on one of the top rungs, at roof level. A sudden gust of the relentless wind slapped a stinging sheet of sleet against his face, and he shivered.

"Dad!" he shouted, trying to be heard above the gale.

His father half turned and peered down at him.

"What are you doing up there?" Jake demanded angrily, his lips taut.

"The gutter's blocked. Had a waterfall right above the front door," the older man called in reply.

It wasn't the first time lately that Jake had found his father engaged in an activity that was far too strenuous for him. Now that the older man was feeling better, he was beginning to act as if he'd never had a heart attack. But today was the worst transgression so far. He shouldn't be on a ladder in *any* weather, let alone what seemed to be the beginning of a southwester.

"I'll fix it later. Come down here right now!"

Even through the gray curtain of rain and sleet, Jake could see the sudden, defiant lift of the older man's chin. "I was only trying to help. And you're not in the navy anymore, you know. So stop giving orders."

A muscle in Jake's jaw clenched and he took a deep

breath, struggling for control. "Will you *please* come down and go inside where it's warm? We're both getting soaked and I, for one, don't intend to get pneumonia."

With that he skirted the ladder and strode into the house, banging the door behind him.

By the time Howard followed a couple of minutes later, Jake had stripped off his wet coat and hung it to drip in the bathroom. His father glared at him as he entered, then stomped into the bathroom and threw his own drenched coat into the tub. When he returned, Jake was waiting for him, his fists planted on his hips, his lips compressed into a thin line.

"Okay, Dad. Let's talk about this. I can't be here to watch you all day. You know what you're supposed to do and what you're not supposed to do. This—" he gestured toward the front door "—is *not* on the list of 'do's,' and you know it."

Howard gave him a resentful glare. "I'm not one of your students, Jake. Or some enlisted man you can order around. I feel fine. I'm tired of being treated like an invalid. I can do what I want. You're not my keeper."

"Yes, I am. I promised Mom years ago—and Rob more recently—that I'd take care of you. And I intend to do just that."

"That's the only reason you let me come up here, isn't it? Because you promised your mother and Rob. Well, I don't need charity. I can do just fine on my own."

"Right," Jake replied sarcastically. "Like that little escapade I just witnessed outside. Suppose you'd fallen? Or put too much strain on your heart? You could be dead right now—or at the very least, in the hospital."

"Maybe I'd be more welcome there."

"That's a fine thing to say."

"Well, it's true. You haven't wanted me around in years," the older man declared bitterly.

"I invited you to live with me, didn't I?"

Howard gave a snort of disgust. "Sure. But only because you promised your mother and Rob. Maybe if you'd bothered to come around once in a while, Clara wouldn't have died—five years ago today, not that you'd remember. You broke her heart, Jake. Just like you broke Maggie's."

Jake drew in a sharp breath. His father's harsh words cut deeply, leaving a gaping wound in his soul. He struck back without even stopping to think, wanting to hurt as badly as he'd just been hurt. "You didn't exactly act like you wanted me around. It wouldn't have killed you to try and understand how I felt. Maybe if you hadn't been so stubborn, we could have worked this out years ago. Maybe it's as much your fault as mine that Mom's gone."

Howard's face went white with shock and anger. He gripped the back of the chair and the look he gave Jake was scathing. Yet there was pain in his eyes as well, raw and unmistakable. "That's a terrible thing to say," he rasped hoarsely.

Yes, it was, Jake admitted, silently cursing his loss of control, shocked at the words he'd just uttered. And more were poised for release, despite his efforts to hold them back. Words that, once spoken, could never be retracted. They'd said too much already, possibly irreparably damaging the fragile relationship they'd built these last few weeks. It was time to stop this tirade, before it got even more emotional and hateful. With one last look at his father, Jake brushed past him and retrieved his damp coat from the bathroom, shrugging into it as he headed toward the front door.

"Where are you going?" Howard demanded, his voice quivering with anger.

"Out. I need to cool down before I say anything else I'll end up regretting."

And then he stepped outside, slamming the door shut behind him.

The sleet continued unabated, but Jake hardly noticed as he drove mindlessly to a nearby spot that overlooked the turbulent, storm-tossed coast. He sat there for a long time as the elements battered his car much as his father's words had battered his soul. So many old hurts had surfaced, so many suppressed emotions had been released. But not in a healthy way. They'd ended up accusing each other of terrible things. All this time, while Jake thought their relationship was stabilizing, his father had been harboring a deep-seated anger against him, borne of blame and resentment. And, in many ways, Jake had felt the same toward the older man, he admitted. No wonder their "progress" had been so slow. Now it had not only come to a grinding halt, but regressed dramatically.

Jake sighed and raked his fingers helplessly through his hair as a wave of despair washed over him. His father clearly didn't enjoy living with him. Was only doing so under duress. But he couldn't go back to Rob's—not yet, anyway. Though Rob had finally connected with a firm that seemed interested in hiring him, his life was still in an uproar and there was a strong possibility he and his family would have to move. So what options did that leave for Howard?

Jake didn't have the answer to that question. And he

probably wasn't going to come up with one in the next few hours, he thought with a weary, dispirited sigh. He might as well go home, as unappealing as that prospect was.

All in all, he decided, it had been one lousy day.

And it didn't get any better when he stepped inside the door and his glance fell on his father's suitcase. Now what was going on? He closed his eyes and drew in a long breath, then let it out slowly.

He could hear his father rattling pans in the kitchen, and slowly, with reluctance, he made his way in that direction, pausing at the doorway just in time to see his father emptying what appeared to be a pot of beef stew into the garbage disposal. The act seemed somehow symbolic of far more than dinner going down the drain, he thought, his gut twisting painfully.

"What's with the suitcase, Dad?" he asked, striving for an even tone.

"I'm going to visit Rob for a week. I called, and he said it was okay. There's a flight out of Bangor in the morning. I'll take a cab."

Jake sighed. "I'll drive you."

"That's not necessary," the older man replied stiffly.

"I'll drive you, Dad. Let's not argue about that, too."

Howard reacted to that statement with silence. And *silence* was the operative word during the drive to Bangor the next morning. The few comments Jake tried to make were promptly rebuffed, so he finally gave up. Only when Howard was preparing to board the plane did he get more than a grunt for an answer.

"When are you coming back, Dad?"

"I'll take a cab to the house."

"I'll pick you up. Just tell me the day and time. Or I'll call the airline and find out."

Howard gave him a withering look, but provided the information—with obvious reluctance.

"Have a good trip," Jake said.

Howard didn't reply, and as Jake watched him trudge down the ramp to the plane, he jammed his hands into his pockets in frustration. How would the two of them ever work out their differences? Or maybe the real question was whether they even could, he acknowledged with a disheartened sigh. He desperately wanted to make things work between them, but he was beginning to think this was one mission that was destined for failure.

Jake was oblivious to his surroundings as he drove back to Castine, his mind desperately seeking a solution to a situation that appeared to have none. Why the retirement home caught his eye he didn't know, but he eased his foot off the accelerator slightly and looked at it with a frown as he drove past. He'd seen it before, of course, but for the first time he examined it with a critical eye. It seemed to be a nice place. Well kept, with spacious grounds in an attractive setting. Maybe... But even as the thought crossed his mind, Jake pushed it aside. How could he even consider such a possibility when he'd promised his mother that he'd never send Howard to an "old folks" home, as she called them?

And yet...he'd also promised to take care of his father. Given the recent turn of events, he was beginning to doubt whether it was possible to keep both promises. His father clearly didn't want to live with him. And Jake couldn't be there all the time to take care of the older man, who was beginning to take chances with his health. Maybe, in the short term, a retirement home was the best solution. His father would have companionship, and better care than Jake could provide. They certainly wouldn't let him climb on ladders, for one thing. And it would only be temporary, until Rob was settled again. His father liked living with Rob. Rob liked having him. Ultimately Jake was sure Howard would move back in with his first-born. Until then, he might be a lot happier—and healthier—away from his younger son.

Yet the thought of packing the older man off turned Jake's stomach. Yes, things were bad between them. But surely there was a way to smooth out their relationship. There had to be. Only, he didn't have a clue what it was, not after last night. And he was reaching the point of desperation. They couldn't live as they had those first few weeks. The tension had been almost unbearable. That in itself was bad for his father's health. The retirement home wasn't a great solution, Jake acknowledged. But maybe his father would welcome the chance to get out from under Jake's roof. At the very least, Jake decided to check the place out. He didn't think it was the answer, but it couldn't hurt to consider all the options.

Maggie's gaze sought and came to rest on Jake's tall, distinguished form across the gallery, and she smiled. He was half turned away from her, engaged in conversation with a patron, looking incredibly handsome in a crisply starched white shirt and dark gray suit that sat well on his broad shoulders. It was the first time all evening that Maggie had been alone, and she savored the respite, heady with elation at the praise her work had received during the opening reception for her show, basking in this moment of glory. And yet...as she lovingly traced the contours of Jake's strong profile, she knew that her happiness tonight was magnified because he was here to share her moment of triumph. His presence made her joy complete.

"And you were worried about having this show."

Maggie turned at Philip's gently chiding voice and smiled. "You were right. I guess I was ready after all."

Philip glanced at Jake, then back at Maggie, and smiled. "For a lot of things, it seems. I take it you two have worked things out?"

She colored faintly and turned to gaze again at Jake, a whisper of a smile softening her lips. "We're getting there. We still have issues, but...I don't know. Somehow I sense we'll work them out."

Philip put his hand on Maggie's shoulder. "I'm happy for you, you know. About this—" he gestured with one hand around the gallery "—and about that." He nodded toward Jake. "You deserve all the happiness life has to offer, Maggie."

"Thank you, Philip," she said softly. "But I'm trying not to rush things. I want to be sensible about this."

Just then Jake turned and glanced around the room, his gaze restless and searching until it came to rest on Maggie. He gave her a slow, lazy smile that warmed her all the way from her toes to her nose, and she heard Philip chuckle.

"Maggie, honey, I know your intentions are good. But trust me. Jake is past the sensible stage. And forgive me for saying it, but so are you. In fact, I'm guessing that wedding bells will be in the air in the not-too-distant future."

Maggie blushed. She didn't even try to deny Philip's words. Because the truth was she felt the same.

* * *

Maggie's eyes were glowing as she set the Sunday paper down on the kitchen table. A review of her work—brief, but highly complimentary—had made the Boston paper! A wave of elation washed over her, and she was filled with a deep sense of satisfaction and accomplishment—and a compelling need to share the news with Jake—in person. He would be thrilled, too. She'd see him in church in two hours—but she couldn't wait!

With uncharacteristic impulsiveness, she tucked the paper carefully into a tote bag, added four of the large cinnamon rolls she'd baked last night and headed out the door. Maybe her impromptu visit would cheer Jake up, even without the news she was bearing. He hadn't shared many of the details about the latest falling-out with his father, sparing her the worry during this last week as she fretted about her opening, but she knew it was serious if Howard had actually gone down to Rob's. She hoped Jake would tell her more about it now that the opening had passed.

Maggie grinned at Jake's look of surprise half an hour later when he answered her ring. She'd never shown up uninvited before, and he was clearly taken aback—but just as clearly pleased.

"Maggie!" He drew her inside, pulling her into his arms as he kicked the door shut with his foot and buried his face in her hair. For a long moment he just held her, loving the feel of her soft, slim body wrapped in his arms. Less than five minutes ago he'd been wishing—praying—for just such a visit, and it seemed the Lord had heard his plea. The last week had been hell as he'd wrestled with the problem of what to do about his father, and he was running out of time. Howard was returning late this afternoon, and Jake still hadn't figured out how to deal with the situation. All he knew with absolute certainty was that they couldn't go on as they had before.

But now, with Maggie in his arms, her sweetness enveloping him, he somehow felt better.

Maggie snuggled closer against Jake's broad, solid chest. His embrace today spoke less of passion than of the need for comfort and solace, almost as if he was drawing strength from her mere physical presence. It was a much different sensation than the usual amorous nature of their touches, but oddly enough, Maggie found it as powerfully affecting in a different way. She remained motionless as he held her, his hands stroking the curve of her slender back.

When at last he drew away, he looped his arms loosely around her waist and smiled down at her.

"Hi." His eyes were warm and tender, his voice husky and intimate.

"Hi yourself," she replied softly, playing with a button on his shirt.

"I'm glad you're here."

"I sort of got that impression. Do you want to talk about it?"

"About what?"

"About why you're so glad to see me."

"You mean beyond the obvious reason?"

"Mmm-hmm."

"Actually, I'd rather talk about you. What's the occasion?"

"What do you mean?"

"Well, you've never shown up on my doorstep uninvited before. Not that you need to wait for an invitation, you understand. It's just a first. And I hope not a last."

She smiled and blushed. "I had some good news, and I wanted to share it with you."

"I could use some good news. Let's have it."

She reached into her tote bag and withdrew the Boston paper, already turned back to the right page, and handed it to him, her eyes glowing.

He tilted his head and smiled, loving the way her eyes lit up when she was happy. She was like a warm ray of sun, a balm on his troubled soul. He reached over and gently stroked her face, letting a long, lean finger trace its way from her temple to her chin, following the delicate curve of her jaw. Her eyes ignited at his touch, and he was tempted to take her in his arms again, to taste her sweet lips until all coherent thoughts were driven from his mind and he was lost in the wonder of her love.

But first he needed to focus on the paper, he told himself. If it was important enough to bring her over without an invitation, it deserved his full attention. So, reluctantly he transferred his gaze. As he scanned the complimentary article, his lips curved into a slow smile, and when at last he turned to her, his eyes held a special warmth.

"I would certainly call that an auspicious beginning, Maggie. I'm very proud of you," he said with quiet honesty. "And in case I haven't told you lately, you are one amazing and incredible woman—not to mention talented, intelligent and drop-dead gorgeous."

Maggie flushed with pleasure at his compliments. "That might be overstating it just a bit."

"Nope. I never exaggerate."

She laughed, so filled with joy that it simply came

bubbling to the surface. All of the pieces of her life were finally falling into place. She'd raised the girls well and sent them on their way in the world. She'd taken a bold step and successfully launched a serious art career. And the only man who'd ever touched her heart had come back into her life and offered her his love. The long, dry years, often filled with drudgery, seemed suddenly a distant memory. She'd made it through the hard times, and now, at last, it seemed that the Lord was rewarding her for her diligence and hard work. Her heart felt lighter than it had in years, and her face was radiant as she looked up at Jake.

"I think you're pretty special, too, you know. In fact, now that we've formed a mutual admiration society, I would say a celebration is in order." She lifted the bag. "I brought some homemade cinnamon rolls."

"Now that's the best offer I've had all day," Jake declared with a grin. He draped an arm around her shoulders and guided her toward the kitchen. Maggie's enthusiasm and euphoric mood were catching, and he found himself feeling better—and more hopeful—by the minute. "I'll pour the coffee if you want to nuke those for a minute."

"Okay."

Maggie tore the foil off the cinnamon rolls, put three of them on a plate and set the timer on the microwave. "Jake, do you have some plastic wrap? I want to leave one of these for your dad."

"Sure. In the drawer, on the right. Boy, they smell great already!"

Maggie smiled and pulled out the drawer. "They're pretty hard to resist, if I do say so myself. My guests always..."

Maggie's voice faltered and her smile froze as the words *Water's Edge Retirement Community* screamed up at her from a brochure, Jake's name prominent on the mailing label. Her stomach clenched into a cold knot, and she gripped the edge of the counter as the world tilted strangely. All of her dreams, all of her hopes, suddenly seemed to dissolve like an ethereal vapor on a frosty morning.

Maggie wanted to shut the drawer again, pretend she'd never seen that brochure, but she knew she couldn't erase it from her memory so easily. Nor could she deny its implication. The man she loved, the man she had come to believe was honorable and could be counted on to remain steadfast in bad times, was reneging on his promise to his mother. He was throwing in the towel on his relationship with his father because things had gotten rough. Or at the very least *considering* throwing in the towel. And as far as she was concerned, that was bad enough. The future that had moments before looked so full of hope and promise now seemed bleak and empty.

"Your guests always what?" Jake prompted over his shoulder as he poured their coffee. When she didn't respond, he frowned and turned toward her.

Jake knew immediately that something was wrong. Very wrong. Her body was rigid, and she was gripping the edge of the counter so fiercely that her knuckles were white. Her face was mostly turned away from him, but what little he could see was colorless. His gut clenched in sudden alarm, and he moved toward her in three long strides, placing one arm around her shoulders.

"Maggie? What's wrong?" he asked urgently.

She looked up at him, and he was jolted by her eyes, dull and glazed with shock. Panic swept over him and he gripped her shoulders, his gaze locked on hers.

"Maggie, what is it? Tell me. Let me help."

As she stared at him, Jake was able to read beyond the shock in her eyes. There was pain and confusion and disillusionment in their depths as well. His frown deepened as he mechanically reached down to close the drawer that separated them. And that's when he saw the brochure.

With a sickening jolt, he came to the obvious conclusion. Maggie had finally given him her trust, had come to believe that he was man who kept his promises and could be counted on to stand fast no matter what the circumstance, and now she had found stark evidence to the contrary.

Silently Jake cursed his carelessness. He'd meant to put that brochure in his room, had barely looked at it when it arrived, feeling in his heart that it wasn't the answer to his dilemma. But Maggie wasn't going to believe him, not now, not considering the look of betrayal in her eyes. And he couldn't blame her. He'd made a mistake in a moment of weakness, and though he recognized it as such now, he knew that for her, the fact that he'd even *considered* such an option indicated that he held his promise as less than sacred.

She began to tremble, and Jake tried desperately to think of something, anything, to undo the damage. But no words came to mind. Instead he silently guided her to the table and gently forced her to sit down, then pulled up a chair beside her. Jake reached for her hand, and she looked at him dully as he laced his fingers through hers.

"Maggie, will you listen if I try to explain?"

"Is there an explanation?" Her voice was flat and lifeless.

"Yes. Although it's not one you'll want to hear, I suspect. But I'd like to tell you anyway. Will you listen?" he repeated.

When she didn't respond, Jake took a deep breath and spoke anyway. "You know that Dad and I have had a rough time of it from the beginning, Maggie. I've made no secret of that. But I was really starting to think that we'd turned a corner. I won't say things between us were completely comfortable, but we were getting along. Life was pleasant enough.

"Then, last Monday, everything just fell apart. I'd had a bad day at school, and I came home to find Dad up on a ladder in the middle of that sleet storm. I was a little too heavy-handed in my reaction, I guess, and Dad took offense. The next thing I knew we were accusing each other of some pretty terrible things. Including the death of my mother."

Maggie gasped, and Jake nodded soberly. "Yeah, it got that bad. On top of everything, it was five years to the day Mom died. Emotions were running pretty high on both sides. Suffice it to say, the situation was pretty tense by the time I walked out to cool off. When I got back, Dad's bags were packed. He left the next morning for Rob's."

Jake paused and stared down unseeingly at the oak table. "I don't know what made me request that information on the retirement home, Maggie. Desperation, I guess. I just felt that I couldn't keep my promise to Mom *and* make sure Dad was taken care of. And I think living with me is the last thing in the world he wants. He's unhappy here, and stressed, which isn't good for

his health. I just didn't know what to do. I passed that
retirement home on the way back from the airport, and
figured it couldn't hurt to check it out. The brochure
came yesterday. To be honest, it's not something I even
want to consider. But I just don't know what's best for
Dad anymore. Do you understand at all how I feel?"

Maggie tried. Desperately. But she was too numb
to even think. "At the moment, Jake, not very much is
clear to me," she said shakily. "But I know one thing.
A promise is a promise. No one ever said life was easy.
But we can't just walk away from our commitments. If
you give your word, you keep it. Period. It's a matter of
honor. And if people don't honor their promises, how
can there ever be any trust?"

Jake flinched. Maggie's words had been said without rancor, but they hit home nonetheless. And she was
right. He'd made a mistake—and it was apparent that it
was going to cost him dearly. Maybe even the woman
he loved.

She stood up then, and Jake was instantly on his feet,
as well. "Don't go yet, Maggie. Please."

"I need to be alone for a while, Jake."

"Will you call me later?"

There was a pause, and when she looked at him her
eyes were guarded and distant. "I don't know."

Jake felt like someone had just delivered a well-
placed blow to his abdomen. He couldn't let the woman
he loved walk out of his life. But he didn't know how
to stop her.

She gathered up her purse and bag, and he followed
her to the door, futilely searching for something to say
that would make her reconsider. When she turned on
the threshold and looked at him, her eyes were filled

with anguish and brimming with tears. His stomach tightened into a painful knot, and he wanted to reach out to her, gather her in his arms, tell her that he loved her and would never do anything to hurt her. But he doubted whether she would believe him. Why should she? He'd hurt her once before. And now he'd done it again. What was that old saying? Fool Me Once, Shame On You; Fool Me Twice, Shame On Me. And Maggie was no fool. Hurt and betrayed a second time, he was afraid she would simply choose to cut her losses and go on alone. She was strong enough to do it. But he wasn't strong enough to go on without her. He needed her. Desperately. For the rest of his life.

"Goodbye, Jake." Her voice was quiet, and though a tremor ran through it, he heard the finality in the words.

And as he watched helplessly while she turned and walked out into the cold rain, the rest of his life suddenly loomed emptily before him.

Chapter Thirteen

Jake turned into the church parking lot and pulled into a vacant spot by the front door.

"What are we doing here?" Howard demanded, giving his son a suspicious look.

Jake shut off the engine and angled himself toward his father, resting his arm on the back of the seat. Ever since the fiasco with Maggie this morning, he'd been praying for guidance about how to mend the rift with his father. But no one upstairs seemed to be listening. And then suddenly, on the drive to Bangor, a plan had formed in his mind. He wasn't sure it would work. In fact, he figured the odds were fifty-fifty at best. But he knew in his heart that this was the only way he and his father might have a chance at a true reconciliation. And so he had to try. He took a deep, calming breath and gazed steadily at the older man.

"I'd like to talk with you, Dad. On neutral ground. In a place where we can't shout, and where maybe some greater power will guide our conversation. I couldn't think of a better spot than here, in the house of the Lord."

His father's eyes were guarded. "What do you want to talk about?"

"Us."

Howard shifted uncomfortably and turned away, staring straight ahead. "Seems like we've done enough talking already. Maybe too much."

"Too much of the kind you're referring to," Jake agreed. "I have something different in mind. Will you give me a few minutes?"

While Howard considered the request, Jake waited quietly, his physical stillness giving away none of his inner turmoil. Only when his father grunted his assent did he realize he'd been holding his breath, and he let it out in a long, relieved sigh.

They didn't speak again until they were seated in a back row in the quiet, dim church. It was peaceful there, and conducive to the kind of talk Jake had in mind. He just prayed that his father would be receptive.

Jake hadn't really prepared the speech he was about to give. There hadn't been time. So he silently asked the Lord to help him find the right words to express what was in his heart.

"I guess it's no secret that things have been rough between us for a long time, Dad," he began slowly, a frown creasing his brow. "Twelve years, to be exact. You didn't approve of my decision to leave Maggie and join the navy, and pretty much told me to my face that I was being selfish and irresponsible. I didn't want to hear that then. It hurt too much. The truth often does."

His father turned sharply to look at him, his face registering surprise.

Jake smiled wryly. "I guess you never expected me to admit that you were right, did you? There's stubborn blood in this family, you know. And a lot of pride. Too much, sometimes. I think that's what got us into trouble through the years. I was too stubborn and proud to admit I was wrong, even though in my heart I knew it was true. Then, to make things worse, the man I had always loved and admired, who I never wanted to disappoint, had rejected me. So...I rejected him.

"It wasn't a rational decision, Dad. It was reactive, a way to protect my heart from the pain of knowing that I had disappointed you and hurt Maggie. After that, we just seemed to grow further and further apart. It's not something I ever wanted. The truth is, I missed you all these years. I missed your humor and your kindness and your guidance. And I missed your love."

He reached over and gripped the older man's hand, the hand that more than thirty-five years before had been extended to him in encouragement as he took his first few struggling steps. Jake was breaking new ground today, too, taking new, faltering steps in their relationship, and he was as much afraid of falling now as he probably had been then.

"Dad, I'm sorry for all the pain I've caused you through the years. I'm sorry I wasn't there for Mom—and you—when you needed me most. I want to try and make things right, but I need your help. That's what I'm asking for today. I've been on my own for twelve years now, and one of the things I discovered is that I need you now as much as I ever did. Maybe more. Please give me another chance."

Jake thought he saw the glint of moisture in the older man's eyes before he averted his glance, but he couldn't be sure. *Please, Lord, if ever You listened to a prodigal son, hear my voice today,* he prayed fervently. *I*

*want Dad back in my life—not to make things right
with Maggie, but because it's the right thing to do. For
Dad and me.*

Several long moments of silence passed, and Jake
saw this father's Adam's apple bob. When Howard at
last turned back to his son, he seemed less stiff, less
aloof than he had at any time since coming to Maine.

"I know your mother would have wanted this, Jake,"
he said, his voice catching. "It was one of the last things
she prayed for before she died. Fact is…I always wanted
it, too. But it was like you said, we sort of took our positions and just dug in. Neither of us was willing to budge.
Can't say it did either of us any good. And it sure did
make your mother sad. She called me a stubborn fool
more than once, told me you'd come back in a flash if
I gave you half a chance. Guess she was right after all.
Clara had a way of knowing about those things. I should
have listened to her. But that West pride got in the way,
I expect. Couldn't bring myself to admit that maybe
I was a little too hard on you. Not that I agreed with
what you did. Still don't. But it was a lot to take on at
such a young age. Looking back, I can understand how
it must have been pretty overwhelming. I guess Maggie can, too, seeing as how you two are getting along
so well these days."

Jake didn't correct him. The situation with Maggie was too fresh, too raw, to even discuss. He would
find a way to deal with it later. He had to. His future
depended on it. But at the moment, he had another relationship to mend.

"Does that mean you're willing to make a fresh
start?"

Howard nodded slowly, his face thoughtful. "I expect we'll still have our differences, though," he warned.

Jake smiled wryly. "I'm sure we will. The key is to agree up front that we'll work them out instead of building walls. We just need to keep the lines of communication open, just like you did with Rob all those years ago."

Howard smiled, and the bleakness that had earlier been in his eyes was replaced by a new warmth. "Even if it takes hot chocolate and sandwiches in the woods?"

Jake grinned. "*Especially* if it takes that. Maggie's converted me to hot chocolate. I even prefer it over a gin and tonic."

"That girl always was a good influence on you," Howard declared with a smile. "I'm glad she's back in your life."

A shadow crossed Jake's eyes, but he kept his smile firmly in place. "So am I, Dad. But we have run into a bit of a roadblock," he admitted. He couldn't say much more, not without revealing *why* they were having a problem, and there was no need to tell his father about the retirement home. That idea was already history, had been almost from the moment he'd sent for the brochure.

"Nothing serious, I hope," his father said in concern.

"We'll work it out," Jake replied with more confidence than he felt. But he had to think positively. Because he couldn't face the alternative. "Are you ready to go home?" he inquired, changing the subject before his father probed more deeply.

Howard nodded. "I don't want to overstay our welcome here in the Lord's house. I expect He has more important problems to deal with than ours."

"I expect He does," Jake agreed as he stood up. "But I'm grateful He helped us through this one."

Now if only He would do the same for him and Maggie.

Maggie paced back and forth in the living room, agitated and unsettled. This time, when Jake called, he hadn't let her put him off as he had on the numerous other occasions he'd phoned. Tonight he'd simply asked if she would be home and announced he was coming over.

She paused in front of the fireplace and gazed down into the flickering flames, a troubled frown creasing her brow. Since the day she'd walked out of Jake's house almost three weeks ago, her emotions had been on a roller coaster. They'd run the gamut from devastation to bleakness to loneliness to grief to anger. She'd berated herself over and over again for allowing her trust to be betrayed a second time—and by the *same* man! How big of a fool could she be?

She'd asked herself repeatedly if she had overreacted. And always the answer came back the same. No. Jake had made a sacred promise to his mother, literally as she was dying, and until recently he had gone to admirable lengths to keep it. Everything he'd done and said in the months he'd been here had seemed to indicate he was a changed man, a man who understood the meaning of duty and honor and responsibility.

Maggie understood Jake's frustration and sense of helplessness over his relationship with his father. She'd had similar moments during the girls' growing-up years, when they'd clashed and said things they'd later regretted. It happened. But you didn't deal with it by turning your back on the problem, by simply shoving it out of sight. You talked about it. You worked things through. You made amends and went on. You didn't walk out.

Yet that's exactly what Jake had contemplated doing when things got rough. The very fact that he'd even *considered* breaking his promise scared Maggie to death. Because if he'd done that with Howard when things got dicey, how did she know he wouldn't do it with her?

And that was one fear she couldn't handle. Life was filled with uncertainties. She knew that. But if she ever married, she wanted to do so secure in the knowledge that the sacred vows of "for better, for worse" would be honored by the man to whom she'd given her heart. And she was no longer sure Jake was that man.

The doorbell interrupted her thoughts, and she jerked convulsively, one hand involuntarily going to her throat. She didn't feel ready to face Jake. Then again, she doubted she ever would. So they might as well get this over with, she thought resignedly.

When she reached the front door, she took a slow, deep breath, then pulled it open.

For a long, silent moment, Jake simply looked at her, his breath making frosty clouds in the still, cold air. He was wearing a suede, sheepskin-lined jacket over dark brown corduroy slacks, and his hands were shoved deep into the pockets. The shadowy light on the porch highlighted the haggard planes of his face, and Maggie suspected he'd suffered as many sleepless nights as she had.

"Hello, Maggie."

She moved aside to let him enter. "Hello, Jake."

He stepped in and shrugged out of his jacket, watch-

ing as she silently hung it on a hook on the wall. Except
for Sunday services, he'd seen nothing of her since the
day she walked out of his house. The faint bluish shadows under her eyes, the subtle lines of tension around
her mouth, were mute evidence of the strain she'd been
under, and his gut clenched painfully. It seemed all he
ever brought this woman he loved was pain and uncertainty, when what he really wanted to give her was joy
and peace.

Of all the failures in his life, his relationship with
Maggie was the one that affected him most deeply. He
wanted to take her in his arms right now, to hold her
until she knew beyond the shadow of a doubt that he
loved her with every fiber of his being. But that was not
the way to convince her. He had another plan in mind.
Not one he particularly liked, but at least he felt it had
a chance to succeed.

She turned back to him then, her eyes guarded and
distant. "Let's go into the living room. I have a fire
going."

She chose a chair set slightly apart from the others,
and Jake sat down on the couch. He leaned forward intensely, his forearms resting on his thighs, his hands
clasped.

"Thank you for seeing me, Maggie."

"I suppose we had to talk sooner or later."

"Well, it was tonight or not for several months. Dad
and I are going to Rob's tomorrow for Christmas. We
won't be back until after you leave for Europe."

That jolted her, and Maggie's eyes widened in surprise. "When did you decide to do that?"

"Last week. Rob invited us, and Dad wanted to go.
It will be a good chance for all of us to have some fam-

ily time together. It's not the way I anticipated spending Christmas, but given the circumstances, I thought it might be for the best."

Maggie's throat constricted, and the ache in her heart intensified as she turned to gaze unseeingly into the fire. She blinked to hold back the tears that suddenly welled in her eyes, berating herself for her lack of control, and took a deep breath before she spoke.

"You're probably right." How she managed such a calm, controlled tone when her insides were in turmoil she never knew.

Jake nodded wearily. "But I couldn't leave with things so unresolved between us." He frowned and raked his fingers through his hair, then restlessly stood and moved beside the fire, gripping the mantel with one hand as he stared down into the flickering flames. When at last he turned to her, his eyes were troubled. "The fact is, Maggie, the whole retirement home idea was a bust, from start to finish. I'm not even sure why I sent for that brochure, except that I was desperate. I wanted to keep my promise to my mother, but I also knew Dad was unhappy, which wasn't good for his health. I was between the proverbial rock and a hard place.

"I guess what it comes down to is this—I'm human. I make mistakes. And that was a big one. But I never pursued it beyond sending for that brochure. Because I realized, even before you walked out, that I had to try harder to make things work with Dad. The two of us had been living under the same roof for months, but we'd never really connected, never really opened up and been honest with each other, never dealt directly with the issues that divided us. And so I decided to tackle them head-on when he got back."

He paused and dropped down on the ottoman in front of her, his eyes so close that she could see the gold flecks in their depths. As well as the sincerity.

"It worked, Maggie. The last three weeks have been the best we've had in twelve years. We admitted to each other where we'd fallen short and agreed to try our best to make things work. And we are. I know we'll still have some rough times. I think that's the nature of any human relationship. But we'll get through them. Because we both want it to work."

He reached for her hand then, and Maggie's breath caught in her throat. It took only this simple touch to reawaken all the longing she'd so ruthlessly crushed since she'd walked out of his house.

"The fact is, Maggie, I feel the same about us. I have almost since the day I took shelter here from the mist. I never realized how lonely the last twelve years had been until then. I know you're disappointed and disillusioned right now. I know you think I betrayed your trust. But I do honor my commitments. I'm a different man in a lot of ways than the twenty-five-year-old who walked out on you twelve years ago. What I did then was wrong, and I make no excuses. All I can do is give you my word that it will never happen again. The retirement home fiasco notwithstanding, I've learned a lot about duty and honor and responsibility in these last dozen years. I can't promise that I won't make mistakes. But I can promise you that in the end I'll always do the right thing. Because I love you with all my heart. And I always will."

The tears in Maggie's eyes were close to spilling

over. With every fiber of her being she wanted to believe him. But hurt had made her cautious. And so had the need for self-preservation.

Jake watched the play of emotions across Maggie's face. He saw the yearning and the love in her eyes, but also the uncertainty and fear. It was what he expected. What he had come prepared to address. Slowly he reached into the pocket of his slacks and withdrew a small, square box, then flipped it open to reveal a sparkling solitaire.

Maggie's eyes grew wide as she gazed at the dazzling ring. "Isn't that…that's the ring…" Her voice trailed off.

"It's the same ring, Maggie. I kept it all these years. I never knew why—until I came to Maine and found you again."

Maggie's voice was thick with unshed tears, and a sob caught in her throat when she spoke. "Jake, I…I don't know what to…"

He reached over and placed a gentle fingertip against her lips. "I'm asking you to marry me, Maggie. But I'm not asking you for an answer right now. In fact, I don't want one tonight. Because whatever you decide, I want you to be absolutely sure. No second thoughts, no regrets. All I'm asking is that you take the ring with you to Europe, as a reminder of my love. Think about my proposal. Give yourself time. And then, when you get back, we'll talk about it again."

Maggie's mind was whirling. This was the Christmas present she'd anticipated with such joy at Thanksgiving. Now…now it left her confused and uncertain—yet filled with a sudden, buoyant hope. But there was still a major unresolved issue between them that had nothing to do with their recent falling-out.

"Jake...there's still something we haven't dealt with," she reminded him in a choked voice. "The family issue. I haven't changed my mind on that."

He looked at her steadily. "But I have. I've given it a lot of thought, Maggie. And bottom line, while I'd like to have children, if it comes down to a choice between you and a family, there's no contest. I love you, and that's enough for me. Anything else would be a bonus. Whatever you decide is fine with me."

Maggie felt her throat tighten at the love and tenderness—and absolute certainty—reflected in Jake's eyes.

"You seem awfully sure."

"That's because I am. It's not so hard to make compromises when you love someone as much as I love you. Besides, I don't come without strings, either."

She frowned. "What do you mean?"

"Think about it, Maggie. I'll bring an aging parent to this union. A lot of women wouldn't want to take that on. You faced marriage once before saddled with a pretty overwhelming responsibility. In a way, you will again."

Maggie smiled and shook her head. "Jake, I love Pop. I don't consider him a burden in any way. In fact, before...well, before we had this problem, I was thinking down the road that maybe if things...well...progressed between us, we might want to live here. And we could turn the little guest cottage into a place for your dad. That way he'd be close by, but still have a sense of independence."

Jake's heart overflowed with love for this incredible woman who was so giving, who always thought of others. Dear Lord, how was he going to survive the next three months without her? And he couldn't even bring himself to consider beyond that if, in the end, she rejected his proposal.

"You are one special woman, Maggie Fitzgerald," he declared huskily. He was tempted to demonstrate the depth of his feelings in a nonverbal way, but he restrained himself—with great effort. Calling on every ounce of his willpower, he stood up, then reached down and pulled her to her feet. For a long moment they simply gazed into each other's eyes, both wanting more, both trying desperately to remain in control.

"Will you take the ring, Maggie?" Jake finally asked, his voice rough with emotion. "Not as a commitment— but as a reminder of my love?"

She nodded. "Yes." Her voice was a mere whisper, and she clutched the small velvet box tightly to her breast. "You know, I...I almost wish I wasn't going now," she admitted tremulously.

Jake shook his head firmly. "Don't feel that way. Savor every minute of this experience. You owe that to yourself after all these years. And I'll be here when you get back."

"I'll...I'll miss you, Jake."

He reached for her then, groaning softly as he pulled her fiercely against him and buried his face in her hair. How could he leave without at least one brief kiss to sustain him during the long months to come? That wasn't too much to ask, was it?

He backed up slightly and gazed down into Maggie's eyes. They were filled with yearning, and his own deepened with passion. No, it wasn't too much. They both wanted this. Needed it. Silently he let one hand travel around her neck, beneath her hair, to cup the back of her head. And then he bent down and gently, tenderly claimed her sweet lips.

Maggie responded willingly, knowing that this moment would be a memory to take with her, to hold in her heart, during the long, solitary months ahead. His lips, warm and lingering, moved over hers, seeking, tasting, reigniting the flames of desire that had smoldered in her heart these last few weeks. But all too soon, with evident reluctance, he drew back. The smile he gave her seemed forced, and his voice sounded strained.

"I'd better go."

Several more moments passed before he released her, however, and when he did it was with obvious effort. She followed him to the hall, watched silently as he shrugged into his coat, walked beside him to the door. He turned there, reaching out once more to touch her face, his gaze locked on hers.

"Bon voyage, Maggie. Think of me."

And then he was gone.

Maggie knew that Jake was doing the right thing, the noble thing, giving her time to sort through her feelings and be sure of her decision. But for just a moment, she was tempted to throw caution to the wind, fling open the door and run impulsively into his arms. It was what her heart told her to do. But her heart had led her astray before, she reminded herself. And so, with a decisive click she locked the door and turned back to the living room. She would take the time he'd offered her to think things through. It was the wise thing to do.

But it wouldn't be easy.

Chapter Fourteen

Jake smiled as he read Maggie's account of her adventures at the Trevi Fountain in Rome. He wasn't surprised that several locals had tried to pick her up. She might be nearing forty, but she was still one gorgeous woman.

"Good news from Maggie?" his father inquired, setting a mug in front of Jake. They had gotten into the habit of sharing hot chocolate—and some conversation—each evening before going to bed.

Jake chuckled. "Seems the Italians are a good judge of beauty after all."

Howard raised his eyebrows. "Oh? Are they asking her for dates?"

Jake smiled. He doubted that "dates" were what they were after, but he let it pass. "Mmm-hmm. But she's holding her own. Sounds like she's having a wonderful time. The art classes are going well, and she says she's made some great strides with her painting."

"Glad to hear it. But I'll sure be glad when she comes back. Seems kind of quiet around here without her."

Jake's smile faded. "Yeah."

"You never said much the night you went to say goodbye to her, Jake," Howard said carefully. "I don't want to pry, but...did you two work things out?"

Jake glanced down into his half-empty mug and sighed. "I don't know, Dad. But...well, I guess there's no reason to keep it a secret. I asked her to marry me."

Howard's eyes widened in surprise. "You did? What did she say?"

"I didn't ask for an answer. All I asked her to do was think about it while she was gone, and let me know when she got back."

Howard drained his cup and rose thoughtfully. He paused by Jake's chair and placed a hand on the younger man's shoulders. "Maggie will come around, son. You'll see. You're a good man, and she'll realize that in time."

Jake stared after his father, his throat tightening with emotion. The future of his relationship with Maggie might still be uncertain, but at least he and his father had reconnected. His father had just touched him with affection for the first time in years. And he'd called him "a good man." That small gesture, those few words, meant more to Jake than all of his other accomplishments combined.

Now if only Maggie would come to the same conclusion.

Maggie tipped her face back to the sun and sighed contentedly as Parisian street life bustled around her. Her fabulous European adventure was drawing to a close, but it had been everything she'd hoped. She felt steeped in great art, had soaked it up until her soul was satiated. And she'd learned so much! The classes had been tremendous, and she'd produced some of her best work on this trip, shipping it home to Philip as she completed it. His enthusiastic response had reaffirmed her opinion that she'd made great strides.

With only two weeks left in her sojourn, her thoughts were now beginning to turn to home, and she reached up to finger the ring that hung on a slender gold chain around her neck. Soon she would have to make her decision. Maggie knew, with absolute certainty, that she loved Jake. She also knew, with equal certainty, that she was afraid. So the question came down to this: Was she willing to take the risk that love entailed? To trust her heart completely to this man who had walked out on her once before? A man who she had come to believe was now capable of true commitment—but whose unexpected lapse had shaken her trust?

Maggie knew what the twins thought. They'd summed it up in three pithy words. *Go for it.* Philip had said much the same thing. And Maggie felt in her heart they were right. She knew that nothing good came without risk. Yet she was still afraid. She'd prayed daily for guidance, asked for a sign, for direction, but so far the Lord hadn't responded to her plea.

Maggie sighed and reached for the mail she'd just picked up. There was a letter from Jake, she noted, her lips curving up into a smile. He wrote practically every other day. And one from Pop, she saw with surprise. Those would be letters to savor. So she put them aside and opened the large brown envelope from Philip, who sorted through her mail at home and passed on things that looked important. She peered inside and withdrew a small package with an unfamiliar New York return address. Curiously she tore off the brown wrapping to find a little box cocooned inside a letter. Quickly she scanned the single sheet of paper.

> Dear Ms. Fitzgerald,
> Millicent Trent gave this to me and asked that I send it to you. I am sorry to inform you that she passed away last week after a brief illness. But she did so at peace with the Lord, and with joy. She said she wanted you to have this because you would understand, and that she hoped your story turns out happier than hers. She also asked me to remind you that very few people get a second chance, and to consider carefully before you let yours slip away. I confess I don't understand the message, but Millicent said you would. May the Lord keep you in His care.

The letter was signed by a Reverend Thomas Wilson. Maggie's eyes filled with tears as she removed the lid from the small box and gazed down at the two-part heart pendant nestled inside. She was deeply touched by Millicent's gift, for she knew that of all the woman's possessions, this was the one that meant the most to her. Perhaps in death she would at last find the reconciliation that had eluded her in life, Maggie thought wistfully, as she silently asked the Lord to watch over her friend.

Wiping a hand across her eyes, Maggie reached next for Pop's letter. It was brief, and written very much in character.

> Hi, Maggie.
> I got your address from Jake. I hope you're having fun. We're not. Don't get me wrong. Things

are good between Jake and me. Real good. Jake turned out fine after all, and I'm proud to have him for a son. But he's been moping around the house like a lovesick puppy, and it's driving me crazy. So please come home soon and put him out of his misery. He misses you a lot. So do I.

Maggie smiled through her tears. Obviously Pop and Jake were getting along fine. Jake had told her he'd make it work, and he had. There was an undertone of affection in Pop's letter that conveyed even more clearly than the words that the two of them were back on track.

And then she settled back in her chair and opened Jake's letter. His notes were typically chatty and warm as he filled her in on his daily life, making her feel that she was sitting next to him on the couch while he shared his day's adventures. But it was always the opening and closing that she reread several times. He never failed to remind her how much he missed her or that he was counting the days until her return. Though he never pressed for an answer to his proposal, she could sense hope—and anxiety—in every line. The closing of to-day's letter especially tugged at her heart.

The days are long, Maggie, and without the sound of your voice and your sparkling eyes, they seem empty. The nights are even worse. I find sleep more and more elusive as I anticipate your return. I hope that you're faring better than I am on that score. And then again, maybe I don't. In my heart, I hope you miss me as desperately as I miss you. I don't know what hell holds for those who sin, but I feel that in the agony of uncertainty I've endured

during these last few weeks I have somehow made
reparation for at least some of my transgressions. I
love you, Maggie. More with each day that passes.
I look forward to the moment I can tell you that
again face-to-face. Until then, know that thoughts
of you fill my days—and nights.

Maggie's eyes grew misty again, and she drew in a
long, unsteady breath. This was the most direct Jake
had been about his feelings. Until now his letters had
been mostly lighthearted, written to make her smile, not
cry. But now he was baring his soul, letting her know
just how much her answer meant to him. It was a courageous thing to do, giving someone the power to hurt
you that way. But it was honest. And from the heart.
And it touched her deeply.

Maggie pressed his letter to her breast as she ex-
tracted Millicent's pendant from the tiny box and cradled it in her hand. She thought about the gift of love
Jake was offering her. And she thought about Millicent's
sad story of love thrown away. She thought also about
all that Jake had done in the last few months to prove
his steadfastness and his ability to honor a promise.
How he had diligently cared for his father and pains-
takingly rebuilt that relationship. How he came to her
aid when she was ill. How he stayed by her side at the
hospital, and was there for her to lean on during the
twins' emotional send-off to college. Since coming back
into her life, he had never once failed to be there when
she needed him.

And suddenly the image of the painting she was just
now completing came to mind. With a startling flash of
insight, she realized that while she had been asking the

Lord for a sign to help her make her decision, it had literally been in front of her for weeks. For she now knew
that she had made her decision long ago, in the hills
above Florence. She'd just been too afraid to admit it.
But today's letters had brought everything sharply into
focus and banished her fear.

With a sudden, joyful lightening of her heart, Maggie gathered up her letters and headed back to her room.

Jake shoved his hands into his pockets and drew a
long, unsteady breath. It had been three months since
he'd said goodbye to Maggie. Three eternal, lonely
months. She'd written regularly, but letters didn't ease
the ache in his heart, nor did they fill his days with joy
and laughter and his nights with tenderness and love.

He sighed and reached up to loosen his tie as he
gazed out into the night. Nothing seemed right without Maggie. He needed her. The thought that she might
ultimately reject his proposal had plagued him inces-
santly, etched faint lines of worry at the corners of his
eyes. And yet he knew he had done the right thing. He'd
given her the time she needed to be sure. Because he
didn't want her to commit to him unless she felt the
same absolute certainty, trust and deep, abiding love
for him that he felt for her.

Jake heard a door open and he turned slowly, his
gaze softening into a smile as Maggie entered. She always looked beautiful to him, but never more so than
right now, as she walked toward him resplendent in her
wedding finery. He held her at arm's length for a moment when she joined him, letting his gaze move over
her slowly and lingeringly, memorizing every nuance of
her appearance as she stood before him, more dazzling

in her radiance than the illuminated Eiffel Tower visible behind her through the French doors on the balcony.

Her hair was drawn back on one side with a cluster of sweetheart roses and baby's breath, a miniature reflection of the bouquet she'd carried as they were married just hours before. Her tea-length white silk gown, subtly patterned to shimmer in the light, was simply but elegantly cut, with slightly puffed sleeves and a sweetheart neckline. Around her neck she wore Millicent's heart pendant, the two halves seamlessly joined by the hands of a master jeweler. Jake would never forget the expression of joy and certainty on her face as they'd exchanged their vows in the tiny chapel she'd reserved. Illuminated only by the mosaic of late-afternoon light as it filtered through the intricate stained-glass windows, with the fragrance of roses sweetly perfuming the air, it had been the perfect, intimate spot for them to exchange the vows that had been so long delayed.

"You look breathtaking," Jake said huskily, the warmth in his eyes making her tremble with joy—and anticipation.

She smiled, and a becoming blush rose in her cheeks. "Actually, I feel pretty breath*less*," she admitted.

He chuckled. "It has been a bit of a whirlwind, hasn't it?" Since her phone call a week ago, life had moved into high gear. Thank heaven her call had coincided with Spring Break! But even if it hadn't, nothing could have kept him from her side.

"Everything happened so fast that I can hardly believe it's real."

"You're not sorry, are you?" he asked worriedly. "Would you rather we had waited, been married at home?"

She smiled and shook her head. "No. We waited long enough. And once I decided, I was determined to have that Paris honeymoon after all."

His eyes deepened with passion, and he reached for her. But when she held back, he looked down at her questioningly.

"Jake, before we…we…well, I have something I'd like to give you first," she stammered.

He smiled indulgently. "Since I've already waited years for this moment, I suppose I can hold out a few more minutes."

"I'll be right back," she promised, extricating herself gently from his arms. She disappeared into the bedroom of their suite, and returned a moment later with a large package wrapped in silver paper. As she held it out to him, she noticed that he'd placed two small packages with white bows on the coffee table.

"Looks like we both had the same idea," he commented with a smile.

"I didn't expect a present, Jake. Not on such short notice," she protested.

"I've had these for a long time, Maggie," he told her quietly. "They were just waiting for this moment."

He sat on the couch and drew Maggie down beside him, then tore off the shiny paper of his package to reveal an impressionistic painting of a man, woman and small child on a hillside picnic, visible only from the back, surrounded by a golden light. The man and woman were seated, and he had his arm around the child. He was pointing into the distance, and the woman's hand rested on the man's shoulder as she leaned close to him. A feeling of intrinsic love and serenity and unity pervaded the painting, making the viewer yearn to be part of the idyllic family scene.

Jake examined the exquisite painting silently, then drew a deep breath as he turned to his wife and shook his head in awe. "This is wonderful, Maggie!" he said in a hushed voice. "All of your work is excellent, but... well, this stands apart. You always paint from the heart, but this...it captures something, some essence, I've never seen before in your work."

"It comes even more from the heart than you realize, Jake," she told him softly.

He looked at her curiously. "What do you mean?"

"I thought a lot about us while I've been here. I knew from the beginning that I loved you. That was never a question. But I was so afraid of being hurt again. I just couldn't decide what to do. I asked the Lord for guidance, but I never seemed to get an answer.

"And then last week I was sitting at a sidewalk café, and I thought about this painting, which I started in Florence. Suddenly I realized I'd made my decision— about a couple of things—a long time ago."

She drew a deep breath and looked at him, her gaze steady and certain. "That's us, Jake. You and me...and our child. I never even realized it until a few days ago. My heart's known for weeks what I wanted to do. It just took a little longer for the message to reach my mind."

Carefully Jake set the painting down, then he reached for her and pulled her close.

"Oh, Maggie." His voice broke, and he buried his face in her hair, holding her tightly. "Are you sure? You're not doing this just because you know I want it?"

"Partly," she admitted, her voice muffled against his chest. "But I'm doing it for me, too. I want to raise our child—together—if the Lord chooses to bless us with one. I want part of us, what we have together, to live on. And I want to share our love with a child."

He drew a deep, shuddering breath, and when he pulled back, the tenderness, love and gratitude reflected on his face brought a lump to her throat.

"I love you, Maggie."

"I love you, too. With all my heart." Her own voice broke on the last word, and he reached over to frame her face with this strong hands, his thumbs gentle as they stroked her damp cheeks.

"Now it's your turn." He retrieved the two small packages, handing her the smaller one first.

Maggie tore off the wrapping and lifted the lid of the small box to reveal an antique, gold-filigreed locket. She flipped it open to find two tiny photos—one of she and Jake taken when they were about nine and ten, and one of them taken by the twins on her last birthday. Those two photos seemed to reaffirm what her heart had long known—that their lives had always been destined to join.

"That was Mom's locket," Jake told her. "I found it when I was cleaning out the house for Dad. Her mother gave it to her when she turned twenty, and it was always one of her most treasured possessions. I know she'd want you to have it. And so do I."

"Oh, Jake! It's lovely! Thank you."

He handed her the other package and waited silently as she tore off the wrapping, raised the lid and carefully folded back the tissue paper. With unsteady hands she withdrew a small, framed document, and her breath caught in her throat as she was immediately transported back to another time and place. At the top, in careful lettering, were the words *Official Document*. Below that it read, "I, Jake West, and I, Maggie Fitzgerald, promise to always be friends forever and ever, no matter what happens." It was dated twenty-eight years before, and they'd each signed it in their childish scrawls. Their mothers had signed also, as witnesses.

"I'd forgotten all about this," she whispered.

"I found it in my mother's fireproof 'treasure box' the same day I found the locket," Jake said quietly. "I meant those words then, Maggie. And I mean them now."

Maggie could no longer hold back her tears. They streamed down her cheeks unchecked as she stared down at the yellowed document in her hands. She thought about the gifts they had just exchanged—the locket that had once belonged to Jake's mother, this sentimental document, her painting. None of them had much, if any, monetary value. But they were worth far more than gold to her, for they came from the heart and were born of love. A cherished line from Matthew came suddenly to mind—"For where thy treasure is, there also will thy heart be."

Maggie looked up at Jake, and he reached over to gently brush her tears away.

"No more tears, Maggie. There've been enough of those in this relationship." He reached down and drew her to her feet, guiding her to the French doors that looked out onto the lights of Paris, the illuminated Eiffel Tower rising majestically into the night sky.

"Remember how we used to talk about Paris? How we thought it was so romantic, and how we dreamed of spending our honeymoon here?" he asked softly.

She nodded, a smile of gentle remembrance touching her lips. "Mmm-hmm."

He turned to face her, his hands resting gently at her waist. She looked up at him, and the intensity—and fire—in his eyes made her breathless. "Well, our honeymoon might have been a little delayed. But I promise you this, my love. I'll spend the rest of my life making up for lost time. Starting right now."

Then he took her hand and drew her back inside, closing the door on the lights of Paris before he pulled her into his waiting arms. And as his lips claimed hers, in a kiss filled with promise and passion, Maggie said a silent prayer of thanks. After all these years, she had at last come home to the man she loved. And it was where she belonged. For always.

Epilogue

Two and a half years later

"Allison, will you run down to the cottage and tell Pop dinner's almost ready?"

"Sure." Allison pulled off a piece of the turkey that stood waiting to be carried to the table and popped it into her mouth. "Mmm. Fantastic! Sure beats the food in the dorms," she declared with a grin.

"Well, you'll only have to put up with the food for one more semester," Maggie reminded her with a smile. "I still can't believe you two are graduating in less than six months!"

"We can't, either," Abby chimed in. "Watch out, world, here we come!"

Maggie laughed. "Amen to that!"

Jake ambled into the kitchen, sniffed appreciatively and headed straight for the turkey. "That smells great!" he pronounced.

But just as he reached for a piece, Maggie stepped in his way. "If everyone eats their turkey in the kitchen, I'll end up having mine alone in the dining room," she complained good-naturedly. "And that's no way to spend Thanksgiving."

"Well, I have to nibble on something," Jake declared. Without giving her a chance to elude his grasp, he reached for her and pulled her into a dip. "I guess your ear will have to do."

Abby giggled. "You two act like you're still on your honeymoon."

Jake's eyes, only inches from Maggie's, softened and he smiled tenderly. "That's because we still feel like we are," he replied as he held her close.

Abby sighed dramatically. "That's s-o-o-o romantic. I sure hope I meet somebody like you when I'm ready to get married," she told Jake.

"I hope you do, too, honey," Maggie agreed before Jake muffled her lips in a lingering kiss.

"Mmm," he murmured. "I like this idea. Start with dessert."

Maggie laughed softly. "That's all you're going to get if you don't let me up before everything burns."

"That's all I need," he countered, raising one eyebrow wickedly.

She blushed. "Well, I don't think the others would agree to defer dinner until after you have…dessert."

With an exaggerated sigh, he slowly released her. "Oh, all right. I suppose I have to be a good sport about this."

"Pop's on his way," Allison informed them as she breezed back into the kitchen.

"Okay, let's get this show on the road, then. Everybody grab a dish and let's eat!"

It took a few minutes for everyone to settle in, and

then they joined hands and bowed their heads as Jake spoke.

"Lord, we thank You today for all the blessings You've given us this past year. For the joy You've sent our way, for good health, for the family ties that bind us to one another with deep, abiding love. Thank You also for watching over us and guiding us through each day, for letting us feel Your loving presence so strongly in our lives. Help us always to be grateful for all that we have, not only today, but every day of the year. Amen."

As Maggie raised her eyes, she was filled with a sense of absolute peace and deep contentment. All of the people she cared about most were with her today, and that alone made her heart overflow with gratitude. Her gaze moved around the table. Pop, who loved living in his own little cottage and now had a thriving woodworking business. Allison and Abby, still incurable romantics, ready to launch their own careers. And Jake. She gazed at him lovingly as he carved the turkey. Every moment with him had been a joy. Each day their relationship grew and deepened and took on new dimensions.

At that moment, one of those dimensions began to loudly demand attention, and Maggie's gaze moved to the high chair next to Jake. Her lips curved up softly and her eyes took on a new tenderness as she gazed at the newest member of their family. For the last nine months, Michael had joyfully disrupted their household, and they'd loved every minute of it. True to his word, Jake had gone out of his way to make sure that this time raising a child was a shared experience. He'd attended every childbirth class, coached her through labor, took most of the night feedings and changed more than his share of diapers. And Maggie loved him more every day.

As Michael demonstrated his hunger in a particularly vocal way, Jake turned to him with a smile. "Hold on there, big fella," he said, reaching over to tenderly ruffle the toddler's auburn locks.

Then he glanced at Maggie, and they smiled across the table at each other. It was a smile filled with tenderness, understanding, joy and love. Especially love. Because both of them realized how very blessed they were to have been given a second chance to find their destiny. And how close they'd come to losing it.

Though no words were spoken, Maggie knew what Jake was thinking. She could read it in his eyes. And it mirrored her thoughts exactly.

It didn't get any better than this.

* * * * *

Dear Reader,

When my husband and I were married, the priest who officiated at the ceremony spoke about the extraordinary gift of ordinary love—how remarkable it was that love could flourish amid the stresses and tribulations of day-to-day life. He went on to point out that it was the everyday kindnesses and caring gestures—more than the fleeting euphoric moments—that formed the solid foundation of lasting love. And he said that this "ordinary" love was to be celebrated and held up as an example to others.

Although I was too caught up in the "euphoric moment" of the wedding to fully appreciate his message that day, ultimately I recognized its truth—and broadened my definition of *romance*. Yes, it's still that enchanted evening when you see a stranger across a crowded room. And it's still that heart-stopping moment when two hearts touch for the first time. But it's so much more! It encompasses all of the levels on which two lives intertwine—intellectual, emotional and spiritual, as well as physical.

I try to capture this multidimensional nature of love in all of my books. But it is perhaps especially present in *It Had to Be You,* which focuses on growth and change in a long-term relationship. I hope you enjoy reading about Jake and Maggie's reawakening love as much as I enjoyed writing about it.

Sincerely,

Irene Hannon

ALL OUR TOMORROWS

He has made everything appropriate to its time.
—*Ecclesiastes* 3:11

With thanks and gratitude to the Lord for the many blessings that have graced my life.

Chapter One

"You'll never guess who I saw today."

Caroline reached for a roll and gave her mother a bemused glance. She never won at this game, which had become a standard part of their weekly dinner. Judy James knew more people than the President of the United States. Or so it seemed. "I haven't a clue, Mom."

"Guess anyway."

Instead of responding, Caroline popped a chunk of the crusty roll into her mouth, savoring the fresh-baked flavor. No question about it—her mom was a whiz in the kitchen, even if she did have a few idiosyncrasies. Like her penchant for outrageous hats. And her eclectic taste in decorating, thankfully confined to the family room, which had done time as a South Seas beach shack, a Japanese tea house and a Victorian parlor—to name but a few of its incarnations. In light of those eccentricities, Caroline supposed this silly guessing game was a tame aberration. And it was one she felt obliged to indulge, considering how much she owed her mother, who had been a rock during the difficult months when grief had darkened Caroline's world, blinding her to everything but pain and loss. She couldn't have made it through that tragic time without the support of the older woman sitting across from her.

"Okay. How about…Marlene Richards."

A thoughtful expression crossed Judy's face. "Goodness, I haven't had any news of Marlene in quite a while. Whatever made you think of her?"

"I reviewed an obit today for a Maureen Richards for the next edition of the paper. No relation, it turns out. But it made me think of Marlene. She was a good Sunday school teacher. A bit unconventional, but all the kids loved her. I wonder what ever happened to her?"

"When she retired, she went on a mission trip to Africa. Liked it so much, she stayed. Last I heard, she lived in a little village somewhere back in the bush and taught school."

At her mother's prompt and thorough response, Caroline smiled and shook her head. "How in the world do you do that?"

"What?"

"Keep tabs on so many people."

"I make it a point to stay connected. And speaking of staying connected…do you want to guess again?"

"Nope." Focusing her attention on the appetizing pot roast, Caroline cut a generous bite and speared it with her fork.

"All right. Then I'll tell you. David Sloan."

The hunger gnawing at Caroline's stomach suddenly turned into an ache that spread to her heart, and her hand froze halfway to her mouth. "David Sloan?"

"Yes. Isn't that a strange coincidence? I was at the post office, and as I was leaving I must have dropped my scarf, because the next thing I knew this nice young man came up from behind and handed it to me. He looked familiar, but it took me a few seconds to place him. He didn't remember me, of course. We only met that one time, just for a few minutes and under such sad circumstances. But when I introduced myself, the oddest expression came over his face." Judy tilted her head in the manner of an inquisitive bird. "Kind of like the one on yours right now."

Caroline lowered her fork to her plate, the pot roast untouched. David Sloan. Her fiancé's brother—and the man who bore at least some measure of responsibility for his death. For a moment, the taste of resentment was sharp and bitter on her tongue, chasing away the fresh flavor of her mother's homemade roll. But then her conscience kicked in, dissipating her resentment with a reminder that she bore the lion's share of responsibility for the tragedy—and triggering a crushing, suffocating guilt that crashed over her like a powerful wave, rocking her world.

"Anyway, he took a new job and moved to St. Louis a couple of months ago. Still, it's a big city. Seems strange that I would run into him, doesn't it?" Judy prodded.

"Yes." Caroline could squeeze only one word past her tight throat. With a shaky hand, she reached for her glass of water and took a long, slow swallow, struggling to rein in her wayward emotions.

"I'm sorry, honey." Distress etched Judy's features as she studied her daughter's face. "I had no idea the mere mention of Michael's brother would upset you."

"I didn't, either." Denying the obvious would be foolish. Her mother knew her too well for that.

Reaching over, Judy patted her hand. "Well, we just

won't talk anymore about it, then. Except I did promise him I'd give you his regards. Now that I've done that, tell me about your day. Any hot news at the *Chronicle?*"

Switching gears wasn't easy. But Caroline appreciated her mother's efforts to distract her. It was a technique that had helped keep her sane during those first few weeks after Michael's death, as her world disintegrated around her. So she tried to change focus. And prompted by Judy's interested questions, she was able to maintain the semblance of a conversation. As the meal ended, her mother even elicited a smile or two from her with an entertaining story about her latest passion— square dancing—and the lessons she was taking with Harold, her reluctant partner and steady beau.

"So I said to Harold, 'Just listen to the caller. He'll tell us what to do. It's like assembling that glider in my backyard. You just follow the directions and it all comes together.' And he says, 'I didn't read the instructions for the glider.'" Judy shook her head in exasperation. "Now I know why the thing seems a little lopsided. And why he ended up with all those leftover parts."

By the time Caroline left, with her almost untouched, foil-wrapped dinner and an extra piece of dessert in hand, she felt a bit more settled. But as she drove home through the dark streets of St. Louis, a shiver ran through her—one that she knew was prompted by more than the damp cold on this rainy March night.

Although her numbing, debilitating grief had ebbed over time, the mention of Michael's brother had dredged it up from the deep recesses of her heart. Along with all the other emotions she'd wrestled into submission these past two years. Guilt. Anger. Blame. Resentment. Some of those feelings were directed at her; others, at

David Sloan. But none of them were healthy. As a result, she'd tried her best to suppress them and to move on with her life. Yet it took only the merest incident, like the passing reference to David tonight, to remind her that they hadn't been tamed, just subdued.

The rain intensified, obscuring her vision, and she flicked on her wipers. With one sweep, they brushed aside the raindrops, giving her a clear view of the road ahead. Too bad she couldn't banish the muddled emotions in her heart with the same ease. But they clung with a tenacity that rivaled the ivy creeping up the side of her mother's brick bungalow, imbedding itself with roots that sought—and penetrated—even the tiniest crack.

As she pulled into her parking spot, the light in the front window of her condo welcomed her with its golden warmth and promise of haven. Set on a timer, it came on faithfully every day at five o'clock, lessening the gloom of coming home to a dark, empty apartment. It might be a poor substitute for the warm embrace of the man she'd loved, but that glow buoyed her spirits, which had a tendency to droop after she left the office. Her hectic days at the newspaper kept her too busy to dwell on her personal life during working hours, but it was harder to keep thoughts of the past at bay when she was alone.

It was getting easier, though. Each day, in tiny increments, the past receded a little bit more. It had been months since she'd had to pull the car over because her hands had begun to shake. She didn't choke up anymore when she heard a song on the radio that reminded her of Michael. She didn't cry herself to sleep every night. And, once in a while, a whole day passed when she didn't think about what might have been. That was progress.

She knew Michael would have wanted her to move on. He, of all people, with his love of life and live-for-today attitude, would have been the first to tell her to get over it and get on with her life. To live, to love and to laugh. To make every day count.

Caroline was doing her best to put that philosophy into action. But it didn't take much—as tonight's brief conversation proved—to remind her that she still had a long way to go before she reached that ideal.

And to make her wonder if she ever would.

David Sloan angled into a parking place, set the brake and rested his hands on the steering wheel as he read the sign a few doors down. *County Chronicle.*

A wave of doubt swept over him, and he hesitated. Was he making a mistake coming here? He hadn't seen Caroline since Michael's funeral, and her attitude toward him then had been chilly at best. Not that he'd blamed her. If he and Michael hadn't argued, Michael would have been more focused when he'd gone to meet that contact in the marketplace. His brother had always had great instincts. That was why he'd been such a successful photojournalist, why he'd risen through the ranks of the Associated Press to be one of their top shooters. It was why they'd sent him to the Middle East, knowing that he'd be able to get into the thick of things, make great images and emerge unscathed. Until that fateful day in the marketplace, when he had no doubt been distracted by their argument, and by concerns for their mother. So David understood why Caroline would blame him for Michael's death. For turning her world upside down. For destroying a man they'd both loved in the prime of his life. He blamed himself, too.

For almost two years he'd grappled with his complicity. But finally he'd come to terms with it—at least as well as he would ever be able to, he suspected. And some good had come out of his struggle, too. After much prayer, he'd reevaluated his life and made some dramatic changes, following a new path the Lord had revealed to him. The work he was doing now might not offer him the kind of income provided by the high-stakes mergers and acquisitions he'd brokered in his previous job, but it paid dividends in human terms. And even though it had been hard for David to let go of the financial security his former position had offered, he'd put his trust in the Lord three months ago and made the change. So far, he hadn't had a single regret.

But he had plenty of regrets about his role in Michael's death. And one of them involved Caroline. He'd always felt the need to contact her, to express his sorrow, to apologize. Though they'd sat side by side at Michael's funeral, her grief had been too thick for words to penetrate. When he had reached out a tentative, comforting hand to her once during those terrible few days, she'd recoiled, staring at him with a look of such profound loss and resentment that it was still seared in his memory. That was the main reason he'd never tried to contact her. Not the only one, but the main one.

As for the other reason…he wasn't going to go there. Until yesterday, it had been irrelevant, since he'd never expected to see her again. Yet the chance meeting with her mother, and the medallion resting in the inside pocket of his suit jacket, its weight pressing against his heart, had prodded him to do what he should have done months before. If she brushed him aside, so be it. He still had to make the effort to reach out to her and apologize. And then he would move on—and do his best to forget about her.

From the outside, the *County Chronicle* looked like any other storefront on the busy Kirkwood street, which still retained a small-town flavor even though it was a close-in suburb of St. Louis. On his way to the front door, he passed Dubrov's Bakery, Andrea's card shop and Fitzgerald's Café, all of which seemed to be family operations instead of the chain stores that were multiplying like rabbits around the country. He liked that. Liked the notion that even in this modern age of megastores and conglomerates—many of which he'd helped to create in his previous job—the entrepreneurial spirit continued to flourish. That people with enough drive and determination could still create a successful business to pass down to the next generation.

As he stepped into the lobby of the *Chronicle,* David tried to calm his erratic pulse. The first moments would be awkward, at best. *Please, Lord, help me find the words to make the apology I came here to offer,* he prayed.

"May I help you, sir?" A dark-haired woman, who looked to be in her early thirties, spoke to him from behind a desk. Her nameplate identified her as Mary Ramirez, receptionist.

"Yes. Is Caroline James in?"

"Do you have an appointment?"

"No. I just took a chance she might be available. I only need a few minutes."

"May I tell her what this is about?" The woman reached for the phone.

"I'm an old…acquaintance. She'll know the name. David Sloan."

The woman didn't look convinced, but she punched in some numbers, anyway. "She's got a very full schedule. I'm not sure she'll be able to see you."

Caroline's mother had told him that she was the managing editor of the paper, so he was sure she was busy. And perhaps not inclined to mix professional and personal business. But since she didn't have a listed phone number—he'd checked that first—he hoped she'd give him a few minutes at the office.

"Caroline, it's Mary. There's a David Sloan here who would like to see you." After several seconds of silence, the receptionist spoke again. "Caroline? Are you still there?"

Shock. That had to account for Caroline's delayed response, David reasoned. Which did not bode well for the reception he was going to get—if he got one at all.

"All right." The woman was speaking again. "Yes, I'll let him know." She hung up and gave David a speculative look. "She'll be out in a sec. Have a seat while you wait." She gestured to a small grouping of furniture with a coffee table in the middle.

Relieved, David nodded and moved to one of the modernistic upholstered chairs. He didn't feel like sitting, but pacing wasn't an option, either. The receptionist was already casting discreet, but interested, glances his way. He didn't want to arouse any more curiosity than necessary. With studied casualness, he sat in one of the chairs, reached for a copy of the newspaper from among those fanned on the coffee table, leaned back and pretended to read the blur of words on the page in front of him. He was more nervous about this encounter than any of the high-powered, deal-making sessions he'd once participated in, when hundreds of millions of dollars had sometimes hung in the balance. Maybe because the capital here was emotional, not monetary. And for another reason he didn't want to consider.

As the minutes ticked by, David grew more apprehensive. What if Caroline had changed her mind? What if she refused to see him? He'd get the medallion to her somehow, he vowed, find another way to apologize. Perhaps he'd resort to a letter. That would be easier than dealing with her face-to-face. But not as personal. Or as noble. Still, if she didn't come out, he'd have to conclude that she didn't want to see him, and he'd be left with no other option. It wasn't ideal, but he...

Suddenly, the door to the inner offices opened and Caroline stepped through. He set aside the newspaper and rose slowly, using the opportunity to do a quick assessment of the woman who stood before him.

She was still gorgeous, no question about it. Michael had always appreciated beautiful women. Just as it had the first time they'd met, David's heart tripped into double time. Caroline was model-tall, just three or four inches shorter than his own six-foot frame. And slender. Maybe too slender now, he corrected himself. A jade-green silk blouse was tucked into her pencil-slim black wool skirt, and a delicate gold necklace dipped into the hollow of her throat. She radiated the same style, class and poise he recalled from their first meeting, when Michael had brought her home for Christmas to introduce his fiancée to him and their mother. Now, as then, he was struck by her sleek, shimmery hair, which was the color of an autumn hillside—rich brown, laced with glints of gold, bronze and copper. She'd changed the style, though. He recalled her hair being shorter. Her new look was longer, just brushing her shoulders.

He noticed other new things, as well. Faint, parallel furrows in her brow. Fine lines at the corners of her eyes, and a deep, lingering sadness in their hazel depths. She'd also aged in some subtle way he couldn't quite identify. He knew she was a year younger than him. Michael had mentioned it once. And it wasn't that she looked older than her thirty-five years, exactly. It was just that there was a weariness in her eyes that hadn't been there before. A timeless, ancient expression not related to age, but to experience. The kind of look shared by people who'd seen too much, been through too much. But at least the animosity he'd glimpsed at the funeral was gone. In its place was wariness.

As David stood there, Caroline looked him over as well, though she had a less vivid picture in her mind for comparison. The Christmas they'd come home to announce their engagement to both families, she'd been focused on Michael. And at the funeral, her grief had been so overwhelming that she'd been aware of David only on a peripheral level. In fact, she'd gone out of her way to avoid him as she'd tried to deal with the avalanche of shock, guilt and resentment that had buried her in a suffocating blackness.

But she had always recognized the distinct differences in the two brothers. David was a couple of inches shorter than Michael, and his hair was dark brown while Michael's had been sandy and sun-streaked. Their eyes also provided a contrast. Michael's had been a sparkling, vivid blue, while David's were quiet and deep brown. Just as their physical appearance differed, so, too, did their personalities. Michael had been an adventurous extrovert. David was a cautious introvert. Or at least that's how Michael had characterized him. He'd always referred to David, five years his junior, as his kid brother, and called him "the suit" in a good-natured way. He'd told Caroline that David was destined for the corporate world and power lunches, that one day he would be rich and famous while Michael continued to tilt at windmills. And that was just fine with Caroline. It was one of the things she'd loved about Michael. His absolute passion for truth and his zeal for his job were the first things she'd noticed about him. The world needed more people like him. Instead, it had one less. Thanks to her—and, to some degree, the man now looking at her from across the room.

Caroline had almost refused to see David. But what good would that have done? Any blame he bore for Michael's death was far less than her own, after all. And Michael wouldn't have wanted her to be unkind to David. Though the brothers had been estranged for several weeks prior to Michael's death, she knew that their break had weighed on his mind. Despite their difference of opinion on their mother's care, Michael had never stopped loving his kid brother. And she suspected the feeling was mutual. She was sorry they hadn't had a chance to resolve their dispute before Michael was killed.

But that was in the past. Right now, David was waiting for her to speak, and she forced herself to walk toward him. Michael would want her to be cordial, she knew. Still, she found the whole situation awkward. And unsettling. Not to mention painful.

"Hello, David." She held out her hand, and her fingers were engulfed in a warm, firm clasp.

"Hello, Caroline. Thank you for seeing me."

His voice sounded huskier than she remembered, and despite the almost palpable tension between them, he exuded a deep-seated, inner calmness that somehow eased her nerves. Yet another difference between the brothers, she mused. Michael's dynamic energy had infused those around him with excitement and enthusiasm. David, on the other hand, came across as calm, steady and in control. Someone who planned before plunging. Michael had always plunged first and planned on the fly. That spontaneity was one of the reasons he'd been so good at his job.

"I'm afraid I don't have much time," she told David.

"That's okay. I took a chance stopping by without warning. But after I ran into your mother yesterday, I decided I'd put this off long enough."

"Mom told me she saw you at the post office. How is your mother doing?"

"She died a year ago. The Alzheimer's progressed far more rapidly than anyone anticipated. And her heart just kept getting weaker."

Her query had been routine and mundane, and she'd expected the same kind of response. Instead, his reply shocked her. Sympathy replaced wariness in her eyes. "I'm so sorry."

"Thank you. It was a shock, but in many ways I'm glad God called her home. Alzheimer's is an awful disease. It robs people of everything that made them who they were. In the end, she didn't know me anymore, or remember anything about the past. The mother I knew had left months before her physical body stopped functioning."

So now David was alone. Michael had told her once

that they had no other relatives. Both of their parents had been only children, and their father had died years before.

"I'm sorry," she repeated.

He lifted one shoulder. "I survived. My faith was a great comfort."

Another contrast between the two brothers, Caroline thought, recalling Michael's skeptical attitude toward religion in general. Though the brothers hadn't been raised in a household where faith played a central role, David had sought out the Lord as an adult. And the Christmas they'd met, Caroline had discovered that he'd found something that she had envied deep in her heart. An inner peace. A sense of greater purpose. Something to cling to through the turbulent seas of life. She'd wanted to question him about it, but the time hadn't been right then. Nor was it now. In ten minutes she was scheduled to do a phone interview with the mayor, and she needed to get focused.

"Well...I do have to get back to my desk. Was there something you wanted to talk about?" she asked when the silence between them lengthened.

With a jolt, David realized that she wasn't going to invite him to her office. Although Mary appeared to be busy, he suspected that she was tuned in to the conversation taking place only a few feet away, and what he had to say wasn't meant for public discussion. But he wasn't leaving without accomplishing the purpose of his visit.

"Is there somewhere private we could speak?" He lowered his voice and angled his body away from the receptionist.

After a brief hesitation, Caroline nodded. "But I have a phone interview to do in a few minutes."

"I'll be brief."

Without responding, she turned and led the way to the inner door, holding up an ID card to the scanner. The door responded with a click and she pulled it open.

The office was much more expansive than David expected. And far more modern than the quaint exterior of the building had suggested. The newsroom was quite large and honeycombed with dozens of cubicles. There was a hum of activity, and staff members stopped Caroline twice to ask her questions as she led the way through the maze.

When they reached her glass-enclosed office, she stepped aside and motioned him in, then followed and closed the door behind her.

"Busy place," he commented.

"And this is a quiet day. You should see it when things are really hopping." She moved to her chair, putting the desk between them.

"I guess I didn't realize that a smaller paper would be so...thriving."

"The *Chronicle* isn't small. It's the second-largest paper in the city, next to the *Post-Dispatch,* and we continue to acquire smaller community newspapers. But I don't need to tell you how mergers and acquisitions work. You deal with that every day."

"Not anymore." At her surprised look, he explained. "I took a new job a couple of months ago. As executive director of Uplink, an organization that pairs gifted high school students in problem environments with mentors for summer internships. That's why I moved to St.

Louis. But it seems you've changed directions, too. I thought you'd be back at the Associated Press by now."

Her eyes went flat. "No. I've seen enough blood, sweat and tears to last a lifetime. This suits me just fine." She checked her watch, and he got the message.

"I know you're on a tight schedule, so I won't keep you." He reached into the pocket of his jacket and withdrew a small, tissue-wrapped object. "When I was packing for the move, I came across this among Michael's things. A few weeks after he...after the bombing...AP sent me some personal effects that had been returned by the authorities. I didn't give them more than a cursory look at the time. It was too hard." He stopped and cleared his throat. "I did notice this, but to be honest, I thought it had been sent to me by mistake, that it belonged to one of the other victims. It wasn't a symbol I would have associated with Michael. But when I was packing, I looked at it more closely and saw the initials. I think it must have been something you gave him. So I thought you should have it." He handed it across her desk, his lean, strong fingers brushing hers as she reached for it.

Curious, Caroline unwrapped the tissue. Nestled inside lay a small pewter anchor on a chain. As she stared at the medallion, the air rushed out of her lungs in a sudden whoosh. She groped for the edge of her desk, and for a brief second the room tilted. Then firm, steadying hands gripped her upper arms, and the world stabilized.

"Are you okay? Why don't you sit down for a minute?"

She drew in a ragged breath before she lifted her head. David's concerned face was just inches from hers as he leaned across her desk.

"I'm fine. It was just a…a shock." Nevertheless, she made a move to sit in her chair, not trusting her shaky legs to hold her up.

As David released her arms, he shoved one hand in the pocket of his slacks. "I was pretty sure the initials on the back were yours."

Turning the anchor over, she traced the familiar inscription with a gentle finger. CMJ to MWS.

"I gave this to Michael the Christmas we got engaged." Her voice was whisper-soft. "He always told me that I was his anchor. That whenever the world got too crazy, he would think about me, and then everything made sense again. That I kept him stable through the storms of life. After I gave this to him, he never took it off. He said it was his good luck charm."

Her voice choked on the last word, and David swallowed hard. No doubt they were sharing the same thought: that he hadn't been so lucky the day he'd gone to the marketplace.

"There's something I've been wanting to say to you for two years, Caroline. I'm sure you know that Michael and I argued about Mom the night before he was…before he died. And that our relationship had been strained for several weeks. You have every right to put at least some of the blame for his death on me. I know he was upset when we talked. And I'm sure he was distracted when he went out on that assignment the next day. I lived with the guilt for almost two years, and even though I found some measure of peace about it after a great deal of prayer, I suspect it will always be with me to some degree. I just want you to know how sorry I am. And that I hope you can find it in your heart someday to forgive me."

The regret and anguish on David's face mirrored that in her heart. Yet she knew hers was far more deserved. That she was even more culpable than the man across from her. No one else was aware of that, though. She'd never spoken to anyone of the part she had played in Michael's death. But now that she realized the depth of David's distress, had glimpsed the burden of pain that weighed down his heart as he shouldered all the blame, she couldn't in good conscience keep her role a secret from him. It wouldn't be honest. Or moral. She might not agree with the steps he'd taken, against Michael's wishes, to institutionalize their mother, but she couldn't let him continue to think that he alone was at fault for the tragedy.

Gripping the medallion in a tight fist, Caroline rose. When she spoke, her voice was taut with tension. "The guilt isn't all yours, David. Or even mostly yours."

"What do you mean?" He sent her a puzzled look.

She tried to swallow past the lump in her throat. "Michael shouldn't have been in the marketplace that day. It was supposed to be me. I was working on a hot story, but I got sick. He volunteered to meet my contact for me." Her face contorted with anguish, and when she continued her voice was a mere whisper. "I was the one who should have been killed by the suicide bomber."

A shock wave passed through David as he digested Caroline's revelation—and tried to comprehend its ramifications. Somewhere, in a far corner of his mind, he realized that her confession had absolved him from a portion of the blame for the tragedy, and he felt a subtle easing of the guilt that had burdened his heart for two years. But in the forefront of his consciousness was the realization that for those same two years the woman across from him had borne a burden even greater than his on her slender shoulders. The man she loved had done her a favor, had taken her place and he'd been killed. He'd thought his guilt had been wrenching. How much more intense it must have been for Caroline, who lived now because Michael had died.

The devastated look on her face bore that out and twisted his gut into a painful knot.

"I'm sorry, Caroline." The words were wholly inadequate, but he didn't know what else to say.

"I'm the one who's sorry," she whispered. "You have every right to hate me."

"How can I hate you for getting sick?"

"Because I shouldn't have let that stop me. I still should have gone. It was my responsibility, not Michael's."

"How sick were you?"

She shrugged. "Pretty sick. I had some weird virus."

"Did you have a fever?"

"Yes. A hundred and three."

"You needed to stay in bed."

"That's what Michael said."

"He was right."

"No." Her voice was resolute. "I should have gone."

"You'd have been killed."

"I know. But it *should* have been me." Her voice broke on the last word.

"Do you think that's what Michael would have wanted?"

David's quiet question startled her. And the answer was obvious. No, of course not. Given a choice between who would live and who would die, Michael would have taken her place in a heartbeat. But that was beside the point. She wouldn't have let him.

She shook her head. "Thanks for trying. And thank you for this." She cradled the medallion in her hand, fighting back tears. She hadn't cried at work in a long time. And she didn't intend to start now.

"Maybe God had other plans for you, Caroline. Maybe that's why He took Michael instead of you."

Jolted, she stared at him. That was a new thought. And a generous one, considering that she was the primary reason David had lost the brother he loved. But it wasn't one she put much stock in. She saw no greater purpose in her life than had been in Michael's, didn't think she had any more to contribute than he had. His work had been Pulitzer-prize quality. She was good at her job, but not as good as he had been. No, that explanation didn't hold up for her.

She was saved from having to respond by the jarring ring of the phone, reminding her that she had an interview to conduct. Even if talking with the mayor right now about the new zoning law was about as appealing as...playing her mother's guessing game.

"That must be your interview. I'll let myself out."

"Thank you for coming today," she said as she reached for the phone.

"It was long overdue."

As she put the phone to her ear, mouthed a greeting and waited to be connected to the mayor, she watched David make a quick exit, then weave through the newsroom toward the front door. When he reached it, he turned back. Their gazes connected, and held, for a brief second. But it was long enough for Caroline to sense that for David, their meeting today had provided a sense of closure. Then he lifted his hand and disappeared through the door. It shut behind him, with a symbolic sense of finality, giving her the distinct feeling that he had no intention of contacting her again. That his visit today had tied up the last loose end associated with Michael's death.

Caroline wished she could find that same sense of closure. That she, too, could shut the door on her past. But for her, the pain, the regret, the guilt, just wouldn't go away.

David, on the other hand, seemed to have found some sense of comfort, some relief, some absolution, in his faith. Not to mention a wellspring of charity. Instead of hating her when she'd revealed her part in Michael's death—as he'd had every right to do—he'd put it in the hands of the Lord, suggesting that perhaps God had other plans for her.

And for just a moment, as she had on that Christmas when they'd met, she envied him his bond with a greater power, which had given him answers and lightened his burdens while hers still weighed down her soul.

Chapter Two

"That's good news on the funding front, Martin. Every donation helps. Thanks for the report." Chairman Mark Holton checked the agenda for the Uplink board meeting. "Looks like you're next, Allison. What's the latest on signing up mentoring organizations?"

"Good news there, too. Several more businesses have agreed to take on student interns over the summer. But a lot of the companies I contacted had never heard of Uplink. I think we need to find a way to generate some additional publicity."

"Point well taken." Mark surveyed the eight-member board, ending with David. "Any thoughts?"

"Well, after only a couple of months on the job, I have limited experience to draw on," David responded. "But I've run into the same issue with my outreach efforts at schools. Some of the administrators are familiar with the program, but most of the students aren't. It wouldn't hurt to have some coverage in the local media."

"I agree." Mark turned to Rachel Harris, the publicity chairperson. "Have we pitched any stories in the past few weeks?"

"No. Not since the *Post-Dispatch* did that piece last fall. It might not be a bad idea to contact the *Chronicle*, considering its wide reach. I can make a cold call, but if anyone has a connection there it would be helpful."

"I know the managing editor," David offered.

"Excellent." Mark jotted a few notes on a pad in front of him.

Now what had prompted him to blurt that out? David chided himself in dismay. He'd had no intention of contacting Caroline again after he walked out of her office a few days before.

"Could you make a call?" Mark asked. "Rachel can follow up, but it might help if you paved the way."

David wasn't so sure about that. But short of explaining his link to Caroline—which he didn't intend to do—he was left with no option but to agree. "Sure. I'll call her later this week."

"All right. Now why don't you bring us up-to-date on your outreach efforts at the schools."

As David gave them a quick overview of his busy schedule of visits to area high schools, he focused on a few institutions in the most troubled parts of the city, where he'd put a great deal of effort into recruiting participants. When he ticked off their names, a few board members shifted in their seats and exchanged uneasy glances.

"Is there a problem?" David asked.

"I think there's some concern about soliciting participants from those schools," Mark told him when no one else spoke. "Many of them have gang problems, and those students may not be the best representatives for our program right now. If any of them cause trouble at their assigned businesses, it could hinder our efforts."

"And if they succeed, it could help our cause."

"It's the *if* we're worried about."

"Let me make sure I understand the issue." David folded his hands on the table in front of him and leveled a direct gaze at the chairman. "I thought the mission of Uplink was to reach out to gifted students who were in environments that might sabotage their continued education. I was working on the assumption that our goal was to offer them an opportunity to develop their talents and encourage them to continue in school by giving them role models and experience in a real-world setting. To provide them with a taste of the kind of life they might have if they persevere despite the obstacles that their present situations might present. Is that correct?"

"Yes," Mark affirmed.

"Then we need to be aggressive in our recruiting or we'll fail."

"We'll also fail if we recruit students who cause problems with the participating businesses."

Stifling a frustrated sigh, David nodded. "Understood. But unless we offer this program to those who need it most, we're doing a disservice to our mission."

"David has a point." All heads swiveled toward Reverend Steve Dempsky, one of the charter board members. "If we play this too safe, the program loses its meaning. Let's not forget that we were heading in that direction under our former director. We brought David in to give the program some punch, to make it more dynamic and cutting edge. I don't think we want to tie his hands at this point. We need to trust his judgment and have confidence he won't take undue risks that put Uplink in danger."

As the board digested the minister's comments, David sent him a grateful look. Steve had been his college roommate, and they'd never lost contact. In fact, Steve had been the one who'd told him about this job and recommended him to the board. He appreciated not only his friend's confidence, but also his willingness to put himself on the line over an issue that was stickier than David had expected.

"Your points are well-taken, Reverend." Mark turned to the other members of the board. "Do we need any further discussion on this?" When those seated around the table shook their heads, Mark nodded. "All right. I'll see you all next month, same time, same place."

The rustle of paper, muted conversation and the scrape of chairs signaled the end of the meeting. David stood, gathered up his notes and made his way toward Steve.

"Thanks for the vote of confidence," he told him.

The sandy-haired minister flashed him a smile and spoke in a low voice. "Just don't blow it. Or we'll both be out on our ear."

A wry smile tugged at the corners of David's lips. "That makes me feel real secure."

The other man laughed and put his hand on David's arm. "Just kidding. I trust your instincts. But if you need a second opinion about any of your candidates, I'll be glad to talk to them, too."

"I may take you up on that."

"Will I see you at services Sunday?"

"Have I missed a week yet?"

"No. You're very faithful. I just wish I could have convinced you years ago to give religion a try."

"The timing wasn't right, I guess."

"Well, I'm glad you finally saw the light. Listen, call me some night next week and we'll go out for pizza. Monica will be in Chicago for a conference, and I'll be scavenging for food."

"You could learn to cook."

"My friend, I have been blessed with a number of talents. But cooking is not among them. My culinary forays have been a disaster. In fact, Monica has banned me from the stove and the oven when she's home. Trust me, she'll be glad if I eat out instead of messing up her kitchen. So call me, okay?"

A chuckle rumbled deep in David's chest. "You've got a deal."

"And don't worry about today's meeting. The board has always tended to err on the side of caution, but the members are working on that. Intellectually, they realize that nothing worth doing is accomplished without some risk, but it will take a little time for that understanding to reach their hearts. In the meantime, follow your instincts."

Another board member claimed Steve's attention, and David turned with a wave and headed toward the door. Despite Steve's parting words, he wondered if he was pushing too hard. Yet he prayed for guidance every day, and he was convinced God had led him to this place for a reason. He was also sure the Lord wouldn't want him to take the easy way out.

But the board's reaction was unsettling. If he made a wrong step, he could be ousted—just as his predecessor had been. And for a man who until recently had put a high priority on financial security, that was a scary thought. Growing up in a blue-collar family, where times had always been lean—and gotten even leaner when their father died too young and their mother had to take a job as a cook in a diner just to make ends meet—David had vowed to find a career that provided an income high enough to eliminate financial worries. He'd achieved that—in spades—in his former job. But over time he'd felt a call to do something else, something that made a difference in lives instead of balance sheets. Steve's call six months ago, alerting him to an upcoming opening at Uplink, had seemed almost providential. David had prayed about it—had even prayed that God not ask him to apply for it—but in the end, the call had been too strong to ignore. So he'd put his trust in God and taken a leap of faith. He just hoped he hadn't leapt into unemployment.

But as Steve had just reminded him, nothing worth doing was accomplished without some risk. And even if he failed, he would be able to take some comfort in knowing that he'd followed God's call and done his best.

David reached for the receiver, hesitated, then let his hand drop back to his desk. He wished he hadn't volunteered to contact Caroline about a story for the *Chronicle.* Seeing her once had been hard enough. Now he had to call and ask for her assistance. At least it was for a larger cause and not a personal favor. Still, it made him feel uneasy. And unsettled. In fact, he'd been feeling that way ever since his encounter with her the week before.

And he knew exactly why.

For one thing, their meeting had dredged up mem-

ories of the tragedy that had robbed his brother of his
life. Had made him recall the day he'd been pulled out
of a major negotiation session to take an urgent call
that his usually efficient secretary hadn't seemed able
to handle. He remembered muttering, "This better be
important," as he swept past her with an irritated glance.
He'd still been annoyed when he'd picked up the phone.
Until he'd heard Caroline's almost hysterical voice on
the other end of the crackling line, telling him between
ragged sobs that Michael was dead.

David's gut had twisted into a hard knot, and he'd
sagged against the desk, almost as if someone had delivered a physical blow to his midsection. He'd been too
shocked to comprehend much else of what she'd said.
And when she'd hung up, he'd sat there in stunned silence, until at last his secretary had knocked on the door
to remind him that the high-powered group assembled
in the next room was waiting for him.

It had been a nightmare day. And the two weeks
that followed had been just as horrendous. He'd decided not to tell his mother, who was slipping away day
by day, fearing that the news—if she even understood
it—would strain her heart, which was already weak.
So he'd stood alone at the funeral. Caroline had been
beside him physically, but she'd been as unreachable
as the distant peaks he'd spotted on his trek in the Himalayas last year. And looking at her devastated face,
watching the way her hands shook, had only exacerbated his own pain—and guilt.

Seeing her again had brought all those memories
back. So he shouldn't be surprised that the incident
had unsettled him. Nor should he be surprised that the
thought of contacting her again made him uneasy.

But he knew it was more than that. Knew that his feelings reflected something far deeper and less obvious, something he'd fiercely suppressed since the day Michael had escorted Caroline through the door of his mother's apartment and introduced her as his fiancée.

The fact was, from the first moment he'd laid eyes on her, David had been smitten. There was no other word for it. Nor any basis for it. He was an adult, after all. He'd been thirty-four when they met, not some teenager whose hormones could be whipped into a frenzy by the mere sight of a pretty face. In fact, he'd been so stunned by his unexpected reaction to her that he couldn't even recall much about that first meeting. He supposed he'd managed to sound coherent, because no one had acted as if he was behaving oddly. But he'd been so thrown that for the rest of Caroline and Michael's three-day visit, he had made it a point to avoid one-on-one conversations with her. He was afraid his tongue would get tangled up or, worse, that it would sabotage him and say something inappropriate. Such as, "I know you're engaged to my brother, but would you marry me, instead?"

That, of course, wasn't even a consideration. David had never intruded on Michael's turf. Not as a child, not as a teenager, not as an adult. He loved his brother too much to do anything to jeopardize their relationship. In fact, if the truth was known, he'd always had a case of hero worship for him. He'd admired his sense of adventure, his willingness to take risks, his easygoing manner, his go-with-the-flow attitude. Not to mention his choice of women. Particularly his fiancée.

But if Caroline's beauty had bowled him over, he'd discovered other qualities about her in the next few days that had only added to her appeal. She'd been patient and kind with his failing mother, who had enjoyed some of her better days during their visit. He'd been struck by her lively intelligence, her generous spirit, her sense of justice and her passion for her work. In short, he'd been knocked off his feet.

In retrospect, David doubted that Caroline had even noticed him much during that visit. She'd had eyes only for Michael, and the soft light of love on her face when she looked at him had made David, for the first time in his life, jealous of his brother. It had also made him think about all the things he'd missed as he focused on launching his career to the exclusion of everything else—including love. Oh, he'd dated his share of women. But he'd never even considered a serious commitment. The trouble was, even though he'd opened the door to that possibility after her visit, he'd never met anyone who measured up to Caroline.

David knew that his impressions of her had been fleeting. Too fleeting to form the basis for any sort of rational attraction. Yet even as his brain reminded him of that, his heart refused to listen. For some reason, in that one brief visit, she'd touched him in a way no other woman had, before or since. She'd done so again, at Michael's funeral, though on that occasion the attraction was tempered by grief. And guilt. Even now, he could explain it no better than he had been able to two years before. He'd assumed that her appeal would dissipate over time, but he'd been wrong. The minute she'd stepped through the office door last week it had slammed against his chest with the same force that it had the first time they'd met.

As for how to handle his feelings—David had no idea. All he knew was that they were irrational, inappropriate and unsettling. Not to mention guilt-inducing. Caroline had loved Michael. She still did, if her reactions last week were any indication. And he couldn't intrude on his brother's turf. It hadn't felt right two and a half years ago, and it didn't feel right now. Even if the lady was willing or interested. And Caroline didn't fall into either of those categories. So his best plan was to make the call, ask for the favor and forget about her.

But considering the way his feelings had returned with such intensity after a two-year gap in contact, he suspected that plan was destined for failure.

"I have David Sloan on line three for you. Do you want to take the call?"

Caroline's hand jerked, making her pen squiggle across the copy she was editing. With dismay, she eyed the erratic red line sprawled across the typed page. So much for her usual neat, legible edits.

Why was David calling her? When he'd walked out the door last week, she'd been convinced that she'd never hear from him again. There had been a sense of finality about his visit, of closure. Now he was back. And she wasn't anxious to talk with him. It had taken her several days after his last visit to rebury the memories and pain it had dredged up. She didn't want to go through that again.

Still, she was curious. David didn't strike her as the kind of man who did things without a great deal of thought. Nor without good reason. Whatever the purpose of his call, she assumed it was important.

Shifting the phone on her ear, she laid down her pen and rotated her chair so that her back was toward the newsroom. "Go ahead and put it through, Mary. Thanks."

A second later, David's voice came over the line. "Caroline?"

"Yes, hi. I didn't expect to hear from you again so soon."

"I didn't expect to be calling. But we had a discussion earlier this week at the Uplink board meeting about the need for publicity, and I offered to contact you to see if the *Chronicle* might be interested in running a piece about the organization."

So this was a business call. She hadn't expected that, either. But it was much easier to deal with. The knot of tension in her stomach eased.

In journalist mode, she swiveled her chair back toward her desk, reached for a pen and drew a pad of paper toward her. "We're always looking for good story leads. But I have to confess that I'm not familiar with Uplink."

"That's the problem. Not enough people are. And that hampers our ability to fully realize our mission."

"Which is?"

"We target gifted high school juniors in difficult environments and match them with mentors in participating businesses for summer internships to provide them with a taste of a real-world work environment. We hope the experience gives them not only a stimulating summer job, but an incentive to continue with their education. Then we follow up with ongoing support groups to ensure that we don't lose them after their internships."

"You mentioned some of this last week. Sounds worthwhile."

"We think so. But the organization is only three

years old—still a fledgling. There's a lot more we could do if this really takes off. For that to happen, though, we need to heighten awareness."

"What sort of article did you have in mind?"

"I'm not sure. One of the board members, Rachel Harris, handles publicity and communication. She can follow up with more information if you're interested in pursuing this. My role was just to get a foot in the door."

"All right." Caroline jotted the woman's name down, then laid the pen aside. "Have her give me a call. If we can find a good angle, it might make an interesting article."

"That would be great. We'd appreciate it."

"Like I said, we're always looking for good stories. But I have to admit I'm curious about how you became connected with the group. This seems far removed from your previous job."

The momentary silence on the other end of the line told her he was surprised by the question. And so was she. She hadn't planned to introduce anything personal to their conversation. The comment had just popped out.

Despite his initial reaction, however, David's tone was conversational when he responded. "It is. I'd been doing a lot of soul-searching for the past few years, and I began to feel a need to do something with my life that had more purpose than just making a lot of money."

A melancholy smile whispered at the corners of her mouth. "Michael used to say almost exactly the same thing."

Her comment startled him. No one had ever compared him to his brother before. It made him feel good, and odd at the same time. "I guess that's true," he acknowledged. "But my impetus was different. It grew out of long conversations with God."

"You're right. Michael was driven by a deep sense of ethics versus faith, and by a desire to help improve the human race."

"I guess our goal was the same, then. Just not the motivation."

"Well…I wish you luck with the job. It sounds like good work. I'll be expecting Rachel's call."

"Great. We appreciate anything you can do. Take care."

The line went dead, and Caroline put the phone back in its holder. She still wasn't sure why she'd asked about his new job. It had moved them out of a safe topic and into touchy personal territory. Maybe it had just been her professional curiosity kicking in. Since asking questions was part of her job, it made sense that she would delve a little deeper with David. Didn't it?

The answer came to her in a flash. No. If she'd wanted to avoid personal discussion, if she'd wanted to get off the phone as fast as possible, she'd have ended the conversation instead of detouring to a more personal line of questioning.

Okay, so much for her first theory. She tried another one on for size. Maybe contact with David made her feel, in some way, connected with Michael. As if, through David, Michael was still somehow part of her life in a tangible way. She and David were the only ones who had really known, and loved, the man she'd planned to marry. Her mother was a great sounding board, and she'd listened with infinite patience when Caroline had reached the stage of grief where she could talk about her fiancé, and share some of her memories.

But her mother had no firsthand knowledge of him beyond that brief Christmas visit to both families.

David, on the other hand, had years' worth of memories of Michael. Ones that Caroline didn't have. His bond to the prize-winning photojournalist was as strong as hers, in a different way. Maybe, on some subconscious level, she wanted to tap into them. To supplement her own memories of the man she'd loved, who had talked of his past only on rare occasions. And maybe she also wanted to shore up her memories. In recent months it had grown harder for her to picture Michael's face without the aid of a photograph. She'd already begun to forget the unique sound of his voice. Along with the feel of his touch. She didn't want to let go of Michael, but he was slipping away, bit by bit. And that frightened her. Perhaps her reaching out to David today had been driven by fear, and by a desire to connect with the one man who had the best chance of keeping Michael alive for her.

Yes, no doubt that was it.

Satisfied, Caroline reached for her red pen and pulled the copy back toward her. Only then did she realize that her jerky squiggle bore a striking resemblance to half of a heart. How appropriate, she reflected with a pang. Half a heart was exactly what she felt like she had. The rest had died along with the man she loved.

And there was nothing David Sloan could do to fix that.

"Here's some information on Uplink. And I asked Mitch about it, too." Tess Jackson laid the material on Caroline's desk, taking the seat the managing editor waved her into.

"Did he know anything?"

"Not a lot. It's targeted more toward inner-city schools. But he made a few calls, and in general heard glowing reports from his colleagues. He thought it would be a very worthwhile feature. I do, too, from a journalistic perspective."

After a quick scan of the material, Caroline leaned back in her chair and steepled her fingers. She respected Mitch Jackson, a former cop whose innovative work as a hands-on high school principal had drawn state-wide notice. His personal interventions had steered dozens of wayward students back to the right path. She also respected his wife's assessment of the story potential. That was why Tess had been promoted in two short years to assistant editor.

"Okay. What kind of angle do you propose?"

"Human interest. I think we should include some history of Uplink, but focus on a couple of the students who've been through the program and talk about what a difference it made in their lives. We'd want to include interviews with the businesses that were involved, the students and the executive director, as well as the chairman of the board."

"Sounds good. Who should we assign?"

"As a matter of fact, I'd like to take this one. I think I have a good feel for the subject, given Mitch's work at the high school. Unless you want to do it. After that story you did on gangs last year, you've got an understanding of the problems out there, and the need for intervention. Besides, it should be a meaty piece, and you like to tackle those."

Caroline had already thought this through. And had come to the conclusion that whatever her motives in yesterday's conversation with David, it wasn't wise to prolong contact with him. In addition to the painful memories that were rekindled, there were too many unresolved questions that she didn't want to dredge up. Like, why had David insisted on putting his mother in an extended-care facility so soon after their visit, breaking a promise both brothers had made to her years before? She'd overheard the two men discussing it one evening, in subdued tones near the Christmas tree, and while she hadn't been able to make out the words—nor had she tried to—the frustration in both voices had been unmistakable.

In the end, she'd sided with Michael. Martha Sloan might have been a bit vague, but Caroline hadn't seen any evidence of advanced Alzheimer's during their visit. Certainly not enough to warrant institutionalization. David had agreed to hold off, but then had called Michael a month later to tell him that he was going to move her into a nursing facility anyway. Michael had asked him to wait until they could discuss it in person, when he and Caroline returned later in the year for their wedding, but David had refused. The brothers hadn't talked again until the night before Michael died, when David had called to tell him that their mother had suffered a mild heart attack.

It was odd, really. Back then, David hadn't struck her as uncaring or cavalier. Or as a man who broke his promises. He still didn't. She found it hard to think of him as someone who would disregard the wishes of a person he loved. Yet the facts all pointed to that. And it wasn't something she respected. Nor wanted to discuss. But if they continued to have contact, it would no doubt come up, since it had been such a point of contention between the brothers. As a result, it was best if she let someone else handle the story.

"No. You do it, Tess. I'll refer Rachel Harris to you when she calls."

"You're sure?"

"Absolutely."

"Okay. I'll dive in as soon as we hear from Rachel. Any special timing on this?"

From what David had said, the group wanted to raise its profile as soon as possible. Of course, that couldn't be a factor in her decision. She had to do what was best for the paper and for the readers. Still, there was a piece about home schooling scheduled for two editions down the road that was pretty timeless. She checked the run list.

"If we bump the home-school piece a week, we could use this March twenty-seventh. Do you think you can have it ready by then?"

"Assuming the Uplink people get back to us right away, that shouldn't be a problem," Tess assured her.

"Okay. Let's shoot for that. But that deadline isn't written in stone. We can shift it later if necessary."

"Got it. Anything else?"

"No. That should do it. Let me know if you run into any snags." Caroline turned back toward her computer.

"Will do. How's the budget coming?"

Grimacing, Caroline shook her head, her focus still on the screen in front of her. "I didn't go into journalism to crunch numbers," she grumbled.

"Somebody has to do it. And better you than me."

With a mirthless grin, Caroline waved her out. "Thanks for the sympathy."

"At least the budget will distract you from the nasty

letters we've been getting about that story we ran on the group home for juvenile offenders," Tess offered as she exited.

"Good point." Though the article had been straight-forward and objective, neighbors of the home had chosen to view it as an endorsement. They hadn't ap-preciated that, and had been very vocal in their disap-proval of the paper's perceived position.

If the budget work distracted her from that can of worms, maybe there was a plus to it, Caroline conceded. And she'd be even more grateful if it distracted her from David. She didn't want to think about him anymore. Despite his calm, in-control demeanor, his presence in her life had been disruptive. For reasons that eluded her, she couldn't seem to quash thoughts of him. Maybe crunching numbers would do the trick. That would re-quire her absolute and total concentration.

And for some reason, she had a feeling it would take something that attention-demanding to keep thoughts of David at bay.

Chapter Three

As he was being introduced, David surveyed the students in the high school auditorium from his seat on the stage. Most looked bored and made no pretense of listening to Principal Charles Elliot's comments. Others were scribbling in notebooks or staring into space. Out of the hundred or hundred-and-fifty juniors, David estimated that maybe ten percent were interested. It was about the same percentage he'd run into in many of the inner-city schools. But if this presentation went as well as previous ones, he expected that percentage would double or even triple. He couldn't ask for more than that. Besides, they only had places for twenty-five students in the program this summer, anyway.

When the principal turned to him, David sent an encouraging glance to the two former Uplink students seated beside him, then rose and moved forward. He shook the man's hand, pulled the microphone from its stand and came out from behind the podium. His stance was casual, his tone conversational, his attitude approachable.

"Good afternoon. As Mr. Elliot said, I'm David Sloan, the executive director of Uplink. With me today are two students who've participated in our program. For the next forty-five minutes, we'd like to talk with you about an opportunity that could change your life forever."

With passion, conviction and enthusiasm, David explained the principles behind Uplink and spoke of the successes already documented by the program. The testimonials from the two students, who were now attending college on scholarships, were also powerful, making it clear that for committed students, Uplink opened doors to a future that would otherwise have been inaccessible. Neither they nor David made it sound easy, because it wasn't. It took talent and dedication to get in, and the rigorous screening and ongoing evaluation process intimidated a lot of kids. Participation required guts and focus and lots of hard work. But for those who persevered, the rewards were great.

By the time they finished, David figured that a good twenty-five percent of the students in the audience had been captivated enough to at least pay attention. Not bad. If five or six ended up applying, he'd consider it a good day's work.

They stayed around after the presentation ended in case any of the students wanted to speak with them one-on-one, but it didn't surprise David when only a couple came forward. In North St. Louis, where drugs and gangs were rampant and academics wasn't always valued or supported at home, few students would publicly acknowledge an interest in a program like Uplink. Those who decided to apply would follow up without fanfare, in confidence. David understood that and didn't push. That first step took courage, and he considered it a good barometer of genuine interest.

As he thanked the two students who had accompanied him, David turned to find Charles Elliot approaching. The man took David's hand in a firm grip.

"I appreciate your coming today. I expect you'll hear from a few of the students."

"I hope so. I understand that we've had a couple of students from here in the program every year since its inception."

"That's right. I'm a great believer in Uplink, and I talk it up whenever I get the chance. Can I walk you out?"

"Thanks."

David reached for his leather jacket, which he'd slung over the back of his folding chair, and slid his arms into the sleeves as they headed toward the exit. The assembly had marked the end of the school day for the juniors, and they'd cleared out with a speed that rivaled a race car in the home stretch. The rest of the students had been dismissed ten or fifteen minutes earlier. The two men's footsteps echoed hollowly as they walked down the long, deserted corridor toward the exit.

A classroom door opened as they passed, and a woman in a paint-spattered smock, her short black hair a mass of tight curls, spoke when she caught sight of them.

"Oh, Charles…I'm glad I caught you. Do you have a second to sign that exhibit application?"

"Of course." He turned back to David in apology. "I'll be right with you. Sylvia is the art teacher, and she's trying to get some of our students' work included in a traveling exhibition sponsored by a national company."

"Take your time. I'm in no hurry."

While he waited, David examined some of the art-work that hung in the hallway near the classroom door. A variety of mediums was represented, and many of the pieces were impressive. He stopped to examine a striking abstract watercolor, then moved on to a pen-and-ink sketch of a mother and child, caught by their poignant expressions of disillusionment. But it was the next series of three black-and-white photographs that mesmerized him.

The first was a portrait of an older woman wear-ing wire-rimmed glasses, her close-cropped black hair peppered with gray. She sat in front of a window, a bit off center, at a chipped, Formica table, one side of her face in sharp relief, the other shadowed. One work-worn hand rested on the Bible in her lap, the other lay beside a daffodil on the scratched surface of the table. Behind her, the paint on the walls was chipped, the windowsill scarred. Part of a calendar was visible, and the photo-graph of the month featured a quiet, peaceful country lane bordered by apple trees laden with blossoms. The photographer had titled the photo "Beauty."

The next photo was just as powerful. Two small chil-dren in mismatched clothes sat on a concrete stoop. The low angle of the shot drew the eye upward, past the bro-ken windows of a dingy tenement to the open expanse of sky above. The children's raised faces were illumi-nated with an almost transcendent light as they gazed at the clouds drifting overhead. It bore the title "Imagine."

The last picture also displayed a masterful use of

light and a stellar aptitude for composition. There were no people visible in the shot. Just the shadow of a man, his hand extended toward another smaller shadow that was reaching up to him. The dark outlines stretched across a good part of the frame, covering the broken bottles and garbage that littered the foreground. They were poised at the base of a flight of steps that led upward and out of the frame to a higher, unknown and unseen place. The camera had caught them as they prepared to ascend. It was titled "Together."

Though the images were stark and bleak at first glance, that wasn't what caught David's interest. While the subjects were different, they shared a powerful common theme—hope. Captured in a simple, but dramatic and symbolic style. David was overwhelmed.

Until Michael had discovered his talent for photography, David had never paid much attention to that art beyond the occasional fuzzy family snapshots his mother sometimes took. But as Michael pursued his passion, as he learned to work magic with a couple of lenses and the striking use of angle and light, David had learned to appreciate the potential and power of a camera in the hands of a master. Like the photographer of these images, Michael had had the ability to touch hearts, to communicate messages that continued to resonate long after people put the photo aside. It was a great gift, one that had allowed Michael to find his true calling. And the photographer of these photos seemed to share that gift.

"They're pretty amazing, aren't they?"

Charles had rejoined him, and David turned to the

principal. "Amazing is an apt description. Were these done by a student?"

"Yes. Jared Poole. They were part of an art assignment for Sylvia's junior class."

Looking back at the photos, David shook his head. "I hope he plans to pursue his talent."

When the other man didn't respond, David turned toward him again. Charles's face was troubled, and he gave a resigned sigh before he spoke. "Jared has some… problems. He got involved with a gang a couple of years ago, and he's had some minor run-ins with the law. Nothing too serious—yet. But he's headed in the wrong direction. Truancy has also been an issue. He has a lot to offer, including very strong writing skills, but he just doesn't make school a priority."

"That's too bad. What's the family situation like?" Since taking the job at Uplink, David had already learned that without support at home, there was little chance that problem students would buckle down at school.

"Not good. He lives with his grandmother. That's her picture, in fact." He indicated the photo of the woman with the Bible. "His father disappeared before he was born. His mother died of a drug overdose when Jared was about eight. It's just been him and his grandmother ever since. I've met her, and I know she loves him very much. But she works nights, cleaning offices, so Jared is on his own a lot. The gang became a surrogate family for him. I've tried to talk to him, but I don't think I've gotten through. I did hear through the grapevine that he's trying to break his gang ties. But even if that's true, it's not easy to do."

In his brief tenure at Uplink, David had heard any number of similar stories. They always left him feeling helpless, wishing he could do more. But he knew his limitations. He couldn't take a personal interest in every troubled teenager he ran across. The best he could do was pour his heart and soul into Uplink and hope that his efforts would make a difference in at least a few lives.

Charles led the way toward the front door, sending David off with a firm handshake and another thank-you.

"Let me know if any of our students contact you. I'll be glad to give you my thoughts on whether they'd make good candidates for Uplink," he offered.

"I'll do that."

As David stepped outside, a gust of bitter March wind assaulted him, and he turned up his collar and stuck his hands in the pockets of his jacket. Late-afternoon shadows from the chainlink fence around the school slanted across the buckled sidewalk, and dilapidated buildings, crumbling concrete and rusty metal were all he could see in any direction. The place reeked of decay and despair.

But inside the building behind him, captured in those stark black-and-white photos, hope lived amidst the gloom and desperation around him. And as he walked to his car, he prayed that the young man who had captured it in those images would also find a way to incorporate it into his life.

A knock sounded on her office door, and Caroline looked up. "Come in, Tess. What's up?"

"Sorry to interrupt, but Bruce was injured at school.

Some scenery he was painting for the school play fell, and he needs a few stitches. Mitch is taking him to the hospital, and I'd like to meet them there."

"Of course. You don't need to ask permission. Just go."

"The thing is, I was supposed to attend a presentation today by David Sloan at one of the high schools, and then interview him afterward at his office. That was the last interview I needed for the story. If I have to reschedule, I'll miss the deadline."

A few seconds of silence ticked by while Caroline considered her options. She could offer to do the interview and pass her notes on to Tess. They'd worked together doing research and interviews on a number of complex stories. But that meant she'd have to deal with David again. Or she could just reschedule the story. The home-schooling piece was finished and could be dropped into the Uplink slot with no problem. That would delay the Uplink story by a week, but they'd made no promises about when it would appear.

"Let's reschedule," Caroline decided.

"Okay. I'll give him a call."

The matter decided, Caroline went back to editing the next week's edition—only to be interrupted again a few minutes later by Tess.

"Sorry to cause problems, Caroline. But David Sloan says he only has one more presentation, and it's not for two weeks. If we put this off, we'll have to push the story into mid-April."

Not good. Caroline had only the home-schooling piece in reserve. If she used it for the next issue, they'd need the Uplink story for the following edition. Or else she'd have to scramble to come up with another meaty feature. All at once her options shrank.

"Okay. I'll cover for you today."

"Are you sure? I guess I could just let Mitch handle things at the hospital."

Caroline heard the uncertainty in Tess's voice and recalled the difficult time her assistant editor had had with her son just three years before, when she'd moved to St. Louis after losing her job due to downsizing at a small-town Missouri newspaper. She'd found a new life in St. Louis—and a new love in Mitch Jackson, who had helped her get her son back on the right path when he'd fallen in with the wrong group. Caroline understood Tess's need to be present today.

"Go ahead. Don't worry about it. Just give me the details and I'll handle this. Emergencies happen."

Gratitude filled the other woman's eyes. "Have I told you lately that you're a great boss?"

A flush crept up Caroline's neck. "Hey, work is important but family comes first. Let David know I'll be taking your place. Then get out of here."

As she watched Tess make a hasty exit, Caroline thought about what she'd just said. She hadn't always been as understanding about personal obligations. There had been a time when she'd put the highest priority on her work, on rising through the ranks of journalism to nab a top spot. A time when she'd looked with disdain on those who put their personal life ahead of getting the story. Then she'd met Michael. Committed to his work, passionate about truth, he'd nevertheless had perspective, recognizing the critical importance of balance.

He'd worked hard, but he'd also made time for other things—and for people.

In retrospect, Caroline had often wondered if he'd known at some unconscious level that his stay on earth would be brief. It was as if he had been driven to savor each second, to suck every drop of sweetness from each moment, to treat each new day as a gift, as an opportunity to learn and to grow and to become a better person. That attitude had carried over to his work, compelling him to portray even the most horrible circumstances with empathy and compassion. Even images that had made her cringe in their rawness had been infused with humanity. And in his portraits, he always captured the essence of those he photographed, putting a face on tragedy in a way that touched people and softened even the most cynical hearts. That had been his gift.

With Michael, Caroline had learned to see with new eyes. And to forge a new perspective, one that recognized the importance of love and relationships. It was a lesson she never wanted to forget. And the situation with Tess was just one way she'd been able to put that philosophy into action.

Unfortunately, it also put her in the line of fire. She didn't relish another encounter with David. But she was a professional. She'd treat this just like any other interview. And when she was finished, there'd be no reason for their paths to cross again. Tess would write the article, the *Chronicle* would run it and Uplink would have the publicity it had sought.

End of story.

* * *

As the principal did the introductions, David scanned the crowd. He'd gotten Tess's message just as he walked out the door of his office, so he knew Caroline would be in the audience instead of the assistant editor. And he had mixed feelings about that.

Even though his primary purpose in going to the *Chronicle* had been to give her the medallion and to apologize, he'd also hoped to discover that her captivating charm had lessened. Instead, he'd found that the opposite was true. And he still had no logical explanation for it. All he knew was that his safest course was to steer clear of her in the future. That's why he hadn't been all that keen on contacting her about the Uplink story. But at least that had been by phone. He hadn't had to look into those appealing hazel eyes. And he'd figured that would be the end of it.

Now she was in the audience. Afterward, she'd come back to his office to do an interview. And despite all of the rational reasons why her presence was bad, he couldn't stop the sudden rush of happiness and anticipation that swept through his heart, like an unexpected, glorious burst of sun streaming through the clouds on a gray, overcast day.

She wasn't hard to pick out. Her hair would give her away in any crowd, but especially here, where the glints of copper shimmered in the bright overhead light, and her fair complexion stood out in the sea of ebony faces. He watched as she withdrew a notebook from her large shoulder bag and flipped it open, then settled back in her seat in the last row and looked toward the stage. When their gazes connected, he gave her a welcoming smile. Her lips turned up just the slightest bit in response before she shifted her attention to the principal, who was just about to introduce David. And he better get focused, too, David reminded himself. He needed to concentrate on the presentation and forget about Caroline for the next forty-five minutes.

It wasn't easy to switch gears, but once he started talking, his focus became absolute, as it always did. No matter how often he gave this talk, his enthusiasm for the program and his passion for the principles it represented came through loud and clear.

None of which was lost on Caroline. Though she'd had only a few minutes to prep, she'd given the material Tess had collected and her assistant editor's notes from previous interviews a cursory review. She'd been impressed by Uplink and what it had accomplished in a short time, and she was just as impressed by David's sincerity and obvious commitment to the program. His presentation was dynamic and engaging, and she noticed as he spoke that a number of students who had at first seemed disinterested began to pay closer attention.

By the time he and the Uplink students he'd brought along had finished, the boredom and cynicism in the audience had shifted toward respect and interest. She'd learned enough about the North St. Louis high school environment while working on her gang series to know that David's accomplishment was no small feat. Outsiders were typically viewed with suspicion. And Caucasian outsiders were often viewed with hostility. But there had been an appreciable change in the mood in the auditorium. Caroline was impressed.

As the presentation wound down and the students

were dismissed, Caroline gathered up her things, rose and slipped on her coat. She waited by the back door as David said a few words to the two Uplink students, shook hands with the principal then made his way toward her.

"Thanks for coming on such short notice," he said as he drew close.

"It wasn't a problem. Tess and I have worked together on other stories."

"She said her son had been injured?"

"I don't think it's anything serious. It sounded like he might need a few stitches. But she had some problems with him a few years ago, and now she tries extra hard to be there for him."

"That's commendable. I wish more parents felt that way. Especially parents of students like these."

"I know. I did a series a year or so ago on gang culture, about the power gangs exert over their members and how gangs become a surrogate family in the absence of a real one. The problem of uninvolved parents is very real. And not just in this part of town."

"It makes you wonder why some people have kids, if they aren't willing to take on the responsibilities of parenthood."

"Mitch Jackson, Tess's husband, could give you an earful on that subject. He's the principal at one of the high schools in a pretty affluent area of the city. His stories about uninvolved parents are unbelievable."

David shook his head. "Throw in a cycle of poverty and a culture that doesn't value education, and the problem is only exacerbated. It's an uphill battle, that's for sure. But at least Uplink is trying to offer a few kids a way out." The somber expression on his face gave way to a grin. "But I'm done lecturing for today. Are you ready to leave?"

"Yes."

As they exited the auditorium and walked down the hall toward the front door, Caroline reached into her bag for her keys.

"Where are you parked?" David asked.

"Just down the street."

"I'll walk you to your car."

"You don't need to do that."

"Yes, I do. This isn't the best area of town."

As they stepped through the door, Caroline gave him a wry glance. "I've been in worse places."

True, David mused, recalling Caroline's quick summary of her career when he'd inquired, shortly after they met. Two years on the crime beat for a paper in Atlanta, three years in Washington, D.C., covering politics, then domestic and European assignments for AP before being stationed in a hot zone in the Middle East. How had Michael managed to live with the knowledge that the woman he loved was putting herself in danger day in and day out?

As he looked down at her face, lifted to his, the afternoon sunlight infused her skin with warmth and highlighted a small scar on her right temple, near her hairline. Without stopping to think, he raised his finger and traced the thin white line with a gentle touch. "Is this a souvenir of one of those places?"

The husky quality of his voice, his tender touch, the deep caring in his warm brown eyes so surprised Caroline that for a second she could only stare at him.

At her stunned reaction, David let his hand drop back to his side. Talk about a dumb move. The last thing he needed to do was tip his hand about the embarrassing—and guilt-inducing—feelings he'd been trying to deal with for two and a half years. Besides, they were all one-sided. Caroline had been head-over-heels in love with Michael. She still was, if her reaction to the medallion had been any indication. David had never even been on her radar, except in a negative way after Michael's death. And he wanted to keep it that way. It was much safer.

Shoving his hand in his pocket, he forced his lips into a smile. "Sorry. That's none of my business." He started down the sidewalk, and Caroline fell into step beside him.

"I didn't mind the question." It had just been the way it was asked that had startled her. "And the answer is no. This is of a more recent vintage."

She didn't offer more, and although he was curious, he didn't press her. He needed to stay away from personal topics. "Do you have directions to my office?"

"Yes. It's in Maplewood, right?" Caroline was familiar with the close-in suburb.

"Mmm-hmm. How about we meet there in fifteen minutes?"

"Sounds good."

By the time Caroline pulled up in front of the modest, storefront office for Uplink, she was still mulling over the few seconds at the school when David had touched her—and the disturbing look in his eyes. Though he'd masked it quickly, she'd had a brief glimpse of something she was tempted to call attraction. But she had to be wrong. They'd only met a few times. Even the Christmas she'd visited with Michael, she and David hadn't spoken at any length. She'd spent more time with their mother, figuring the two brothers might want some time alone. And she'd thought little about him since. She hardly knew him. Yet he'd looked at her in a way that made her feel he knew her. And that he'd thought about her a great deal.

Still, she could be jumping to conclusions. David seemed to be a caring man. His involvement with Uplink was proof of that. Maybe he looked at everyone in that same kind, concerned manner. Yet that didn't make sense, either, not after the way he'd treated his mother, breaking a promise both brothers had made to her and disregarding Michael's wishes. In any case, she figured she was reading far too much into a three-second interlude.

Putting thoughts of the incident aside, Caroline slung her bag over her shoulder, stepped out of her car and walked down the busy street toward David's office. Maplewood was enjoying an incredible resurgence, and she made a mental note to do some brainstorming at the next *Chronicle* staff meeting to see if they could come up with a story to highlight the transformation.

When she stepped through the door, a solid, big-boned, middle-aged woman smiled at her from behind a reception desk. "You must be Caroline. Come right in, honey. David had to take a call, but he'll be with you in a minute. Can I get you some coffee?" Her husky voice had a pleasing, rough-around-the-edges quality.

"Yes, thanks. That would be great."

"Cream or sugar?"

"Black is fine. But I can get it." Caroline took note of the coffeemaker off to one side as she dropped her shoulder bag on a chair.

Ignoring her, the woman came out from behind the desk and headed toward the small cabinet. "You just sit. Take the load off. Not that you have much load to take off." A chuckle rumbled deep in the woman's chest as she filled the cup. Then she turned back toward Caroline with a smile that showcased the dazzling white teeth in her dusky face. "Here you go, honey. Nothing like a good cup of coffee late in the afternoon to give you a second wind. I'm Ella, by the way. After Ella Fitzgerald. My mother was a great fan of hers. Hoped I'd be blessed with a voice like she had, too. No such luck, though. I could never carry a tune in a bucket."

With a smile, Caroline took her proffered hand. "It's nice to meet you, Ella."

"I'll let David know you're here."

"Thanks."

While Caroline waited, she surveyed the small reception room. Though the surroundings were pleasant and clean, they were pretty bare-bones. Ella's desk was an older-style metal unit, and the wall behind her was lined with two utilitarian file cabinets. The small grouping of furniture in the waiting room was an eclectic mix of pieces that made Caroline wonder if they might be donations from a variety of sources. There were a few homey touches, though, including a plaque that said, "Bloom where you are planted," and some photos of students receiving awards, plus a table next to the window laden with a variety of flourishing plants.

"Someone has a green thumb," Caroline commented when Ella returned. "Or should I say green hand?"

"David says that I'm turning the office into a greenhouse," Ella told her with another chuckle. "But I like to watch things grow. Plants—or people. Those were all half-dead castoffs when I inherited them. But they just needed a little attention. TLC goes a long way."

Before Caroline could respond, the door behind Ella opened and David motioned her in. "Sorry for the delay. I see Ella took care of you." He nodded to the coffee cup in her hands.

"Yes. It was just what I needed."

"She has a knack for that." David sent the receptionist an affectionate look.

"Now that one's a flatterer," Ella warned Caroline, though it was clear she was pleased by David's compliment. "And I could tell you some other things about him, too."

"Uh-oh. I don't like the sound of that. Come on in, Caroline, before Ella says something I'll live to regret."

Caroline smiled and moved past David into his office. As she took a seat at the small table he indicated in the corner, she again noted the bare-bones nature of the Uplink offices. David's U-shaped desk module and the conference table were wood-grained Formica, while the filing cabinets were gray metal. It was obvious that very little of the money intended for the Uplink program was funneled to administrative expenses. A few personal touches warmed up the room, including some family photos that she surveyed with interest, and an exotic-looking woven wall hanging.

The contrast between David's present work environment and the plush offices he must have enjoyed in his old job struck Caroline. Michael had said he brokered multimillion-dollar mergers and acquisitions, rubbing elbows with the movers and shakers in business. What had made him give all that up?

"I'm new at this interviewing game. What can I tell you about Uplink that Tess hasn't already covered?" David asked, interrupting her musings.

Uplink. That's why she was here, Caroline reminded herself, refocusing her attention. From Tess's notes, she knew the other woman had most of the background information she needed. And Caroline had jotted down a great deal of information during the presentation that could be used to flesh out the story. A few quotes from the executive director would round out the article.

"I don't need much," she told him. "Tess has done a thorough job already. And the meeting today was very helpful. Just tell me a little bit about your role."

David complied, explaining the fundraising, recruiting and administrative duties of the job. But he focused on the recruiting aspect, which he considered to be vital.

"We want to attract the students who can benefit the most from our program," he explained. "For the first few years, my predecessor devoted his time to getting the program established. Now that it is, we're taking a more aggressive approach to recruiting, doing outreach and presentations in schools where there is a high incidence of students who drop out, or where truancy is a problem. The mission of the organization is to reach out to those most in need of intervention, and since I took over on the first of the year, we've moved more and more in that direction."

"Tell me a little about your background, David. This seems like quite a switch from your previous job."

"It's night and day," he acknowledged, then proceeded to confirm what Michael had told her about his high-stakes business career.

"What prompted you to make such a radical change?"

"A friend of mine is on the Uplink board. He told me several months ago that the position would be opening up, and asked if I'd be interested. I don't think he expected me to say yes, but I surprised him. And myself, I might add. I'd been doing a lot of soul-searching about where I wanted to be five years down the road, and I'd come to the conclusion that I needed more to show for my life than a list of mergers and acquisitions I'd helped broker. I wanted to be able to say that my life stood for something more lasting, more important, than dollars and deals. I took to heart something Mother Teresa once said—'God has not called me to be successful, God has called me to be faithful.' And after a lot of prayer and discernment, God led me here."

"This isn't a faith-based organization, though, is it?"

"No. But helping young people get their lives together is one way of doing God's work."

Caroline was again struck by the quiet, deep faith that seemed to guide David's life. Since she hadn't had a chance to probe about it when they'd met, she took advantage of the opportunity. Closing her notebook, she laid it aside. "Can I ask you a question, off the record?"

A flicker of surprise—followed by caution—registered on his face. "Sure."

"Michael told me once that you weren't raised in a home where faith was discussed very much. And his faith was marginal, at best. How did you find your way to God?"

A smile touched the corners of David's mouth. "To be honest, I didn't. He found me."

Curious, Caroline studied him. "If this gets too personal, just tell me to back off, but I'd be interested to hear more about that."

"May I ask why?"

It was a fair question. If she was making personal queries, he had a right to do the same. "I guess I'm intrigued by faith. Maybe even drawn to it. I was raised in a household where faith was important, but over time I just drifted away. When we met that Christmas, there was something about the way you talked about your faith that caught my attention. I'd have liked to talk more to you about it then, but there just wasn't time. Then Michael died, and I didn't think about God for a long time. But in the past few months my interest has started to grow again. To be honest, I'm not sure why."

"I don't think that's an uncommon experience. My initial forays were pretty tentative, too, and I didn't understand the reason. I just felt the need to connect with something bigger, some higher power. And when I did, three or four years ago, my life started to change. Not always in ways that were comfortable, though. This job is a good example. I'm sure Michael told you that we grew up in a lower-income, blue-collar family. Money was always tight. Too tight. I decided that when I grew up I would find a career that gave me financial security. But once I had that, I realized it wasn't enough. That's when I started to listen to the Lord's voice. To put my trust in Him, and to follow the path He was leading me to."

"So one day you just woke up and decided to give up the life you'd created and take this job?"

"It wasn't quite that simple." He leaned back in his chair, and his face grew thoughtful. "I struggled with it for a long time. But my options were limited before Mom died."

Caroline wanted to ask why, but he continued before she had a chance to voice the question.

"After she was gone, I talked to my friend on the Up-link board, who's a minister. I also forced myself to get out of my rut, out of my usual environment, away from the familiar, hoping that a change of scene would give me some new insights. One year, I took a trip down the Amazon. The next, a trek in the Himalayas. That's a souvenir from the second trip." He indicated the woven wall-hanging Caroline had noticed earlier.

Taken aback, Caroline stared at him, trying to reconcile this David with the picture Michael had painted of his cautious, introverted brother, whose idea of an "adventure" vacation—according to Michael—was spending four days camping on the shores of Lake Michigan.

He flashed her a brief grin. "I surprised myself, too. As Michael obviously told you, risk-taking isn't in my nature, and those trips were a stretch for me. But they did help me think about things in a different way. Get a new outlook. Other than those adventures, though, I've led a pretty boring life."

Caroline's eyes grew flat, like landscape thrown in shadow by a dark cloud. "Boring isn't so bad."

Her sudden bleak expression didn't get past David,

and he recalled her comment at the *Chronicle,* that she'd seen enough blood, sweat and tears to last a lifetime. "It can be if it traps you in a life that keeps you from growing in your faith or as a person."

"Maybe." She didn't sound convinced.

"Anyway, after a lot of thought, a lot of prayer and a lot of conversations with my friend, I found my way back to God. And that's how I ended up here."

"Any regrets?"

"Not a one. At least not about the job, and about turning my life over to God." Then his face grew pensive. "But there are other things I would do differently if I had a second chance."

Caroline wondered if he was thinking about his decision to institutionalize his mother. Or about his estrangement from Michael. But she'd asked enough questions today. If she delved any deeper, he could very well turn the tables on her and ask about her regrets. And that wasn't something she wanted to discuss.

Reaching for her tote, Caroline stuffed her notebook inside and slung it over her shoulder, then rose. "Well, thank you for your time today. We're planning to run the article in next week's edition."

Standing, David reached over to grip her hand with his strong, firm fingers. "Thanks for the coverage."

"Like I said when you called, we're always looking for a good story."

When he continued to hold her hand, she searched his eyes. They were a soft, quiet brown, as still and deep as a spring tucked into the shadowed crevices of a woodland grotto. She had the oddest impression that he was looking right into her heart, touching her pain, seeing the secrets and doubts she'd kept long buried.

Feeling off balance, she pulled her hand free and turned to go. "We'll send you some extra copies."

"I'd appreciate that."

He opened his office door, and when she stepped through Ella gave her a smile.

"Well, that didn't take long. Did you get everything you need, honey?"

"Yes. Thanks."

"I figured David would take care of you."

As Caroline exited the office and made her way back to her car, the receptionist's words echoed in her mind. She knew the woman's comment had been in reference to the story. But for some reason, Caroline sensed that it was true on a deeper level. That if she gave him the chance, David would take care of her in far more personal ways as well.

She had no idea where that absurd intuition had come from. She and David had nothing in common beyond a link to Michael. They didn't even know each other very well. She must be losing it.

There was a time when Caroline had relied on her instincts, when she'd trusted them. But if today's experience was any indication, she'd better be a little more cautious about putting her faith in them in the future.

Because this one had been way off base.

Chapter Four

Jared Poole.

The name stared back at David from the Uplink application. So his presentation had reached the gifted photographer. The student who, according to his principal, was trying to break his gang ties. The student who had a truancy problem. The student whose stark black-and-white images on the high school wall had reflected great talent and hope—though the latter was perhaps unconscious, much as Michael had been unaware of his underlying theme of humanity until his mentor had pointed it out.

Jared Poole was exactly the kind of student David was trying to reach with Uplink. But he suspected Jared was also exactly the kind of student the board would classify as high-risk.

As David perused the application, several things became clear. Jared wasn't the strongest student. His grades were marginal, at best. Yet a letter from his art teacher praised his creativity and visual gifts. And as David read the essay required by the application, he had to concur with the English teacher, whose enclosed assessment commended the boy's writing talent.

What he couldn't gauge from the application was Jared's determination and commitment. Much as he wanted to reach out to students like Jared, he understood—and respected—the board's wishes not to take unnecessary risks with the program at this early stage. Jared could be a great success story—or he could spell disaster. And from the pieces of paper in his hand, David couldn't tell which was more probable.

Pulling his school directory toward him, he scanned his list of principals for Charles Elliot's number, then tapped it in.

"David! Good to hear from you. I was just wondering this morning if any of our students had applied to Uplink."

"As a matter of fact, that's why I'm calling. I'm just starting to sift through the applications from all of the high schools, and one of the first ones I came across is from Jared Poole."

A couple of beats of silence ticked by before Charles spoke. "I have to say I'm surprised."

"I am, too, based on our last conversation. He doesn't fit the profile of our typical applicant. At least up until now. In any case, I wanted to take you up on your offer to give me an evaluation of students from your school who applied. How high of a risk do you think he'd be?"

Again, a few beats of silence. "If pressed, I'd have to say fifty-fifty. At best. I wish I could be more positive, but he's got a very spotty record. It's not that he doesn't have the ability to perform. When he wants to, he can apply himself. He just doesn't seem to want to most of the time."

David knew that the board members would have apoplexy if he told them he was even toying with the idea of considering such a high-risk student. "His art and English teachers included pretty strong letters of recommendation."

"Like I said, he can do great work when he's inclined to. Art and English are his two best subjects—as I'm sure you realized, if you checked the transcript required by the application."

"Yes. I saw that."

"I'd hate to be the one who derails his chances, though. With the right support and motivation, he could surprise us all."

Leaning back in his office chair, David looked out his window. The first buds of spring were just starting to come out on the flowering trees that lined the street, waiting for the warmth of the sun to coax them into blossom. Given the right conditions, and some TLC, almost any living thing could thrive. Ella's table of salvaged plants, which had withered and almost died in the hands of a variety of owners, had flourished under her care and attention. People reacted the same way. If he didn't believe that, he wouldn't have taken the job at Uplink.

With sudden decision, he turned back to his desk and pulled Jared's application toward him. "I think I'll talk to him," he told Charles.

"Good idea. You can tell a lot more in person than you can from a piece of paper."

As David hung up the phone, his face grew thoughtful. From his years of negotiating high-stakes deals, where he'd had to rely on his instincts and his ability to do a quick and accurate assessment of the players, he should have the skills to make this determination.

Then again, he hadn't had many dealings with troubled teenagers. Maybe his skills wouldn't hold up with someone like Jared.

But in his heart, he knew he had to try.

At the knock on his door, David looked up.

"Jared Poole is here." On the threshold, Ella rolled her eyes and nodded behind her.

Over her shoulder, David could see a tall, lanky teen slouched against the far wall of the reception area. When Jared looked his way, the defiance in his eyes was unmistakable. Yet David sensed the boy's nervousness beneath the cover of that brash look. Though his posture appeared relaxed, indifferent even, there was an almost palpable tension about him that told David he cared about this interview. And the fact that he'd not only shown up, but was right on time, was also a good sign.

"Thanks, Ella." As she returned to her desk, David rose and walked to the doorway. "Come in, Jared."

The boy pushed away from the wall and moved toward David, taking his time. When David offered his hand, the boy hesitated for a brief second before he took it.

"Come on in and make yourself comfortable." David gestured toward the table. "Would you like a soft drink?"

"No." As an afterthought, he tacked on a mumbled, "Thanks."

David reached for Jared's application from his desk, then took a seat at the table beside him. With his baggy, low-slung pants, torn jacket, scuffed sneakers and dreadlocked hair, he didn't look anything like a typical Uplink applicant. David suspected that if the board were present right now, Jared would get a thumbs-down before he even had a chance to speak. But David was determined not to make any rash judgments.

"I saw some of your photographs on the wall at the school. Very impressive."

The boy shrugged. "They're okay, I guess."

"Tell me a little about your photography. How did you get involved with it?"

"I did some photos for an art project last year with a disposable camera. I guess Mrs. Thompson, the teacher, thought they were pretty good, because she let me borrow the department camera so I could do more complicated stuff."

"What kind of camera is it?"

"An old Olympus manual thirty-five millimeter. Some rich dude donated it to the school when he got tired of it."

"Who taught you to use it?"

He lifted one shoulder. "I just played around with it until I figured it out. And I've read some books about photography."

Self-taught. Impressive. "Why black-and-white instead of color?" David asked, leaning back in his chair.

"I do color, too. But black-and-white is better for... ideas."

"That's what my brother used to say."

"Is he into photography?"

"He was a photojournalist with the Associated Press. Spent years covering the world's trouble spots. He was even nominated for a Pulitzer prize once."

A flicker of interest sparked to life in Jared's eyes. "Is he still doing that?"

"No. He was killed by a suicide bomber in the Middle East while he was on assignment."

The shocked look that ricocheted across Jared's face before his mask of indifference fell back into place told David that the boy wasn't quite as thick-skinned as he tried to appear. "That's tough," he said.

"Yeah. He was very gifted."

"Is he the reason you noticed my stuff on the wall at school?"

"I guess it would be fair to say that. After Michael got involved with photography, I learned to appreciate the power of a camera in the right hands. And I learned to recognize talent." When Jared didn't seem to know how to react to that compliment, David switched gears. "Tell me why you want to be part of Uplink."

"It's all in the essay." Jared gestured to the application lying on the table in front of David.

"I want to hear it from you."

"Look, man, I'm not that good with words."

"That's not what your English teacher said in her letter of recommendation."

"Words on paper, that's okay. I don't speak words that well."

That could be true, David conceded. Some people expressed themselves better in writing—or through photos—than they did verbally. Still, he needed more from Jared. The boy didn't exactly seem to be bubbling over with enthusiasm about the opportunities Uplink provided, and David couldn't offer an internship to someone who didn't appreciate it when dozens of others were desperate for the chance.

Pulling Jared's essay toward him, David scanned it again. It was concise and well-written, but it didn't convey compelling interest. Maybe David should let this go. Maybe he was only pursuing this because something in Jared had reminded him of Michael in his younger days. His brother had also been directionless and floundering until someone had recognized his talent and given him an entrée into the world of photography, putting him on a path that had changed his life. But once discovered, Michael's passion for photography had consumed him, his fervor so intense it was almost tangible. David wasn't sensing anything close to that in Jared. It either wasn't there, or the boy was hiding it well.

Laying the essay back down, David leveled a direct look at the young man across from him. "Let me give this to you straight, Jared. I saw something in your photography the day I was at your school that impressed me. That's why your application stood out—even though your grades overall aren't as high as those of students we've considered for this program in the past. I decided to talk with you because I respect your creative gift. But that gift isn't enough. I want students in Uplink who are passionate about the things they love to do, who have dreams and who are willing to work hard to overcome any obstacles that life might have put in their way to achieve those dreams. I look for drive and determination and commitment. I can overlook grades to some extent if all of those other things are present. But to be honest, I'm not picking up enough energy or ambition or intense motivation from you to convince me to go out on a limb and take a chance."

For several long seconds, the boy stared back at

him. Indecision and defiance battled in his eyes. Defiance won.

"Hey, man, I don't need this program. Not enough to grovel." He stood and shoved his hands in his pockets, squeezing his hands into tight fists.

"I don't expect you to grovel. I just expect you to show some interest and enthusiasm. I need people who are willing to make a commitment to the program and work hard while they're in it. I couldn't tell your level of commitment from your application, but I thought I might be able to in person. I was wrong. I can't get inside your head, Jared. You're very good at masking your feelings."

The boy glared at him, his shoulders stiff. "It's called survival, man." He turned and strode toward the door, tossing a parting remark, laden with sarcasm, over his shoulder before he exited. "Thanks for your time." A few seconds later, David heard the front door open, then close.

Frustrated, David raked his fingers through his hair. All his years of experience working with hard-nosed business people hadn't helped him one iota in dealing with Jared. The boy was as tight as a clam with his feelings. Yet he had to be interested. He wouldn't have gone to the trouble of applying otherwise. But none of that came through in person. There was no way David could send a student like Jared into any of the current Uplink hosting companies. They wouldn't put up with his attitude.

"That boy has got one big chip on his shoulder." Hands on her hips, Ella regarded him from the doorway.

"Yeah. Tell me about it."

"He's got a big hurt in his heart, too."

"Why do you say that?"

"You can see it in his eyes."

"All I saw was defiance. And suspicion."

Shaking her head, Ella folded her arms across her chest. "You've got a lot to learn about young people."

"Tell me something I don't already know." David rose and walked over to the window, then stared out at the trees. Each day, coaxed by the sun, the buds were opening a little more, revealing their inner beauty bit by bit.

"It'll come. You've got to remember that these kids aren't rich businessmen who are into power and money. Those folks are confident and they're successful. If one deal falls through, it's not a big thing. They know there's always another one coming along. A lot of the kids in the poorer neighborhoods have never tasted success. They have no confidence. All they know about life is that it stinks. They've never had a break, and even when one comes their way, they're suspicious. Why shouldn't they be? They've learned that nothing comes free. They've been conditioned to believe that they're losers. It takes a lot of guts for a kid like Jared to even take a first step like this."

"Are you saying that I should consider him for Uplink?" David turned back to her.

"That's your call. I'm just saying that maybe he wants it more than you think."

"Even if he does, I can't overlook his insolent manner. And I doubt any of our sponsoring companies could, either. They don't need or want people with attitudes. The only photography/writing slot I have available is at the *Post*, and I guarantee they wouldn't tolerate that chip on his shoulder for a day."

"Maybe you could find another place for him, with someone who's a little more tolerant and willing to take a personal interest in his development."

An image of Caroline flashed through his mind. She struck him as someone who would be willing to look deeper, who would take the time to dig through the layers of defiance and wariness to find the real Jared. Under her tutelage, the boy might blossom.

But even if he was willing to contact her again— and that was a big if—Jared still represented a major risk. Until Ella had walked into the office, he'd been prepared to write off the boy—albeit with regret. Now he wondered if he'd been too hasty.

As he pondered that, a movement down the street caught his attention. A city bus had come to a stop with a squeal of breaks, and as the doors folded open, he saw Jared disengage himself from his slouched position against one of the flowering trees and walk toward the door. His shoulders were slumped, and the confident strut he'd used in the Uplink office had become a weary shuffle. With his hands in his pockets, and his head bowed, his posture spoke of discouragement and despair. He stepped on board, the doors closed and the bus rumbled off.

All at once, the significance of what has just transpired became clear. Jared had taken a bus—probably several—to get to this interview after school. Without a car, public transportation had been the only option available to him. Yet he'd made the effort—again confirming his seriousness about the program. In fact, all of his actions spoke of his interest. It just hadn't come across in person. Yet Ella had seen something in him that he'd missed.

He turned back to the receptionist. She was still standing in the doorway, her head tilted to one side, her arms folded across her chest, her face placid and nonjudgmental. That's one of the things he liked about her. She was always willing to express her opinions, which were well thought out and insightful, but she didn't take offense if he disagreed. She respected his views, just as he respected hers.

"I think I'll give this a little more thought," he told her.

"Good idea. We always make better decisions when we think things through. Don't forget you have that conference call at five o'clock with Feldman and Associates."

"Right. Thanks." The architectural firm was considering taking an Uplink intern for the summer, and David strode toward his desk, shifting gears as he prepared to do a sell job with the management of the company. The addition of that firm would be a real plus for Uplink.

The question was, would Jared?

Lord, please give me some direction on this, David prayed as he gathered up his notes in preparation for the conference call. *I want to help Jared, but I don't want to hurt Uplink. Help me make the right decision.*

"That's a new necklace, isn't it?"

Reaching up, Caroline fingered the pewter anchor that hung on a slender chain around her neck. She'd begun wearing it on a regular basis, but she hadn't thought about her weekly dinner at her mother's home when she'd put it on this morning. If she had, she wouldn't have worn it, knowing it would prompt questions. "Yes. I gave it to Michael right before we became engaged."

"I don't remember ever seeing you wear it before."

"That's because I didn't have it until a couple of weeks ago. David dropped it off at the office. He found it among Michael's things when he was packing for his move."

"You've seen David?"

Her mother's startled reaction didn't surprise Caroline. Her meeting with David would have been a logical bit of news to share during one of their frequent phone conversations or at dinner. Caroline wasn't sure why she hadn't.

"Yes. He stopped by the *Chronicle* for a few minutes."

"Why didn't you tell me?"

"It was only a quick conversation. Nothing worth reporting." The excuse was lame, and Caroline knew it. The meeting alone would have been worthy of mention in her mother's mind.

"Of course it was! He seems like a nice young man. And I told *you* when *I* ran into him."

There was no arguing with that. "It was no big deal, Mom."

"Well...considering how you reacted when I mentioned his name a few weeks ago, I suspect it was a bigger deal than you're letting on." Her mother shoved her green beans around on her plate with more force than necessary.

Feeling guilty, Caroline tried to make amends through further disclosure. "Actually, my visit with him yesterday was more interesting."

Her mother went from miffed to curious in a heart-beat. "You've seen him twice?"

"Yes. Tess is doing a feature story about the organization he heads, and when she had a family emergency yesterday, I interviewed him in her place."

"And you weren't going to tell me?"

"I'm telling you now."

It was a hedge, but at least her mother let it pass. "So what is he doing these days?"

"He's the executive director of an organization that sets up summer internships for talented high school students from impoverished backgrounds."

"Sounds very worthwhile. But isn't that quite a switch for him? Didn't you tell me once that he was an investment banker?"

"Close. He handled merger and acquisition negotiations for multinational companies."

"What prompted the change?"

"He said it was something the Lord had called him to do."

"Then he's a religious man?" Her mother looked pleased.

"It seems so."

"Well, good for him. It's not often you hear of someone giving up a successful career to take a job for far less money, just because they think it's the right thing to do. It sounds like he has good values, and a lot of integrity."

Yes, it did sound that way, Caroline acknowledged. But she knew what he'd done to his mother. And it wasn't consistent with either of those qualities.

"You look puzzled, dear."

Her mother didn't miss a thing, that was for sure.

"I'm just trying to reconcile this David with the one I met two years ago."

"Has he changed?"

Shrugging, Caroline speared a bite of pork tenderloin. "All I know is that he did something a few weeks before Michael died that doesn't seem in keeping with either good values or integrity."

"Do you want to tell me about it?"

The rift between the two brothers wasn't something Caroline had ever talked about. It had seemed too personal. But it was history now, and her mom did have good instincts. Maybe she could shed a little light on the situation that would give Caroline some new insights.

After taking a sip of water, Caroline set her glass back on the oak table in her mother's breakfast room, where so many confidences had been exchanged over the years.

"Remember I told you that Michael's mother had Alzheimer's?"

"Yes. Poor woman! What a terrible disease."

"I know. When I met Michael's mother the Christmas we got engaged, she seemed a little vague, but she was a very kind, sweet lady. I wouldn't call anything she did abnormal. But I overheard Michael and David talking about her while we were there, and Michael told me later that David wanted to break a promise they'd made to her years before and put her in an extended-care facility. Michael was upset, and I didn't blame him. At the time, she was still living on her own, and David had arranged to have someone stay with her during the day. There didn't seem to be an immediate need to take more dramatic measures."

"What happened then?"

"David agreed to wait. But a few weeks later he called Michael and reneged. They had a huge argument about it, and Michael asked him to hold off making any decision until we came home for the wedding, when they could discuss it in person. But David refused and moved ahead. They didn't talk again until the night before Michael was…before he died…when David called to say that their mother had had a mild heart attack. It was a bad situation all around."

The story had held Judy's rapt attention, and when Caroline finished her mother leaned back in her chair, a thoughtful look on her face. "Did Michael tell you why David wouldn't wait?"

"He said that according to David, we'd seen their mother on a few good days, and that she'd gotten much worse in the weeks that followed. David thought she needed constant care and was worried about leaving her alone. Not just at night, but even long enough for a caregiver to run to the grocery store or take a shower."

At Caroline's skeptical tone, Judy sent her a curious look. "And you don't believe that?"

"It doesn't matter if I believe it or not. All I know is that Michael didn't. He knew David's career was demanding, and he figured he just didn't want to be bothered."

"That's easy to say if you're thousands of miles away and not the one who has to deal with a situation like that day after day."

Shocked, Caroline stared at her mother. "You think David was right to break the promise he and Michael made to their mother?"

"I'm not going to judge him, Caroline. All I know

is that Alzheimer's patients can be a handful. Remember Rose Candici?"

Now there was a name from the past. It took Caroline a few seconds to place her. "Your high school classmate? The one you play bridge with?"

"Yes. I never saw a woman who loved her mother more. And she had to deal with the same issue. She tried to care for her mother at home for as long as she could. They even built a self-contained suite onto their house for her, and brought in specialized care when she got worse. Rose was determined to keep her mother at home. But in the end, she needed round-the-clock care. It got to the point where she had few lucid days and no longer recognized her family. Plus, she began to have other medical problems that needed daily monitoring. The solution seemed pretty clear-cut to her friends, but Rose agonized over the decision. I'm not sure she ever reconciled herself to it."

"I don't think Michael's mother was that bad."

"Then you think David was lying?"

Caroline's reaction was immediate. No, David wouldn't lie. She didn't know him very well, but he radiated honesty—and honor. Unless her powers of intuition were way off, David was a man you could count on to do the right thing.

"I can see on your face that you don't," her mother continued, when Caroline didn't respond.

"To be honest, I don't know what to think."

Rising, Judy reached for Caroline's plate, then picked up her own. "I always believe in giving people the benefit of the doubt. That young man has caring eyes. I can't see him doing anything to hurt someone he loved. And remember…there's always at least two sides to every story. Maybe you can ask him about it sometime, if it's still on your mind. Now, how about some split lemon cake?"

It took Caroline a second to respond after the abrupt change in topic. "Sure. That would be great."

"I made it this morning. I just love the combination of tart and sweet. It's a perfect springtime dessert."

And a perfect complement to her mood, too, Caroline reflected, recalling again the events that had led to Michael's death. Even though he'd been in the market-place because of her, she'd always believed—*wanted* to believe—that if he hadn't been distracted by his argument with his brother, he might have sensed danger. And avoided it. So for two years, she'd had tart, almost bitter, memories of David. Yet in the past couple of weeks she'd seen glimpses of sweetness, of innate goodness, that had tempered her image of him, countered her resentment and anger, mitigated the sour taste that thoughts of him usually left in her mouth.

Until now, Caroline had always assumed that Michael's position in regard to his mother had been the right one. That honor had been on his side because of his commitment to keep the vow they'd made to her. After all, Caroline had seen the woman herself mere weeks before. She couldn't have degenerated that much in such a short time.

Could she?

It wasn't a question Caroline had asked until now. She'd never allowed for the possibility that David might have made the right decision. But maybe he had. Maybe, if asked, he would explain his motivations. Her mother had even suggested she give him that opportunity.

There was just one little problem with that idea. Caroline never expected to see him again. What was the point? It just resurrected painful memories best left buried. So reaching out to him was not a good idea.

And she had the distinct impression that the feeling was mutual.

Chapter Five

"I think you'll find the letter on top very interesting." Ella set the morning mail in David's In basket.

Focused on the computer screen in front of him, David reread the last line in his follow-up letter to Feldman and Associates, then sent Ella a distracted look. "Can it wait?"

"Sure. Jared probably figures you won't respond, anyway. Kids in that kind of environment haven't been programmed to expect much."

Thoughts of Feldman and Associates vanished as David stared at her. "Jared wrote me a letter?"

"Yeah. How about that? I guess maybe he was more interested in Uplink than you thought."

Flashing her a grin, David reached for the letter. "Thanks for not saying, 'I told you so.'"

Shrugging, she turned away. But he caught a quick glimpse of the twinkle in her eyes. "I'll save that for another time," she told him.

She would, too, David thought with an affectionate chuckle. Ella had been a godsend as he'd plunged into his new job, her advice sound, her insights sure. She'd become a trusted advisor and a reliable sounding board, helping to make his transition far smoother than he'd anticipated.

The letter from Jared was typed, just as his essay had been, David noted. And again, his punctuation, spelling and syntax were flawless. But as he read the text, David realized that there was one significant difference between the two writing samples. This one had heart.

Dear Mr. Sloan: After our interview yesterday, I thought about your comment that I didn't seem to have the commitment or drive or determination you look for in Uplink students. That you wanted students with dreams, who were willing to overcome any obstacles that might keep those dreams from coming true.

Well, I've had plenty of obstacles in my life. If you talked to Mr. Elliot about me, you probably know about some of them. But I figure the biggest obstacle to my success right now is me. I don't trust a lot of people. Especially white folks. And they pick that up real quick, just like you did. I know I need to change my attitude, and I'm trying. As for hard work, I'm not afraid of that. Not if it will open doors. I don't want to waste my life in the ghetto. I want to count for something, to make a difference, to leave a mark. And Uplink seems like a way to get me started on the right path. Maybe the only way.

When I left your office, though, I figured I'd blown it. That's what I told my grandmother when

I got home. And she sat me down and read me the riot act about my attitude. She said if I really wanted this, I should try again. That maybe you'd give me another chance. So that's what I'm asking for, if it's not too late. I know I haven't been the best student, and that my commitment to school hasn't been as strong as you might want. But if you give me this chance, I won't disappoint you. I can work hard when I want to, and I don't break my promises. I want this opportunity very much, and if you take me, I'll give it my best shot.

Like I said when we met, I'm not very good at talking about my feelings. I guess I have to work on that, too. But for now, I hope you'll accept them in writing. And that you'll give me a second chance.

Thank you.

The letter was signed in Jared's scrawling hand.

David leaned back in his chair. He'd never expected to hear from Jared again, but the image of the dejected, slump-shouldered boy had been on his mind ever since he'd watched him get on the bus three days before. And he'd been praying for him, asking God to help Jared find a way out of his present situation, to give him an opportunity to nurture his talent. Now God had put the ball back in his court.

With sudden decision, David reached for the phone and tapped in Steve Dempsky's number. When he answered on the second ring, David gave him a quick recap of the situation, then asked for his input.

"It's a bit sticky," the minister acknowledged. "One of those things that could go either way."

"I know."

"If you brought this before the board, I doubt they'd be willing to sign Jared on."

"I know that, too. But I don't have to go to the board for this. I have the authority to choose the candidates for interviews."

"How risky do you think this is? Could he jeopardize the program?"

Leaning back in his chair, David looked out at the flowering trees. "That's the sixty-four-thousand-dollar question. I do know he's exactly the kind of student who needs Uplink the most."

"What does your gut tell you about the risk?"

"Three days ago, after I interviewed him, I'd have said it was high. He has a real attitude problem that I knew none of our sponsoring companies would put up with. I'd more or less written him off. Then, when I saw him getting on the bus, he was the picture of dejection. And today I got the letter. I think he wants this, Steve. And I know he needs it."

"Would you like me to talk to him?"

"I was hoping you'd offer. I know it's still my decision, and I'll take full responsibility for it, but I'd value your input."

"Glad to help. Just have him give me a call."

"Thanks, buddy."

"Hey, what are friends for?"

As David replaced the receiver, a sense of peace came over him. He still wasn't sure what his decision would be. But he knew he would do everything he could to give the boy a chance. That's what Uplink was supposed to be about. If Steve concurred that Jared was worth the risk, David would take it. And put the outcome in God's hands.

"You want me to talk to a preacher?"

From the tone of Jared's voice, you'd think he'd asked the boy to walk over hot coals barefoot, David reflected, a wry smile touching his lips. Their phone conversation had started off well enough, although Jared had seemed surprised that David had followed up on his letter. It was as if he'd expected nothing from the effort. Or hadn't allowed himself to expect anything. Just as Ella had suggested. But at least his tone had been cordial, and it had been obvious that he was making an attempt to keep his attitude in check. Until David mentioned Steve.

"That's right," David affirmed. "He's a member of the Uplink board and an old friend of mine. I value his opinion, and when he offered to speak with you I took him up on it."

"Do you send all the Uplink candidates to talk to him?"

"No." David decided that absolute honesty was the best way to proceed with Jared. He suspected the boy would respect that in the long run. "But your situation is a bit unique. In general, we wouldn't consider someone with your GPA or attendance record. But as I said when we spoke before, I'm impressed with your talent. I think you have a lot to offer, assuming you buckle down. Your letter makes me think you're willing to do that. But I want a second opinion."

There was silence for a few seconds before Jared responded. "I'm not a religious kind of person."

"Religion isn't on the agenda for your meeting with Reverend Dempsky."

"Then what's he going to ask me about?"

"A lot of the same things I did."

"And he won't get into that Jesus stuff?"

"No. Uplink isn't a Christian organization, even though it lives the gospel principles."

There was a moment of silence while Jared thought about that. "Yeah, okay. I guess that's fine. When does he want to talk to me?"

"You two can work that out. Just give him a call." David recited Steve's number while Jared jotted it down.

"What happens after that?"

David heard the anxious note in the boy's voice. "We'll be notifying all of the finalists by May first. There will be one more interview after that, with the sponsoring organization. The internships run ten weeks and start in early June. Do you have a portfolio of writing and photography samples, Jared?"

"No."

"Put one together. It doesn't have to be fancy. Just a collection of some of your best work. And include copies of the letters from your English and art teachers. I'd like you to show it to Reverend Dempsky, and you'll need it for an interview with a sponsoring organization if we get that far."

"Okay."

"Any other questions?"

"No."

"All right. I'll talk to you soon, then."

"Listen…thanks, okay? I—I didn't really expect you to give me a second chance."

That comment probably summed up the breadth of the boy's experience, David thought with a pang. "Everyone deserves a second chance, Jared."

"A lot of people don't feel that way."

"Well, Uplink does. Just make the most of it, okay?"

As David rang off, he wasn't sure the board would agree with him about second chances. Not when it came to someone like Jared, who could be a high risk. But Michael had been a risk, too, when a mentor had stepped forward and taken a chance on him. It was something Michael had never forgotten, and he'd vowed someday to repay that debt by helping another young person. In the end, he'd never had the opportunity to follow through on that pledge. His life had been cut way too short, and despite Caroline's confession, David still felt somewhat responsible for that. Perhaps, by fulfilling Michael's vow for him, he could in some way make amends for any role he'd played in his brother's death.

Still, he wasn't going to take unnecessary chances or let his judgment be clouded by personal feelings. He had to do what was right for Uplink. But if Steve considered Jared to be a worthy candidate, David would take the boy on in a second.

"David? Steve. Got a few minutes?"

This was it. Jared was on spring break, and David knew Steve had met with him earlier in the day. His grip on the phone tightened, and the muscles in his shoulders bunched. "Yeah. How did it go?"

"Let me just say that I can see why you wanted a second opinion."

Uh-oh. Not good. "You weren't impressed?"

"I didn't say that. He's got talent, no question about it. He brought along a very impressive portfolio. But I picked up on the attitude, even though it was clear he was trying to keep it in check. Plus, I think he was very uncomfortable with the whole notion of talking to a minister. I tried to put him at ease, but I sensed a lot of wariness and suspicion."

That sounded like Jared. "Anything else?"

"Yeah. His appearance. I could live with the dreadlocks. But I can't see most of the organizations we work with allowing that kind of attire. Most of them have dress codes, and even though casual clothes are okay at a lot of places, his concept of casual falls way below that line. I know the Lord teaches us not to judge by appearances, but most businesses aren't that forgiving."

"We could work with him on that."

"True."

"Well, what do you think? Yea or nay on letting him into the program?"

"It's not an easy call, is it?"

David could hear the uncertainty in his friend's voice. "No."

"I guess you're just going to have to go with your heart on this one. I do think Jared wants this. But I also think he's a risk. I talked with him a little about his gang ties, and he claims he's cutting those, like his principal told you. That's hard to do, though, and there's no guarantee of success. And what if he gets into the program and then loses interest halfway through? Or can't get along with his coworkers? Or does something worse? Did you check to see if he has a juvenile record?"

"Yeah. Charles Elliot, his principal, says he's had a few minor brushes with the law, but there's nothing on record. At this point, he's officially clean."

"Well, that's good news, at least."

David had hoped for a definitive opinion from Steve. But his friend's feelings seemed as mixed as his own.

"What did you think of the photos?"

"Like I said, impressive. Even though the images are stark, there's a certain optimistic quality to them that suggests...goodness, maybe. They make me think there's a light deep in his soul, waiting to be released. Frankly, without the photos I suspect I'd write him off as too risky. But those pictures tugged at my heart."

So Steve had noticed that, too. David had made it a point to keep his impressions about the photos to himself, wondering if Steve would pick up on the same qualities he had, qualities that not only reflected Jared's good eye for photography but also offered a window into his soul. Qualities that suggested the boy wasn't quite as jaded as he might first appear, that there was a chance he could make something of his life, with assistance. The kind of assistance Uplink offered.

"They had the same effect on me," David responded.

"What are you going to do?"

"Think about it. And pray."

"Sounds like a good plan. I'll support whatever decision you make."

"Thanks."

"Just one question. Where would you place him if you decide to take him on? I can't think of any organization on our roster that would help him develop his writing and photography talent. Or take the time to give him the kind of personal attention I suspect he'll need."

Until now, David hadn't let himself dwell on that issue. He'd been too busy to worry about a problem that might never materialize. But Steve was right. He needed to start thinking about lining up a spot for Jared if he was getting serious about taking the boy.

"The *Post* might work, but it's such a big organization that I doubt he'd get the kind of one-on-one assistance he may need to blossom. I'll have to find a new place," David responded.

"It's getting pretty late in the year to start recruiting new businesses."

"I know." In the end, the decision to take Jared might come down to whether they could find somewhere to place him.

"Well, let me know what you decide. Like I said, I'm with you either way."

"Thanks, Steve. I'll be in touch."

As David replaced the phone, he'd already decided that Jared was a risk he was willing to take—if he could find a place where the boy would receive the kind of attention and support he would need to succeed. That was a big if. Most businesses were too busy to devote a lot of attention to a student intern. And too many of them just gave the teenagers busy work. David had addressed that issue with the offending organizations on Uplink's roster after reading evaluations by previous participants. That had been the single biggest complaint by students, who were anxious to spread their wings and be exposed to new experiences. A few organizations hadn't lived up to their end of the bargain.

But Jared's case was even more difficult. He not only needed exposure to the business world, but step-by-step guidance. And someone who believed in his potential.

David was too new in town to have a lot of contacts yet. He was still making the rounds of area businesses, selling in the program, meeting the right people, answering questions. He couldn't just pick up the phone and secure the perfect spot for Jared.

Or could he?

"Caroline, I have David Sloan on the line for you. Do you want to take the call?"

Surprised, Caroline stared at the thank-you note from David on her desk, expressing his appreciation for the story that had run earlier in the week about Uplink. Tess had received a similar note. Though few people bothered with such niceties after the *Chronicle* ran a story, she hadn't been surprised when David's handwritten note arrived. It had just seemed like something he would do.

But she *was* surprised by his call. With the story finished and his note sent, she'd expected that to be the end of their contact. Had hoped it would be, in fact. She still found it difficult to deal with him. And was disturbed by the questions that his reappearance in her life had raised. It had been easy to paint him as the villain in the dilemma with his mother when all she had to go on was Michael's angry assessment of the situation. It had been a whole lot harder to reconcile the living, breathing man, who exuded character and integrity and honor, with the uncaring, selfish portrait of him that Michael had painted in his fury after David had reneged on their promise.

Of course, that was all over now. The rift between the brothers was history. It didn't much matter who had been right and who had been wrong. Yet every time she heard from David, the questions were stirred up in Caroline's mind. Had she been too harsh in her judgment of David? Had she been unfair in accepting Michael's judgment at face value? And at this point, why should she care? Caroline didn't have the answer to any of those questions, especially the last one. And she wasn't even sure she wanted to find them. That's why she preferred to cut all contact with David.

"Caroline?"

"Sorry, Mary. I got distracted for a minute." She could refuse his call. But that wasn't a very mature way to behave, she supposed. She'd had the distinct feeling that he hadn't intended to contact her again, either. If he was doing so, there must be a good reason. She might as well talk to him. "Okay, put him through."

After her greeting, his voice came over the line. "Thanks for taking my call, Caroline. I know you're busy."

"No problem. What can I do for you?"

"I have an idea I'd like to run by you, if you could spare a few minutes."

She glanced at her watch. "I've got about ten minutes now, if that works."

"I'd prefer to do this in person. There's a show-and-tell component."

"Is this personal or business related?"

She didn't try to disguise the wariness in her voice. Nor did he miss it.

"Business." His reply was prompt and definite.

The tautness in Caroline's shoulders eased. Curiosity replaced tension, and she reached for her calendar. As usual, almost every second of her day was booked. She flipped to the next week. Not much better. But she had one open slot late on Thursday.

"How about April thirtieth at three o'clock?"

A frown creased David's brow. That was pushing it. Finalists were scheduled to be notified by May first and interviewed the following week at sponsoring businesses. "Is there any way you can squeeze me in sometime this week? I'm sorry to push, but this is important and there's some urgency due to our deadlines."

Flipping back the calendar, Caroline scanned her schedule as she spoke. "Do you want to give me a hint what this is about?"

No, he didn't. David knew from experience that it was too easy for people to say no over the phone. He wanted Caroline to see Jared's work before she made a decision. But her question was legitimate. In her place, he'd ask the same thing. Time was at a premium in most jobs.

"I have an unusual Uplink applicant whose talent has blown me away. I'd like to get a second opinion before I try to place him, and his skills are in your area of expertise. Since I'm new in town, you're the only journalist I know well enough to call." Okay, that wasn't the whole truth. But he'd rather press his case for the *Chronicle*'s involvement in person.

"Okay. I can do that." She scanned her schedule

again, doing some rapid mental rearranging. She'd planned to run a couple of errands over lunch tomorrow, but they could be deferred. "I've got about forty-five minutes tomorrow at noon. Would that work?"

"Only if you let me buy you lunch."

She seemed surprised by the invitation. But no more than he was. Since he'd planned to keep this strictly business, introducing a social component wasn't a good idea.

"That's not necessary," she assured him.

"At least let me bring some sandwiches."

"Really, David, you don't have to do that."

"Would turkey be okay?"

He wasn't going to relent, she realized. Besides, it wasn't that big a deal. She should eat lunch, anyway. If he didn't bring food, though, she knew she'd skip. Again. She'd never regained the weight she'd lost after Michael's death, and her mother was always on her about eating more.

"Turkey's fine. Thanks. About noon?"

"I'll be there. I appreciate your time, Caroline."

"No problem. See you tomorrow."

No problem. The words echoed in his mind as he hung up. Maybe not for her. But seeing Caroline again was a big problem for him, given his feelings for her. Only a compelling need to help Jared would have prompted him to make another contact. To take that risk. And risk was the right word—one that had been on his mind a lot in recent weeks, thanks to Jared. Taking a chance on the troubled teenager put Uplink in a high-risk situation. Not to mention the risk he was taking professionally. If things didn't work out, his new career could be toast.

But all at once that risk paled in comparison to the one he was taking on a personal level by seeing Caroline again. Because when it came to his emotions, he was on dangerous ground with her. And he felt far less confident about controlling *that* risk.

Chapter Six

"Caroline, David Sloan is here."

Shifting the phone to her other ear, Caroline reached for a pad of paper and a pen. "Thanks, Mary. Can you show him to the conference room? Tell him I'll be with him as soon as I return a call."

"Sure thing."

By the time Caroline joined him a few minutes later, David had unpacked the lunch and eating utensils, and set a three-ring binder on the table. He rose as she entered and held out his hand, taking her slender fingers in a firm grip.

"Sorry to keep you waiting. I had to return an urgent call," she apologized.

"I'm just glad you could squeeze me in." He waited until she took her seat, then sat as well. "There's a little deli near my office that makes a great turkey on whole wheat. I picked up a few other things, too."

Surveying the containers of pasta salad, potato salad and fresh fruit salad—not to mention brownies—Caroline shook her head. "This is more than I eat for lunch in a week."

"You can afford to indulge."

As she reached for her sandwich, she angled a bemused look his way. "Now you sound like my mother. She's always on me about my weight."

"You do look thinner than I remember."

Her hand stilled on the plastic wrap for a fraction of a second before she continued to unwrap her sandwich. "Life keeps me busy. Sometimes too busy to take time for meals. But I have a healthy appetite when I do eat." As if to illustrate her point, she took a big bite of her sandwich, then scooped a large serving of pasta salad onto her plate. "Is this the work of the student you mentioned?" She nodded toward the portfolio as she chewed.

"Yes. Jared Poole. I saw some of his photographs on the wall when I did a presentation at his school, and later found out he's a talented writer as well. But he isn't a typical Uplink candidate. He has gang ties, which he's trying to break, and is only a marginal student overall. He also has a truancy issue. Not to mention an attitude problem. The chip on his shoulder is more like a boulder."

Tilting her head, Caroline gave him a puzzled look. "With all those negatives, why are you considering him? The gang connection in particular is troubling."

"I agree. But without help, his future looks pretty bleak. His father disappeared before he was born, his mother died of a drug overdose when he was a little kid and he's being raised by a grandmother who has to clean office buildings at night just to keep food on the table. From what I can tell, no one's ever given him a break. Uplink could make a huge difference in his life."

"Maybe. But he sounds risky."

"He is."

Her perceptive hazel eyes missing nothing, Caroline scrutinized his face. "There's more behind your interest, isn't there?"

Instead of giving her a direct response, David slid the portfolio closer to her. "Take a look."

Wiping her hands on a napkin, Caroline opened the binder. Writing and photo samples had been slipped into plastic sheets, and she took her time reviewing each one. The minutes slipped by, and David continued to eat, watching in silence as she gave her full attention to the material in Jared's folder.

She spent a long time examining the three photos that had first caught David's attention, and when she at last closed the binder and looked over at him, he could see that she was impressed even before she voiced her single-word assessment.

"Wow."

"That's what I thought. But I'm not an expert."

"How old is he?"

"Seventeen."

She shook her head. "His writing is very good. But the photos…they're exceptional."

"Now you can see why I didn't want to let him slip through the cracks. A talent like his needs to be nurtured."

"I agree."

"Here's the issue, though." David wiped his lips on a paper napkin and leaned forward, his face intent as he folded his hands on the table in front of him. "Taking Jared on would require a huge commitment from the sponsoring organization. He's going to need personal attention and understanding and patience. He'll need to be challenged and held accountable. That's assuming we find an organization that recognizes his talents and can put them to good use."

As Caroline gazed into David's serious, deep brown eyes, a wry smile touched the corners of her lips—even as her heart did an odd flip-flop that threw her off balance for a brief instant. "I think I'm beginning to see why you offered to buy me lunch."

"Not that you've eaten any of it." David was well aware that she'd taken only a couple of bites of her sandwich and a forkful of pasta salad before she'd become absorbed in Jared's portfolio.

"This happens all the time. There are way too many interruptions at the office to make take-out worthwhile. But this is really good." She reached for her sandwich and took another bite.

"So…what do you think? Would you even consider taking Jared for the summer? Assuming you wanted him after an interview, of course."

Her face grew speculative as she chewed, and she sipped her soda before responding. "We've never hired an intern. They tend to require significant training time from a staff already stretched too thin. And just when we start to get some productivity out of them, the internship ends."

"I understand those concerns. It's no great bargain for the sponsoring organizations, although the students do work for minimum wage, so it's not a big financial commitment. But it does require staff time from one or two people. We like students to be assigned to a mentor or two who can guide them through the process and make sure they're getting the most out of the experience. The rewards for the student are incalculable, though."

Once more, Caroline opened the portfolio to the black-and-white photos. Her face softened as she studied them, her lunch once again forgotten. "Michael once told me about the mentor who recognized his talent and set him on the right path. He always talked about how much he owed him, and how he wanted to do the same someday for some other young person."

She turned to the next page, to the photo of the two children looking toward the sky. "Jared's photos make me think of Michael," she continued, and the quiet wistfulness in her voice tightened David's throat. "Even though there's a desolation to them, something shines through that touches my heart. Michael's photos made me think of the preciousness of each individual life. These make me think of aspirations and hopes and dreams."

When she looked up, the pensive expression on David's face made her suspect that the parallels hadn't been lost on him, either.

"I thought the same thing," he confirmed, after clearing his throat.

"So are you doing this for Jared? Or for Michael?"

He hesitated, then gave her an honest answer. "Maybe both."

Indecision flickered in her eyes, and David prayed she'd at least consider taking Jared on.

"Let me think about it. I'd also like to share Jared's work with our chief photographer, Bill Baker. He'd be the logical mentor on the photography side. Can I get back to you tomorrow with an answer?"

"Sure." He'd hoped for an affirmative response today. But at least she hadn't said no.

Checking her watch, Caroline rose. "I'm sorry to run, but I have an interview at one and I need to prep."

David stood as well and began gathering up the remnants of their lunch. "I understand. I appreciate your giving up your lunch hour to see me."

"And I appreciate the lunch."

"You didn't eat much of it."

Reaching for her sandwich, she rewrapped it. "I'll finish this later."

"I'll leave the rest, too."

"Thanks. My mother would love that pasta salad. And I'm going to see her tonight."

"Perfect. Give her my best." David held out his hand. "I'll wait to hear from you."

She took it, and as his lean fingers closed around hers and their gazes met, her heart did that funny flip-flop thing again. He had wonderful eyes, she realized. Warm and insightful and caring. And his grip was sure and strong, yet gentle and comforting. By look and by touch, he made her feel protected and cherished. Did he have this effect on everyone? she wondered, feeling a bit dazed.

As they stared at each other, Caroline sensed an almost imperceptible tightening of his grip. A flash of something she couldn't identify ricocheted through his eyes, come and gone with such speed that she wondered if she'd imagined it. Then, with a move that startled her by its abruptness, David released her hand and took a step back.

"I hope you find time to finish that." He gestured toward the sandwich she was clutching in her hand. With a brief nod, he turned away and strode out of the conference room.

For a full minute, Caroline stared after him, trying to figure out what had just happened. Whatever had flared to life in David's eyes had made her heart trip into double time, and for a brief second she'd felt...attracted to him. But that was impossible. She'd resented him for two years. Besides, he was the brother of the man she'd loved. The man she *still* loved. She shouldn't feel anything for him except friendship. *Couldn't* feel anything. It would be wrong. A betrayal of Michael. Of their love. Whatever had just happened must have been simply a fluke. And no doubt she'd read far too much into it.

Even so, discussing his visit with her mother wasn't going to be easy. And she refused to consider why.

"This is great pasta salad! A perfect accompaniment to our first barbecue of the year." Caroline's mother, Judy, helped herself to another serving as the sun dipped behind the trees at the back of the yard, dimming the light on the brick patio.

"I'm glad you like it." Before her mother could comment further, Caroline switched topics. "Now tell me how the square dancing lessons are going. Is Harold catching on?"

"He's trying, let me just say that. And you have to

give a man credit for trying." She took a closer look at the pasta salad. "I think there's avocado in here. Where did you get this?"

Caroline took a deep breath and plunged in. "I had a meeting at noon with David Sloan today. He brought lunch. This was left over."

Judy stared at her daughter, the pasta salad now forgotten. "You met with David again?"

"Yes. He wants the *Chronicle* to take an Uplink intern for the summer."

"Are you going to?"

"I don't know yet. This particular student has problems. And it takes a lot of staff time to deal with an intern."

"But time well spent, I would think, from what you've told me about Uplink."

It was hard to argue with that. "I gave Bill the student's portfolio. I want to see what he thinks about his potential."

"What kind of problems does this student have?"

As Caroline gave her a brief overview, Judy shook her head. "It makes you appreciate your own blessings when you hear a story like that. The boy sounds like he could use a break."

Tracing the ring of moisture left by her water glass on the patio table, Caroline's face grew melancholic. "His situation reminds me a lot of Michael's. Not the upbringing. But the raw talent, just waiting to be recognized and directed."

"Maybe that's what caught David's attention, too."

Her mother's insight never failed to surprise Caroline. Despite her sometimes flighty ways, she had a keen sense of human nature. "I think you're right."

"You know, it must be hard on him."

Confused, Caroline gave her mother a puzzled look. "What do you mean?"

"I was just thinking how alone David is. He had no one to comfort him when Michael died. Now he has no family left, he's living in a strange new town where he probably hasn't had much chance to make friends and he's trying to learn a new job. You should ask him to join us sometime for our weekly dinner."

Speechless, Caroline stared at her mother.

"Why do you look so surprised?" Judy asked. "It would be an act of Christian charity to invite him. Mentioning his name doesn't seem to upset you, like it did a few weeks ago when I told you I'd run into him, or I wouldn't even suggest it. And it might give you a chance to ask him about that situation with his mother, which seems to bother you."

"It doesn't bother me. It's ancient history. Why should it bother me?"

"I didn't say it should. Just that it seems to. But that's up to you, of course. In the meantime, tell him I enjoyed his pasta salad."

Her mother moved on to a new topic, and even though Caroline tried to keep up, thoughts of David kept disrupting her concentration. The fact was, the disagreement between the brothers did bother her, history or not. And somewhere, deep inside, she wanted to hear David's story, sensing at some intuitive level that it might absolve him from guilt. Why that was important to her, she had no idea. In fact, if David had been right, that would mean Michael had been wrong. Why would she want to believe that? And why did it matter at this point, anyway?

There were no easy answers to those questions. Nor were they ones Caroline necessarily wanted to find. Because she had the oddest sense that if she delved deeper, if she heard David's side of the story, she would have to rethink and reevaluate a whole lot of things. And she wasn't sure she was ready to do that.

"This kid has talent." Bill Baker strode into Caroline's office without knocking, plopped Jared's portfolio on her desk and sat in the chair across from her.

"Have a seat, Bill." She smiled as she reached for the portfolio.

Social nuances were lost on the brusque, craggy-faced photographer. With his shaggy white hair pulled back in an elastic band, his startling blue eyes rimmed with fine lines and his standard attire of blue jeans and T-shirt, he wasn't a typical *Chronicle* staff member. He didn't waste time on office politics, and tact wasn't his strong suit. But he had a heart of gold. Not to mention the best photographic skills in the business. The newspaper was lucky to have him.

"Do you have time to work with him if we decide to take him on?"

"I can make time. But I can't help him much on the writing end."

Caroline had already thought about that. And decided that she'd mentor him in writing if they proceeded. They'd lost a couple of people through attrition in the past few months, and the top brass in the parent organization had made the decision not to replace them. She couldn't ask any of her busy staffers to take on yet another responsibility. Besides, from her conversations with David, she understood that Jared was a high risk. She wanted to give this her best shot if she decided to take him on.

"I'll handle that. Do you have any concerns about the issues he has?" She'd already given Bill an overview of Jared's background.

"Some. But if he's willing to work hard, I'm willing to give him a chance."

"Okay. I'll set up an interview."

Rising, Bill nodded toward the portfolio on Caroline's desk. "I'd hate to see a talent like that go to waste. And I like challenges." Without giving her time to respond, he exited.

As Caroline watched him leave, she hoped they wouldn't live to regret Bill's words. She liked challenges, too. But she had a feeling that Jared Poole was going to be a bigger challenge than either of them imagined.

What in the world had David been thinking?

Caroline stared in dismay at the young man who took his time rising when she stepped into the lobby to greet him for the interview. Jared's low-slung pants, scuffed sneakers, muscle shirt and dreadlocks made Bill's appearance look preppy. Tall and lanky, his complexion the color of rich café au lait, he had dark, brazen eyes that stared back at her with a bravado she suspected was more wishful than real.

But she tried to keep an open mind. If David thought

Jared had the right stuff, if he was willing to take a chance and put his career on the line for this young man, Caroline at least owed him the benefit of the doubt. Summoning up a smile, she moved toward him and extended her hand.

"Jared, I'm Caroline James. Welcome to the *Chronicle.*"

After a brief hesitation, he rubbed his palm on his thigh, then took her hand. She thought she detected a slight tremor in his fingers, but he retrieved his hand and shoved it in his pocket before she could tell for sure.

"Thanks," he mumbled.

"Come on back to the conference room. Bill Baker, our chief photographer, is waiting." She held her ID card to the scanner, then led the way into the newsroom. Jared followed close behind her, giving the beehive of activity around him a discreet, but interested, perusal.

At the door to the glass-walled conference room, Caroline paused. "Can I get you a soda?"

"No. Thanks." The latter was tacked on as an afterthought.

"Okay. Then let's get started."

After she introduced him to Bill, they all took seats at the long table, Caroline at the head, Bill on one side, Jared on the other. Jared's portfolio lay in the center.

For the first few minutes, Caroline kept the conversation general. But it was like pulling teeth to get the boy to open up. The writing in his portfolio and the letter David had shared with her showed a different side of Jared than he was revealing in the interview. And the attitude David had spoken of was very apparent. An attitude that screamed, "Why would you do this for me and what's in it for you?" A kaleidoscope of emotions—suspicion, anxiety, belligerence and longing—shifted across the face of the rigid-shouldered young man sitting beside her, his hands tightly clasped on the table in front of him. She suspected he was trying to control his attitude, trying to sort through his jumbled feelings, but he was having limited success.

Since small talk wasn't putting the boy at ease, Caroline decided to plunge right into the guts of the interview. "Okay, let's talk about the internship, Jared. You're here because David Sloan believes in you, and because he and I and Bill all agree that you have talent. We're sure that if you apply yourself, you can succeed. What we're not sure about is whether you'll do that. If we bring you on board, we think there's a risk. David seems convinced that it's a risk worth taking. We need you to convince us of that, too."

He swallowed. "I want to do this."

"Tell us why we should give you this chance when there are a dozen other students we could take who have better grades and better attendance records."

He swallowed again. Hard. "Look, I don't want to spend my life in the ghetto. And this may be my best chance to get out. I'll try hard not to disappoint anyone. I like working with words and I...I love photography. But I need help to get better at both. The kind of help I can get through Uplink."

"Do you still have gang ties?" It was the first question Bill had asked.

"I'm working on breaking them."

"Work harder. What about drugs? You'll have to take a drug test to work here. Standard procedure."

The boy stiffened. "I'm clean."

"Good. Keep it that way. You'll have to do something about your clothes, too. There's a dress code here. Not that you'd know it, looking at me."

Jared turned to Caroline, elegant as always in a slim black skirt, silk blouse and gold necklace. "I don't have fancy clothes."

"You don't need fancy clothes. Bill's at one end of the clothes spectrum. I'm at the other. Some of that is by necessity. Bill's work out in the field takes him to places that aren't always conducive to nicer clothes. Jeans allow him to climb on walls, get down on the ground, do whatever it takes to get the shots he needs. The important thing to remember is that journalists or photographers never call attention to themselves. We strive to blend in. The focus should be on the subjects, and we need to do everything possible to make them feel comfortable so that we can get the best story or the best photo. We can work on the clothes, as long as you're agreeable."

"Yeah. I guess so."

"Okay. I'll want you to do a writing test before you leave. That's also standard practice for new hires. We'll give you some facts, and ask you to write a story. I'll set you up at one of the empty workstations when we're done here. Bill, anything you want to ask about first?"

"Just a few technical things." He pulled Jared's portfolio toward him and flipped it open to the photo of the two shadows. "Tell me a little about this. Why you framed it this way, what kind of lighting you used, why you chose this angle."

As the two of them discussed the photo, Caroline

leaned back and observed. Jared became more animated the longer they conversed, and she saw something flicker to life in his eyes. Something she'd seen in Michael's eyes as he talked about his work. Passion. Excitement. Conviction. It wasn't as easy to spot in Jared. He'd learned to mask his feelings. But it was there. His eyes might be hard, but they weren't yet calcified. Meaning there was hope for him.

When Bill was finished, Caroline settled Jared into a workstation and gave him the material for a story. Once she was sure he understood the word processing program, she stood. "Take your time. When you're finished just knock on my door. I'm right over there." She gestured toward her office near the back wall.

Half an hour later, Jared appeared at her door, his portfolio tucked under his arm. "I'm done." He took a step into her office and handed over two double-spaced sheets of text.

"Great." She scanned the first couple of lines, impressed by the lead. The piece looked promising. "That wraps it up, then. Let me walk you out." She set the sheets on her desk and led the way to the front. If the rest of the article looked as good as the lead, she was pretty sure she was going to take him on—pending Bill's agreement, of course. This was going to have to be a team effort.

After pushing through the door to the lobby, she turned to shake hands with the teenager. "Thanks for coming in, Jared. Bill and I appreciate your time. I'm sure David Sloan will be in touch with you soon."

He wanted to ask more. She could read the question in his eyes. But she didn't have an answer for him. Not yet. Besides, it wasn't her place to tell him the outcome. However, it took all of her willpower to keep her expression placid, when she could see the yearning on his face.

"Yeah. No problem." He returned her handshake. Then, after hesitating a moment, he swaggered to the door. As if to say, I have my pride. I don't need you. I'm just fine on my own.

But Caroline knew otherwise. So did David. And in his heart, she suspected Jared did, too.

She just hoped he was smart enough to recognize that Uplink was the opportunity of a lifetime and to follow through on his promise to give it his best shot.

Chapter Seven

"Jared? David Sloan. You're in."

Several beats of silence ticked by on the other end of the line before Jared responded. "For real?"

"Yeah. For real."

"Okay, man. That's good."

Although the teenager was trying to sound cool, David could hear the undercurrent of excitement in his voice. "I'll send you an official letter, but I figured you'd want to know right away."

"Yeah."

"There's a meeting for all of the participating students and their mentors from the sponsoring organizations a week from Saturday, from nine to eleven. The details are in the letter, but I just wanted to give you a heads-up."

"I'll be there."

"Any questions in the meantime?"

"No."

"If you think of any, don't hesitate to call me. We'll look forward to having you in the program, Jared. Caroline James and Bill Baker were impressed with your talent, and they'll both be serving as mentors for you at the *Chronicle*. They'll be at the meeting."

"Okay." He hesitated, then tacked on a single word before breaking the connection. "Thanks."

As David hung up, he found Ella regarding him from his office doorway, a pleased look on her face. "You took him."

"Yes. After a lot of soul-searching. But I still think he's a risk. I'll be praying that he recognizes this for the fabulous opportunity it is and takes advantage of it."

"He strikes me as a smart young man. And Caroline James impresses me as a very caring, compassionate person. Working with her, I think he'll do fine."

"You just met each of them one time. Do you always jump to conclusions based on first impressions?"

Shrugging, she laid some correspondence in his In basket. "Don't discount first impressions. It doesn't take long to pick up people's vibes, if you listen with your heart. And kindness can produce amazing results."

As she exited, David swiveled toward his window, his face thoughtful. The trees had now been coaxed into full and glorious bloom by the warmth of the spring sun. Though they'd looked dead and lifeless a month ago, under nurturing conditions they had flourished.

David prayed the same would be true for Jared.

The meeting room at Matejka Industries was packed with Uplink students and their mentors. Stefan Matejka, a Bosnian immigrant who was one of Uplink's biggest supporters, had donated the use of his facilities for the orientation meeting, as he had since Uplink's inception. Thanks to the generosity of people like him,

Uplink was beginning to establish a strong foothold in the community.

As David surveyed the room, he recognized the students he'd interviewed over the past month. All had been eager, interested and grateful for the opportunity, and he could feel the excitement and electricity in the room. It was a good feeling—one he'd never experienced in his previous career. Yes, there had been satisfaction when he'd closed a deal. But once he'd walked out the door, he'd forgotten about it. It was business. His work had involved dollars, not lives. It had made no lasting contribution to society. This job, in contrast, was about people. About recognizing talent and ability, and finding ways to nurture it. It was about changing lives for the better. Most of all, it was about hope.

Once more, David scanned the crowd. Almost every seat was filled. Even the board was on hand. The expectant faces turned his way reminded him that it was time to begin. But there was one little problem.

Jared was nowhere to be seen.

When David spotted Caroline, seated with Bill about halfway back, she sent him a questioning look. He gave a slight shake of his head and lifted his shoulders. As he watched, she leaned toward Bill, said a few words then rose and made her way toward him. He met her at the side of the raised platform, and as he leaned down she spoke.

"I take it you have no idea where Jared is?"

"No." Once more David surveyed the room, a frown marring his brow. "I knew he was a risk, but I didn't expect him to go AWOL this soon." Sighing, he raked his fingers through his hair. "There's no reason for the two of you to stay if he doesn't show."

"Maybe he just got delayed. We'll hang around for a while. Do you want me to try calling him?"

"If you wouldn't mind, that would be great." He checked his watch. "I need to get started, or I'd do it myself. Ella has all the students' numbers with her. She's probably still at the registration table."

"Okay. I'll give it a try."

Ten minutes later, Caroline reappeared and slipped into her seat. She mouthed "no answer" when he looked her way. An hour later, at the break, David tried himself—with the same result.

"Look, I hate to waste your time," he told Bill and Caroline before he went back to the front to resume the meeting. "If you need to take off, I understand."

"You'll be wrapping up in forty-five minutes. I'll hang around," Bill said.

"Me, too," Caroline added. "Maybe there's a good explanation for Jared's absence today. If he's still going to participate, Bill and I need to be part of this orientation."

"All right. Thanks."

By the time the meeting broke up, Jared had still not appeared. David was kept busy answering questions from mentors and students for another fifteen minutes. By then, the crowd had dispersed. Bill had left, but Caroline was still sitting off to one side, talking on her cell phone as Ella collected the stray printed material in the chairs and on the information table.

David approached Caroline, waiting while she finished her conversation. Then she stood, dropping her phone into her tote. "Sorry. A bit of a crisis at the *Chronicle*."

"No problem. I appreciate that you and Bill stayed for

the whole thing." He shook his head. "I just can't figure this out. Jared promised he'd be here when I spoke with him, and I thought he was sincere. Either my judgment is way off base, or something's wrong."

"Why don't you try him one more time before I leave? I'm a little worried myself."

"Are you sure you don't mind waiting?"

"I've invested this much time. Another couple of minutes won't hurt."

"Okay." He withdrew his cell phone and hit redial, hoping for an answer but not really expecting one. When a woman's voice came over the line, his face registered surprise. "Hello. Is Jared there?"

After a couple of seconds, she responded in a cautious tone. "Yes. But he can't come to the phone right now."

The woman had to be Jared's grandmother. Her voice sounded older—and a bit fearful, David noted. He'd seen her name on Jared's application, and he searched his memory, trying to call it up. Grace. Grace Morris.

"Ms. Morris? This is David Sloan from Uplink. We had an orientation meeting this morning for our new student interns, and we were concerned when Jared didn't attend. I wanted to follow up and make sure everything was okay."

Again, a hesitation. "No, Mr. Sloan, I'm afraid it's not. Jared had a…a run-in with his former gang last night."

Twin furrows appeared on David's brow. "Is he all right?"

"I'm taking care of him. But I'm afraid he's going to have to drop out of the program."

Whatever had happened last night must have been

worse than she was letting on. "We'd hate to lose him, Ms. Morris. He's a very talented young man."

"I know. And I'm very sorry that he's going to miss this opportunity. But I think it's…better…this way."

Safer was what she meant, David guessed. But there had to be a way to make this work. He wasn't giving up on the boy without a fight. "Look, Ms. Morris, I appreciate your concerns. I know you want what's best for Jared. Why don't you let me come down and talk this over in person? Maybe we can figure something out to help Jared take advantage of Uplink without causing any further problems."

"I don't see how, Mr. Sloan." Her voice was weary—and resigned.

"Will you at least give me a few minutes of your time to talk this through?"

"I guess that couldn't hurt."

Consulting his watch, David did a rapid mental calculation. "I can be there in half an hour. Would that be okay?"

"Yes. That's fine. But I think you're wasting your time."

"I'm willing to take that chance."

"All right. I'll see you about noon."

As David ended the call, Caroline gave him a troubled look. As she'd watched his face and listened to his side of the exchange, she'd gotten the gist of the conversation. Something had happened to Jared. And he was dropping out. Questions sprang to her lips, but she waited while David gathered his thoughts and let him speak first.

"Jared had a run-in with his old gang last night. I got the impression they roughed him up. Enough to give his grandmother—and maybe him—cold feet. I'm assuming it was an intimidation tactic, to keep him from straying too far. They must have found out about Uplink. She says he's going to withdraw from the program."

"But you're going to talk to her?"

"Yes. I'm not sure what good it will do. Her mind seems to be made up. But I can't let him walk away from this without exploring every option first."

"I agree. Why don't I come with you? Maybe between us we can convince her to let him continue."

The offer surprised him, but before he could respond, Ella came up beside them. "Sounds like a good idea to me. Two heads are always better than one." She gave the room a quick scan, then directed her next comment to David. "I've gathered up all the extra material. Do you need me for anything else today?"

"No. Thanks for your help, Ella. I'll see you Monday."

"I'll be there. In the meantime, you work on that grandma. Together." She gave Caroline a wink. "And don't be shy, honey. You just speak right up to that lady. Go for the heartstrings. You'll be much better at that than David." With a wave, she went to retrieve her purse.

A smile touched the corners of David's lip. "I guess I have my orders."

"It seems I do, too," Caroline replied, amused.

"Let's give it a try, then. We can take my car. Since it's not the best part of town, we ought to stick close."

His suggestion made sense, so Caroline just nodded and reached for her purse.

Twenty minutes later, as they pulled up in front of the apartment building where Jared lived, David's lips settled into a grim line. Calling the dilapidated, five-story building with a dozen plastic-covered, broken windows and a small bare patch of earth in front a tenement would be too generous. A few youngsters were playing with a cardboard box in a side yard, and rap music blared from one of the open windows. In a vacant lot next door, a clump of wild tiger lilies had somehow managed to gain a foothold, providing the one touch of beauty in the desolate setting.

When David turned to Caroline, it was clear that the abject poverty and dismal environment had made a deep impression on her as well. Her face reflected sadness as she stared at the surroundings, and when he caught a glimmer in her eyes, he knew she was fighting back tears. All at once he was sorry he'd brought her. If he thought it was safe, he'd suggest she wait in the car and spare her a visit inside, which he suspected was as bad—or worse—than the outside. But there was no way he was leaving her alone in this neighborhood.

Reaching out, he laid a gentle hand on her shoulder. "This wasn't such a good idea. It's not very pretty down here."

His tender, caring touch choked her up even more, and she tried to swallow past the lump in her throat. "I've seen worse. I spent time in the Middle East, remember? But I'm always blown away when I come across poverty like this in our country. In a land where so many have so much, where a few miles from here people drive Mercedes and belong to country clubs and live in five-thousand-square-foot homes." She took another second to compose herself, then turned to him. "Ready?"

"Yes. I'll get your door."

She waited for him to come around, and he took her arm as they walked toward the entrance. A group of teenage boys sat on a stoop at the next building, and as he and Caroline picked their way over the cracked and buckled concrete sidewalk, whistles and catcalls followed their progress. David's grip on her elbow tightened in an instinctive, protective gesture. Once more, he regretted bringing her into this environment.

By unspoken mutual consent, they climbed the stairs instead of taking a dark, dingy elevator ride to the third floor. But the stairwell wasn't much better. The smell of stale urine assailed their nostrils, and garbage was wedged in every corner—except for the one where an older man slept with an empty whisky bottle beside him. More than ever, David resolved to do everything in his power to help Grace Morris find a way to feel comfortable—and safe—letting Jared participate in Uplink. It might be the boy's one and only chance to escape from this world.

When they reached the third floor, a long, dim, deserted corridor stretched before them, echoing with the noise coming from behind the dozens of closed doors. Shouts, curses, rap music, the blare of a TV set turned to full volume, a child crying—the cacophony of sound assaulted their ears. Resolving to get out of the hallway as fast as possible, David urged Caroline forward. She followed without protest, making it clear she was of the same mindset. Three doors down they came to Jared's apartment, and David knocked.

Within seconds, a woman's muffled voice came from the other side. "Who is it?"

"David Sloan."

A lock slid back, and an older woman cracked the

door to peer out at them. Then she pulled it open and stepped aside, motioning them in. With a firm click she shut the door behind them and slid the lock back into place. "How do you do? I'm Grace Morris." She extended a gnarled, work-worn hand.

Both recognized her at once from Jared's photo. David took her hand first. "I'm David Sloan. This is Caroline James, from the *Chronicle,* who has agreed to be one of Jared's mentors at the newspaper. She was at today's meeting and offered to come with me."

Caroline took the woman's rough, sinewy hand as well—a hand that spoke of too much exposure to hard work and abrasive detergent. "It's nice to meet you, Ms. Morris."

The woman gestured toward a couch and rocking chair in the tiny living room. "Please sit down. May I offer you something to drink?"

Glancing at Caroline, David shook his head. "No, thanks. We're fine."

As she and David took a seat on the couch, Caroline gave the room a discreet perusal. Though the furnishings were shabby and the ceiling bore water stains, the apartment was tidy and spotless. A hand-crocheted afghan draped over the couch camouflaged the threadbare patches in the fabric, and a bud vase containing one of the lilies from the vacant lot next door sat on a small table beside a worn Bible. Photos of Jared at various ages were grouped in cheap frames on a small credenza, and pictures of scenic vistas—the kind found on many calendars—brightened the walls.

As Grace Morris sat in the rocking chair at a right angle to the window, the sunlight threw the lines in her face into sharp relief. She looked like a woman who had

had a hard life, one filled with care and worry. Yet her demeanor and bearing conveyed dignity and strength. As if she'd found a way to deal with the unfair hand life had dealt her without growing bitter. Caroline's gaze flickered to the Bible, and she suspected that book was the sustaining force in the woman's life. Jared's photo had suggested as much.

"Thank you for seeing us, Ms. Morris," David began. "I hope you don't mind that I brought Caroline along, but she's taken a great interest in Jared as well."

"I appreciate that very much."

"Is he here?"

She glanced toward the bedroom. "He's been sleeping. I didn't want to wake him."

"Can you tell us what happened last night?" David prodded gently.

A shadow passed over the woman's face. "He went out to pick up some medicine for me at the pharmacy. On the way back, some of the members of his gang jumped him. He's been trying to break off with them." Pausing, she reached over and laid her hand on the Bible. "I've been praying for that for a long time. Those boys are bad news. And they don't like defectors. They were putting pressure on Jared to get more involved, and when they heard about Uplink, they figured he was slipping away for good. Last night was a strong message that he better come back into the fold." She removed her glasses, closing her eyes as she massaged the bridge of her nose. Then she replaced the glasses and looked at David and Caroline. "I want Jared to find a way out of here. I want something better than this for my boy. But I also want him to have a long life. And I'm afraid if he continues with Uplink, that might not happen."

His face intent, David leaned forward. "How badly hurt is he, Ms. Morris?"

"Enough that we spent twelve hours in the emergency room. At first he didn't want to go. He knew there'd be questions. But he was having trouble breathing, which scared him—and me, too. By eleven last night I convinced him that we needed to get help."

"What did the doctors—"

A door opened down the hallway off the living room, and David stopped speaking. The sound of shuffling feet followed. Neither he nor Caroline had a view of the hall from where they sat, but it was in Grace's line of sight. She rose just as Jared appeared in the doorway, leaning against the wall and clutching his side.

"Nan, the bandage on my arm came off. Do we have any…"

Caroline shifted in her seat, and the movement caught Jared's attention. Startled, he jerked his head their way and stared at her, then at David. "What's going on?" He directed the question to his grandmother.

"Mr. Sloan called to see why you missed the Uplink meeting, and asked if he could visit to talk with me. Ms. James came along."

As the two conversed, David took a quick inventory of Jared. It was clear from his bent posture that the boy was in pain from injuries David couldn't see. But there were plenty of visible injuries as well. Jared's right eye was almost swollen shut, his lip was puffy and split, and on his upper arm, just below the sleeve of his T-shirt, there was a jagged line of stitches.

A quick glance in Caroline's direction told him that she was just as shocked as he by the boy's condition.

Jared tried to straighten up, but the effort was too

much and he winced. "Didn't you tell them I'm dropping out?"

"Yes."

"We'd like to find a way for you to stay in the program, Jared," David said.

The boy looked at him, his face bleak. "It ain't gonna happen, man. I won't put Nan through the worry."

"But there has to be a way," Caroline countered. Now that she'd seen his living conditions, she was more determined than ever to help him find a way out. She didn't want the gang's intimidation tactics to rob Jared of the best opportunity he might ever have to escape this environment.

"I already have two broken ribs. I'm not angling for two more. Or worse."

"Look, why don't you sit down for a minute while we discuss this?" David rose and moved toward the boy, whose instinctive reaction was to recoil. Slowing his advance, David stopped short of Jared and reached out a hand. "Just lean on me, okay? There's nothing wrong with admitting you need some help. We all do at times."

For several seconds Jared stared at David. Then his shoulders slumped. "Okay. Thanks," he mumbled.

David moved closer, and the tall, lanky teenager grasped his arm as he shuffled toward the couch. Caroline moved over to make room for them both, and David eased the boy down before taking his own seat.

"Okay. Let's think about this a little. It's obvious that we need to get you out of this environment. Ms. Morris, is there anywhere else Jared could live for the summer? A relative who might take him in, in a different part of town? Somewhere away from the gang, a place where they might be less likely to bother him?"

"I have one sister. A widow. She lives in Webster Groves, but we haven't spoken in a long time."

"Webster is close to the *Chronicle*. And far enough away from North St. Louis that the gang might leave Jared alone." It sounded like the perfect arrangement to David.

"I've always taken care of Jared by myself. No one's ever offered to help, and I've never asked. I don't plan to start now," Grace replied. "Besides, like I said, my sister and I haven't spoken for years."

A family rift. David could relate to that. He knew he was treading on sensitive ground, stepping onto a potential minefield, by pursuing this. But he had to take the chance, for Jared's sake.

"Ms. Morris, I admire the fact that you've always cared for Jared on your own. You deserve a lot of credit for that. But maybe the best way you can take care of him right now is to ask your sister for help. I understand why that may not be easy. I had a rift with my own brother, and I've always regretted the fact that we didn't resolve it before he died." His voice grew hoarse on the last word, and he cleared his throat. "There's still time for you, though. And in the process, you'll be doing your best to take care of Jared, just as you always have."

Grace considered that for a moment. Then she reached for the Bible on the table beside her and cradled it in her hands. "I tried to contact her once, to mend our fences, when her husband died three years ago. But she didn't want any part of a reconciliation. I doubt she's changed her mind since then."

"And there's no one else?"

"No."

Stymied, David leaned forward and clasped his

hands between his knees. He couldn't dismiss Grace's worry. Leaving Jared in this environment while he participated in Uplink was asking for trouble. But there seemed to be no other option. Unless...unless Jared lived with him for the summer. It wasn't ideal, of course. The board had warned him early on not to get personally involved with individual students. Too many of them had stories of hardship, and the emotional toll could be great. As a result, the board preferred that the executive director be compassionate but maintain a professional distance. Yet if David didn't step over that line, Jared would be out. And he couldn't let that happen.

"Look, Ms. Morris, this isn't something in my job description. But I care about what happens to Jared. If there's no other option, he would be welcome to stay with me over the summer."

All three people in the room stared at him. Jared looked shocked. Ms. Morris seemed taken aback, but touched. Caroline looked... He didn't want to dwell on the soft warmth in her eyes. So he turned back to Jared's grandmother and focused on her.

"I don't know what to say, Mr. Sloan," she told him.

"I hope you'll say yes."

Something flickered to life in Jared's eyes. Something that looked a lot like hope rekindling. He turned to his grandmother. "I'd like to be part of Uplink, Nan."

Indecision registered on her face. She looked down again at the Bible in her lap, then shook her head. "That's a very kind offer, Mr. Sloan. But it's too much of an imposition."

For most of the visit, Caroline had remained silent. But she could feel the tension in the boy beside her, knew at some instinctive level that even though

he might not be very good with the spoken word, he
wanted this opportunity. Very much. Yet he would defer
to his grandmother's wishes. At the same time, she understood the woman's reluctance to accept David's generous offer. It *was* a tremendous imposition. That left
only one other option.

Leaning forward, Caroline spoke to the older
woman, her voice earnest and empathetic. "Would you
consider contacting your sister again, for Jared's sake,
Ms. Morris? I know you said you tried three years ago,
but many things can change in three years…or three
months…or even overnight." The shadow of pain that
darkened her face wasn't lost on David, and he had to
stifle an urge to reach over and give her hand an encouraging squeeze. Instead, he linked his clasped hands
more tightly. "Maybe it would be worth trying to contact her one more time. You wouldn't have anything to
lose, and perhaps you'd have a lot to gain."

Jared's grandmother looked at the three people sitting across from her on the sofa, waiting for her decision. If two strangers were willing to go out of their
way to give her boy the chance she'd always prayed for,
how could she refuse their appeal to make one more attempt to contact Dara? Maybe her sister would rebuff
her again. But maybe, just maybe, she'd listen this time.
And with God's help, they might even be able to recap-
ture the closeness they'd once shared. Its absence had
been a great sorrow in Grace's life. Perhaps the woman
from the *Chronicle* was right, and Dara's attitude had
changed. But even if it hadn't, she couldn't argue with
Caroline James's other comment. She didn't have anything to lose by trying.

With sudden resolve, Grace clutched her Bible to

her chest and took a deep breath. "All right. I'll give my sister a call."

As she voiced her decision, the looks of elation on the three faces across from her were almost enough reward in themselves.

Chapter Eight

"That was a very generous offer you made to Jared."

As David merged into the traffic on the highway and headed west, he risked a quick glance at Caroline. "I want him to succeed. That seemed like the only way to make it happen."

"Most people wouldn't make such a personal investment."

A rueful look settled over his face. "Nor does the board encourage it. This whole business with Jared has been risky from day one."

"Yet you're willing to take a chance on him."

"Yeah. And for a guy who's been risk-averse most of his life, it's a bit unsettling. But I think Jared has a lot to offer, and I'd hate to see his talent go to waste. I assume that's why you're taking a chance on him, too."

When she didn't respond, David sent her an inquisitive look. She was staring out the front window, her face troubled. "What's wrong?"

At his comment, she turned toward him. "I wish my motivations were that selfless. He is a very gifted writer and photographer, and I'd like to help him find his calling. But I also keep thinking about Michael, how a mentor helped him get his act together and develop his talent. And how Michael always wanted to pay back that kindness by doing the same for another young person. I guess, in a way, I feel like I need to do this for Michael, as a final tribute. And as an atonement for the part I played in his death."

Her voice choked on the last word, and without stopping to think, David removed one hand from the wheel and reached over to touch her cheek. She turned to him in surprise, and he found his hand cupping her chin, her skin smooth and silky against his fingers.

Clearing his throat, he retrieved his hand and transferred it to the wheel, curling his fingers around it in a tight, steadying grip. "I feel the same way," he admitted, his voice a bit rough around the edges. "I guess neither of us has purely altruistic motives."

After that unexpected touch, it took her a second to refocus. "I—I suppose the important thing is that good may come out of it. And I think Michael would be pleased, don't you?"

"Yeah, I do. Jared's exactly the kind of kid he would have chosen to help if he'd had the opportunity."

"Do you think his grandmother will have any luck with her sister?"

"Hard to say, since we don't know what prompted the falling-out." He consulted his watch. "Listen, I don't know about you, but I'm starving. I just grabbed a doughnut this morning at the meeting. Can I interest you in some lunch?"

The man was full of surprises today, Caroline thought, taken aback by the suggestion. She turned to him, noting the strong chin, the firm lips, the well-shaped nose revealed in profile. Sometimes it was hard to believe that he and Michael were brothers. There was little physical resemblance. And their personalities were just as different. Michael had crackled with energy, infusing those he met with excitement and enthusiasm. David was more steady, more solid, instilling trust and confidence in everyone around him. Michael had lived on the edge, carrying a whiff of danger with him; David resided on a firm foundation, and he made people feel safe and protected.

After their first meeting weeks before, Caroline had vowed to cut all ties to David. Being with him had dredged up unhappy memories and resentments. But as their paths had begun to cross—and would continue to cross throughout the summer if Jared ended up participating in Uplink—she'd come to see his warm, compassionate, caring side. And as she'd witnessed his deep faith and integrity, she'd found herself not just enduring his company, as she'd expected, but enjoying it.

So the idea of sharing lunch with him held a certain appeal. Besides, it might also give her a chance to ask a few questions about the rift between the two brothers, as her mother has suggested. Already her perspective on that had shifted, and she had a feeling that if she heard David's side of the story it might shift even more. For reasons she didn't quite understand, she was beginning to hope it would.

When the silence between them lengthened, David flicked her an amused glance. "If it's taking you that long to decide, you must not be as hungry as I am."

With a start, she forced her thoughts back to the present. And made her decision. "As a matter of fact, I am. Lunch would be nice. Thanks."

For a brief instant, David seemed as surprised by her acceptance as she'd been by the invitation, but he recovered quickly. "Great. Any suggestions on a place? I'm too new in town to know the good spots yet."

"How about Café Provençal, in Kirkwood? They have a great patio and the weather is perfect today for outdoor dining."

"Sounds good. But you'll have to direct me."

She did so, and once seated at a wrought-iron table under the large awning, he nodded his approval. "I like this. Do you come here often?"

"No. I've been here for dinner a few times. But it's more of a special-occasion place at night. During the day, it's pretty casual."

"I don't know. I think a special-occasion place is defined more by the company than the ambiance."

His tone was conversational, but something in his eyes sent an odd tingle up her spine. Caroline was saved from having to respond by the appearance of the waitress, who recited the list of specials. As she departed, a man about David's age, dressed in khakis and a golf shirt, rose from a nearby table and walked over to them.

"David? I thought that was you."

At the greeting, David turned in surprise. Then he smiled and rose, extending his hand. "Chuck Williams! What are you doing here?"

"I'm on vacation, visiting my wife's family." He gestured toward a table in the corner, where an attractive woman was seated with an older couple.

"Chuck, this is Caroline James. Caroline, Chuck was

an associate of mine at my old firm in Chicago until he switched companies about a year ago."

After they exchanged a few pleasantries, Chuck turned his attention back to David. "So what are you doing in St. Louis?"

"I took a job here with a nonprofit organization almost six months ago."

"No kidding? When you turned down that fabulous offer in New York right before I left because you didn't want to disrupt your mom's life by moving her again, I figured you'd be in Chicago forever. How is she?"

"She passed away a year ago. Not long after you left."

Sympathy suffused the man's face. "I'm so sorry, David. That had to be tough. I know how much she meant to you. And what great care you gave her."

"Thanks. It's been hard. But I have a new life now, doing something I love. It seems all things work toward God's plan."

"Well, I'm happy for you, then." He turned back to Caroline. "It was nice to meet you. And good luck with the new job," he told David.

"Thanks."

As the man returned to his table and David took his seat again, Caroline reached for her water glass, trying to buy herself a few seconds to digest the information she'd just heard. David had turned down a major promotion in order to remain in Chicago because he had felt it was in his mother's best interest. It was yet another piece of information confirming that David hadn't been selfish in his decision to put their mother in a nursing facility, as Michael had thought.

"You look a bit pensive."

At David's comment, Caroline tried for a smile. "I

was just thinking about Michael." That was true. Sort of. And it might give her an indirect avenue to ask the questions that were on her mind.

"Anything in particular?"

"About his passion for life. And his spontaneity. And how much he cared for the people he loved."

"Yeah. I agree. I always admired him for his loyalty and his willingness to embrace life without agonizing over every little decision. I had a case of hero worship for him ever since I was a little kid. He always seemed larger than life, somehow. I tried to emulate him, but we were just too different. He was athletic, I was academic. He was the daredevil type, always looking for adventure, while I was the cautious one. Even though I sometimes cringed at his recklessness, I couldn't help but admire his fearlessness." A smile touched his lips, and the firm planes of his face softened in recollection. "I remember one time, when he was about ten or eleven, he was convinced that he could jump from the roof of our garage to the roof of the toolshed next door. So he put on his superhero cape and climbed up on the roof—a feat which, in and of itself, seemed incredibly brave to me at the time. Then he proceeded to attempt the jump."

"What happened?"

"We all took a trip to the emergency room while he got a dozen stitches in his chin." David chuckled and shook his head. "The whole incident seemed to bother us a lot more than it bothered him. By the next day, he was ready to try it again. And he would have, too, if my dad hadn't threatened to pull him out of soccer if he did."

That sounded like Michael, Caroline reflected, her

own lips turning up into a wistful smile. "Well, you may have had a case of hero worship, but Michael also had great admiration and respect for you. He was always bragging about his little brother."

That was news to David. Michael had never been the type to give voice to those kinds of thoughts. At least not to him. The love between them had been strong, but not often verbalized. "Thanks for telling me that. It means a lot. And that's another way that Michael reminds me of Jared. Verbal communication wasn't his strong suit."

Caroline gave David a surprised look. "I thought he was very good with words."

"Maybe he was with you. At least, I hope he was. An engaged woman has a right to hear what's in the heart of the man she loves. But with most people, Michael kept his feelings to himself. He might have been willing to take chances physically, like the day he jumped off the garage roof, but he was a lot more cautious about sharing what was in his heart. That's why it was difficult to talk to him about the situation with Mom."

A perfect opening, Caroline thought. But she needed to proceed with caution. "He was very upset about that," she ventured.

"I know. We both let anger get in the way of communication. I'm sorry we never resolved our differences. I'll regret that until the day I die."

With the tip of her finger, Caroline traced the trail of a drop of condensation down her glass, thinking how much it looked like a tear. When she spoke, her voice was soft and tinged with melancholy. "I have to admit that I resented you for a long time after Michael died. I felt that your argument with him was on his mind that day in the marketplace, that maybe it distracted him and made him less alert than usual. That if he'd been focused on the situation, he might have noticed something awry and stayed out of harm's way. The fact is, though, suicide bombers don't often tip their hands."

"Maybe not. But I've always felt guilty about it, anyway. Still, I don't know what I'd do differently. When you visited at Christmas, Mom had a couple of good days. But right after that, she went downhill so fast that even I had a hard time believing it. And it had to be much more difficult for Michael to grasp the extent and swiftness of her decline from thousands of miles away. Within weeks, I was afraid to leave her alone for even a few minutes. Once, on a Saturday, I left her in the kitchen for less than three minutes and came back to find that she'd turned on all the burners on the stove and put empty pots on each one. Another time, I took her to church and when I stopped to talk with a friend, she disappeared. Ten frantic minutes later I found her wandering down the middle of the street."

Taking a deep breath, David raked his fingers through his hair. "To make matters worse, I was having a harder and harder time finding reliable help during the day. Since night help was even more difficult to arrange, I started sleeping at her house. I cut down on my business trips as much as I could, because it was almost impossible to find anyone to stay with her for extended periods. I know Michael wanted me to wait until you came home for the wedding before taking any action, but there was no way I could do that. I didn't want to break our promise to Mom any more than he did, but for her own sake, she needed round-the-clock supervision. There just wasn't any other option. Michael wouldn't—or couldn't—accept that. And, to be honest, I resented him for abdicating his responsibility in dealing with the issue. He left it all to me, then got angry when I addressed the problem. It was a bad situation all around."

As Caroline listened to David's explanation, her heart began to ache for him. Until now, she'd never realized the weight of the burden he'd carried. It also became clear to her that despite Michael's angry assessment, David's decision hadn't been arbitrary. It had been born out of necessity. Distance had insulated Michael from the harsh reality of their mother's condition. And perhaps he simply hadn't wanted to acknowledge it, as David had implied. It was hard to come to grips with breaking a promise to someone you loved, even if it was in their best interest. Yet David had had the courage to do that, to handle the heart-wrenching situation alone in a way that reflected deep love and great integrity. Earlier in the day she'd admired his generosity for the offer he'd made to Jared's grandmother. Now her admiration grew yet again. Respect and esteem for this special man filled her heart, easing out any lingering resentment.

The waitress delivered their food then, and Caroline searched for an appropriate response to David's story. She settled for something simple. Reaching over, she laid her hand on his. "Thank you for sharing that with me, David. It gives me a different perspective on the whole situation."

Startled by her touch, David looked at her—and his lungs stopped working. In her hazel eyes he saw kindness and caring and empathy—and no trace of the wariness or resentment that had lurked in their

depths until today. For the first time she was seeing him as a unique person—not as a future brother-
in-law, not as an enemy, not as a business associate.
But as David Sloan, the man. The individual. And it
just about did him in.

Swallowing, he dropped his gaze to her slender fingers, delicate and pale against his sun-browned hand.
And a sudden yearning swept over him—a yearning
to touch her, to hold her, to let her warmth fill his life
and chase away the loneliness that had plagued him for
the past couple of years, when his first sight of her had
awakened a hunger in him for all the things he'd been
missing by putting love on the back burner.

As she removed her hand and turned her attention
to her lunch, David forced himself to do the same. But
he knew that the hunger inside him, the empty place in
his heart, could never be satisfied by the chicken salad
sandwich on his plate.

Grace Morris reached for the phone, then let her hand
drop back to her lap. She'd had to do a lot of hard things
in her life. Bury her husband. Watch her one child, her
beloved daughter, die of a drug overdose. Do menial,
physical work that left her bone-weary. Raise her grandson alone. But calling Dara ranked right up near the top.

Reaching for her Bible, as she had during many of
the hard times, Grace opened it to Matthew, to the passage that had given her comfort and sustained her in her
darkest days. Once more she read the familiar words.
"Come to me, all you who labor and are burdened, and
I will give you rest. Take my yoke upon you, and learn
from me, for I am meek and humble of heart—and you
will find rest for your souls."

Closing her eyes, Grace added her own prayer. *Lord, please help Dara find it in her heart to understand. Please help her to see the truth, to know that I love her and would never do anything to hurt her. Help us to be sisters again. But even if that can't be, please fill her heart with compassion for Jared so that he can have a better life. Amen.*

Once more, Grace reached for the phone. This time she tapped in the number. Though her hand was trembling, she felt steadier inside, her courage bolstered by her prayer. When her sister answered on the third ring, she forced the words past her tight throat.

"Dara? It's Grace." Holding her breath, Grace waited for a response, praying that it wouldn't be just a hang-up. *Please, Lord, at least let her talk to me.*

Several seconds of shocked silence passed. But at last the other woman spoke in a cautious voice. "Hello, Grace."

"Thank you for not hanging up on me."

"I've gotten past that, I guess."

That was a good start, Grace thought. "It's been a long time since we talked."

"Yes. It has."

"I'm sorry for all the misunderstanding between us. I've missed having a sister."

After a few seconds, Dara responded. "I have, too." Her quiet admission surprised Grace. As did her next comment. "I even thought about calling you once or twice. But I could never bring myself to do it. The fact is, I should never have gotten angry at you. It was just easier, somehow, to blame you than to accept the fact that George was…that he wasn't the most faithful husband."

Grace thought back to that Christmas when George had cornered her in the kitchen after having one too many drinks. Recalled how he'd backed her against the refrigerator and kissed her, suggesting that he'd be happy to ease her loneliness now that she was a widow. Grace had heard rumors for years that George had a tendency to stray, but she'd never believed them. Never wanted to believe them. Then Dara had come into the kitchen at the worst possible moment. She'd stormed over, yanked George away and lit into Grace about seducing her own brother-in-law when he was half-drunk. She'd said a lot of bad things that had hurt Grace and incited her own anger. How could the sister she'd loved all her life make such terrible accusations?

That had been nine years ago, right before Jared had come to live with her. Though Grace had made an overture to mend their fences when George died, her sister had rebuffed it. She and Dara hadn't talked since.

"I never encouraged him, Dara."

"I know that now. All the stories I heard after he died confirmed what I'd suspected for years, but refused to accept. Ever since then, I've wanted to call you. But pride got in my way. I didn't want to admit that I couldn't even keep my own husband interested."

"The problem wasn't in you, Dara."

"Sometimes I wonder about that. But it's over now, anyway. And more and more I realize how much I miss having you in my life. I was just afraid it was too late. I said some awful things to you."

"I was angry about that for a long time," Grace admitted. "But I prayed a lot about it through the years, and I finally let the anger go. I've been wanting to call you for a long time, but I was afraid you'd cut me off."

"Fear and pride. Two destructive emotions. We're quite a pair, I guess. What's that saying about an old fool? But at least you tried to reconnect when George died. Considering how I treated you then, I'm surprised you tried again. I figured the next attempt would have to come from me."

Now came the moment of truth. And Grace figured honesty was the best way to handle it. "I guess maybe that would have been the case if I wasn't worried about Jared."

"Is there something wrong with him?"

Plunging into the story, Grace gave Dara the highlights, then summed up the impetus for her call. "So unless I can find a place for him to stay for the summer where he'll be away from the gang, he's going to have to turn down the opportunity. I just don't want to risk losing him. But I do want him to have a better life. I guess my love for him helped me overcome my fear about calling. I need your help, Dara. If you can find it in your heart to give him a room for ten weeks, it could make all the difference in the world to him."

When her request was met with silence, Grace fought down the panic that welled up inside her. "I know this is coming at you out of the blue, Dara. I don't expect an answer right away. You can call me back after you think about it. And if you don't want to take this on, I'll understand. I realize what an imposition it would be."

"You did take me by surprise, Grace."

"I'm sure I did. Like I said, I'd just be grateful if you'd consider it. For Jared's sake, not mine."

"Is he a good boy?"

"He's good at heart. That's why he's trying to break his gang ties and make something better of his life. He's honest, and if he makes a promise, he keeps it. But I won't lie to you. He's had some rough stretches. His grades aren't the best, and I've had a tough time keeping him in school. That's why Uplink is such a godsend. I've been praying for the past two years that something will help him turn his life around, and I think this is it."

"I'm not sure I know how to deal with a teenager, Grace. Since George and I never had children, I don't have any experience with young people."

"Jared is very self-sufficient. All he really needs is a place to sleep. I'll be happy to contribute toward his meals and any other expenses he might incur."

"Are you still working?"

"Yes."

"Doing what?"

"The same thing I've always done."

Dara shifted the phone on her ear. George might not have been faithful, but he'd at least given her a comfortable life and left her well-fixed. She could afford to take the boy on for the summer. And with two empty bedrooms, she had plenty of room. "I'd like to meet the boy, at least," she said.

Grace said a silent prayer of thanks before she responded. "He'd like to meet you, too."

"Why don't you bring him out on Saturday?"

"You want me to come, too?"

"Of course. I don't remember Jared very well. It will be less awkward if you're there. Besides, we have a lot to catch up on."

"I doubt we can make much headway in one meeting."

"I'm hoping it's the first of many."

A cleansing wave of happiness swept over Grace,

washing away the debris of their broken relationship and leaving a smooth, fresh expanse in its wake.

"We'll be there, Dara."

"Make it about eleven, if that's okay. And plan to stay for lunch."

"All right. And thank you."

"Thank *you*. For having the courage to take the first step. I'll see you Saturday."

As Grace replaced the phone, she reached over once more to pick up her Bible, her heart overflowing with gratitude. And as she placed it against her heart, she smiled.

God was good.

Chapter Nine

"Take a look at these."

Ignoring her half-shut door, Bill Baker strolled into Caroline's office without knocking and dropped several black-and-white photos on her desk.

If he wasn't such a great photographer—and if he didn't have a heart of gold—Caroline wondered if she'd be willing to put up with Bill's brusque style. As it was, she just set aside the layouts for the next week's edition and reached for the photos, her mind still on the changes she needed to call into the production department.

But her focus shifted abruptly as the photos caught her attention. The subject of each was a child with some sort of disability. One little boy was laughing in delight as he was lifted from his wheelchair to the back of a horse. A young blind girl was engrossed in shaping a vase on a potter's wheel, her face alight with wonder as her hands molded the clay. The joyful expression of a boy with Down syndrome had been caught at the perfect instant, as he reeled in a fish. Each of the remaining photos was just as compelling, capturing expressions and moments that spoke of joy and hope in the midst of problem-plagued lives.

When she finished, she looked up at Bill. "Let me guess. Jared."

"That's right." He propped a hip on the corner of Caroline's desk. "I sent him to cover a day camp for disabled children. It was his first solo assignment. My only instruction was to capture the spirit of the event, and this is what he came back with."

Leaning back in her chair, Caroline steepled her fingers. "Amazing."

"That's the word for it. I figured you'd want to see these before I turn them in to production."

"You were right. Thanks. How's everything been going in general?" Three weeks into the internship, Jared seemed to have settled in. There'd been a few rough patches at first as he adjusted to his new living arrangement and the eight-to-five working world, but nothing that had caused Caroline any great concern.

"Better and better. The attitude problem is disappearing, and he's done a good job at all the shoots he's been on with me. He remembers every critique I make of his work, and incorporates my suggestions into the next assignment. That's why I figured he was ready to go solo for the camp story."

"You figured right."

"How's he faring from the writing end?"

"Also improving. He doesn't take as much offense when I offer constructive criticism. And we're going to run a bylined piece in the next edition."

"He'll like that." Bill rose, gathered up the photos and headed toward the door, glancing across the newsroom through Caroline's glass-walled office toward Jared's cubicle. The boy was concentrating at his computer and oblivious to their perusal. "I need to catch him before he takes off. I'll talk to you later."

As Bill strode toward Jared, Caroline assessed the changes in their intern. He'd appeared the first day in jeans, new loafers and a golf shirt—a great improvement over the baggy pants and ripped shirts that seemed to be his typical attire. After two weeks, the dreadlocks had been sheared into a clean-cut, close-cropped style. Although the employees had been welcoming, he'd kept to himself at first, standing apart in the break room when other staffers gathered to chat over coffee, and rebuffing lunch invitations. But in the past couple of days, she'd noticed him leaving at lunchtime with two of the younger employees who frequented a local sandwich shop. She'd seen that as a good sign, an indication that he was adjusting and beginning to feel comfortable.

If Caroline's relief at the smooth transition was considerable, she knew David's was even greater. He'd put his career on the line by taking a chance on Jared. A chance that seemed to be paying off. She and David spoke on a regular basis, and he'd stopped by a couple of times to visit Jared on the job site, as he did with all of the interns. For reasons she didn't want to examine too closely, she found herself looking forward to those visits. Much more than was prudent. When Jared's internship ended, there would be little reason for David to stay in touch. Considering her antipathy toward the man just a few weeks before, she should be happy about that. Instead, she felt melancholy, which in turn made her feel uncomfortable. Again, for reasons she wasn't inclined to scrutinize.

To distract herself, Caroline turned toward her credenza and opened the top drawer. Withdrawing the envelope she'd placed there last week, she scanned the announcement from the national journalism association about a competition for high school students. Winners would attend a two-week intensive program in New York conducted by major names in the fields of journalism and photography. The entry required at least one letter of recommendation from a member of the professional organization, as well as a feature story written and photographed by the entrant. When Caroline had seen it, she'd thought of Jared at once. With some judicious coaching, she'd pit his work not just against other students, but against many pros she'd met. Since the deadline wasn't for six weeks, she'd been biding her time, waiting to see how things worked out with the internship. But at this point, she saw no reason to delay suggesting that he enter.

Just then Jared rose, and Bill laid a hand on his shoulder. Where once he would have flinched, now she saw a quick grin flash across the boy's face. Another positive sign, she thought. As she headed for her door to discuss the competition with him, he reached for his backpack under the desk. Checking her watch, she noted that it was already after five—and he had a bus to catch. His great-aunt's home wasn't far, but the bus schedule in the county was somewhat limited, and if he missed his ride it would be a long walk. Deciding that their discussion could wait until first thing the next morning, Caroline put the competition materials aside and went back to work.

Almost three hours passed before quitting time came for her. The day before the paper went to press was always grueling. Then again, she hadn't gotten into journalism for its regular hours, she thought, a wry grin tugging at her lips as she reached for her tote. Hoisting it on her shoulder, she was just about to switch off the light in her office when her phone rang.

The temptation to ignore it was strong. She wasn't anxious to extend her already long day. Nevertheless, she circled back around her desk to check her caller ID, hesitating at the unfamiliar number. What if it was a hot lead for a great story? Her journalistic training kicked in, and ignoring the hunger pangs that told her it was well past dinnertime, she reached for the phone.

"Caroline James."

"Caroline, it's David. I tried your home number, but when I didn't get an answer I took a chance you might still be at the office."

The sound of his voice brought a smile to her lips. "Mondays are always late nights for me because we go to press on Tuesday. I was just heading out."

"Well, I don't want to delay you. I was just in the neighborhood and thought I'd drop off the midterm evaluation form instead of mailing it. We always ask our mentors to give us a brief written progress report on their intern halfway through the program. Is there a night slot I could leave it in?"

"How far away are you?"

"About five minutes."

"I'll just wait for you in the lobby."

"Are you sure you don't mind?"

"No. I could use a couple of minutes to sit and veg."

"Okay. I'll be there soon."

As it turned out, David didn't arrive for almost fifteen minutes. When she finally saw him striding down the sidewalk, his suit-and-tie attire suggested that he, too, had had a long workday. She met him at the door before he could even press the buzzer.

"Sorry for the delay," he apologized. "I got stopped by a train a few blocks up on Kirkwood Road."

Smiling, she reached for the envelope he held out to her and slid it into her shoulder tote. "It happens all the time. There's a route over the tracks, but only the locals know about it. I'll give you directions sometime."

"Thanks."

When he hesitated, Caroline searched his face. He looked tired, she thought. As if he'd not only been putting in long hours, but perhaps investing too much of himself in his job—worrying about the students, worrying about making the program a success, worrying about fulfilling the plan he seemed to feel that God had for him. That was another difference between the two brothers, she mused. Michael hadn't been a worrier. Or much of a planner. He'd always lived for the moment, choosing to let tomorrow take care of itself. A worrier herself, Caroline had found that quality appealing—and liberating. But while she'd agreed with Michael that worry taken to extremes was counterproductive and could rob you of today, in retrospect she realized that he may have erred too much in the other direction. Worry in moderation could be constructive, allowing you to avoid mistakes. It could also foster compassion. The trick was finding the balance.

Caroline suspected that David hadn't done that yet. That he still took on the cares of those entrusted to him as if they were his own. Including every student in the Uplink program. And one student in particular. His next question confirmed her suspicion.

"How's Jared doing?"

"Great. Bill showed me some photos today that Jared took on his first solo assignment, a day camp for disabled children. They were fabulous. Every one displayed the signature quality we noticed in the work in his portfolio. And we're going to run a bylined story in the next edition. His writing was good to begin with, but it's gotten even better."

The subtle relaxing of David's features told her he welcomed that news even before he spoke. "I'm glad to hear it." He glanced over her shoulder, to the darkened offices. "Are you the last one here?"

"The managing editor is always the last to leave. At least on pre-press days. It goes with the territory."

"Can I walk you to your car?"

Surprised, she shook her head. "Thanks, but that's not necessary. There's a lot right behind the building. I'm just going to set the night alarm and pull the front door shut behind me, then head down the alley." She punched some numbers into the keypad beside the door, then stepped outside.

As she twisted the handle of the door to confirm that it had locked, David gave the narrow, dim passage a quick look. "I'd feel better about it if you'd let me see you to your car. My mother always told me that a gentleman should never let a lady walk down a dark alley alone." His lips quirked into a grin.

David was a gentleman, no question about that, Caroline reflected as she hoisted her shoulder tote higher. Even her mother would approve of his good manners. Not that it mattered, of course. It wasn't as if they were dating or anything.

But I wish we were.

The wistful but startling thought came to her unbidden. How in the world could she even think such a thing? This was the brother of the man she'd loved. The man she *still* loved. She wasn't interested in getting involved with *any* man, let alone this man. It just felt…wrong.

As David waited for Caroline's response, he wasn't quite sure what to make of the expressions flitting across her face. But he hoped she wasn't insulted. In today's politically correct world, it was sometimes hard to know just how chivalrous to be with women. "I know the offer is a bit old-fashioned, and to someone who's spent time in the Middle East it may seem like overkill. I hope I didn't offend you."

With an effort, Caroline reined in her wayward thoughts and tamped down the sudden staccato beat of her heart. "No. Not at all. I guess I've just gotten so used to taking care of myself that the offer surprised me. Thank you." Without waiting for him to respond, she headed for the alley.

He followed close behind her, since the passage wasn't wide enough to accommodate them side by side. Most of the time Caroline exited out the back door, right into the parking lot. She'd only used this route once or twice. And never in the evening. Even though it stayed light quite late this time of year, dusk had settled, and the deep shadows between the buildings were a bit unnerving. Despite the fact that she considered Kirkwood safe, and that she'd been alone in far more dangerous situations on assignments, she found David's presence comforting. It made her feel protected. While his offer might have been prompted by mere courtesy, it nevertheless made her feel cared for. And special, somehow.

When they emerged into the dimly lit parking area,

he moved into step beside her. She gestured toward her car, which was wedged into a far corner of the lot. "I had to run an errand at lunch, and when I got back that was the only spot left. Most of the time I park much closer to the door." She stopped and turned to him. "Thanks again."

"I'm beginning to think you're trying to get rid of me."

"No, of course not." Her protest came fast. Too fast. The line from Shakespeare flashed through her mind, and a flush crept up her neck.

"Then I'll finish the job." His hand moved to the small of her back and he urged her forward with a firm, sure touch.

At his prompt, Caroline moved toward her car, deciding that silence was her best response. She had no idea what was going on with her equilibrium, but all at once she felt off balance and ill at ease. Later, when she was alone, she'd think this through. Right now, she just needed to get into the car and away from the man beside her, who seemed to be the cause of her problem.

Trying not to run, she picked up her pace. As she approached the car, she fumbled in her shoulder tote for her keys. "Are you just heading home from the office, too?"

When her question produced no response, Caroline sent David a questioning look. He was staring at the passenger door of her car with an odd expression, and when she turned in search of the cause, it hit her like a slap in the face.

Scratched into the maroon paint was a warning—"Back off"—followed by a single, crude term directed at her. She gasped at the vulgar reference.

David's hand tightened on her waist, and she turned to him. His mouth was set in a grim line, and all levity had vanished from his face. When he looked down at her, she saw worry in the depths of his brown eyes. "Do you have any idea what that might be about, besides the obvious?"

Although his tone was quiet and controlled, she could sense the tension in his body. The "obvious" was Jared, of course. But she didn't want to believe that.

"Maybe it's not what you assume."

"Can you think of any other explanation?"

In truth, she couldn't. She'd taken flak for stories in the past, but there was no issue hot enough right now to raise anyone's ire to a level that would push them to take this kind of action. "No."

"That's what I figured." David reached into his pocket and withdrew his cell phone.

"What are you doing?"

"Calling the police."

"I doubt it will do any good. The lot's deserted. This could have been done hours ago."

"It still needs to be reported. For insurance purposes, if nothing else."

She put out a hand to restrain him. "Look, David, I don't want to cause trouble for you or Jared. If this gets back to the Uplink board members, they'll give you a lot of grief. And it could jeopardize their willingness to take a chance on students like Jared. It's not worth that risk."

His hesitation was so brief she wondered if she'd imagined it. Then he punched in 911. "I'm not taking chances with you, either. That's a threat." He gestured toward the car. "It has to be reported." Before she could respond, his call was answered, and while he provided the requested information, she stared at the warning. Instead of intimidating her, it strengthened her resolve to help Jared. If gang members were responsible for this, as David suspected, their plan had backfired.

"All right. Thanks." David flipped his cell phone shut and slipped it back in his pocket as he turned to Caroline. "An officer should be here within a couple of minutes." He scanned the parking lot, then nodded toward the building. "Why don't you wait inside?"

Her chin lifted a notch. "I don't run away from trouble, David. I'll wait here with you."

As he studied her in the shadowed light, noting the resolve in her squared shoulders, the determined look in her hazel eyes, the uncompromising line of her lips, he found himself admiring her strength and tenacity. No wonder she'd been such a good reporter.

But he found himself admiring other things, as well. The delicate column of her slender throat. Her classic cheekbones. The graceful line of her jaw. As a sudden gust of wind whipped a few strands of silky hair across her face, he was tempted to reach over and let them drift through his fingers. Instead, he watched, motionless, as she lifted her hand to brush them aside with a graceful gesture. In the distance, a flash of lightning zigzagged across the night sky, followed by the muted rumble of thunder. The clouds that had been gathering on the horizon must have moved closer, because the air was now charged with electricity. Soon the storm would break. If they didn't take evasive action, they would both be caught in it.

"Maybe we should both go inside where it's safe."

His voice rumbled deep in his chest, just like the thunder, sending a little shiver down her spine.

Although she couldn't see the expression in his shadowed eyes, Caroline sensed David's intensity. Heard the rough timbre of his voice. Felt her own pulse leap in response.

And suddenly knew that nowhere with David would be safe.

Before she could find her voice, a police car turned into the parking lot.

"Too late," David murmured, his gaze holding hers captive.

His comment was rife with meaning. And she couldn't agree more. But right now she needed to focus on the immediate problem. Her car. She could worry about everything else later. Forcing herself to turn away, she looked toward the police.

Two officers emerged from the patrol car and walked over to them. The older one withdrew a notebook. "Good evening, folks. I'm Officer Scanlon. This is Officer Lowe. I understand you reported some vandalism?"

"Right there." David pointed toward Caroline's car.

The two men examined the damaged car, then scanned the ground with their flashlights. "I take it this is your car, ma'am?" The younger officer directed his question to Caroline.

"Yes."

"Any guess on when this might have happened?"

"I took the car out at lunch. It was okay then."

"Any idea who might have done it?"

David stepped in and gave them a brief overview of the situation, then voiced his own suspicions.

"A gang-related crime, huh?" The older officer took

a closer look at Caroline, recognition dawning in his eyes. "This isn't your first run-in with gang violence, is it, Ms. James? Looks like the forehead healed up just fine, though."

Caroline felt David's intent gaze on her even before he spoke. "What does that mean?"

Forcing a nonchalant tone into her voice, she lifted one shoulder in an indifferent shrug. "Remember that series I told you about, the one I did last year on gangs? Someone didn't appreciate it. This—" she lifted her hand to touch the hairline scar "—was the result of a rock thrown at a window in my condo. I just happened to be standing in the wrong place when it came through. A voice mail at work the next day confirmed that it was related to that series."

A muscle in David's cheek twitched.

"Lucky for you it didn't take out an eye," Officer Scanlon said.

If Caroline had been the victim of gang violence once already, David realized that it could easily happen again. This time with far worse consequences. "Aside from the vandalism, what about the threat in that warning?" he asked the policemen.

"It could end right here. Or they could follow through. There's no way to tell. The easy solution is to end the internship."

"No way." Caroline folded her arms across her chest. "I won't be intimidated."

"Look, Caroline, maybe we need to talk about this," David interjected.

She turned to him and planted her hands on her hips, her eyes fiery. "No. I'm not going to deny Jared this chance."

David understood her commitment to the teen. He felt the same way. And he wouldn't care if the threat had been directed to him. He'd be just as adamant about seeing the thing through as Caroline was. But he felt a whole lot different knowing that she was a target—and that he was the one who had put her in the line of fire. Yet her resolve was strong. He doubted whether he was going to be able to convince her to back off, as the warning had instructed.

Jamming one hand in his pocket, he raked the fingers of the other one through his hair as he turned back to the policemen. "Is there anything you can do to track down the person or persons responsible for the vandalism?"

"Very little. We could dust for prints, but experience tells me we won't find any. Even small-time crooks and street kids know better than to leave that kind of evidence. And there's nothing in the immediate area that could have been used to do this. Right, Mark?" He turned toward his partner, who had continued to search the ground. The man nodded.

"Okay. What about Ms. James's safety?" David persisted. "What can you do to protect her, assuming whoever scratched that into her car intends to follow up on the threat?"

"We'll beef up patrols here at night." He turned to Caroline. "Do you still live in the area?"

"Yes."

"What's the address?" He jotted it down as she recited it. "We can schedule a few more patrols past your home, too. Other than that, I would just advise that you use caution. Avoid dark places by yourself at night—including this parking lot. Play it safe. And if you have any concerns, don't hesitate to call us."

When the officers finished filling out their report and headed back to their car, David gave Caroline a worried look. "I don't feel good about this."

She didn't, either. But there was no way she was going to let him see her fear. He'd just press her to send Jared packing, and she had no intention of doing that. "Everything will be fine, David. I'll be careful."

"I still don't like it. Neither will Jared. He was going to pass up this program to ease his grandmother's mind when she was worried about his safety. I suspect he'll feel the same way about you once he knows his presence is putting you in danger."

"Then we won't tell him."

"We have to."

"No, we don't. There's a possibility this incident isn't even gang-related."

"You don't believe that."

"It's possible," she insisted, her chin lifting in a stubborn tilt. "Promise me you won't tell him, David."

There had been a few times in his life when David had been torn between two less-than-ideal options. This was one of them. There just wasn't a good answer. No matter what course they followed, he'd worry.

Sensing his indecision, Caroline played her trump card. "If you tell Jared and he drops out, you'll need to explain it to the board. And that won't do Uplink any good. Let's just let things ride for a while. My guess is that this will be the end of it."

Even though her tone was confident, Caroline wasn't sure she believed that. Judging by his face, David didn't seem to, either. But she knew how much Uplink meant to him. She hoped he'd go along with her in order to safeguard the program, if for no other reason.

After several seconds, he conceded her point and capitulated—with reluctance. "Okay. But you have to promise me that you'll use extreme caution, and that you'll report anything suspicious, no matter how insignificant it seems."

"Of course." Then, brightening her tone, she reached for her door handle. "I don't know about you, but it's way past my quitting time. I'm out of here."

He beat her to the handle, then held the door open while she slid into the driver's seat and put her tote bag on the floor beside her. "I'll follow you home. It sounds like you live pretty close. I bought a small bungalow in Brentwood, so it won't be out of my way."

Words of protest rose to her lips, but she stifled them. Considering he'd let her win on the Jared issue, it might be best not to push her luck. And lightening things up a bit wouldn't hurt, either. "Your mother would be proud of your good manners," she told him, forcing a smile to her lips.

David figured that was true. But as he shut her door with an instruction to wait on the side street while he retrieved his car, he knew that good manners weren't his only motivation for following her home. His reasons went far deeper than that.

When David had met with Caroline to pass on Michael's medallion, he'd hoped that whatever infatuation had plagued him for two and a half long years would fizzle out once he was back in her presence. It hadn't. And as he'd gotten to know her better, as she'd dropped her wall of resentment and worked with him to help Jared, his feelings had deepened. Over the past few weeks they had evolved to respect and admiration and an attraction based on far more than the hormones that had surely triggered his initial reaction to her. In fact, as time had passed, his infatuation had begun to move toward love. But he'd resolved to put his feelings on hold during the summer, as they worked with Jared. He'd never believed in mixing business and pleasure.

Besides, he still had guilt and loyalty issues to work through. How could he pursue his brother's fiancée? Wasn't that wrong, somehow? Even though he was gone, Michael cast a long shadow. And Caroline's love for his brother had been deep and abiding. If and when she was ready to love again, would she, too, think it odd to consider the brother of the man she'd planned to marry as a potential suitor?

None of those questions had easy answers. And David hadn't planned to focus on them yet. Not while they were involved in a business relationship. But things had changed tonight, when he'd discovered that Caroline was in danger. He'd have to stick a whole lot closer to her than he'd planned, and he wasn't sure how he could do that without tipping his hand about his feelings—far sooner than she might be ready to accept them. And far sooner than he was prepared to reveal them.

But if she was going to put herself in jeopardy, he didn't plan to let her face the danger alone. He had to get more involved. There was just no way around it.

And he also planned to pray. For both of them.

Chapter Ten

Caroline jotted a final notation on the layouts for the next edition of the paper, then forked the last spear of broccoli in her Chinese take-out dinner. At least one good thing had come out of the vandalism incident, she mused. For the past two Mondays, David had appeared at her office at about seven o'clock, dinner in hand for both of them, and planted himself at an empty desk with his laptop while she finished up for the day, explaining that he didn't like the idea of her being alone at the *Chronicle*. And he especially didn't like her walking to her car by herself at night. So he'd taken up the job of bodyguard for one night a week, providing dinner to sweeten the deal.

As it had turned out, his considerate gesture had been unnecessary. Nothing more had come of the incident. But Caroline hadn't minded his attention. Capping her pen, she glanced his way, tracing his strong profile as he gave the document in front of him his full attention. During both visits he'd left her alone while she worked, saying that he didn't want to disturb her.

Yet he'd done just that.

Reaching up, Caroline fingered the medallion that rested near her heart. She'd started wearing it more often, to remind herself that her growing attraction to David was inappropriate. And perhaps to warn him to keep his distance. But she wasn't sure how much longer it would have the desired effect. On herself—or on David.

The fact was, Caroline's feelings for David were deepening. Even though she felt guilty about it, she couldn't put the brakes on the sudden acceleration in her pulse when David appeared, couldn't contain the rush of tenderness that swept over her when she looked into his caring, compassionate eyes, couldn't suppress the yearning that filled her heart when she was near him. Nor could she understand her reactions. She still loved Michael—a good, decent man who had taught her how to embrace life and who had added a zest to her days that had forever changed her outlook on the world.

But David was a good, decent man, too. Though the brothers' different approaches to life each had appeal and charm, more and more she was beginning to think that in the long term, over a lifetime, David's quiet, measured style suited her better. And that not only made her feel guilty, but also disloyal.

As if sensing her scrutiny, David looked her way. For a brief second his eyes darkened, sending a rush of warmth to her cheeks. When he rose and walked toward her door, her lungs stopped working and a tingle of anticipation raced up her spine. He paused on the threshold, his gaze flickering down to her hand, which gripped the medallion around her neck, before it moved back to her face. For several seconds he just looked at her.

"I'm going to get some water. Would you like some?" he asked at last.

The innocuous comment was so at odds with the intense look on his face that it took her a second to regroup. "N-no, thanks. I should be done here in another twenty minutes."

"No rush. Take your time."

As he disappeared, Caroline's lungs kicked back into gear. She'd dated enough men to recognize David's expression. If it were anyone else, she'd have expected something to follow that look. A touch, perhaps even a kiss. But since David had never exhibited any romantic inclinations, maybe she was wrong. Maybe she was jumping to conclusions. Maybe her assessment of what had just transpired was simply wishful thinking. Whatever it was, though, she needed to get her emotions under control and stay at arm's length. She didn't need the kind of complication in her life that a romance with David would bring.

When he reappeared a few minutes later and went back to work, Caroline tried to ignore him. During her years composing copy in noisy, chaotic newsrooms, she'd learned to tune out distractions and stay focused. Yet those skills deserted her now. Like it or not, David was one big distraction. Finally, realizing that she was just spinning her wheels and wasting both their time, she reached for her tote and rose.

When she appeared at her door, David looked up in surprise. "Ready so soon?"

"Yes. I'll finish up tomorrow."

"You're not rushing because of me, are you?"

Yes. But not for the reasons you think. "No. It's just been a long day. What's left can wait until tomorrow."

"Okay." He swept his papers into a neat pile and slid them into his briefcase, then stood and followed her to the back exit. After she tapped in the code to set the night alarm system, they stepped out into the July heat.

"I didn't realize St. Louis was so muggy in the summer." David reached up to loosen his tie, giving the parking lot a quick but thorough scan as he walked with her toward her car.

"This is just a preview. Wait until August."

"That's encouraging."

She chuckled. "It does take some getting used to. Especially if you're from a place like Chicago that has a more reasonable climate in the summer."

"I prefer your winters, though."

"We've been lucky the past few years." Caroline was grateful for the small talk. It was easier to deal with than more personal subjects. And safer.

As usual, he opened her door, and she reached in to put her tote bag on the passenger seat before thanking him. But the words died in her throat when she straightened up and once more caught the unguarded look in his eyes. For the briefest second, she saw a warmth that made the July heat seem tame. A warmth suffused with yearning that told her in no uncertain terms that she wasn't alone in the attraction she'd been feeling. Unfortunately, she had no idea how to deal with that revelation. Or this situation.

David stared at the woman beside him, just inches away, and his fingers itched to reach out to her. To stroke her silky skin. To pull her close and wrap her in his arms. To protect her and shield her and love her. That urge had been growing stronger every time he was in her presence. And he was losing his battle to keep his distance, to maintain control.

But not tonight, he told himself, shoving his hands in the pockets of his slacks before he did something with them that he'd regret. He'd already revealed too much in the office a few minutes before, when he'd looked up to find her watching him. The temptation to touch her had been so strong that he'd actually walked to her office. Only the medallion around her neck had stopped him. The message it communicated, to back off, was as clear as the one that had been scratched onto her car two weeks before. Meaning that moving too soon would be a mistake. One that he might not be able to fix. And he wasn't about to take that chance.

"I'll follow you home." He tried to keep his tone conversational, but his voice was uneven, at best.

Instead of speaking, she just turned and slipped into her car. He shut the door and then headed for his own car a couple of spots away. And as he slid into the driver's seat and put his key in the ignition, he knew that one of these days, despite his best efforts, he was going to have to follow his heart. He just prayed that the Lord would give him restraint until the time was right.

In the days that followed, Caroline found her thoughts straying far too often to David. Her concentration slipped, and she wished she could focus on something—anything—except the man with the compelling, deep brown eyes.

Two weeks later, when the phone rang one afternoon in her office, she got her wish. And was sorry she'd ever made it.

"There's a bomb inside the *Chronicle*. You've got fifteen minutes to get out."

The muffled voice on the other end of the phone was almost indecipherable, but the message came through loud and clear. Caroline sprang to her feet, stabbing in 911 with a shaking finger even as she rose.

As soon as her call was answered she spoke, struggling to keep her voice steady. "This is Caroline James, managing editor at the *County Chronicle*. The paper has just received a bomb threat. The caller said the bomb would go off in fifteen minutes."

"We'll dispatch a bomb squad immediately. Evacuate the building and move away from the perimeter walls. The police should be there within a couple of minutes. Call back from a secure location if you need more instructions before then."

"Okay. Thanks." Caroline severed the connection, then called each of her department heads to relay the information and to ask that they make sure all of their people left the building. By her third call, there was already a flurry of activity outside her office as staff members began to rise in panic and rush toward the exits. When she finished the last call she grabbed her tote, pulling her cell phone out as she headed for her office door.

"Tess!"

Her assistant editor stopped in mid-flight, then hurried toward Caroline. The color had drained from her face, and she looked as shaken as Caroline felt. "Aren't you leaving?" Tess asked.

"Yes. But I'm going to do a walk-through first to

make sure everyone's out. The police and bomb squad are on the way. Will you talk to them until I get out there?"

"Sure."

"Okay. Now go."

Caroline did a rapid inspection of the office. Only when she was convinced that everyone was out did she head for the door, tapping in David's office number as she strode through the lobby toward the front door.

"David? Caroline. We've had a bomb threat."

She heard the crash of a chair, as if David had jumped to his feet. "What!?"

"We've had a bomb threat. The police and bomb squad are on the way."

"Are you safe?"

"I'm leaving the building now."

"I'm on my way."

"Look, you don't need to come. I just wanted you to know."

"I'll be there in fifteen minutes. Are you out yet?"

She pushed open the front door and stepped into the late-afternoon sunlight. The police had already blocked off the street and seemed to be evacuating the surrounding buildings. Employees and curious onlookers were gathering in a parking lot across the street, and Caroline headed in that direction. "Yes. I just walked out the door."

"Okay. I'll see you in a few minutes."

By the time David arrived, Caroline had spoken to both the police and the bomb squad. She'd also dismissed the staff. It was late, and she doubted whether they'd get back inside before the workday ended. A lot of staffers were hanging around, though, including Jared. And news crews from the local TV stations were also arriving.

Weaving his way through the crowd, David made a beeline for Caroline. When he reached her he grasped her upper arms, relief flooding his features. "Are you okay?"

"Of course."

But she didn't look okay. Her face was drained of color, and he could feel the tremor in her muscles beneath his fingertips. Like the besieged rudder on a storm-tossed boat, his resolve to keep his distance snapped and he pulled her into his arms, pressing her close. Only then did he truly believe she was safe. It took every ounce of his willpower to finally release her and take a step back. "What happened?"

She stared at him, wide-eyed, as if the embrace had thrown her even more off balance. "A—a threat was called in. He said it would go off in fifteen minutes. That was twenty minutes ago."

"So it was a hoax?"

"I guess so. But they're not treating it that way." She inclined her head toward the police activity on the other side of the yellow tape that had been used to rope off the area.

"I would hope not. Has anyone given you an update?"

"Officer Scanlon is here. About five minutes ago he told me that they hadn't found anything yet. And they asked me a lot of questions about the security system." She looked toward Jared, still standing off to one side, then moved closer to David and lowered her voice. "Based on the incident with my car, the police seem to think this may be gang-related, too. They want to talk to Jared."

David had come to the same conclusion. And he was sure Caroline had, too, or she wouldn't have felt it necessary to call him right away. He looked over at the teen, who was still watching the activity from the sidelines, before turning his attention back to Caroline. "I can understand their concern. They probably think this is another intimidation tactic." He raked his fingers through his hair and fisted one hand on his hip. "This incident isn't going to be as easy to downplay as your car."

Surveying the TV cameras, Caroline nodded. "I know. But we don't have to tell the media about the potential gang tie-in. The police will be discreet, too, unless they find some direct evidence linking this to gang activity. And I doubt they will."

Caroline's cell phone began to vibrate, and she reached for it distractedly, her attention still focused on the scene before her. But when she answered it, she realized that the caller was the same person who had made the bomb threat, and her grip tightened, turning her knuckles white.

"This was just a warning. Next time it will be for real unless you get rid of Jared," the muffled voice said before the connection was severed.

As a look of shock passed across Caroline's face, David's eyes narrowed. "What's wrong?" When she didn't respond, he gripped her arms again, pinning her with an intense gaze. "Caroline, what's wrong?"

"It...it was the same person who called earlier. He said this was j-just a warning, but that next time it would be for real. Unless I get rid of Jared."

David's face grew hard, and he led her over to a low wall at the edge of the parking lot, urging her down as he motioned for a nearby officer. When the man joined them, David spoke. "Ms. James just had another call from the person who issued the bomb threat."

The man turned and gestured to another policeman, just as a reporter from one of the local TV stations honed in on them, camera crew in tow.

"Ms. James? Angela Watson, KMVI. Could you tell us what's going on?" The woman shoved a microphone in Caroline's face.

"I have no comment right now."

"We see bomb-sniffing dogs. Was there a bomb threat?"

"The police are still investigating. It would be premature to comment."

When the woman started to ask another question, David stepped between her and Caroline. "The lady said she has nothing further to say right now."

The reporter gave him a venomous look, then stalked off. When he was sure she didn't intend to return, David sat beside Caroline and reached for her ice-cold hand, twining his fingers with hers and giving them an encouraging squeeze. Although her responses to the reporter had been composed and professional, the trembling he'd felt earlier had increased. "Hang in there, okay?"

She tried to summon up a smile. "Yeah."

Several police officers gathered around as Caroline relayed the latest message.

"We'll continue to sweep the building, but my guess is there's nothing inside—this time," Officer Scanlon said. "And now that the caller has tied this to your intern, we need to talk to him as soon as possible."

"But he cut his gang ties weeks ago," Caroline said.

"Maybe. But even if he did, it's clear that his presence at the *Chronicle* still poses a risk."

She couldn't argue with that. It appeared she and David might lose their gamble with Jared after all—through no fault of the teen's. If the threat had remained directed just against her, Caroline wouldn't budge. But she had dozens of staff members to worry about. She couldn't endanger them. And David couldn't endanger the entire Uplink program for one student, no matter how talented he was.

Caroline faced the officer. "So are we just supposed to let that gang scare us into submission?"

"I don't like it, either, ma'am," he replied. "Why don't you let us check out your security system? If it's adequate, and if your staff is on high alert and no strangers are allowed in without proper clearance, there's little chance that a bomb could be placed inside. We'll also check out your maintenance crews. That could be a weak spot. If everything looks clean, you'll probably be okay."

It was the "probably" that gave her pause. And another quick glance at David confirmed that he felt the same way.

"I don't like playing the odds," he said, a frown creasing his brow.

"You folks will have to make that decision, based on our evaluation. In the meantime, I'd like to talk to your intern."

"He's right over there." David nodded toward Jared. "Can you let me lead off? We didn't tell him about the car incident, so he has no clue that any of this is related to him."

"Sure."

As David rose and motioned Jared over, Caroline stood and noted the curious looks being directed at the teen as he wove his way through the crowd. She turned to the officer. "Could we have this discussion somewhere in private?"

The policeman gave the scene a rapid survey, then pointed toward an insurance office a couple of stores down. "I know the owner there. I'm sure he'll let us use his conference room. Let me check it out."

As the man strode down the sidewalk, Jared joined them. His body was stiff with tension, and there was a look of caution on his face. "What's up?" he asked.

"The police have a few questions," David told him, placing a hand on his shoulder.

"What kind of questions?" Fear licked at the edges of his voice.

The officer reappeared on the sidewalk and motioned to them. "Let's talk about it in private," David suggested, leaving his arm around the boy's tense shoulders as he guided him toward the insurance company.

The small group remained silent until seated in the conference room. David spoke first, his tone measured and nonaccusatory. "Jared, today's bomb threat was gang-related."

Surprise widened the teen's eyes before they narrowed in suspicion. "How do you know?"

"Ms. James just got another call, telling her that unless we let you go, there will be another threat. And next time it will be for real. This isn't the first incident, either. A couple of weeks ago, Ms. James found a warning scratched onto her car, telling her to back off. We weren't sure at the time that it was related to your internship, but this confirms it."

"I didn't have anything to do with any of this." Jared's tone was defensive, but fear etched his features.

"We believe you, Jared. But the police still have a few questions."

A bleak look settled over his face and he slumped in his seat. "I'm sorry I caused problems," he told Caroline.

"None of this is your fault, Jared," she assured him.

"At least as far as we can tell," Officer Scanlon qualified. As all three sets of eyes focused on him, he faced Jared and continued. "I understand you're trying to cut your ties to the gang."

"I did cut them."

"That's not easy to do."

"Yeah. Tell me about it."

When he didn't offer any more information, David stepped in, relaying the story of Jared's trip to the hospital.

"Is that right?" the officer asked Jared.

"Yeah."

"Why didn't you report it?"

The teen stared at him. "I already had two broken ribs. I didn't want more. Or worse."

After a moment, the officer gave a curt nod. "Okay. I know they play rough. I can appreciate your caution. But we're in a different league now. This bomb threat endangers dozens of people. We need information."

Jared swallowed. "I don't know anything."

"Names would help."

"Look, man, I've been out of touch with the gang for weeks. People come and go."

"Not the leaders."

Shifting in his seat, Jared looked from David to Caroline. The distress on his face was so agonizing that

Caroline's heart ached for him. Reaching out, she covered his hand with hers. "We have to cooperate with the police," she said softly. "If we don't, the gang will win. And we'll all have to live in fear."

He looked down at her hand. He'd been in some tough situations, but this was one of the toughest. For most of his life he'd figured he didn't owe anybody anything, except maybe Nan. No one had ever done him any favors, given him a break. Sure, a couple of teachers at school had made him feel pretty good, had seemed to believe in him. But nobody had ever put themselves on the line for him like Mr. Sloan and Ms. James had. So he owed them. Giving the police the information they wanted was dangerous—for him. But he didn't see any way around it. Not if he wanted to be able to live with himself.

With an effort, he swallowed past the lump in his throat. Then he looked over at the cop. "Okay. I'll give you the names. But I'm not even sure they're still in charge. And even if they are, they're smart. You're not going to be able to tie them to this."

"Let us worry about that." Officer Scanlon flipped open his notebook and took out his pen, scribbling down the names as Jared ticked them off. "Okay. That's a start, anyway," he said when Jared finished. "We'll check them out. In the meantime, we'll do a security assessment of your facility," he told Caroline. "You might want to have people work from home tomorrow." He stood and tucked the notebook in his pocket. "I'll be in touch. And you did the right thing," he told Jared.

The boy drew a long, unsteady breath. "Yeah."

"We'll need you to hang around for a while," the officer told Caroline. "In case there are any other questions."

"Okay."

As he exited, David turned to Jared. "Can I give you a ride home?"

"No. I can still catch the bus." Without waiting for a response, Jared rose and walked toward the door, then looked back at Caroline. "So I should stay home tomorrow?"

"Yes. I'm going to contact all the staff members."

"What about the next day?"

"Let's wait and see what the police say."

At her noncommittal response, a weary resignation settled over Jared's face. "Okay. See you around."

As they watched him exit, Caroline's phone once more began to vibrate, and she reached for it automatically, her heart thudding in her chest.

"Another call?" David asked.

"Yes."

After she hit the Talk button and put the phone to her ear, she found her free hand taken in a firm, reassuring grip. David's powers to protect her were limited, but his strong hand holding hers calmed her, giving her an illusion of safety. It wasn't a good idea to let him hold her hand, of course. Not if she wanted to keep him at arm's length. But she couldn't summon up the strength to pull away.

"Caroline James."

"Caroline? I've been calling your office for an hour. I finally tried the receptionist but I couldn't get an answer there, either."

Closing her eyes, Caroline expelled a relieved breath.

"Hi, Mom. We had to evacuate the building. There was a bomb threat."

"What?!"

"Everything's fine. It was a false alarm."

"What on earth prompted that?"

"It's a long story."

"All right. You can tell it to me at dinner. If you're still coming, that is."

With all that had happened, their weekly dinner date had slipped her mind. She checked her watch. Her mother always went to a lot of trouble to prepare a nice meal and she hated to disappoint her, but she wasn't sure how long she'd be delayed.

"I'd like to, Mom. But the police asked me to stay around for a while. And I have some things to discuss with David."

"Is he there?"

"Yes."

"Then this whole thing must have something to do with that young man from Uplink you told me about."

Her mother would have made a great detective, Caroline decided. "That's right."

"Well, he needs to eat dinner, too. I made plenty. Bring him along."

The suggestion startled Caroline, even as it tempted her. But spending a cozy evening with David at her mother's house wasn't a good idea. "I'm sure he has other plans, Mom."

Tilting his head, David gave her a quizzical look.

"You don't know that unless you ask him," her mother persisted.

"Is she asking about me?" David inquired in a soft voice.

Nodding, Caroline spoke into the receiver. "Hold on, Mom." She touched the mute button, trying to figure a way out of this without lying. "I'm supposed to go over there for dinner. Mom thought you might like to come, but I know it's last minute, and I don't expect…"

"I'd love to," he cut her off. "I haven't had a home-cooked meal in a long time."

Caroline stared at him. Maybe he was just angling for a good meal. Considering that her hand was still held in his protective clasp, however, she knew she was just fooling herself. No doubt, his motivations were far more complicated than that. And she had a feeling her life was about to become a lot more complicated, too. But she didn't see any way around it.

Taking her finger off the Mute button, she spoke. "We'll be there as soon as we can, Mom."

"Great! I'll see you in a little while."

Her mother sounded pleased, Caroline thought, as she severed the connection. But no more pleased than David looked. The smile that lit his eyes warmed her all the way to her toes, and the gentle squeeze he gave her hand as they rose and headed back outside seemed to be part thank-you and part reassurance that every-thing would be okay.

But Caroline wasn't sure about that. Earlier, the bomb threat had scared her, making her afraid for her physical safety. Yet the fear she felt now was just as strong. Except this time it was her heart that was in peril.

It had been years since Caroline had prayed. And she wasn't sure why she turned to the Lord now. Maybe it was because David's quiet, deep faith had rubbed off on her. Maybe it was because she didn't know where else to go for help. Whatever the reason, she sensed a need for assistance from a higher power.

Lord, I haven't talked with You much in recent years, she prayed as David left her for a moment to speak with the two officers. *Life got pretty busy, and I let my faith lapse. I forgot that I need You. But now I realize that I do. Please help us through this situation. Help us find a way to protect everyone's safety without being forced to give up on Jared. He has so much to offer, and I'm afraid that if this opportunity falls through, he'll end up on the street.*

And please help me deal with my feelings for David. I don't want to be disloyal to Michael, but David is so kind and caring and wonderful. And he's here, Lord. Michael always believed in living today without being constrained by the past. I think he'd want me to move on. It just seems awkward—and wrong, somehow—to move on with his brother. Please help me figure out how to deal with this situation. Because I don't want to pass up a second chance for love.

Chapter Eleven

"That was a wonderful meal, Mrs. James. Thank you again for inviting me."

"Please, call me Judy," Caroline's mother told David, who stood as she picked up the creamer. "And it was my pleasure. We were due for a little male companionship at one of our weekly tête-a-têtes. Overdue, in fact." She gave Caroline a pleased smile—one of the many she'd sent her daughter's way during the meal. A meal that had been served in the dining room—on the good china—instead of their usual spot in the kitchen or on the patio. "Now I know you and Caroline have things to discuss about Jared. You just sit here and get on with it while I load up the dishwasher."

"I'll help, Mom."

Caroline started to rise, but Judy put a hand on her shoulder. "Not tonight. You two have some decisions to make."

Although her mother had listened with interest as Caroline and David spoke at dinner about Jared and the threats that had been issued, in an uncharacteristic display of reticence she'd made few comments and offered even fewer opinions. While Caroline sometimes found her mother a little *too* opinionated, she valued her insights and was curious about her take on the whole situation.

"What do you think about all this, Mom?" she asked, settling back in her seat.

Shaking her head, Judy reached for the butter dish. "It's an unfortunate situation. Jared sounds like a bright, talented young man who's trying to improve his life. But that gang is treacherous. I'd be lying if I said I wasn't worried. About everyone. And about you in particular." A spasm of distress tightened Judy's features as she looked at her daughter. "But I worried about you in the Middle East, too. I guess I'm used to it by now. And I've always been proud of your sense of justice and integrity, and your willingness to stand up for what you believe in. Those are some of the reasons I love you so much. I just hope you'll be careful." She turned to David. "What do *you* think?"

The look he gave Caroline was steady and sure. "I couldn't have said it any better."

A satisfied look settled over Judy's face. "That's what I figured. In the meantime, I guess I'll just keep bending the Lord's ear, like I did when you were in the Middle East."

As her mother bustled out of the room, Caroline stared at David. Had he just implied that he loved her? Or was he just agreeing with her mother's comment about being careful?

Instead of continuing that discussion, however, David switched topics. Steepling his fingers, he leaned forward, his face intense. "Your mother was right about Jared. We need to make some decisions."

Caroline exhaled a relieved breath. "I know. But I think we should wait until the police assess the security risk at the *Chronicle*. I don't want to give up on him yet. What about the Uplink board's reaction to all this?"

Twin furrows appeared on David's forehead. "As it happens, we have a regular board meeting tomorrow morning. I'm not sure how detailed the news coverage on the bomb threat will be, and I doubt Jared will be mentioned. But I owe it to the board to explain the situation. I had resistance from the beginning on taking high-risk students, and I need to be honest about the situation. However, I'm going to suggest that the board not take any action until we get the police assessment of the security risk."

"Do you think the members will go along with that?"

"I have no idea. But I'm going to pray that they do. Uplink needs to be there for students like Jared. Otherwise, it's not doing justice to its mission. Assuming the police come back with an encouraging report, how do you feel about keeping him on in light of all that's happened?"

"As long as I can be assured that danger to the staff is minimal, I plan to see this through."

"What about the danger to yourself?"

"I've been in dangerous situations before."

No doubt that was true. But it didn't make David feel a whole lot better.

At the odd expression on his face, Caroline tilted her head and gave him a curious look. "Are you having second thoughts?"

"Not about helping Jared. I just never expected things

to escalate like this. I thought we might have some trouble from Jared himself, but I didn't think the gang would bother him once he moved."

"Gangs don't look kindly on deserters. I learned a whole lot about how they operate when I did that series last year for the *Chronicle*."

"The one that earned you this." He leaned over and traced a gentle finger along the scar at her hairline.

She stared at him, trying in vain to stifle the sudden yearning that sprang to life at his touch.

"If you knew that much about gangs, I'm surprised you took Jared on." His voice was as soft as the finger that still rested against her temple.

"H-he deserved a chance."

"But the stakes are a lot higher now."

"I'm not a quitter, David."

He already knew that. But while he admired her commitment, it was playing havoc with his peace of mind. Knowing he was taking a risk, knowing it might be too soon, he reached for her hand, enfolding her fingers in his without ever breaking eye contact.

Her own eyes widened in surprise, and a pulse began to beat frantically in the hollow of her throat, but she didn't pull away.

"Caroline, I have to be honest with you. I'm having a real problem dealing with the danger you're in as a result of your involvement with Uplink—an involvement I initiated. The fact is, my feelings for you have..."

"Did I leave the lid for the butter dish on..." In one quick but comprehensive glance Judy took in the scene at the table, then turned on her heel. "I'll check later," she said over her shoulder, disappearing into the kitchen.

Caroline didn't know whether to be grateful or dismayed at her mother's interruption. But she did know that she wasn't ready to hear whatever David had been about to say. Giving her hand a gentle but firm tug, she pulled free from his grasp. "I'll be fine, David. But I appreciate your concern."

As she reached up to touch Michael's medallion, David drew a slow, steadying breath. Her message was clear. She wasn't ready yet to hear what he had to say. So he'd have to wait to tell her what was in his heart. But in the meantime, he was still going to worry.

After checking his watch, he rose. "I think I'll head out. It's been a long day. If you're ready to leave, why don't I follow you home?"

"I'm going to stay awhile and visit with Mom. But you go ahead. You need to be rested for your confrontation with the board tomorrow."

"I hope it won't come to that."

"I hope not, either. But you need to be in fighting form, just in case," she said with a smile.

"You're probably right." He rose, reaching for their plates.

"Leave the dishes, David. Mom and I will take care of them."

"Nope. I always clean up my own messes. Just lead the way to the kitchen."

Considering the firm set of his jaw, Caroline decided arguing would be fruitless. She pushed through the swinging door, with David close on her heels, and Judy turned from the sink when they entered.

"He insisted on helping clear the table," Caroline told her.

"That's very nice. But not necessary."

"Many hands make light work. I'll bring in the rest of the dishes while you two ladies straighten up out here."

A few minutes later, when the table was cleared and the dishwasher loaded, they walked with him to the front door.

"Thank you again for a lovely evening, Judy. I haven't had such a good meal in a long time."

"It was my pleasure. You're welcome anytime."

"I'll remember that. Good night."

They watched as he headed down the front walk, returning his wave when he lifted a hand in farewell before striding toward his car. As her mother closed the door, she turned to Caroline. "He's quite a man."

"Yes, he is. But don't get any ideas."

"Considering the cozy scene I interrupted in the dining room, I don't think I'm the one with ideas."

A flush suffused Caroline's face. "All right. Let me rephrase my response. Don't get your hopes up. Whatever you saw isn't going anywhere."

"Why not?"

"Because I loved Michael. I still do."

"I feel the same way about your father. My love for him didn't die when he did. But that doesn't mean I can't also find room in my heart for someone else. Like Harold."

"That's different. Harold wasn't Dad's brother."

Her mother gave her a speculative look. "You know, back in Biblical times, it was very common for a man to marry his sister-in-law if his brother died."

"That was centuries ago."

"Good ideas never go out of style."

Propping her hands on her hips, Caroline stared at

her mother. "Are you suggesting that I should *marry* David?"

"Only if you love him."

"I hardly know him!"

"Baloney."

"Okay, I guess I know him pretty well," Caroline conceded. "But there's nothing romantic between us."

"Hmph. You can believe that if you want to. But I saw the way you two looked at each other tonight. My body may be older, but my heart's still young and my eyesight is just fine. I know attraction when I see it. And I'll tell you something else. David may be Michael's brother, but he's also a keeper. I'd think long and hard before I discouraged his attention." With that, Judy headed back toward the kitchen.

If she could have mustered an argument, Caroline would have. But her mother was absolutely right. One day soon Caroline would have to deal with the thing simmering between her and David. She just wasn't yet ready to do so.

Mark Holton banged the gavel and called the Uplink board meeting to order. "David asked to be first on the agenda today because of an urgent issue that has arisen. We'll push the publicity report to second place, if that's okay with you, Rachel."

"Sure. No problem."

"David, you have the floor."

Standing, he faced the board. He could count on Steve to back him up. The rest he wasn't as sure about. But he wasn't going to back down—even if it put an end to his fledgling career. *Give me the right words to touch their hearts, Lord,* he prayed. *Help me make them understand that taking Jared on wasn't a mistake, even if it's put us in a difficult position. That helping kids like him is what we should do, even if it involves risk.*

"I don't know if any of you caught the late news last night, or read the paper yet this morning. If you did, you might have seen the story about the bomb threat at the *Chronicle,*" he began.

Several heads nodded, and Allison spoke. "I noticed it because the *Chronicle* is one of our new sponsoring organizations."

"That's right. Jared Poole is working there this summer," David confirmed. "And that's what I'd like to talk about this morning."

For the next few minutes, David gave them an overview of the situation, beginning with Jared's successful internship and ending with the final threatening call Caroline had gotten yesterday, along with the security review being done by the police. As he spoke, the expressions in the room changed from curious to uneasy to anxious.

"None of this information has made the press, and there's been no connection drawn between Uplink and the bomb threat. At this point, my recommendation is that we withhold action pending the police report. Assuming the security at the *Chronicle* checks out, I'd like to let Jared complete his internship," he finished.

The board members exchanged nervous looks, but remained silent.

"I'm not anxious to put anyone in danger, David," Mark spoke up.

"I'm not, either. That's why I think we need to wait until we have the police report before we make a decision. But I wanted to brief all of you on the situation."

"Rachel, you're our publicity expert. What's your assessment of the long-term implications if the connection leaks?" Mark asked.

"Depends on how it's spun. We don't want to come across as a reckless organization that makes arbitrary decisions about the students we select and puts our hosting organizations in danger. On the other hand, if Jared is a success story, we could generate some great press for the positive impact Uplink has had by taking a few risks."

"Allison...what about the reaction of other hosting companies?" Mark asked the liaison chairperson.

"No company is going to want its operations disrupted or its employees put in danger. This could be a problem if more details leak or something else happens. What's the reaction at the *Chronicle?*" She directed her question to David.

"Caroline James, the managing editor, isn't easily intimidated. And she believes in Jared. At the same time, she's concerned about putting her staff at risk. She's agreed to wait until we have the security evaluation from the police before taking any action."

"Not every organization would be that cooperative," Mark noted.

"I realize that," David replied.

For the first time, Steve spoke. "I think the course of action that David has outlined is prudent."

"But there's still a risk," Mark pointed out. "Even if the police evaluation comes back positive and the *Chronicle* continues with the internship, there's no guarantee that something else won't happen. This gang seems to be persistent. And based on the attack on Jared, the members aren't averse to violence."

"I can't argue with that," David responded. "There is some risk. And there are no water-tight guarantees. But if we allow ourselves to be intimidated, we'll be closing Uplink to all the Jareds of the world. And compromising the integrity of the program."

"It's a tough situation. I think we're going to have to take a vote." Mark looked around the table. "All in favor of David's recommendation, raise your hand." Four hands went up—a couple with less-than-encouraging confidence. "All in favor of pulling Jared out of the program now, raise your hand." Three hands rose. "Let the record show that the vote was four to three in favor of continuing with the program given a limited-risk assessment by the police. You win, David. Just keep us apprised of the situation. We can call an emergency board meeting if necessary, should things change. Rachel, you're up."

As he took his seat, David expelled a relieved breath. But as for winning...he wasn't sure about that. Although the board had sided with him, the margin had been slim. It was pretty clear that he was on thin ice. If much more weight was brought to bear, he suspected his support would give way and he'd go under—perhaps taking the Uplink program with him.

He just prayed that if that happened, no one would get hurt in the process. Especially the woman who had stolen his heart.

"Caroline James called. She said it was urgent."

That wasn't the kind of message David had hoped to be greeted with when he arrived at his office after the board meeting. His adrenaline, which had almost returned to normal since the charged meeting had ended, shot back up as he strode toward his office.

"How long ago?" he asked Ella over his shoulder.

"About half an hour. I said I'd have you call the minute you came in."

"Thanks."

He shrugged out of his suit jacket, tossed it onto the conference table and loosened his tie as he punched in Caroline's number. "What's up?" he asked as soon as she answered.

"David? How did the board meeting go?"

"They're with us. For now. Ella said your call was urgent."

"Yes. I heard from Jared this morning. He wants to withdraw from the program."

Sucking in a deep breath, David dropped into his chair and raked his fingers through his hair. If every internship was fraught with this much difficulty those few flecks of silver he'd noticed at his temples last week would spread as fast as weeds in a spring lawn. "What's the story?"

"He said he didn't want to cause any more trouble for anyone. And I think he was really shaken by the realization that if the gang follows through on its threat, a lot of people could be hurt."

"Did you hear anything from the police yet?"

"So far, so good. We've always had a first-rate security system, which the police verified. And they seem pretty comfortable that at least in terms of a bomb threat, we should be safe—especially if we follow our access security protocol. They're still checking out the maintenance crew, but it doesn't sound like that will be an issue, either. I'll have the final report this afternoon."

"Does that mean you're willing to see this through?"

"Yes."

"Okay. Then we need to talk with Jared."

"He sounded pretty firm."

"Let me give him a call. I'd like to get him into my office this afternoon, maybe with his grandmother, even his great-aunt, and talk this through. Could you join us?"

"Of course. Just let me know the time."

"All right. I'll be in touch."

The grim faces of those squeezed around his small conference table that afternoon didn't offer David much confidence that his persuasive skills would be effective. But after all the effort he'd expended getting Jared into the program, he wasn't about to let him walk away without a fight. And based on Caroline's determined expression, neither was she. At least he had one ally in the group.

Jared, on the other hand, looked beaten. His grandmother seemed sad. His great-aunt was a new player, and David studied her for a few seconds. She bore a faint resemblance to her sister, but she was dressed more upscale, in a tasteful linen suit. Her ebony hair was coiffed in a contemporary style, and her polished fingernails made it clear that her hands spent little time immersed in detergent—in sharp contrast to her sister's chapped, work-worn hands. Although she carried herself with poise and confidence, fear lurked in the depths of her eyes.

This wasn't going to be an easy sell.

"Can I offer anyone a soft drink?" David asked.

When everyone declined, he took his seat and directed his opening comments to Jared. "A lot of people have gone to a lot of effort and taken a lot of risk to help you succeed, Jared. Including those in this room. Before we write this internship off, I thought all of us should talk it through."

"There's nothing to talk about. I've already decided to drop out."

"Why?"

"Like I told Ms. James, I don't want to cause any more trouble."

"So you're going to let the gang win?"

"No. I'm not going to rejoin."

"But you *are* going to let them deprive you of an opportunity that could change your life forever."

"So what do you want me to do?" Jared demanded, frustration nipping at the edges of his voice. "Stay and put everyone in danger?"

"We're still waiting for the final report from the police, but Ms. James has spoken with them. We're pretty sure they're going to conclude that security at the *Chronicle* is sufficient to reduce the risk of an actual bombing to almost zero."

"That doesn't mean the gang won't try something else. Hurt someone else. They already warned Ms. James. Maybe next time it will be Nan. Or Aunt Dara. Or even you."

"David and I are willing to take that risk." Caroline glanced at David as she spoke, then looked back at Jared. "And I have a feeling your grandmother feels the same way."

"I don't care how she feels. The apartment's not safe. It would be too easy for the gang to hurt her."

"Then she'll just have to come and stay with me." At

Dara's statement, everyone turned to her in surprise. She looked back at them, tilting her chin up a notch. "Well, why not? I have two empty bedrooms. My neighborhood is secure. It's the best solution."

There was a suspicious sheen in Grace's eyes as she reached over and took her sister's hand. "You've already done more than enough for us. We couldn't ask you to take this on, too."

"You didn't ask. I offered." She leaned forward, her face intent, the fear in her eyes replaced by determination. "I want to do this, Grace. Besides, if we stick together, we can protect each other. There's safety in numbers, remember? And there's a nice young police officer who lives next door to me. He'll watch out for us, too."

"Are you sure about this, Dara?"

"More sure than I've been about most things in my life."

"Jared?" Grace looked at her grandson.

"I guess...I guess that would be okay." He turned toward David and Caroline, his face puzzled. "Since Nan and Aunt Dara are family, I can kind of understand why they're willing to take a chance for me. But I still can't figure out why you are."

"This is what Uplink is all about, Jared. Taking a chance on teens who have talent and potential. And from a personal standpoint, it's just the right thing to do. The Lord said to love one another, and I can't think of a better way to demonstrate that love than by giving a deserving young person a helping hand."

"We're also repaying a debt," Caroline added softly, her gaze flickering for a brief second to David. "A stranger once helped a man we both loved get a start

in life. That man always wanted to do the same for another young person. But he never had the opportunity.
So we're doing it for him."

Looking from one to the other, Jared shook his head.
"I don't know what to say."

"*Thank you* would be good," Nan prompted.

A grin tugged at the corners of Jared's mouth. "You
always were a stickler for etiquette."

"We may be poor, but that's no excuse for bad manners."

"Yeah. Okay. Thanks," he said, directing his comment to David and Caroline.

"Is there anything else we should do?" Dara asked.

"Praying might not be a bad idea." David's somber
demeanor underscored the seriousness of his suggestion.

"I've been doing that. But I'm going to do a whole lot
more," Grace declared, making a move to stand. "Thank
you both." She extended her hand to David and Caroline in turn. Dara and Jared did the same.

"I'll see you at the office tomorrow," Caroline told
Jared.

"I'll be there."

As the three exited via the front door, Ella handed
David a stack of messages. "These all came in during
your meeting."

"No rest for the weary, I guess," he replied, flipping
through them as he spoke.

Caroline retrieved her purse. "I need to be going,
anyway."

"I'll walk you to your car."

"No need. I'm right in front." She pointed to her
car, visible out the window. As Ella answered yet an-

other call, Caroline motioned to the messages in David's hand. "It doesn't look like you'll be leaving for a while."

"I'm hoping I can get through these quickly. I'm meeting a friend for pizza tonight."

Caroline stared at him. It had never occurred to her that David might be dating someone. Of course, there was no reason he wouldn't have an active social life. He was a handsome, intelligent, caring man. Any woman would be happy to spend time with him.

Realizing that she had misinterpreted his comment, David hastened to explain. "I might have mentioned Steve Dempsky to you once. The guy I went to college with, who's a minister now and is on the Uplink board. Sometimes when his wife travels, we meet for dinner. I see him every Sunday at church, but our dinners keep our friendship strong."

Relief coursed through her, reminding Caroline that she cared far more about this man than perhaps was prudent. "He's the pastor of your church, too?" It was an inane comment, but she didn't know how else to respond.

"Yes. He gives a great sermon. You'd be welcome to join us anytime. The congregation is very friendly, and you might find the experience worthwhile."

"Maybe I will. Well…" She consulted her watch. "I need to be off. Have a nice evening. See you later, Ella."

"You take care, honey," the woman responded.

From his position by Ella's desk, David was able to follow Caroline's progress toward her car. He couldn't help but feel encouraged by the shocked look on her face when she'd thought he had a date tonight. It had told him she cared for him at a far deeper level than she perhaps wanted to. But he was also aware that she was fighting the attraction, just as he was. They both still had issues related to Michael that they needed to resolve before they could move forward. But he was working on his. And he hoped she was working on hers. Until now, he'd been able to rein in his feelings and keep them under wraps. But it was an ongoing battle. One he figured he was going to lose sooner rather than later.

He turned to find Ella watching him, a knowing look on her face. "She is one sweet lady. But I guess I don't need to tell you that, do I?"

And as she turned back to her computer, David realized he'd already lost the battle.

"Listen, thanks for voting in my favor today." David reached for another slice of pizza as Steve took a swig of his soda.

"I just followed my conscience. But that doesn't mean I'm not worried."

"Me, neither. Caroline got the police report this afternoon, though, and the *Chronicle* security system got an A-plus. They think there's little chance that a real bomb could be planted."

"That doesn't mean the gang won't try something else."

It was the same concern Mark and Jared had voiced. And it was the same one that was keeping David awake at night.

"Yeah, I know." David put down the piece of pizza, his appetite vanishing.

"You realize you might be putting yourself in danger, don't you?"

"I can take care of myself. I'm more worried about Caroline, since she's already had a direct threat. I'm not sure I could live with myself if…" His voice choked, and he cleared his throat.

Leaning forward, Steve scrutinized David's face. "Do I detect more than professional interest here?"

David raked his fingers through his hair. "You and everyone else, it seems. I thought I was doing a pretty good job disguising it, but Ella's picked up on it. I think Caroline's mother has, too."

"What's wrong with that?"

Although he and Steve had been close for years, he'd never talked to his friend about his connection to Caroline. When he'd first met her, he'd been so overwhelmed—and guilt-ridden—by his attraction to his brother's fiancée that he hadn't discussed her with anyone, afraid that he'd reveal his inappropriate feelings. But maybe now was the time to bring it up. Especially since that original infatuation had mushroomed into full-blown love.

Reaching for his glass, he took a long swallow of soda, then gave Steve a direct look. "Caroline was Michael's fiancée."

Steve stared at him. "Your brother, Michael?"

"Yeah."

"But…I thought he was engaged to a reporter in the Middle East?"

"He was. Caroline worked for AP then. After Michael died, she came home to St. Louis."

"And you two kept in touch?"

"No. I didn't see her until I stopped in one day after I moved here to give her something of Michael's that had been returned to me with his personal effects. I never planned to see her again after that."

"Why not?"

"I'm not sure how to…it's just that I've always… ever since we met I…" He stopped and shook his head, gripping his glass with both hands. "Sorry. I've been struggling with this for more than two years. To use an old cliché, I've been carrying a torch for her since the first time I saw her."

"You mean you're in love with her?"

"I am now. Back then…I don't know. I guess it was infatuation. I've never believed in love at first sight."

"I never did, either. Until I met Monica."

"You fell in love with your wife the first time you met?"

"I don't know if it was love, exactly. But right away I knew she was something special. Since we got married eighteen months later, I guess my instincts were right. And I learned not to discount first impressions. Besides, what's the problem?"

"In a word…guilt."

A light dawned on Steve's face. "You feel disloyal to your brother."

"Bingo."

"He's been gone for more than two years, David."

"He wasn't when I first felt this way."

"You didn't do anything about it then, did you?"

"No. But I was tempted."

"Temptation is part of being human. The real test of our character and faith is whether we act on those temptations. You didn't."

"Are you saying it's okay to fall in love with my brother's fiancée?"

"Considering the situation, I don't see a big issue from an ethical or moral standpoint."

A couple of beats of silence ticked by. "There's more," David told him.

"I kind of figured there was. Want to tell me about it?"

A wry smile lifted one corner of David's mouth. "This was supposed to be dinner, not a counseling session. You do enough of this during the day."

"I may be a minister, but I'm also your friend. And friends are there for each other. If you want to talk, I'll be happy to listen."

His role in Michael's death was something else David had kept to himself. Only Caroline knew about it. In many ways, that was even harder to talk about. But guided by Steve's quiet questions, he told him the story about their mother's rapid decline and the argument the night before Michael died, which had no doubt distracted his brother—and maybe even caused his death.

"So I feel doubly guilty about Caroline. Not only is there a good chance that I contributed to my brother's death, but now I want to claim the woman he loved," David finished.

"I see your dilemma," Steve sympathized. "Guilt can be a powerful force for good, when applied in the proper circumstances. But it can also hold us back or result in unnecessary self-denial when misapplied."

"Do you think that's what's happening here?"

"Only you can answer that question. But from what you've told me, I don't see how denying your love for Caroline is going to help anyone. Maybe your feelings for her were inappropriate when you first met, but since you didn't act on them, there's no reason for guilt. I can't say what role your argument played in Michael's death. Maybe none. No one will ever know. But blaming yourself for it for the rest of your life isn't going to bring Michael back. It may be time to give it to the Lord, ask His forgiveness for any responsibility you might bear and then let it go."

"I've tried that. And I thought I'd made my peace with it. But when Caroline came back into my life, I realized the guilt was still there."

"Then try again. Ask the Lord to help you let it go, to lift the burden from your shoulders. Put it in His hands and move on with your life. With Caroline, if that's where your heart leads you. Assuming she feels the same way, of course. Does she?"

"I think so."

Reaching over, Steve laid his hand on David's shoulder. "Maybe it's time you found out."

Chapter Twelve

The organ music swelled, and for the dozenth time Caroline tried to figure out how she had wound up in church, beside David, on this bright August morning.

When he'd suggested earlier in the week, after their meeting with Jared and his family, that she consider attending his church, her response had been a polite, "Maybe I will." While she admired David's deep faith and felt a growing need to connect with a higher power herself, she'd made little effort to do so aside from a few recent prayers in the quiet of her heart. Life had just been too busy. But that had always been her excuse, she acknowledged. Finding time for God hadn't been one of her priorities during her hectic years with AP. She'd been too focused on building her career, surviving in new and sometimes hostile environments…and falling in love with a man for whom religion had never been top-of-mind. At best, Michael had been an agnostic. While he hadn't denied the existence of God, he hadn't bought into Christianity. Although Caroline had been raised Christian and still believed the basic tenets of the faith, she hadn't practiced it in any formal way for years. And except for an occasional sense that there was a spiritual emptiness in her life, she hadn't missed it.

But when she'd met David the Christmas she and Michael visited, she'd been intrigued by the sense of purpose his deep faith seemed to give to his life. And ever since then, she'd been drawn toward the source of that purpose. Vague at first, the call had grown steadily stronger after Michael's death. Though she'd done little to heed it, and in fact sometimes found it annoying, the quiet voice deep in her soul had persisted. As a result, when David had called yesterday and invited her to join him for services, she'd said yes.

While she'd been afraid that the situation between them might be awkward after that interrupted moment at her mother's house, David had worked hard to ease any tension, sticking to safe subjects and even eliciting a few laughs with a story about how Ella's plants were taking over their offices. By the time they arrived at the small brick church with the tall white steeple, she'd been relaxed and receptive to the experience.

So far, she'd enjoyed the service. Steve Dempsky had merry eyes and a ready smile—as well as a great singing voice that soared above the choir. He conducted the service with an infectious joy and enthusiasm that seemed to capture the true spirit of Christianity. Caroline had been concerned that she would feel self-conscious and ill at ease in church after such a long absence, but to her surprise the experience seemed more like a homecoming. It felt right to be back in the house of the Lord.

As the minister moved to the pulpit to deliver his sermon, Caroline aimed a sideways glance at David.

He was focused on the sanctuary, giving her a good view of his strong, appealing profile. Although he came across as a composed, disciplined person who could be counted on to analyze any situation and make a sound judgment, Caroline suspected that beneath his calm, restrained exterior, David was a man of strong passion, whose feelings ran deep. She'd glimpsed that side of him once or twice when he'd looked at her in an unguarded moment. And on some intuitive level she knew that he was the kind of man who, when he loved, would give release to his feelings with such intensity that the mere thought of it took her breath away.

So captivated was she by these wayward musings that Caroline missed a good part of the minister's sermon. Only with great effort—fueled by guilt at her inappropriate thoughts in this house of God—did she shift her attention to the front of the church and focus on his words.

"And so I think that our reading today from Ecclesiastes will always remain timeless. To everything there is a season...that's just as true today as it was three hundred years before the birth of Christ, when this passage was written. Each of us has experienced seasons in our lives. Times of happiness and times of sadness. Times of putting down roots and times of pulling them up. Times of grieving and times of rejoicing. We know that there are times to be silent, and times to speak. Times to draw close, and times to stay apart. As the author of Ecclesiastes reminds us, the Lord has made everything appropriate to its time.

"Those words are a great source of comfort. They help us understand that the ebbs and flows of life are natural, that we're not alone in the difficulties we encounter. But they also bring a challenge. Because they leave some of the choices about the seasons of our lives in own hands. Grief is a good example. While we don't choose our times to grieve, we do choose the duration of our mourning. Clinging too long to grief can blind us to other joys God sends our way. The same is true of hate. Clinging too long to this destructive emotion can harden our hearts. Likewise, clinging too long to baggage from our past can clutter our lives, leaving no room for anything new to enter."

The minister surveyed the congregation before him, his expression kind and compassionate. "My friends, while this passage provides a reassurance that we're not alone when we experience the diverse seasons of our lives, it also serves as a wake-up call. A reminder that sometimes it's up to us to step from one season into the next. To go from weeping to laughing, from scattering to gathering, from losing to seeking. And as we move through these seasons, we have one advantage the writer of Ecclesiastes didn't have: an understanding of the purpose and plan for our lives, which the Lord provided during His time on earth. We also have someone to turn to when we need guidance for our journey. When we need courage to choose a new season. Let us always remember the beautiful words from Matthew: 'Ask, and it shall be given to you; seek, and you shall find; knock, and it shall be opened to you.' The Lord waits for our call. Don't be afraid to ask Him for help as you journey through the seasons of your life.

"And now let us pray…."

As the minister continued with the rest of the service, the words of his sermon resonated in Caroline's mind. It was almost as if he'd looked into her heart and chosen a topic that would have special significance for her first visit back to church. His talk had captured many of the conflicts and feelings she'd been experiencing these past few weeks, since David had reentered her life. And it had made her question her doubts about pursuing a relationship with him. Was she clinging too long to grief? Was the baggage she was holding on to from her past robbing her of her future? Was it time to ask for forgiveness for the role she'd played in Michael's death and move on? Michael would want her to, she knew. And maybe the Lord did, too.

Bowing her head, she closed her eyes in prayer. *Lord, I listened to the words today from Your book with an open heart. And I listened to the minister as well. For the past two years I've been living in an emotional vacuum, consumed by grief and guilt and hate. I hated myself for the role I played in Michael's death, and I resented David for his role. I don't resent him anymore, Lord. And I'd like to stop hating myself. I want to move on. It's time. I've lived in the darkness of winter for too long. I want to move to the next season, to spring and the new life that will bring. A life that I'd like to share with David.*

I ask Your help, Lord, in making that transition. Please give me peace of mind about the decision, relieve me of the guilt I feel and give me the courage to enter this new season. I'll always love Michael, but as Mom told me recently, loving one person doesn't mean there's no room in your heart for someone else. I used to think that it was a coincidence that David's new job brought him here. Now I think maybe it was more than that. That maybe You brought him to me. And that

You're leaving the next step to me. Please give me the courage to take it.

With trembling fingers, Caroline reached up and touched the medallion around her neck. It had served as an expression of her love and devotion to the man she'd planned to marry—and a warning to the man beside her to keep his distance. A warning David had respected. But it was time to remove the wall that had kept him away—and kept her safe. She knew that tearing it down would expose her to risk. Yet even though the wall had protected her, it had also isolated her, leaving her heart cold and dark and lonely. And more and more, her heart was yearning for sunlight and warmth.

Summoning up her courage, Caroline lifted her hands and sought the clasp behind her neck. Without giving herself time for second thoughts, she opened it, letting the medallion and chain slide into her waiting hand. And as she felt the weight in her palm and closed her fingers around it, the oddest thing happened. Though the sky had been dark and ominous when they'd arrived at church, a sudden shaft of sunlight darted through the stained-glass window beside her, painting her hand—and only her hand—with a rainbow-hued mosaic of rich, bright, vibrant color. She froze, and her breath caught in her throat as she stared at it. Several seconds ticked by, and then David reached over and covered her hand with his. Startled, she turned to him. The tender expression on his unguarded face told her that he'd observed her symbolic maneuver, understood the significance—and approved.

And as she glanced down at his fingers, protectively covering hers, the mosaic of color seemed to deepen in intensity and expand to accommodate David's larger hand. Once more her gaze sought his. The pensive look on his face told her that he, too, was pondering the odd timing of that shaft of vivid light. And that like her, he wondered if, in this subtle way, Michael was giving them his blessing.

Caroline wasn't the type of person who believed in signs. She was too practical by nature, too much of a journalist, always wanting proof and impeccable sources. She was from the Show-Me state, after all. The play of light was probably just a coincidence, she told herself.

Yet deep in her heart, she sensed it was more than that. And all at once she experienced a feeling of release, of liberation. Of absolution, almost. Maybe it was just wishful thinking. But even so, the effect was the same. And bowing her head in gratitude, she uttered a silent prayer of thanks.

After one more quick scan of Jared's entry for the journalism contest, Caroline handed it over to the intern. "I'd say we're almost there. I just have a few more minor editing suggestions, and Bill has recommended some slight cropping revisions on the photos. See what you think."

As Jared dropped into a seat across from her desk and looked over his mentors' comments, Caroline leaned back in her chair and flexed her shoulders. With the deadline looming in two days, she and Jared had stayed far later than usual to finish the entry. It had been too hectic at the *Chronicle* to work on it during normal business hours. But she didn't mind putting in the extra time. Jared had written a stellar piece on the plight of residents at an underfunded nursing home, and his dramatic photos of the elderly inhabitants had reinforced his powerful words. Caroline had no doubt that he'd be a finalist, if not one of the winners.

Reaching for her bottle of water, she took a long sip, hoping to stem the hunger pangs in her stomach until David arrived in half an hour to take her out to dinner. A smile curved her lips at that thought. Since their church visit four days earlier, they'd had almost no time together. Just as the service ended, she'd been paged about a breaking story and had to leave right away for the office. David had been sequestered in wrap-up meetings all week with Uplink hosting organizations as the internships wound down. Plus, she'd been staying late for the past few days to work with Jared on his entry. But now that she'd resolved her issues, she was anxious to move forward with their relationship. To explore the opportunity that had blessed her life and see where it led. As a result, when David had suggested a late dinner, she'd responded with an immediate yes.

"These comments all make sense," Jared said, interrupting her thoughts. "I can make the changes before I leave. But you don't need to hang around to give me a ride home like you did the other nights. Aunt Dara said she'd come and get me if I needed to stay extra late tonight to finish this up."

"I don't mind. David and I are going to dinner, and he'll be swinging by at eight o'clock to pick me up. We can drop you off on our way to the restaurant."

Even if he wasn't coming by, Caroline wouldn't have left. While things had been quiet since the bomb threat, and Jared's internship would be over at the end of the following week, she wasn't confident that they'd heard the last of the gang. She figured there was safety in numbers.

Rising, Jared fingered the papers in his hand. "He's a good guy."

"Yeah. He is."

"I thought he was going to write me off after my first interview. I wouldn't have blamed him if he had."

"He recognized your talent and wanted to give you a chance to develop it."

"I guess. But I...I couldn't figure out why, in the beginning. Then I realized he was into the Jesus stuff, like Nan and Aunt Dara. And everything kind of fell into place at that meeting we all had, when I asked him why he was going out on a limb for me, and he said it was just the right thing to do. That he was following the Lord's commandment to love one another."

"I'd say that's a pretty accurate assessment of his motives."

"I think that's pretty cool, you know? I was never much into religion, even though Nan dragged me to church when I was a kid. But nothing in my life ever convinced me there was really a God who cared about me. Then all this good stuff happened this summer. And people like you and Mr. Sloan and Mr. Baker believed in me." He looked down and shifted his weight. "Anyway, I started going to services with Nan and Aunt Dara. And I thought maybe you might want to tell Mr. Sloan. He never talked to me about going to church, but I think he might like to know, since it's so important to him."

A warm smile lighted Caroline's face. "I know he would. I'll be sure to pass it on."

"Thanks. Listen, these changes won't take long. Just give me ten or fifteen minutes."

"No rush. I have plenty to do here. And David's not coming for half an hour, anyway."

Twenty minutes later, with Jared still intent on his revisions, Caroline signed off on the last piece of copy in her review stack and reached for her purse. She still had time to pay a few bills before David arrived, and a couple of them were bordering on overdue. She'd just been too busy to get to them until now.

A quick search in her purse reminded her that she'd tucked her checkbook under the front seat of her car the day before—a bad habit she'd gotten into years before when she'd often traveled without a purse. One of these days she needed to correct that, she reminded herself.

"Jared, I'm going to run out to my car to get something. I'll be back in a couple of minutes," she called to the teen across the empty newsroom.

He swallowed the bite of sandwich he'd been chewing while he worked. "Okay. I'm almost done."

Pausing in the break room, Caroline pitched her empty water bottle and spared a quick glance in the mirror, reminding herself to apply some lipstick before David arrived. By the end of the day, every speck had usually vanished. Most of the time she didn't care. But tonight…well, tonight she cared.

Since the gang-related incidents, Caroline had been cautious, putting herself on high alert whenever she was alone—especially around the *Chronicle.* But as she pushed through the back door into the muggy, oppressive August twilight, her thoughts were so distracted by the evening ahead with David that she didn't notice the fragments of glass on the pavement next to the exit—all that was left of the security light. And she didn't see the two figures in the shadows until they lunged toward her.

By then, it was too late to do much. The hand clamped over her mouth stifled the scream that rose to her lips, and her arms were wrenched behind her with such force that she gasped in pain. On instinct alone, with no conscious thought, she used the only part of her body that was still unconstrained. With one swift kick, she slammed the door shut behind her, drawing some measure of relief when it locked with a decisive click. At least Jared would be safe inside. Thanks to the *Chronicle*'s heightened security, the electronic access card reader had been temporarily disabled. No one could enter from the outside without the security combination.

But her action drew the ire of her two assailants. Their faces were indistinct in the dusk, but she could tell they were young. One looked to be about fifteen or sixteen, the other perhaps a bit younger. The identical bands they wore on their arms beneath the cutoff sleeves of their T-shirts told her at once that they were associated with a gang.

"That wasn't very smart," one of the boys snarled, tagging on the same vulgar term that had been scratched into her car. "Open the door." They shoved her next to the keypad and released one of her arms. "We want Jared."

Fighting down her suffocating fear, Caroline tried to prod her paralyzed brain into action. She knew she couldn't open the door, couldn't expose Jared to the danger these teens represented. But the consequences of noncompliance sent a new wave of terror rippling through her.

"Open the door!" One of the teens twisted her arm, and the sharp pain that shot through her wrist bent her double. "Stand up and open the door." The pressure on her arm eased and she was pulled upright.

Please, Lord, help me! she prayed in desperation.

When she still hesitated, the younger thug grabbed a fistful of her hair, then slammed the side of her face against the metal door. For a second, pinpoints of light exploded behind her eyes, obscuring her vision. She sagged against her captor as a wave of dizziness swept over her.

"Hey, man, be careful. She ain't gonna be no use to us if she passes out."

"Yeah, well, we ain't getting nowhere this way."

"She must have an access badge. Hold on to her." The older of the two moved in front of her and put his face close to hers. "You gonna give it to us, or you wanna do this the hard way?"

When she didn't respond, his eyes narrowed. "Okay. You asked for it."

Caroline closed her eyes and tried not to cringe as his hands moved over her body in a rough and thorough pat-down.

"It ain't here," he pronounced when he finished.

"So whaddaya wanna do?" The younger kid was starting to sound nervous.

"I got an idea."

Although her vision was still slightly blurred, Caroline had no trouble identifying the shiny silver object he withdrew from his belt as a knife. The boy put the point to her throat and his face hardened. "Okay, you got ten seconds to open that door. If you don't, we're gonna keep doing this until you do." In a flash, he removed the point of the knife from her throat, pulled one arm from behind her back and slashed the blade down her forearm. Immediately blood began to ooze from the four-inch gash.

Stunned, Caroline stared at the wound. For a second she thought she was going to faint. Not from pain. So far she felt nothing. It was fear that caused her light-headedness. She'd been in some dangerous situations in her journalism career, but none where she was the intended victim. This was a whole different ballgame. There was no doubt in her mind that these two punks would follow through on their threat. Their expressions were cold, detached. As if hurting people—or taking a life—was no big deal. And maybe it wasn't, for them. That's what made this situation so terrifying.

"Let's try it one more time." The teen who had produced the knife, the older of the two, gestured to the kid behind her, who once more shoved her face close to the keypad.

She had to do something. Stall, if nothing else. Maybe the police would come by. They'd been patrolling the area with increased frequency for the past few weeks. They could appear at any second.

Slowly she lifted her hand. The cut on her arm was bleeding more now, bathing her arm in red. But that was the least of her problems at the moment.

Taking as much time as she dared, Caroline punched in a set of numbers. The wrong numbers. A fact that became apparent to the two thugs when they tried the door and it didn't budge.

Once more, she was jerked around and her arm was yanked forward. "I guess we'll have to do some more persuading," the older boy sneered.

Just as he positioned the knife, the back door opened. All three heads swiveled toward Jared, who stood on the threshold, staring at the scene in shock. He must have come to check on her because she'd been gone for too long, Caroline realized, her panic escalating. In the next instant, she was shoved to the ground as the two youths sprang at the teen.

For a few seconds she lay unmoving, the breath knocked out of her. She was aware of a scuffle taking place, of the dull sound of fists hitting solid flesh, of grunts textured with pain, but little else registered. By the time she could react, the two youths had subdued Jared, who had fallen to his knees. Blood streamed from his nose, and his breathing was labored.

As she struggled to her feet and opened her mouth to scream, the older teen once more brandished his knife. "Make a sound and we'll finish him off right now."

She froze and looked over at Jared. There was fear in his eyes, but also anger. "I don't know these dudes." He spoke fast, in quick gasps. "But they're from my old gang…some kind of initiation rite."

"Shut up." The guy with the knife kicked him in the side—the side with the healing broken ribs. Caroline flinched and a wave of nausea washed over her, followed by a fresh surge of fear. She'd learned enough about gangs to know that initiation rites often involved senseless and random acts of violence.

"Now that we got the traitor, whaddaya wanna do with *her?*" The younger kid motioned toward Caroline.

"I don't know." The youth with the knife gave her a speculative look. When he spoke again, his tone was almost jovial. "But maybe two is better than one. Or even three, if someone else shows up."

David! He would be here any minute, Caroline realized with a jolt. If she didn't answer the front buzzer, he'd no doubt come around to the back. And walk right into this volatile situation. Just as Michael had done the day he died—also because of her. It was a replay of the nightmare that had haunted her for two years. She had to do something!

Catching Jared's eye, she inclined her head slightly to the guy beside him, with the knife. Then did the same toward the guy behind her. Judging by his nod, he got the message. They might not succeed in resisting their attackers, but it was better than waiting for these two thugs to finish them off. At least they'd go down fighting.

Jared was poised for her signal, his face frightened but resolute.

This is it, Lord, she prayed. *Give us strength and courage. Be with us no matter what happens.*

And with that, she nodded to Jared.

Chapter Thirteen

As he pressed the night bell for the second time, a tingle of unease raced along David's spine. He knew Caroline and Jared were here. He'd called Caroline less than an hour before to confirm their dinner date. Why wasn't she answering?

Once more, he pressed the bell—and held it. But again, there was no response. His apprehension escalated to alarm. Just as he reached for his cell phone to call 911, he spotted a police car on routine patrol heading his way. *Thank You, Lord!* David prayed as he flagged down the vehicle.

Officer Scanlon got out of the car as David approached. "Can I help you, sir?"

"David Sloan, officer. We met the day of the bomb threat. I had an appointment with Caroline James this evening, but there's no answer. She was here an hour ago and planned to meet me. Our Uplink intern, Jared Poole, is with her." His tone was clipped and curt as he fought down his rising panic.

The policeman turned to his partner, who had

emerged from the vehicle on the other side. David recognized Mark Lowe as well.

"Call headquarters and report suspicious activity at the *Chronicle*," Officer Scanlon instructed. "Request silent back-up. I'm going around to the rear. You cover the front."

Without waiting for a response, he withdrew his gun and took off at a trot toward the corner of the street, avoiding the alley. When David started to follow, he waved him back.

For a second, David hesitated. He wanted to do something to help. But he didn't want to get in the way, either. Torn, he stared after Officer Scanlon, who had already disappeared around the corner.

"Sir, I'd suggest that you take cover behind the car." Mark came up beside David as he, too, reached for his weapon. "This may be a false alarm, but it would be safer if you stayed out of the line of fire, just in case. We don't like to put civilians in danger. Back-up will be here in a couple of minutes."

Again, David hesitated. He wasn't a civilian. He was the man in love with the woman inside this building. And if this *wasn't* a false alarm, she was directly in the line of fire.

"Look, can I help in some way? I can't just hide behind…"

A woman's scream suddenly pierced the air from behind the building, followed by a gunshot. The surge of adrenaline that shot through David sent his pulse off the scale, and without waiting for Lowe to react, he turned and raced toward the alley.

"Hey! Not that way!" the man shouted.

Ignoring the warning, David plunged down the dark,

narrow passage. A second later he heard the sound of running feet behind him.

When David emerged into the parking lot a couple of seconds later, the sight that met his eyes rocked the foundation of his world. Jared was on the ground, with Caroline kneeling beside him, holding his hand, while Scanlon trained his gun on two young thugs a short distance away. A knife lay on the ground beside them, and blood stained the pants of one of the punks at thigh level. The blood that caught—and held—David's attention, however, was on Caroline and Jared. Despite the deepening twilight, he could see that the lower part of Caroline's left arm was almost solid red. But the dark splotches on her green silk blouse were even more frightening. Jared's face was bloody, and there was a bright red stain on one side of his beige sport shirt.

Officer Lowe pushed past David, gun drawn, as he radioed for more back-up and an ambulance.

"Cuff them," Scanlon barked over his shoulder.

As Lowe complied, David's lungs kicked into gear again and he sprinted toward Caroline and Jared, dropping to one knee beside them. "Caroline?" His voice was so shaky he almost didn't recognize it.

She turned to him, dazed. One side of her face was as pale as a blank sheet of newsprint. The other was puffy and scraped raw, and there was a large, discolored lump on her temple. "David? Are you all right?"

His gut twisted. Despite her own injuries, her first worry was for him. "Yeah. But you're not."

"I—I'm okay. But Jared's hurt." The words came out choked and shaky as she transferred her attention back to the intern.

"You're not okay. Your arm is cut. Your face is swollen. There's blood on your blouse."

"The blood is from my arm. My face is fine. But they hurt Jared. They punched him, and kicked him in the ribs, and then they...they stabbed him in the side." Her voice broke, and her eyes filled with tears. "Please, David. Help him! Do something!"

Taking her assessment of her own condition at face value, David moved to Jared's other side. The boy looked up at him, his eyes glazed with pain, and when David took his hand, it was cold and clammy. Shock was setting in. Meaning he needed help. Fast. Just as David turned to call for assistance from the police, a sudden wail of sirens sent relief coursing through him. "Hang in there, Jared. Help will be here in a couple of minutes. Okay?"

"Yeah." The boy's voice was so soft it was almost inaudible.

David looked across Jared's prone form toward Caroline. The tears had spilled out of her eyes and begun to trickle down her cheeks as she focused on the boy, her face a mask of worry. She seemed oblivious to her own injuries, but David couldn't ignore her battered face or the blood that continued to ooze from a gash on her arm. Nor did he miss the limp hand that lay in her lap. He wouldn't rest easy until the paramedics had checked her out.

The tense wait seemed interminable, but finally help arrived. Within seconds, it seemed that cops were swarming all over the scene, and the paramedics went into action, easing David and Caroline aside as they bent over Jared. While Caroline recounted the attack on Jared and pointed out his injuries, David motioned to another paramedic. "She needs attention, too. Right away," he told the man, inclining his head toward Caroline.

"Okay." When Caroline finished discussing Jared, the EMT touched her shoulder. "Ma'am, let's move over to the side. I need to take a look at you."

Annoyed, she shook her head. "Later. I want to stay with Jared."

David stepped in. "*Now,* Caroline." He moved beside her and drew her to her feet with a firm hand.

Caroline opened her mouth to argue, but all at once her legs buckled and she sagged against David. He caught her, and before she realized his intent he reached down and tucked his arm beneath her knees, lifting her in one smooth motion.

"Where do you want her?" he asked the paramedic, his voice tight with tension.

"The stretcher over there." He pointed toward the ambulance.

As David strode toward it, Caroline spoke. "You're going to get blood on your suit. Put me down." She'd meant to sound forceful. Instead, her comment came out weak and shaky.

In any case, David ignored her. She had a good view of the solid set of his chin as he held her firmly against his chest, and she figured she might as well give up the fight. Besides, after the horror of the past twenty minutes, the haven of his arms felt good. And safe. And right.

"Right here, sir."

At the paramedic's instruction, David eased her down onto the stretcher. But he stayed close while the man checked her out. The EMT asked a series of questions as he worked to ensure he wasn't missing any serious injuries. He was joined a few minutes later by Officer Scanlon, who had his own set of questions. Caroline answered them all, and as she recounted the terrifying, violent experience she began to shake. David reached for her hand, enfolding it in a firm clasp as he turned to the policeman. "Can this wait until later? She's not up to all these questions right now."

"No problem. I just needed a few preliminaries."

"How's Jared?" Caroline turned to David as the officer left and the EMT cleaned the gash on her arm.

"I don't know."

"Can you find out?"

He didn't want to leave her. But he understood her concern. With a brief nod, he rose and made his way back to the paramedics clustered around the teen. "Can you tell me anything about his condition?"

One of the EMTs spoke without turning as he continued to work on Jared. "Stab wound. Appears to be superficial. Bruised nose. May be broken, but we won't know without X-rays. Possible broken ribs. Again, we need to confirm with X-rays. The preliminary prognosis looks good."

"Thanks."

By the time he returned to Caroline, the paramedic was just standing up, and David asked him the same question about her.

"Severe bruising on her face. The hospital will want to do some X-rays to check for a concussion and broken bones. The gash on her arm will require stitches. Looks like she has a sprained wrist. X-rays will confirm that, too. We're going to load her up now. Do you want to follow?"

"Yeah."

David dropped down to balance on the balls of his feet beside her. As he took her hand, her slightly unfocused eyes, shallow breathing and the strain around her mouth communicated her pain. His throat tightened, and when he spoke his voice was hoarse. "I'm going to follow you to the hospital, okay?"

"How's Jared?"

"It sounds like he'll be fine."

Relief eased some of the tension in her features. "Good."

The paramedics moved into position, and David leaned close. "I'll meet you at the hospital."

She tried to reach out to touch his face, wincing in pain at the effort.

Grasping her arm, he laid her hand gently on her chest and smoothed the hair back from her face. "Don't move, sweetheart."

"I was s-so afraid that y-you would walk into the middle of this and end up like M-Michael. I d-didn't want to lose you, too." Tears pooled in her eyes and her voice choked.

Once more his throat tightened with emotion, and he stroked her uninjured cheek. "I'm fine, Caroline. It's you I'm worried about."

"Sir, we need to get moving."

At the paramedic's voice, David rose and stepped aside. Weeks ago, he had acknowledged his love for this woman, who'd stolen his heart more than two years before. And he'd seen signs that she felt the same way. Yet she'd put up barriers—which wasn't surprising, considering all the baggage that came with their relationship. He hadn't pushed, believing that she'd let him know when the time was right. But tonight, in the midst of a narrowly averted tragedy, she'd given him a glimpse into her heart with that simple comment: "I didn't want to lose you, too."

And now that he knew her feelings paralleled his, it was time to take some action.

David pulled to a stop in front of Caroline's condo and wiped a weary hand down his face. Tonight had been a nightmare, but it was over. Caroline didn't have a concussion or any broken facial bones, the sprained wrist was mild and twenty-two stitches had taken care of the gash on her arm. Jared's ribs had been bruised again, but neither they nor his nose was broken. The puncture in his side had required some work, but it was a flesh wound and should heal with no complications. His grandmother and great-aunt had kept vigil with David and Caroline's mother until the wee hours, and now everyone was on their way home. No one was going to get much sleep this night, David realized, checking his watch. But at least they were all safe. When he thought about what could have happened... Sucking in a deep breath, he closed his eyes. *Thank You, Lord, for letting this end well.*

Looking over at his sleeping passenger, David's heart contracted with tenderness. From the first moment he'd seen her, David had been drawn to Caroline. Some instinct had told him that she was a one-in-a-million woman. Over the past few weeks, as he'd gotten to know her—and grown to love her—that initial impression had been confirmed over and over again. And he intended to tell her that as soon as possible. Not tonight, of course. But as soon as she was back on her feet.

"Sweetheart? You're home." He reached over and stroked the uninjured side of her face, which was closest to him.

Her eyelids flickered open, and for a second she seemed disoriented. Then, as her face cleared, she struggled to open her seat belt.

"Leave it." He stilled her hand with a touch. "I'll get it from the other side. Sit tight and I'll come around."

She didn't argue. She was too exhausted. Her face throbbed, her wrist ached and the numbing shots in her arm were wearing off. All she wanted to do was curl up in her bed and sleep for days.

A few seconds later, her door was pulled open. As David leaned across to unclasp her seat belt, taking care to avoid contact with her injured arm and face, her heart contracted with tenderness and gratitude. She wanted to reach out to him, to touch him, to ask him to hold her as he had done earlier in the evening. Not because she was injured and hurting. But for different reasons entirely. Except this wasn't the time, she realized, noting the smudges beneath his eyes and the lines of worry etched in his face. The night had been fraught with too much emotional trauma already. They both needed to get some rest.

Calling on every ounce of her strength, she swung her legs to the ground and stood. David tucked an arm around her waist as he pushed the door shut with his free hand, and she leaned into him. She'd always prided herself on being a woman who could stand on her own two feet, but neither her feet—nor her legs—felt steady enough to support her weight right now.

"Want me to carry you?" David murmured, his worried voice close to her ear.

In truth, she did. But she shook her head. "I'll be okay as long as I can lean on you."

"Anytime."

Their progress was slow, and negotiating the three steps to her door taxed her energy to the limit. As if sensing how close she was to collapse, David took the key from her trembling fingers, inserted it in the lock and guided her inside.

"Are you going to be okay here by yourself tonight?" he asked.

"The night's almost over."

"You know what I mean."

"Yeah. I do," she said softly. Although she'd been in a lot of pain earlier, at the *Chronicle,* she hadn't missed his murmured endearment then—or just now, in the car. He'd called her sweetheart. And with that single word, she'd known that his feelings for her ran deep and strong. Just as hers did for him. Now, as she looked at him, the banked fire in his deep brown eyes threatened to erupt into a consuming flame. But this man of discipline and self-restraint, this man of prudence, this man who always thought things through and seldom acted on impulse—this man she loved—managed to contain it. As if he, too, realized that now wasn't the time to explore their feelings for each other. "Will I see you tomorrow?" she asked.

A spark escaped from that contained fire, flaring with searing intensity for a brief second before it dimmed. "Count on it."

As she stood there, David reached over and touched her cheek. No words were spoken. None needed to be. Then he turned and walked to her door, pausing on the threshold before exiting for one more look that was loaded with meaning—and promise. And if Caroline's legs hadn't already been shaky, that look alone would have turned them to Jell-O.

David adjusted one of the red roses in the massive bouquet in his arms, then reached over and pushed Caroline's doorbell. He hoped he wasn't too early, but he'd stayed away as long as he could. What little sleep he'd managed had been fraught with nightmares of the possible tragic outcomes of last night's confrontation. Those heart-pounding dreams had wrenched him awake, adrenaline pumping, his breath lodged in his chest. He hoped Caroline had fared better.

But when she answered the door, he knew she hadn't. There were dark circles under her eyes, and even though her cheek was no longer as puffy, a huge bruise, deep purple against her colorless skin, had replaced the redness. While she looked just as appealing in her cutoff shorts and T-shirt as she did in her usual chic, elegant wardrobe, her attire also revealed yet another large bruise, this one on her knee. Nevertheless, she managed a smile.

"I didn't expect you quite this soon. I thought you'd be at work. But those aren't your usual work clothes." She gave his worn jeans, which fit his lean hips like a second skin, and the sport shirt that hugged his broad chest a swift perusal.

"Not today."

"Well…come in." She stepped aside to let him enter, her stiff movements a clear indication of the physical trauma her body had endured. "How's Jared?"

"I talked to his grandmother this morning. He's doing okay. And I also talked to the police. The two punks who attacked you were happy to spill everything to save their own skin. They gave the police enough information to link the gang leaders to a couple of recent crime sprees and keep them off the streets for the foreseeable future. Without their leadership, the police think the gang will be history."

"I'm glad to hear that."

As she shut the door, David nodded to the crystal vase of flowers in his hands. "Where would you like these?"

"On the coffee table in the living room. Thank you. They're beautiful."

After depositing the flowers, he turned as she came up behind him. His compelling, intense eyes locked on hers, holding them captive as he took a step toward her, erasing the distance between them. When he was a whisper away, he reached up and brushed her hair back from her face, letting the silky strands glide through his fingers. Then, moving slowly—but with clear, deliberate intent—he leaned toward her and brushed his lips against hers in a brief kiss that was as light as a drifting leaf.

When she could find enough breath to speak, Caroline opened her eyes and stared at him. "I—I guess we have some things to talk about."

"I guess we do."

At the husky timbre of his voice, her heart stopped, then raced on. "Do you w-want to sit down?"

"Not really." He stroked a gentle finger down her cheek. "I want to kiss you again. I've been waiting to do that for…for a very long time. But I guess I can wait a few more minutes."

When she could drag her gaze away from his, she

eased onto the couch. He sat beside her, angling his body to face her. "How about if I start?" he said.

Since she couldn't seem to find her voice, anyway, that sounded like a good plan, so she nodded.

Reaching out, he cradled her good hand in his, stroking the back of it with his thumbs as he spoke. "I have to be honest, Caroline. After I gave you the medallion, I never planned to see you again. I felt too guilty. You already know about the guilt I felt in connection with Michael's death. It took me a long time to work through that. What you didn't know about was the guilt I felt over my feelings for you." At her puzzled look, David drew a deep breath. "The fact is, you bowled me over the first time we met. And I couldn't get you out of my mind. Since you'd already given your heart to Michael, I tried my best to get over you. I told myself that what I felt for you was just infatuation. That in time it would fade. But the truth is, it never did. And once our paths started to cross again here in St. Louis, that original infatuation, or fascination, or obsession—or whatever it was—evolved into love. So my first instincts about you weren't that far off base after all."

A troubled look crossed his face, and David shook his head. "The thing is, I felt that my feelings for you were somehow wrong, even though Michael is gone. I struggled with that for a long time. Finally I talked it over with Steve, who helped me gain a little perspective. And to acknowledge something my heart has known with absolute certainty for a very long time—that all our tomorrows were meant to be spent together. He also helped me realize that if you felt the same way, I shouldn't let anything stand in the way of seeking out the love that the Lord seems to have guided us toward.

Last Sunday in church, when you took off the medallion, I began to believe that maybe your feelings for me had evolved as well. That maybe, in time, you might come to love me—as I love you."

For most of their relationship, Caroline had sensed that David was a man of strong, but restrained, passion. A man able to mask what was in his heart, to maintain control of his emotions. She'd witnessed a few slight slips in the past several weeks. But nothing had prepared her for what she now saw. Gone were the barriers. Gone was the restraint. Gone was the mask. His eyes invited her to look deep into his heart. And the absolute love and devotion she saw there took her breath away.

Struggling to contain her tears of happiness, Caroline reached over and touched David's face. "I already do," she whispered.

Relief and thanksgiving and wonder washed over his face, intermingling, leaving joy in their wake.

"I know I should do this right…with candlelight and flowers and music…but after last night, I don't want to wait one more second. So…" He dropped to one knee and took her hands gently in his. "Would you do me the honor of becoming my wife?"

Her throat constricted with emotion, and she blinked back her tears. "I can't believe I've been blessed with a second chance for a happy ending."

"Is that a yes?"

A smile illuminated her face as she echoed his words from the night before. "Count on it."

At her positive response, a matching smile chased the anxiety from his features. "I'd like to seal this engagement with a proper kiss, but I think we'll have to be content with something simple until that bruise goes away." Regret tinged his voice as he surveyed her cheek.

"I'm a fast healer."

Her quick comeback brought a smile to his lips, and a chuckle rumbled deep in his chest. "That's good news. But in the meantime, let's try this on for size."

As he leaned close to claim her lips in a tender, careful kiss, Caroline closed her eyes, savoring the gift of love, of passage from winter to spring, that this special man had offered her. With him, and with trust in the Lord, she'd found the courage to leave yesterday behind, embrace today and face tomorrow with joy. In other words, she was claiming the legacy Michael had left her by living the very philosophy that had guided his life.

And somehow, deep in her heart, she knew he would be pleased.

Epilogue

"I thought you were supposed to *cover* stories, not star in them."

Jared turned with a self-conscious grin toward Steve Dempsky, who was holding the latest issue of the *Chronicle*. Splashed across the front page was a feature article on the Uplink intern's recent first-place win in the national photography/journalism contest. "I'm kind of embarrassed by all the attention."

"Hey, enjoy the moment. It's not every day that a St. Louisan wins such a prestigious award. You deserve all the accolades you're getting."

"At least Nan seems proud. And Aunt Dara." He looked toward the two women, who were helping themselves to pizza and cookies from the long table in the *Chronicle*'s conference room.

"David told me you and your grandmother have moved in permanently with your great-aunt. How's that working out?"

"Great! The new school is cool. And they have an awesome photo studio." He looked around the room, then shook his head. "I still can't believe Ms. James went to all this effort for me after the trouble I caused." The entire *Chronicle* staff had been invited to the party celebrating Jared's win, along with his family, Charles Elliot and his former art and English teachers, and the Uplink board.

"She's one fine lady."

"Yeah." His grandmother motioned to him, and he waved back. "Excuse me. I need to see what Nan wants."

As Jared walked away, David joined Steve. "Hard to believe he's the same young man we interviewed, isn't it?"

"I'll say. But you had him pegged from the beginning. All he needed was a chance."

"And lots of TLC," Ella chimed in. She handed David a paper cup. "You forgot your punch."

"Thanks." He took it from her, then looked across the room to where Caroline was chatting with Bill Baker. Eight weeks after the attack, the bruises on her face had disappeared, the splint was off her wrist and a long-sleeved blouse hid the four-inch scar on her arm that would take a lot longer to fade. His gaze softened, and a smile touched the corners of his lips. "Caroline can take most of the credit for the TLC. She worked with him every day. I just provided moral support."

"Considering that rock on her finger, I think you provided a little more than that," Ella teased.

He turned to her. "Only after the fact. I don't mix business and pleasure."

"Honey, I'm not at all concerned about when. I'm just glad it happened," Ella retorted with a grin. "You two were made for each other. Now I'm going to get me a piece of that pizza before this hungry horde devours every last scrap."

As Ella headed toward the table, intent on her purpose, Steve smiled at David. "She's right, you know."

Still focused on Caroline, David nodded. "Yeah. I know."

As if sensing his scrutiny, Caroline glanced his way. For a long second they just looked at each other. Then she turned back to Bill, said a few words and headed toward the two men.

"Uh-oh. Looks like my cue to exit," Steve remarked. "You know what they say about three being a crowd."

"You don't have to leave," David protested. "There's a whole roomful of people here."

"Maybe. But she only has eyes for you. And the reverse is true as well. Dinner next week?"

"It's on my calendar. See you then."

With a wave to Caroline, Steve sauntered away.

"I didn't meant to chase Steve off," she told David as she approached, a slight frown creasing her forehead.

Circling her waist with his arm, he pulled her close. "He left of his own accord. Mumbling something about three being a crowd."

"Should I go after him?"

His arm tightened. "Don't even think about it."

Smiling, she relaxed against him. "And you claim to be his friend."

"Hey, good friends know when to stick close—and when to get lost. Steve's a good friend."

She chuckled, then surveyed the room in satisfaction. "It's a nice party, isn't it? I think Jared was really touched."

"I know he was."

"He deserves it. That win is quite a coup for him. And for Uplink."

"I'm hoping it will smooth the way in the future for us to recruit kids like him. The ones who need us most."

"It can't hurt." Caroline let her head rest against David's shoulder as they watched the revelers. Jared's award-winning story and photos had been enlarged and were displayed on the one solid wall of the glassed-in conference room, and most of the guests were as impressed by the work as the contest judges had been. Although the internship had been fraught with difficulties, Caroline was glad she'd seen it through. In a way, she felt as if she'd paid back Michael's final debt, freeing her from any lingering guilt.

"What are you thinking?"

David's lips were close to her ear, his breath warm on her temple. She wanted to tell him, but she wasn't sure how to do it in a way that didn't sound like she was dwelling on the past. "About paying debts. And giving someone a chance," she replied softly. "And about moving on."

"I feel the same way."

Angling her head, she looked up at him. His eyes were warm and understanding, as if he could see right into her heart and knew exactly what she was feeling. That today, this moment, marked a turning point for them. It was as if they'd come to the end of the chapter in which Michael had played a major role, and tomorrow they would turn to a new, blank page waiting to be filled by the two of them.

Michael would always be a part of their lives, of course. But David sensed that the man they'd both loved would move away now as Steve just had, giving them the space they needed to create their own story. When Steve winked, grinned and gave a thumbs-up signal, David sensed another parallel, as well: that like Steve, Michael was smiling, too.

And as he rested his cheek against Caroline's silky hair, he gave thanks. For the woman he loved. For work that fulfilled him. For a faith that sustained and guided him. And for a brother who had taught him to see with fresh eyes—and to risk everything for the things that mattered most.

* * * * *

Dear Reader,

As I write this letter, I am enjoying the end of spring, with my office window wide-open. Air-conditioning has not yet insulated me from the fresh scent of newly mown grass nor muted the song of the birds. I love this season, which has always represented hope and new life to me. It's a time to put the dark days of winter aside and step into the sunshine.

In *All Our Tomorrows,* Caroline and David learn to do just that with their lives. And as they leave the darkness of grief behind, step into the light of hope and embrace the promise of a new beginning, they trust that the Lord will lead and guide them on their journey together. I hope that their story uplifts and inspires you.

I'd like to invite you to visit my website, at www.irenehannon.com, where you can find news about my upcoming releases (not to mention scrumptious recipes!).

May you enjoy this season of sunshine, and may love grace your life this summer.

Irene Hannon

Questions for Discussion

1. When David reappears in Caroline's life, she must reevaluate her negative opinion of him, which was based on secondhand information from his brother. Have you sometimes formed opinions about people—even judged them—based on others' interpretation and bias? Why is this dangerous—and unfair? What does the Bible tell us about judging others? Cite some instances from Scripture where the Lord speaks to this topic.

2. Distance insulated Michael from the harsh reality of his mother's condition. Nor did he seem to want to acknowledge it when informed. Can you think of any instances in your own life when you didn't want to face a difficult situation? Why not? How did your faith help you it address it?

3. As a youngster—and even into adulthood—David admired his outgoing older brother. But it can also be difficult to live in the shadow of a successful, popular sibling. Have you ever experienced this in your life? How has it affected your relationship with that sibling?

4. Following his mother's death, David reevaluates his life and takes a job where he hopes to improve lives, not just balance sheets. In explaining his decision to Caroline, he quotes Mother Teresa, "God has not called me to be successful, God has called

me to be faithful." Why does it often seem difficult in today's society to follow this call?

5. In *All Our Tomorrows,* the Uplink board is nervous about reaching out to inner-city students like Jared. Yet David is convinced that those are the students most in need of the organization's assistance. All of us are faced with risky choices in our lives, choices that have great potential for good—but which can also backfire and do irreparable harm. Have you ever faced a situation like that? What did you do?

6. David and Caroline are struck by Jared's hope-filled photos. Why do you think Jared was able to hold on to hope despite his dismal surroundings? What role did his grandmother play in his attitude?

7. Jared pursues the Uplink internship despite the risks and threats. What gives him the courage to do so? How much impact did others' belief in him have on his willingness to persevere? Discuss examples from your own life where perseverance reaped positive results. How has your relationship with the Lord been a source of courage?

8. At first, Jared's grandmother is too proud to ask her sister for help when Jared needs a place to stay. Only when she realizes that asking for help is the best way to express her love, is she able to put her pride aside. What does the Bible tell us about the danger of pride? How can pride get in the way of our relationship with others—and the Lord?

9. A number of the characters have to deal with relationships gone awry. David and Michael experienced a rift; Jared's grandmother and her sister are estranged; Caroline and David start out on shaky ground because of resentments and misunderstandings. How might better communication have affected these relationships? What are some of the hallmarks of good communication?

10. In the end, both Caroline and Jared find their way back to God. Discuss their journeys and the factors that helped lead them home. Do any of their experiences parallel your faith journey?